SECRETS OF THE SAPPHIRE SOUL

BOND OF A DRAGON

A J WALKER

An A J Walker Publishing Novel.

First published in the United States in 2019 by A J Walker Publishing

Paperback first published in 2019 by A J Walker Publishing

Copyright © A J Walker Publishing 2022

Formatting by A J Walker Publishing

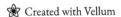 Created with Vellum

To MZM

Acknowledgments

I want to thank all those who've helped me in creating the Bond of a Dragon series. This idea started when I was a young man and has grown into this magnificent story it is because of the help and inspiration of many people. Thanks to my parents, family and friends for their support and encouragement along the way.

Many of you might find it hard to believe that reading and writing didn't come naturally to me, as I am severely dyslexic. I wouldn't have developed the skills necessary to create these works without the support from my family. Thanks to Susan, the brilliant woman who spent long hours combing through my many mistake-ridden drafts. Your help has been instrumental in creating these stories. Thank you to my loving wife who's always inspired me to chase my dreams and desires no matter how ridiculous or far-fetched they may seem. And Thanks to you, the reader, for allowing me to express my creativity on these pages.

Special thanks to:

Susan Penner – copy and developmental editor

Mark Reid at authorpackages.com – cover design

Maggie Walker – Kartania Map, watercolor

Advanced Reader Team

ONE

A NEWLY BONDED RIDER

Anders groaned with frustration in having to trot yet again after another fearful warrior. His muscles strained with fatigue as he jogged through the battle's aftermath. Bodies of orcs, kurr, and humans lay scattered along the valley floor, a sight Anders hated having to return to. Though he and Zahara attempted to aid those wounded in the battle beneath Merglan's fortress, the young rider quickly grew frustrated as each Rollo Islander fled upon seeing his dragon. Anders thought he would've felt a deep sense of fulfillment in using the simple healing spells his mentor, Ivan, had hastily taught him before returning to the battlefield. Each conscious patient, however, met Anders with hostility toward his association with elves and his bond with his dragon, Zahara.

The injured Rollo warrior glanced frantically over his shoulder as he attempted to flee, his mangled arm flapping uselessly at his side. The warrior, still looking back at Anders, tripped over an orc's corpse, falling to the ground. Rolling onto his back, the warrior held out his uninjured arm, motioning for Anders to stay back. Shaking furiously and muttering in native Rolloan, the warrior kicked, shuffling through the dirt on his back as Anders knelt to examine the disfigured arm.

Speaking clearly, Anders attempted to calm the warrior as he reached for the limp arm. A glint of steel flashed in his peripheral vision; Anders moved deftly to block the warrior's blade. With a backhanded punch, he knocked the panicked warrior's right arm aside, forcing him to drop the dagger. Anders pounced on the man, holding him still while Zahara quickly came to his aid.

Growling at the warrior, Zahara flared her nostrils and bared her teeth causing the man to cease squirming instantly. With her large head looming over the Rollo warrior, Anders could release his grip on the man, seamlessly reaching down and tossing the dagger out of arm's reach. With his dragon ensuring the warrior couldn't escape, Anders was finally able to examine the warrior's arm before deciding which spell to use to attempt to heal him.

Anders closed his eyes, feeling the surge of energy Zahara gifted him rising through his body. With his hand hovering over the fractured arm, the warmth of the magic pulsed as it emitted from his palm, washing over the wounded Rollo Island warrior's skin. He ignored the shouts from the warrior as Zahara kept him from escaping as Anders worked the spell. Anders opened his eyes, watching the angle of the man's arm move slightly and then snap back into place. The exposed bone that just a moment before had protruded from the warrior's forearm slid under the skin, the fibers of his muscle tissue slowly stitching themselves back together. Anders shook briefly with a chill as he ended the spell, the bone healed and the gash now closed, a faint scratch the only evidence of the injury. Stepping back, Anders allowed Zahara to release her grip on the man. The warrior scurried to his feet, scrambling to get away. For an instant, the warrior hadn't noticed he was using his injured arm to push himself up. Stopping only for a moment, the warrior examined his healed arm, awed and confused. The islander glanced once more at Anders and Zahara before fleeing toward camp. Anders shuddered, slumping to his knees in exhaustion.

Careful Anders, Zahara's voice entered his mind. *Remember what Ivan said. The elves have more skilled healers among their camp. We only learned how to use this spell a few hours ago. Ivan warned us how it draws energy. If we try to heal everyone's broken bones, we'll die of exhaustion before supper.*

Anders rubbed his hands together, trying to rid himself of the chill left behind from using the spell. Shivering, he said, *I'm being careful.*

You need to rest before we continue. There are more wounded returning from the battle. If you use up all of your energy now, we won't be able to help anyone, Zahara warned, sensing his fatigue.

Anders rose, leaning against Zahara's sturdy front leg as he observed groups of warriors hobbling their way to camp from the battlefield. At the moment, drained from battle and then performing magic, he felt significantly older than his nineteen years. *I'll rest once everyone's back,* Anders said, looking up at the iridescent green and blue dragon. *I at least owe them that much. These people fought with us to free my family.*

Zahara shifted, glancing to the sky as Anders pushed off her leg and began trotting toward the warriors making their way back. Ruffling her wings, she wondered when the two riders that left Cedarbridge with her and the elves would be returning. As she peered toward the mountains, a surge of fear suddenly wrenched her insides. Her gut pained with the thought of what Merglan could've done to them. Allowing her gaze to linger on the peaked horizon, she forced the unhappy thoughts from her mind and bounded after Anders. *Just promise me you won't take this healing too far,* she said catching up with him.

I promise. I won't become a liability, Anders said, heat returning to his body as he walked.

CAMPFIRES BURNED along the valley floor as the Rollo Island warriors gathered close to the recently rescued people of their tribe. Joyous sounds of the reunion of long-lost loved ones rang throughout camp as those who fought through the night to victory celebrated.

Completely exhausted, physically and emotionally, Anders followed the last of the wounded into the temporary camp the victors had established on the grassy plain at the base of Merglan's fortress following the battle.

Anders and Zahara walked numbly as they made their way toward the medical station near the edge of the encampment. The smell of roasting lamb, pork and game-bird filled the air as Anders stumbled wearily past fires scattered throughout the sea of tents near Merglan's fortress. After the gate had been destroyed, the warriors had located Merglan's food supplies, ravaging them and sharing the wealth throughout their newly established camp. Rolloans, elves and the small miscellaneous band of those who'd been attacked at the Grandwood Games had lit campfires to cook meals and warm themselves in the daylight after a night's battle.

Anders perked up slightly when he saw Ivan usher an

elf into the medical tent. Too exhausted to shout, Anders reached for Ivan as he entered the tent.

Ivan stopped abruptly when he caught sight of Anders, "Anders, you look exhausted."

"Have you seen Maija, Max or my cousins?"

Ivan pointed past Anders and gave a quick nod toward the fortress wall, "They've set up a few tents near the northeast end of camp, just past the fortress wall."

Anders bobbed his head and turned to head where Ivan had pointed.

Ivan caught him by the arm as he turned and said, "Get a bite to eat and some rest while you can. The other two dragonriders haven't returned. We'll give them a few more hours, but if they're not back by dusk you, Zahara and I will need to go look for them."

"Okay," Anders said through a long yawn.

"I'll come find you after a bit. I need to meet with Red before we leave," Ivan said. "He's gone back to the battlefield to mourn his father."

Anders' eyes moved awkwardly to his feet. Jorgen's death and the battle with Thargon seemed a lifetime ago. So much had happened over the course of the last day that hours were beginning to blend into one long blur of action and emotion. "Give him my sincere condolences," Anders managed to say.

Ivan looked to Zahara before responding, "I'm sure Red will want to thank both of you for avenging his father's death. If it weren't for your timely arrival, Zahara, we would've all been taken by Thargon's axe."

Thank you, she said, using their telepathic link. *I wish all of the warriors shared that same sentiment.* Zahara peered around at the gathering of Rollo Island warriors.

Anders had forgotten that none of the Rolloan people

had spent time around dragons. Zahara's arrival as the battle was raging must've shocked them.

There are still many here who would like to see me dead, or in chains, she said squinting her large purple eyes and glaring at a warrior as he walked past.

"As long as the elves are here, you're safe," Ivan said reassuringly to Anders and Zahara.

Her loud exhale came out with a soft growl. She flicked the tip of her tail to one side.

"Thanks, Ivan, we'll see you after a short while," Anders said and started off toward his family and friends.

As they made their way across the encampment, Anders found it oddly pleasing how those in their way parted for them.

Once at the far side of the Rolloan camp, Anders spotted Max, Bo and Maija sitting in the grass with his cousins. As they approached, Anders' mouth began to water at the smell of lamb roasting on their small cookfire. Bo and Kirsten shuffled to the side, making a place for Anders to join them. Zahara lay down directly behind them, keeping her eyes fixed on the turned heads of several Rollo Island warriors. Anders sighed audibly as he plopped down on the ground. He leaned back against Zahara's large neck, folding his arms behind his head and closing his eyes.

"You look exhausted," Kirsten said.

"Here. Have some food," Maija said, moving to hand him the spit of mutton she'd been roasting.

Anders reached out gratefully and smiled as their hands briefly touched. Hardly able to keep his eyes open, he said in a hushed voice, "Thank you. This is exactly what I need right now."

Giving him a quick wink, she passed the backside of her forefingers along the side of his head, brushing back his tangled hair as he smiled up at her. After a sweet moment of exchanged looks, she returned to the other side of the fire and sat back down by Thomas and Max.

While Anders chewed on the delicious mutton, the rest of the group looked at him wide-eyed, waiting for him to speak. They wanted to hear about how he'd suddenly acquired the bond of a dragon. Anders didn't notice their looks; he merely put his head back against Zahara's scaled body and chewed the roasted meat with his eyes contentedly closed.

Zahara suddenly pulled away from him and rose to her feet, leaving Anders to topple backward onto the flat of his back. *All this good-smelling food is making me hungry*, she said before running a few steps and leaping into the air, her wings spread and flapping as she flew away.

"Hey," Anders shouted rising to the flat of his elbows on the grass.

I'm going fishing, she said as she flew off toward the sea.

Turning his gaze back to the fire, Anders, at last noticed the dumbfounded looks of his cousins, Maija and Bo. "I'm sorry, I forgot you guys can't hear what she's saying," he said as he pointed the stick of meat in Zahara's direction. He swallowed a bite and explained, "The smell of the lamb was making her hungry, so she decided to go fishing." He took another large bite from the skewer and looked at them as if nothing out of the ordinary had just happened.

"Well," Kirsten said, gesturing expectantly as she leaned forward over her crossed legs.

"Well, what?" Anders said through his mouthful.

"Tell us how the heck you all of a sudden have a dragon and can use magic!" she shouted in a mix of frustration and excitement.

"Oh yeah, right," Anders said, swallowing and continuing in a calm tone. "It all started after I found her one night on the Bareback Plains. I guess that isn't entirely true, though; she was the one who found me. I snuck out from our campsite in the middle of the night. I wanted to walk alone to clear my head. At first, I thought she was a bear about to maul me. Long story short, she was lost and lonely and had a feeling about me, so she showed herself to me. She's a very young dragon and was separated from her parents. Anyway, I kept our meetings a secret from Ivan, Red and Max."

"Who are Ivan and Red?" Thomas interrupted.

"Oh yeah, you don't know Ivan and Red yet. We have so much catching up to do, don't we? Red is the large dark-haired Rollo Island warrior who you might've noticed in my heat during the Grandwood Games. And Ivan, well you haven't met him yet I suppose, but well, um, he was friends with Uncle Theodor during the War," Anders said, hesitating when he saw the still-fresh pain of the loss of their father on their faces.

"Okay," Thomas said clearly urging Anders to continue talking about the dragon and not their murdered father.

"I suppose I should first tell you how I met them," Anders said.

"That's alright," Kirsten said. "Max told us how you got here. With the Rollo warriors, shipwreck, orcs, elves and all."

"He just forgot to mention their names," Thomas added, looking over to Max. Max shrugged, letting out an effortless excuse for his lack of detail when recounting their story, "hey, so I forgot to mention their names."

"Anyway," Anders continued. "After the first night, I continued to meet Zahara in secret while everyone else slept. She followed us as we traveled toward this fortress.

8

She told me how she'd been searching for her family, but everyone she'd come across up to that point had scared her. She hadn't approached anyone for help until she showed herself to me.

"She followed us for several weeks as we headed first to the land of the elves. When we were attacked by orcs, she came to our aid, fighting brilliantly for a young dragon. I went to check on her after the ordeal and that's when we learned that Ivan was planning to counsel the elves in their capital city, Cedarbridge. I convinced Ivan to take us with him because that's where Zahara said her parents were heading when they became separated. Once we got there, I asked around and, sure enough, the elves found her parents for us. It was hard at the time, but we had to leave one another once she'd found her family."

"Wait, so how come she's here if you left her with the elves?" Kirsten asked, pointing toward the sky where Zahara circled over the sea. "And why does she need her parents? She seems old enough to be on her own."

"She might not look it, but Zahara is only two years old," Anders said.

The group gasped collectively. "She's only two?" Maija said in surprise, turning back to watch Zahara looping and diving into the water in pursuit of her meal.

Anders nodded, "I know. Hard to believe, right?"

"So, you left her with the elves?" Kirsten asked, waiting for Anders to explain how Zahara came to be with him now.

"Yeah, I knew we had a special connection, but I couldn't keep her away from her family, especially at such a young age," he said.

In awe, Maija tilted her head to the side and put her hands up to her heart.

Anders blushed and smiled, then continued, "That's when Nadir joined us," he paused, seeing their blank expressions. "He's an elf prince. The elf king sent him with us when we left Cedarbridge. The elves were supposed to meet us here before we marched on the fortress, but they were waylaid en route and arrived after the battle had begun. Sensing danger, I guess, Zahara decided to follow them to find me. In the height of the battle, Zahara suddenly appeared, saving me and many others who would've been defeated by Thargon, and that's when she gave me the gift."

"What gift?" Thomas asked.

"Magic," Anders said.

"That's how it works?" Thomas asked.

"Apparently," Anders held his arms out in front of his body turning them over as he examined them before resting them back behind his head. "She gave me the use of magic and now it flows within me. I have no idea how it works, apart from what Ivan's tried to explain to me. He was bonded during The War of The Magicians, but his dragon was killed before the end of the war. The small bit I've attempted to use is hard to control. I've pretty much been using it constantly since she gave it to me and, as a result, I've never been more tired in my life." He blinked heavily, letting his eyelids remain closed for several seconds before opening them again. "Once I've eaten a little more, I'm going to take a much-needed nap."

"Wow," Kirsten said. The rest of them sat in silence for awhile thinking about all that Anders had told them. He continued to eat several helpings of roasted mutton.

Zahara flew back overhead, returning from her fishing excursion. With the subtleness and gentle paws of a barn cat, she landed just behind Anders as he nibbled the last shreds of meat off the roasting stick. She let her body sprawl out on the green grass around them, closing her eyes as she enjoyed the warmth of the early afternoon sun.

"Yep, that seems about right," Anders said and walked over to where she lay stretched out on the ground and bedded down next to her, closing his eyes and letting sleep overtake him.

Everyone else at the fire suddenly also felt the effects from their long night. Max and Bo joined Anders and his dragon, lying back on the ground where they'd been sitting around the cookfire. Maija walked around to where Anders and Zahara were napping and joined them only a short distance away.

Before Thomas and Kirsten joined the rest of the group in their afternoon nap, Kirsten asked her brother, "When should we tell Anders about what we found in Merglan's chambers?"

Thomas shrugged, "Let him get some rest. We can tell him when he wakes up."

Kirsten nodded and looked over to see her cousin soundly sleeping on the grass next to his dragon. She couldn't believe all she'd experienced in the last several months. "I'll tell him when he wakes up," she said looking back to Thomas. But Thomas was already sprawled out on the ground, eyes closed.

When Anders awoke, he couldn't immediately make the distinction between the darkness behind his eyelids and the darkness of the night sky. He shivered, feeling the cold ground beneath him sucking energy from his body. He sat up a bit confused.

I thought Ivan was going to come and get us before going to search for the missing dragonriders?

Anders searched the area around him, looking for

Zahara. As his eyes adjusted, he began to make out his surroundings. The grassy patch on the valley floor beneath the fortress walls where they'd been napping no longer was beneath him and he couldn't locate Zahara.

He snapped his head around, searching for the cookfire where he'd last seen his friends and family. The fire was gone and there wasn't a soul around. He squinted into the darkness, but couldn't see any sign that anyone had been there.

Anders rose to his feet and took several steps forward. The crunch of dirt and rocks beneath each step echoed through the night. He definitely wasn't in the same place where he'd fallen asleep. Anders' heart began to beat faster.

Where am I? he wondered. Anders remembered how Ivan used his magic to sense the people near him. *Maybe I can do that now.*

He closed his eyes to focus on creating a mental grid of the area around him, searching for any signs of life. He stretched himself out, feeling the cold dirt surrounding him continue farther and farther afield. As he strained his mind to maneuver through the space surrounding him, Anders heard a noise. Opening his eyes, he swiveled to face where he thought it had come from.

"Hello!" he shouted into the darkness. With no immediate response, he turned his right ear to the direction where he thought the noise came from, waiting for an answer. There was none.

"Is anyone there!?" Anders shouted and again thrusting his ear out into the darkness.

Then suddenly he heard it again. A reply to his call. Anders heedlessly ran toward it, not letting himself think about whether the noise he was running toward was a trap or a friend or family member. He didn't care what had made the sound, he just knew that he needed to find it.

"Where are you?!" Anders shouted as he ran.

The noise replied again, this time turning into what sounded like muffled words. He couldn't hear exactly what was being said, but he was able to pinpoint where the noise came from.

As he approached it, he could see the outline of several trees in the darkness. Under the trees there loomed a shadowed shape, darker than the night around him. Coming closer, he began to make out a distinct form... *a dragon.*

Anders skidded to a halt. *Could it be, Merglan?*

He heard the person call to him again.

"Help. Please, help me." It was a woman's voice.

That can't be him, it's a woman, and she's hurt, he thought.

He started running again toward the dragon. As he drew closer, he could see the dragon was lying on top of the woman who'd called out for help. He rushed to the woman's side and heard his feet splash as he ran through something wet. Looking down, Anders nearly lost his dinner when he realized that he was standing in a pool of crimson blood.

Forcing his last meal back down with a hard swallow, he bent down onto one knee and began to examine what kind of trouble the woman was in. Her long brown hair covered her face. She was being crushed under the weight of the bloody dragon's body. He opened his mouth to ask her if she was okay but was cut off when he heard Ivan calling his name. Anders looked up in surprise wondering how Ivan had found him in this desolate place.

"Anders, wake up," Ivan said, shaking Anders by the toe of his boot.

Anders opened his eyes, the setting sun momentarily blinding him with an unexpected jolt of light. Realizing he was no longer next to the woman crushed under the dragon, he bolted upright not sure what was happening to him. Just a moment ago he'd been in a dark place next to a strange woman and a motionless dragon lying in a pool of blood. Now he found himself back in the grass lying beneath the towering walls of the fortress. He put his arm along his brow to block the setting sun so he could see Ivan's figure more clearly. Squinting, he could see that Zahara was still lying next to him, sprawled out sleeping. Max, Bo, his cousins and Maija were chatting around the smoldering remains of their cook fire. He looked back at Ivan, who continued to stare down at him.

"Anders, get up. We are going to search for the missing riders," Ivan said with a stern expression.

"Hold on," Anders said as Ivan began to walk away. "I was just with a woman."

Ivan stopped, cocked his head to the side, and asked, "What?"

"It was dark. I was somewhere else. No one was around. I called out into the darkness and heard a noise. It was a woman. I ran to her. She was under a tree lying in a pool of blood. A dragon lay on top of her." Somewhat breathless, he looked up at Ivan who was now back standing over him.

"Was it a dream?" Anders asked, already knowing better. "It seemed too real to be a dream..."

"That was no dream; you saw one of the missing riders. We must leave at once," Ivan said sternly.

Anders hopped up onto his feet. Zahara had awoken and stood ready to take Anders where they needed to go.

"I need to grab my sword and bow," Anders said,

feeling the place at his side where he usually kept his weapons.

"I'll get Nadir and inform him of your vision," Ivan said. "He'll be joining us on this mission."

"Okay, I'll be quick." Anders ran to his small pile of belongings at the edge of the campfire.

"Hey, what's the rush? Are you going somewhere?" Max asked. He'd been watching when Ivan went to wake Anders.

"I had a vision of one of the dragonriders," Anders said. "We're going to search for them."

"Need any help?" Max, Bo, Maija, Thomas and Kirsten all stood up at the same time, ready to leap into action.

"No, you stay here. Who knows if Merglan is still out there? This is my task to handle."

"Anders wait," Thomas said while Anders was strapping on his sword belt.

Anders faced his cousin.

"You should know about the crystals," Thomas said, glancing over at Maija and Kirsten.

"What crystals?" Anders asked. Just then Ivan called to Anders, waving his hand and urging him to hurry up. He nodded to show he was coming and turned his attention back to Thomas

"I found several crystals in the mine and each time I did the soldiers would confiscate them," Thomas said.

"Merglan's soldiers would bring them into the fortress and straight up to his personal chambers," Kirsten interrupted. "Maija and I found a secret door that led to a room where he was keeping the crystals guarded by a dragon. During the last night, we were there, just after Merglan left, we found that he'd taken the dragon and the crystals with him," she said in a rush.

"Interesting," Anders said. "I'll have to tell Ivan." Anders thanked them before he and Zahara ran to join Ivan. The two climbed onto Zahara's back and held on tightly as she took to the sky. Nadir ran along the ground below them keeping up as they journeyed away from the camp in search of the missing dragons and riders.

CHAPTER
TWO

HONOR FOR A WARRIOR CHIEF

Kirsten and Maija watched as Anders and Ivan climbed onto Zahara's back and took off into the afternoon sky. Nadir, the elf prince, ran beneath them at an alarmingly fast pace.

"Are all elves that fast?" Kirsten asked Max while he sat sipping a mug of hot water.

"Yeah," he said. "It took us three days to walk from the elf city to the Eastland Mountains and we were moving at a steady rate. The entire elf army made the whole trek in one day." He held up his index finger emphasizing his point.

"That's incredible," Kirsten said in astonishment.

"If I had that ability, I would've seen the entire world by now," Bo added, prodding the fire with a stick. "Imagine the places you could go with that kind of speed."

Max bobbed his head as his gaze drifted to the fire's embers, "That would be something else, wouldn't it?"

"It's Bo, right?" Maija asked, leaning forward over her crossed legs and gesturing toward Max's brother.

"Yep, my full name is Beauregard, but it's too much of a

mouthful to say. Also, I got teased a bit when I was younger," he added.

"You were with us on the ship and in the fortress?" Maija asked.

Bo nodded, "I was locked up on that stinking ship, and then they put me to work in the mines."

Maija frowned, "It's crazy to think we went through such a horrible experience together, yet we never met. I'm sure there are lots of others who went through the same thing with us who I wouldn't recognize unless they told me."

"I remember seeing you down in the pit," Thomas said from across the fire.

"I saw you as well," he replied. "You had that guard that all the others didn't like."

"That's why he was such a grouch," Kirsten commented, more to herself than the group.

"He sure was. Nobody seemed to like him much, so he took his frustrations out on all of us," Bo said smiling slightly.

"The way he addressed me when he showed us to the chambermaid's room made my blood boil," Kirsten said, clenching her fists. "Maija had to hold me back from hitting him for his snide remark."

Laughing, Bo said, "He wouldn't have like that. I would've paid money to see anyone hit that grump."

"She did get him in the end though," Thomas added.

"That's right," Maija said, straightening up where she sat and smiling. "When Merglan left before the battle, all of the chambermaids were sent out to work in the pit with you guys. Come morning when the guard came back, Kirsten grabbed his whip and used it on him."

Maija's recounting of the incident drew a hearty laugh

mixed with relief from the group and Thomas added between gasps, "You should've seen the look on his face." He tried to mimic the man's facial expressions as Kirsten pretended to chase Thomas with an imaginary whip in her hands around the fire.

"Now that's got to be the funniest thing I've heard in weeks," Bo said, wiping away his tears of laughter. "When we get back somewhere that has a pub, I'm buying you a drink for that."

Kirsten felt her cheeks flush scarlet and she looked bashfully down at the ground. She'd never been offered a drink before, especially from a boy her age; she'd never even been in a pub before. Theodor let them have a single glass of wine with their dinner after they'd turned fifteen, but he didn't allow them to go to town and have drinks. 'Nothing good ever came from having drinks in a pub,' he would warn them, but they all knew he was known to stop in for a drink or two on his way home from the Grandwood market.

Sensing an awkwardness building, Max broke the silence, "So, what will you do now that this is all over?"

Kirsten looked to her brother and shrugged, "I'm not sure. I guess we'll go back to Grandwood? I haven't really thought about it yet. I think I'm still getting over the fact that we're really out of that evil fortress," she thumbed over her shoulder.

"Yeah," Thomas said, rubbing his hands together. "I'm not too sure, our home is back in Grandwood. If it survived the attack, we could go back and try to pick up where we left off," he paused for a moment, recalling what it was like. "Our father was the heart and soul of that place. With him gone, I'm not sure we could run the farm by ourselves. We could probably manage it alright with

Anders' help, but it doesn't look like he'll be headed that way any time soon."

"Why not?" Bo asked, not really knowing much about Anders or the others.

"I bet Anders will have his hands full in trying to fight Merglan," Thomas responded. "Now that he's been gifted magical abilities and has bonded with Zahara, it could be a long while until his role in this whole thing is over. The last war against Merglan and his evil forces lasted for years. I don't know what Anders' fate will be, but I doubt he'll have the option to return to Grandwood with us."

"You're right, the elves are probably going to want Anders to do some kind of magic training before they face Merglan again," Max said. "Well, if it makes you feel any better, Bo and I don't really know what we're going to do either. Our foster parents don't really care to have me around anymore, now that I'm old enough to fend for myself."

"I don't know what's coming next, but I do know that I'll stick by your side big brother," Bo said slinging his arm around Max's shoulders.

"Thanks, Bo," Max replied with a bashful smile.

Kirsten caught Bo's eye; she thought they did share some resemblance. They both had slightly narrowed eyes, firm jawlines and dark straight hair, but if she hadn't known they were brothers, she wouldn't have guessed they were related. For a moment Kirsten found herself being sucked into Bo's dark eyes. Before it became too apparent to the others, she looked away slightly embarrassed.

"What's happening over there?" Maija asked pointing past their heads toward a gathering crowd of Rolloan warriors.

Max shrugged, "I don't know? We better find out."

Together they walked away from the smoldering embers of their cooking fire. They pushed their way through the crowd until the mass of bodies was so thick that nobody could squeeze any farther.

"I can't see anything," Kirsten said frustrated.

"Here, climb on," Bo said turning so his back was facing her and squatting down.

Kirsten hesitated, she didn't really know Bo; they had only just met recently. Despite her self-consciousness, she did have a good feeling about him and decided to go with her gut.

Placing her hands on his shoulders, Bo squatted lower and Kirsten straddled his head.

He grasped her shins firmly and said, "Ready," then lifted her up off the ground.

Instantly Kirsten was the tallest person in the group. Bo was slightly above average height, so when she sat on his shoulders, she towered over everyone. "What can you see?" he asked.

Kirsten peered across the ocean of dark islander hair swarming around them. In the center of the group, she saw several tall warriors carrying a body. "Some warriors are carrying someone on a board," she said. Bo, Maija and Thomas seemed confused, but Max nodded with a sorrowful expression.

"You know who it is?" Bo asked his brother.

Max pursed his lips and nodded, "It's Jorgen, the lead chief of the Rollo people. He was one of our companion's father."

"Red?" Thomas asked.

Max bobbed his head slowly, "I was there when it happened. Ivan had just faced Thargon in single combat on the battlefield. Thargon had the upper hand and was about

21

to end Ivan's life when Jorgen came rushing at him from his blind side. He tackled Thargon to the ground. In a short-lived effort to distract Thargon, Jorgen was taken by the kurr's axe. I could hear Red's screams from a distance. He was blocked from them by a large group of orcs. That's when Anders faced Thargon head on."

"Wow, that's really how it all happened?" Thomas asked.

"Yeah, shortly after that Zahara and the elves showed up and cleaned house," Max said. "Now I would imagine that the Rollo people will have a funeral for their dead leader and then choose someone to replace him."

"Red won't succeed his father?" Maija asked.

"I don't think that's how leaders are chosen in their culture. My guess is that the top clan members decide who will become their new chief."

Kirsten moved her eyes away from Max and back to the group of warriors carrying their dead leader's body. She recognized Red as one of the people carrying Jorgen. Tears were rolling down his face and into his thick black beard.

"I want to see what it looks like," Maija said, looking expectantly at Thomas and Max.

Max glanced at Thomas and raised his eyebrows.

"Hop on Maija," Thomas said bending down low to the ground.

She climbed onto his shoulders just as Kirsten had done on Bo's. Thomas rose to his feet and Maija joined her friend high above the rest of the crowd. She watched in silence as Red and the other warriors carried his father's body across the camp. The crowd was beginning to shift and people were moving toward the beach.

"Where are they going now?" Max asked Maija and Kirsten.

"It looks like they're taking him to the beach," Kirsten said.

The five of them moved with the crowd. It was so thick that they didn't have much choice other than to continue in the same direction.

"Is there anywhere where we would be able to see what's happening from a distance?" Thomas asked, also wanting to see the proceedings.

"It looks like some cliffs are overlooking the beach that we might be able to scramble up," Kirsten said, pointing to the rock walls separating the black water bay from the rest of the Eastland coastline.

"Let's do it," Thomas said eager to escape the crowd.

Forcing their way through the mass of people still gathering, Max led them away from the center. Kirsten and Maija remained on the shoulders of their carriers because there wasn't much room once they'd started moving for the boys to crouch down and let them off.

"Almost there," Kirsten said to Bo while patting him on the head.

"Thanks for the encouragement," Bo responded sarcastically.

"Sure thing, my little pony," she said teasing him.

When they finally broke away from the crowd, Kirsten took two handfuls of Bo's mid-length hair and said, "Whoa, pony!" He shook his head and bent down to let her off. She hopped off and thanked him for the ride. Kirsten lightly punched him the shoulder and said, "You're pretty strong."

"Your pretty light," he responded tapping her shoulder lightly with his fist.

"Come on, you two," Max said, waving for them to catch up as they were already making their way down the beach to the cliffs.

Bo and Kirsten jogged, catching up as the group walked swiftly around the mob and up to the base of the cliffs that created the secluded bay. Picking the least vertical route, they began to scramble up the rocks. Max and Thomas led the way, pointing out which hand- and footholds were the best to use. Bo went last behind Maija and Kirsten. Soon they were standing on top of a small cliff. Behind them was the Black Water Bay where Bo, Maija and Kirsten were forced off Thargon's ship. To the northwest and away from the bay, they could see the long sandy Marauder's Sea coastline and beyond the beach to the distant base of the Eastland Mountains.

"Not a bad view," Thomas said when Bo reached the top alongside them.

"Not bad at all," Bo replied. The sun hung low over the Marauder's Sea to the west. The sky was just beginning to turn shades of deep purple, vibrant red and bright orange as the sun set.

"If we weren't watching a funeral this would be a pretty romantic place to bring a girl," Max said, sitting down and resting his forearms on his knees.

"Or a boy," Thomas said, mimicking Max and smiling at him, eyebrows raised slightly.

Max looked at him a little taken aback by the comment and said, "Or a boy, if that's what you're into."

Maija looked at Kirsten, eyes wide and head tilted a little sideways. Kirsten responded by shrugging and smiling slightly.

"They're almost at the beach," Bo said pointing down to the group carrying Jorgen's body.

Everyone watched as they hauled the dead chief out onto the sand. They placed his body into a small boat that sat waiting on the beach. The boat was decorated with blooming flowers collected from the valley floor. Jorgen appeared to still be wearing his battle armor. They watched as Red placed a shield at his side and his sword in his hands, gripping the hilt at his chest.

The group of people who had carried Jorgen to the boat now stepped back while Red pushed the craft out into the sea's receding tide. As he did so, the entire Rollo contingent began to sing. The song was sung in native Rolloan, so none of the other humans and elves watching could sing along.

After several verses, the five of them hummed to the repeating tune. This mass of people all singing in honor of their fallen leader was quite a spectacular sight to see. Despite their history of being tricked and ambushed by the Rolloans, even the elves stood to watch in respect for the dead chief. A Rolloan archer came forward and lit an arrow in a fire on the beach. He aimed the arrow, angling it skyward before loosing it toward the drifting boat. The shot was true and hit its target, thudding into the wooden boat. Kirsten expected the boat to burst into flames, but nothing happened. The flame on the arrow blew out, but just as the archer bent down to light a second arrow, the boat suddenly burst into flames.

"How did that happen?" Kirsten asked. "I saw the flame go out on the arrow."

"I would guess that one of the elves did that with magic," Max said. "They probably didn't want the Rolloans to suffer the embarrassment of not having the arrow set fire to the ship." They all nodded, realizing he was probably correct in his assumption.

After the singing ended, the five of them remained up on the rock until the sun was nearly below the horizon. The ship continued to burn as it drifted into the distance.

Through shivering teeth, Kirsten said, "I'm going back to camp; it's getting cold up here." She stood up and began to climb down.

"I'll go with you," Bo said following her.

Max, Thomas and Maija watched the sun fully set before they climbed down off the rocks.

Thomas and Maija waited for Max to catch up with them after returning to the ground, but he called to them, "I'll meet you two back at camp. I need to talk with someone for a minute."

"Okay," Thomas said and split off with Maija.

Max turned, following the sharp line where grass turned to sand along the beach and into the edge of the camp. He needed to find Britt and knew she liked to set up her tent and build her fire along the outskirts of the camp.

After the sun had set, the sprawling encampment was illuminated by the glow of hundreds of campfires. Max walked among the tents and campfires looking at the faces of those lit by the fire. He was searching for anyone he recognized from Britt's crew, or the Captain herself.

Eventually, he noticed her somber-looking face staring blankly into the flickering flames of her fire. Most members of her crew weren't with her. Max was relieved to finally see her again and get a chance to talk to her alone.

Her campfire was near the edge of the camp, just as it had been when Anders and Max first met the Rolloans. The elves were close by, but not interspersed with the warriors. The tension between their two peoples was not relaxed enough for them to be sleeping and cooking among one another, but they had both seen battle recently and were not in any mood for fighting with each other.

"Captain," Max said as he moved out of the shadows and into Britt's view.

Britt's expression lifted to a smile when she heard his voice, but she didn't say anything in response. Looking at Max, she simply scooted over and patted the spot on the log next to her, inviting him to sit beside her. Max strode across the gap between them and sat down, exhaling as he did so.

"I'm sorry to hear about Jorgen," he said.

"He was a strong leader and a well-minded person," she said not lifting her gaze from the fire.

"Shouldn't you be celebrating with the rest of the warriors? I thought it was an honor to die in battle," he said, motioning toward the other groups of people dancing, whooping and shouting nearby.

Britt remained silent for a moment eyeing the other warriors before she spoke, "I'm happy that many of our people got to die an honorable death..."

"But..." Max said, trying to coax out the rest of what she was thinking.

"But I am sad. I'm sad to have so many of my friends gone from this world forever. I lost several good people from my crew, even though I know they died with the highest honor. I was there to see the pain and fear in their eyes when they were cut down," she sniffled and wiped a tear from the corner of her eye.

"Is that why you're sitting over here by yourself?" he asked. "Because you're sad and you don't want any of the other warriors to see you mourning the loss of your friends?"

She snapped a twig in half and threw it into the fire, shrugging. With her legs extended straight out in front of her, heels dug into the ground, she began to wiggle her feet nervously. "I feel so... ugh," she said.

Max gently grabbed her by the forearm, "It's normal to be sad for the people in your life who have died."

27

"Not for my people," she retorted. "If they see me like this, they'll think I'm weak and no longer fit to lead."

"Britt listen," Max said moving his grip down and taking her hand. She looked surprised, seeming to just then notice that he was touching her. She looked at his hand and then at him. "Everyone grieves. And everyone does it in a different way. You can't let anyone tell you how to feel, because each person handles it differently. You may be crying and feeling sad while someone else is laughing because they're remembering something happy about that person. Then five minutes later they will be in tears and you will be laughing about something funny that you remember happening with the lost person. It's normal to feel the way you're feeling now."

Britt shifted her gaze back into the fire and asked, "You've lost people close to you before?"

Max nodded, "Yes, more times than I'm comfortable with. And each time I felt something different. When it was the person closest to me, I was too young to understand it. The more I wanted to cry and weep along with everyone else, the more I couldn't. People looked at me like they thought I didn't care. I was just as sad as anyone else, but for some reason, I couldn't shed tears."

"That's kind of like what's happening to me now, except the opposite," Britt said wiping away more tears. "I'm the one who can't stop crying and they're all happy and wondering what is wrong with me that I can't join them."

"Don't worry about what other people are thinking now. Everyone knows you're a good Captain and a strong warrior. I would gladly sail alongside you any day," Max said. He realized he was still holding her hand and let it go.

Britt smiled and turned her upper body to face him,

then gave him a hug. "Thank you," she whispered through her sniffles.

For a moment he was taken by surprise by her show of affection, then he embraced it and hugged her back. "Well, I hope that's the last time I have to be serious for a while," he said when they pulled away from each other's embrace.

"It's not like you to say such wise things," Britt said. "You usually crack jokes, not words of wisdom."

"Yeah, I know," he shivered and brushed his arms and legs as though he was trying to get something off his body.

"What're you doing?" Britt asked.

"Trying to get all this serious off me," he said smiling at her.

She laughed, "Did you mean it when you said you'd sail with me any day?"

Max stopped wiggling around, "Of course. You're a great Captain."

"Well I am in need of more warriors after that battle..." she said raising her eyebrows and cracking a thin smile.

Max looked up and to the left thinking for a moment about what it would be like and answered, "Can I bring my brother, Bo?" When she nodded, Max added, "Well you know, I'm not one to turn down an adventure."

She hugged him again and he laughed, holding her friendly embrace. "Good, I need more people like you in my life," she said.

When Maija and Thomas returned, Kirsten and Bo were sitting close to one another near the fire, Kirsten with her legs crossed, and Bo with his forearms wrapped around his knees. They had already begun preparing a meal for everyone.

"Where's Max?" Bo asked, seeing his brother wasn't with them.

"He went to talk to someone in camp, I guess," Thomas said taking the bowl Kirsten had handed him.

When the four of them had almost finished their rice and root vegetable medley, Maija asked, "I wonder if Anders and Zahara have found the dragons and riders they're looking for?"

Through a mouthful of food, Thomas said, "I bet they'll find them quick enough. Anders is an excellent tracker. My guess is they'll be back by morning."

Kirsten put her hand on Maija's shoulder and said comfortingly, "They'll be okay; Anders always comes back."

Maija felt slightly relieved by the sentiment but had a strange feeling in her stomach about it.

Later that night after Max returned and the others were asleep, Maija sat alone by the campfire. She listened to the many sounds of festivities coming from the camp thinking it strange that the elves didn't make as much noise as the Rollo Island warriors. She strained her ears, but couldn't hear anyone clearly. She found it troubling that her previously exceptional hearing had suddenly returned to that of a normal human. She fiddled nervously as she tried to distract her mind from worry. As she ventured to her tent and lay down, Maija couldn't help feeling horrified that Anders would come across something dangerous during his search.

CHAPTER

THREE

A TRACE OF MERGLAN'S WRATH

Anders turned his head slightly, looking down toward the valley floor as Zahara climbed higher into the air, flapping her enormous wings. He could see their camp shrinking as they quickly moved east along the Eastland Mountain Front. Nadir soon became a dark speck moving swiftly across the valley floor, chasing Zahara's shadow as she flew overhead. Anders strained his neck to catch one last glimpse of the camp and thought he could just make out people gathering near the camp's center.

Wondering why the Rolloans would be gathering led Anders to one conclusion: *They must have brought Jorgen's body back for a proper Rolloan funeral.*

Turning back to face the rushing wind, Anders dipped his chin slightly, the air pushing his hair back in the breeze as they flew. When remembering the horrific way in which the Rolloan chief's life had come to a sudden end, Anders suddenly felt an unexpected swelling of emotion. He found that tilting his head back allowed the cool air to dry his welling eyes. The evening air bit at his cheeks, reddening

31

and stinging his exposed skin. This chilling sensation brought his focus back to the task at hand; they had to find the two dragonriders who'd flown to their aid earlier and not returned after confronting Merglan.

Suddenly Anders became acutely aware that Zahara had been observing his string of waffling emotions. Embarrassed by exposing this vulnerability, he quickly created a distraction, remarking, *Isn't the sunset gorgeous from up here?*

I guess. It's just like every other one I've seen, she said through their connected minds.

Not for me, he replied. The realization that very few people in the world had been so lucky to see the sunset from the back of a dragon mid-flight hit him like a ton of bricks. *After all the chaos and madness we've seen, how crazy is it that I can enjoy something so constant and fundamental as the setting sun?*

Your mind is different from most, that's why. And that's why I was drawn to you in the first place. There's a natural goodness in you, something that not many people have, she told him.

Anders didn't reply and they remained silent, pondering the past several days' events until the last remaining glimmers of the sun faded beyond the horizon. Darkness consumed them and the cold that came with it sent shivers through Anders as he tried to huddle in closer to Zahara's neck, hoping her head would provide a windbreak, but his efforts proved useless. Within a matter of minutes after the darkening night surrounded them, they reached the spot along the Eastland Mountains where Merglan and his dragon had intercepted the elves on their way to assist the Rollo Island warriors and Anders' small crew.

Reminding them that he was along on the flight, Ivan

said, *We should begin searching with our minds for the dragons and their riders, but be careful. Merglan and his dragon could be close.*

Anders hesitated, he didn't know how to search with his mind, as Ivan suggested. It was too dark for him to see very far by sight, and he wasn't sure what Ivan meant by searching with his mind.

"How do I do that?" Anders asked aloud over his shoulder to the old rider sitting behind him on Zahara's back.

"I thought you'd done this by now when you were using magic during the battle?" he asked.

"I'm not really sure what I did during the battle," Anders answered "For everything other than the basic healing spells you showed us, I've just been acting on instincts. I don't understand how to control this power yet."

"I'm sorry. It's been so long since I learned how to control my powers. Even when I began, I had training before I formed my bond with Jazzmaryth."

Anders' curiosity was piqued at the mention of Ivan's dragon, "That's the first time you've mentioned your dragon's name."

"Oh," Ivan said, fumbling for new words like a youngster caught telling a lie.

"I like that name," Anders said.

Me too, Zahara added. *It's regal.*

Clearing his throat, Ivan continued aloud, "In order to use the magical energy in your body through a focused channel, you must first void your mind of all thoughts. It is hard to do at first, especially with so many distractions like mourning for lost ones during a battle or flying on the back of your dragon for the first time, but there are a few tricks I know that helped me all those years ago when I was training. I like to close my eyes and imagine that I'm standing alone on a dark plain. There's nothing on the dark plain, not even ground under my feet, just a sea of darkness. Once I'm alone with nothing around to distract me, then I can begin to use my mind to reach out and search. Try it, perhaps it will help you."

Anders was doubtful that this exercise would work, but he didn't know any better way to begin, so he closed his eyes and attempted to picture himself in total darkness. Instead of a dark plain, Anders found himself standing outside his home back at Highborn Bay. The salty scent of the bay filled his nostrils as he stood alone beside the large oak tree in front of their house. He'd spent many nights staring up at the starry sky in this very spot. Clanging noises sounded behind him – Kirsten and Theodor cooking in the kitchen. He knew this was a fabrication of his memory and attempted to make them disappear. *Darkness, you're in total darkness,* he told himself. The harder he tried to imagine himself alone, the more the memories of times spent on the familiar farm kept forcing their way into his head.

"This isn't working," he said in frustration at his inability to clear his thoughts.

Try something else then, Zahara said in an encouraging tone. *Before using my mind to sense things around me, I like to remember the time I spent in my egg. It was a warm and comfortable place, where the noises of the outside world were muted. The muffled sounds couldn't distract me. Maybe you can remember when you were in your egg and then you will be able to clear your mind?*

Anders chuckled slightly, *I didn't hatch from an egg like you did.*

That's weird, Zahara said.

34

One of the many differences between our species, Anders commented, forgetting how little time Zahara had spent among any race other than her own.

Anders closed his eyes, trying to remember his mother and father. At first, he felt a warming presence, but the harder he worked to focus on what his parents looked like, the less he could see. He was about to voice his frustration again when he had an idea. The warm presence he'd felt when he first thought of his parents was the most comforted he'd felt in years. He decided not to try to remember what his parents looked like, but instead to search for the feeling he had of them being near. He felt the warming presence return, which cleared his thoughts completely.

"Hey, it worked! I actually did it," Anders said surprised at the method he'd used.

Did my egg trick help? Zahara asked.

Oddly enough, it did, but in a slightly different way.

"Okay," Ivan said, continuing his teaching aloud. "Once your mind is clear of all distractions, you can begin to reach out with it, letting the magic within you sense the areas around you. The sensation will be strange at first, but you'll soon learn what to look for. Start out by reaching out in a specific direction before trying to use a multi-directional sweep," Ivan said.

Anders nodded, preparing to replicate what he'd managed to do. Again, he thought of having his parents nearby. The comforting warming sensation gave him the ability to void his mind of all distractions, bringing his mental faculties to attention.

He knew Nadir would be running slightly behind them, so he decided to test his abilities by sensing for Nadir. Keeping his focus on the empty space between Zahara and the valley floor beneath them, Anders let his mental search cast out. The vast empty space behind Zahara felt cold as his thoughts searched further in a linear direction down toward the world below. Anders felt as though his body were falling through an endless sky, waiting for the ground to arrive. His head ached with the numbing chill that came from the space between them and the ground below. Like a flash of light, the sudden appearance of the features below came into Anders thoughts. He could feel the blades of grass along the valley floor, the dips and rises of the topography as he extended out behind them. Suddenly he could sense a warmth. This warmth was different from that of his memories. This warmth was physical and felt near. He focused in on it with excited anticipation. For a moment he thought he'd come across an animal moving along the plains, but quickly noticed the pace at which it was running and recognized the form to be their elf companion, Nadir. Anders identified the elf's familiar presence and let his connection break away.

Wow, he thought to himself, shaking his head in alarm. *That's freaky.*

Next, he searched out in front of them, expanding his mind to the area where the elves encountered Merglan. The slopes of the mountainsides felt burnt, trampled and disturbed. He couldn't explain how he knew it, but he'd become increasingly aware of the tremendous amount of pain and anguish resonating from the area. Unable to keep his mind locked on the location, he winced away, gasping for air as his mental search broke.

That's where he attacked them, Zahara said.

"Can you feel that?" Anders asked over his shoulder to Ivan.

Ivan nodded, responding over the rushing of the wind

as they flew. "My skills are not as powerful as they used to be, but I can feel the place where they were attacked. It isn't as strong a sensation for me as it might be for you and Zahara, but I'm aware of the mark it's left on the land."

Zahara circled the site of initial attack several times, soaring lower with each pass. After ensuring no one was in the immediate surroundings, they landed on the hillside where the fight began. Anders and Ivan hopped off Zahara's back, coming to land on the scorched earth. The burnt area continued to smolder where the dragons had begun to engage in combat. This extended out for several acres in each direction. The dead trees along the forested hillside hung askew, snapped and mangled after large dragons had crashed into them. In the center of the turmoil, Ivan found a significant depression in the ground, presumably where one of the dragons had crashed into the side of the mountain with great force.

"Anders. Over here," Ivan called to him. As Anders approached the edge of the shallow craterlike depression, Ivan pointed into it and said, "Look."

A small puddle of blood pooled on the burnt ground.

Anders stepped into the depression and knelt, examining the scene. "The dragon must have been injured after the impact," he said.

Ivan nodded, "If the injury occurred during the impact, the blood would have splattered. It appears as though the dragon who crashed here sustained this injury after making its initial impact."

Nadir came rushing into view, quickly coming to their side. Anders was surprised to see the elf hadn't even broken a sweat and did not seem to be out of breath in the slightest.

He doesn't even look tired, Anders said to Zahara, astonished that the elf had run all that way without showing any evidence of exhaustion.

Elves are funny like that, Zahara replied. *They're able to travel great distances very quickly, just like us dragons. Except that my species' means of transportation is much more efficient than stumbling along the ground like a fool.*

He doesn't seem to have stumbled. It's incredible how they can do that.

Zahara sighed.

With a sweep of his eyes, Nadir quickly examined the crater where Anders knelt. He crouched down next to Anders and swiped his finger in the puddle of dragon blood, bringing his crimson-tipped finger up for a closer look. He eyed it carefully for a moment, then said, "They fought along the mountains to the north."

"You can tell that from the blood?" Anders asked amazed at his tracking abilities.

"No," he said smugly. "I was here when the attack began. I saw them battling farther to the north. The riders were trying to draw Merglan farther away from his fortress."

"Oh," Anders said his cheeks flushing with embarrassment.

"Let's get back to the skies and continue searching," Ivan said.

Anders and Ivan climbed back onto Zahara, settling on her scaled back. They had to hold on tightly as she ran down the hillside to get more lift for takeoff.

Once they'd returned to the sky, the three of them continued searching the area with their minds. Anders slowly began to get the grasp of using the magical energy within him to mentally explore an area in one direction. Recalling and then disregarding Ivan's warning, he decided to attempt to sweep out in multiple directions at once. Anders focused all of his attention on imagining that his mind was like many arms reaching out in all directions. This resulted in the overwhelming sensation of understanding each element in the topography sprawling out around them. The many cliffs lining the mountain slopes gave him sudden pause as they were abrupt changes in his mental world.

Suddenly his head snapped back as if he'd just smashed into a wall. Anders felt a vice-like grip pinching down on his brain, squishing it with increasing pain. In the sudden attack on their bonded minds, Anders noticed that Zahara was beginning to lose control of her flight path. She must have been feeling the same pinching pain that Anders was because she dipped and lulled, swaying through the sky. Anders reached up, gripping his head in hopes that the pain would somehow go away. Zahara let out a loud roar and began to fall rapidly. Her wings no longer carrying them through the sky, she was going straight down toward the ground.

Over the tremendous pain attacking his mind, Anders could barely tell that Ivan was shouting to them both. Anders couldn't hear him clearly and, judging by the lack of response from the dragon, Zahara couldn't hear Ivan's shouts over the excruciating pain either. Blinking his eyes rapidly from the pain, Anders saw the ground fast approaching as they fell. Zahara struggled to regain control of their descent, but every time she tried to open her wings, something seemed to force them back in tight to her body. Anders clenched, flexing every muscle in his body as he braced for impact.

Zahara slammed into a patch of trees on the leeward side of the mountain, snapping the thick conifers in half with their initial impact. The fibers of each individual tree exploded upon the force of Zahara's body pushing through. The loud popping and whipping branches sounded through Anders' ears; he knew they were about to hit the ground. Zahara's body recoiled when it skidded into the mountainside, sending Anders rocketing forward and feeling his body leave the perch on his dragon's back.

He and Ivan flew into the air, thrown from Zahara's back as she began to tumble after the initial impact. Anders flailed his arms like a windmill as he tried to keep himself from hitting the ground headfirst. As hard as he tried to avoid it, the angle at which he was thrown off Zahara was such that he toppled headlong over the ground where she collided with the mountain. His head tilted downward while his legs came overhead. He tucked forward trying to protect his head from the eventual impact. Thinking the ground would soon break his trajectory, Anders was surprised to feel himself continuing to tumble through the air. He soared through the air with his legs and feet up over the rest of his body; he tucked his head up to his waist, trying to force himself to rotate to put his feet back under his body. The only things Anders could see while he continued to fly through empty space were his legs and feet and the dark sky behind them.

As he drifted through the openness, he thought to himself, *When am I going to hit the ground? I should have hit the ground by now; when am I going to hit the ground? Oh no, I'm going to break my back. If I survive this, my back will be broken.*

Suddenly Anders could see the rushing of a rock wall moving past his head. As soon as he'd seen the rushing rock, his feet passed through the edge of a tree's thinly spread branches.

Oh sh... he thought and slammed into the ground, with his shoulder blades breaking his fall. He tried hard to keep his head tucked on impact, but it wasn't enough to prevent the whiplash. Flattening out from the force of the crash, he bounced off the ground and rocked forward again. He flipped in the air and hit the slope with the front of his shoulder this time. The steep mountainside where he landed left him tumbling out of control. His forehead grazed the side of a tree. The impact, though not direct, was enough of a blow to knock him unconscious momentarily. Coming to seconds later, he could feel that he'd stopped tumbling and was now sliding down the hillside. Anders slowly came to a stop. He dared not move, worried that his spine had been broken in the fall.

The air had been knocked out of his lungs in the hard landing and the struggle for breath made him sit upright. Straightening his neck and opening his mouth as wide as he could, he tried desperately to get some oxygen back into his lungs. As hard as he tried, he couldn't get any air. A terrible thought surfaced – he began to wonder if Merglan was near and had created a spell that removed all oxygen from the air. He continued to gasp. Just as he thought he would suffocate, air rushed back into his lungs. The sudden inhalation made him cough violently. He sat on the side of the mountain heaving, relieved there wasn't a spell corrupting his ability to inhale. At last, he could breathe freely again.

Well, I guess my spine is okay, he thought as he stood up and stretched his battered body.

Looking around at where he'd finally come to a stop, he quickly searched, but couldn't see Zahara or Ivan.

Maybe I'll try seeing where they are with my mind, he thought. He quickly dismissed the notion, because though the vice-like grip on his mind had disappeared only moments before, he was hesitant to try again after the mental attack. The initial pain was gone, but his head pounded from both the attack and the impact of the crash. He put his hand on his forehead and squeezed it slightly hoping that the applied pressure would lessen the pain. It didn't work. When he lowered his hand, he noticed it was covered with his own blood.

Anders looked up the slope he'd just tumbled down. Although it was dark, his eyes had adjusted to the night and he could see farther than he expected. A cliff band stretched the width of the slope above him. Zahara had initially crashed even higher up the mountain above the band of exposed rock. He looked left and slowly out to the right of the cliff. He could see a chute where water and fallen rocks collected on their way downhill. The rock barrier looked unavoidable in all other directions. If he wanted to get back up to their initial crash site, he was going to have to ascend the steep chute.

Anders slogged uphill to the base of the chute and began scrambling up the steep chimney. He hoped Zahara was not too badly hurt from the crash. His deep concern for her kept him moving despite the difficulty of the climb. He wondered what exactly had happened to her when he was thrown from her back. She'd tumbled out of view. He could only see sky until he landed.

Anders felt his muscles straining and hardening while scrambling up the steep chute, but he ignored his body telling him to stop or slow down. With great relief, he reached the top of the draw and found himself back above the cliff band.

Bending over and placing his hands on his knees, he breathed heavily while he began searching the top of the cliff for Ivan and his dragon. He identified the uphill side of the small meadow where he was standing. The trees above the clearing were snapped where they'd broken through. The ground was gnarled and torn where Zahara's body had crashed. Anders followed this path across the clearing and over a small horizon. He rushed to the edge of the slope where he saw her body. She was lying on the side of the cliff, her tail draped over the edge. She wasn't moving.

"Zahara!" he shouted and ran as fast as he could to her side. Sliding onto his knees, he grabbed her head and said with worry, "Zahara wake up."

Her large eye quivered for a moment, then opened. Anders asked, "Are you okay?"

She closed her eye and lifted her head. Rolling over onto her stomach, she got her four feet under her body and opened her eyes again. Anders stood with his hand on her neck trying to support her. She pushed herself up, wavering slightly. Realizing she was on the edge of the cliff, she took several steps uphill before sitting down.

Are you ok? Anders asked again, this time silently.

I think so, she said and, seeing Anders' torn clothes and face covered in blood, added, *You don't look so good*.

Anders put his hand up to his forehead again and then looked at the sticky blood on his hand, *Yeah, but I feel good enough*. He sat down, his body sore and tired, his head still throbbing. Together they remained still, taking a moment to recuperate from the crash.

Where's Ivan? Zahara asked.

Anders shrugged, *I don't know*.

I'll search for him with my mind.

"No, don't!" Anders shouted aloud, raising his arms and waving his hands. "We were attacked when our minds were searching before. Ivan said Merglan could still be out

43

here and I think he might have been the cause of our crash. We shouldn't take the chance of being attacked again."

Okay. We should find him then.

Yes, Anders agreed, groaning in pain as he stood up.

The two went back to the indentation in the side of the mountain where they'd crashed. Anders remembered seeing Ivan fly off at the same moment that he did, so they stood in the tilled soil and looked in the direction he would have gone. Anders looked over the cliff edge into the darkened area before them. First, he eyed the area at the base near the spot where he had landed. It took awhile to search the space below through the darkness, but after not seeing anything on the ground, he decided to run his gaze across the trees that rose up in front of him. It didn't take them long to spot Ivan climbing down from a tall tree.

"Ivan!" Anders shouted. Ivan looked around and saw Zahara and Anders standing on top of the cliff. "Are you okay?" Anders asked, cupping his hands around his mouth to make his voice carry farther.

Ivan waved and shouted back, letting them know he was not seriously injured from the crash. "Stay there. I'll meet you at the top of the cliff," he called back.

Anders and Zahara did as he asked, taking the time at the top of the cliff to rest up. Before Ivan reached them, Nadir ran down from the ridgeline above.

"Are you okay?" he asked, his face furrowed with concern. After making sure the two were not terribly hurt, he asked about Ivan. Anders pointed over the cliff and told him Ivan was on his way up.

"What happened?" Nadir asked. "I was following you and all of a sudden you started faltering. Before I knew it, I saw you plummet over the mountainside."

"I don't know exactly what happened," Anders replied,

still mystified. "We were searching the area with our minds and I think we were attacked. It could be that Merglan is still in the area and attacked us while we were vulnerable."

Nadir drew his sword and looked around at the tree line along the meadow, ready for an attack at any moment.

"I doubt he's that close," Anders said. "He would've attacked by now if he was going to. We've been exposed for awhile."

"I'm not going to take any chances," the elf said, gripping the handle of his sword tightly.

Just then Ivan's head emerged over the horizon line of the cliff. He had climbed the same chute Anders had to get to Zahara. Anders and Zahara rose back to their feet.

"What happened to us?" Anders asked him. "Were we attacked by Merglan?"

"In a way," Ivan said, walking up to them and brushing the dirt and pine needles from his body. "We must have hit some form of an airmine."

"An airmine?" Anders asked confused as to what exactly that meant.

Rubbing more dirt and needles from his hair, Ivan said, "Yes, an airmine. It's a technique only the most skilled sorcerers can use to knock their enemies out of the sky. He must have placed one here when he was being pursued by the other riders.

"You can create a sphere of energy around a particular location that will disrupt the minds of other sorcerers. A trained magic user can see them coming from a mile away and avoid them. It is a desperate attempt to shake your pursuers or attackers."

How come you didn't see it coming? Zahara asked, her voice sounding in both Ivan and Anders' minds.

"As I have told you before, after the loss of my dragon,

my abilities diminished greatly. The only things I can still do fairly well are sense and locate people, not traps laid by powerful magicians. You two are not yet at the level of training that you would have noticed it. It was lucky that we weren't severely injured in the crash." As the words came out of Ivan's mouth, he noticed the blood covering Anders' face and gave him a strange look.

Anders noticed Ivan's reaction and said, "It looks worse than it is. Head wounds bleed a lot, I guess."

Is it safe to continue searching for the others? Zahara asked.

"Yes, I don't feel Merglan's presence in the immediate area. I think we're safe to continue our search," Ivan said. "How are you holding up?" Ivan asked Nadir, noticing he was still clutching his sword.

"I'm fine. A little slower than you, but I'm enduring just fine," Nadir said, placing his sword back into its scabbard on his back.

"Good. Well, if we have all recovered, then we should continue our search. Given the airmine, it seems we are on the right path," Ivan said.

Anders nodded, "Yeah. I just hope there aren't any more airmines around."

"If Merglan's near, airmines are the least of our worries," Ivan said cautiously.

Zahara crouched, letting Anders and Ivan climb up onto her back. Once they'd properly seated themselves as best they could without a saddle or ties to hold them on, she pounced, spreading her wings as she leapt over the edge of the cliff. Gravity did most of the work as she took flight while Anders tried to keep himself from sliding forward as she gained speed.

Glancing behind them, Anders caught glimpses of

Nadir as he ran below, rushing in and out of the forested mountainside. Carefully and with a very short, one-directional advance, Anders used his mind to search for any signs of the missing dragonriders. Zahara circled high over the mountaintops, forcing Anders to expand his reach when he thought he felt something. Homing in on the large object, Anders thought it wasn't a part of the natural landscape, yet it wasn't living either.

"I think I found something," Anders said, calling to Ivan over the roar of the wind.

"Where?" he asked.

"Directly in front of us and down below the midpoint of the mountainside," Ander replied.

Zahara dipped toward the location Anders had described. Ivan soon acknowledged that he felt it too.

"Do you have it?" Ivan asked Zahara.

Yes, I do, she said as she angled herself over the spot.

"Land us close, but not directly on it. It could be another trap," Ivan said to her.

She did as he asked and landed in a close gap among the trees, just wide enough for her body to slide in. Climbing off Zahara's back, Anders nearly fell under the ache of his body. He caught himself on a tree and gave Ivan a nod to assure him he was okay to continue. Ivan led as they crept quietly through the forest.

Do you think I should stay here? Zahara asked Anders with their mental link.

Yes, you stay here and wait for Nadir. I'll let you know what we find and if it's safe to continue. Okay, be careful.

Anders continued to focus his senses on whatever thing lay in waiting among the trees before them. As far as he could tell, it was massive and motionless. As they drew closer, Ivan stopped, putting his arm out to the side and motioning for Anders to do the same. Anders watched Ivan's face as he squinted through the darkened forest. His eyes widened and mouth slackened, opening with horror.

"What is it?" Anders whispered.

"It's not a trap," Ivan said, trying to remain stoic, but Anders could tell whatever he saw shook him to the core.

Anders stepped closer and peered into the shadows where Ivan was gawking. He could see a large ominous shape, somehow darker than the blackness of the forest, slumped in a pile on the ground. Taking longer than Ivan, Anders slowly recognized what it was. His heart sank and he called to Zahara.

It's safe to approach, but you should prepare yourself mentally.

What is wrong? Zahara asked, sensing his sorrow.

You'll see when you get here, he thought as he and Ivan approached the dark mass.

Anders walked slowly alongside Ivan, approaching the wilted body of a dead dragon. The dragon was much larger than Zahara, indicating the creature was more advanced in age. Lying on the ground next to the dragon was its rider, who also seemed to be lifeless. There was no blood on the ground as he'd seen in his dream or back at the initial point of attack that they found in the crater. Anders thought that this dragon and rider pair couldn't be the ones from the crater or his dream. That meant the other was still out there and most likely wounded, or he or she, too, was dead. Given the lack of blood at the scene, Anders speculated that Merglan had killed them using some kind of spell or curse. He and Ivan came to a halt just short of the bodies, staring at the gruesome scene.

The dead dragon's body lay mangled and contorted in a

terrible way. Zahara shielded her emotions from Anders when she came to stand at their side.

After sniffing the ground and air around the lifeless body, she once again opened the line of communication between them, *I didn't know them very well, only from our short venture from Cedarbridge to where Merglan attacked them.*

I'm sorry, Zahara. It's not what we were hoping to find, Anders said, trying to bring both of them some comfort. "What do we do now?" he asked Ivan. "Should we bury them?" As the question left his mouth, he regretted asking it when he thought about how long it would take to dig a grave for the enormous dragon, and, to add to the ill-thought-out question, they didn't have a shovel.

"We should burn them," Ivan said shortly. "When a dragon dies, you shouldn't bury it. Burning them transfers their magic back into the form that flows within the earth. Once their energy is restored to the natural force of the earth, they'll be allowed to rest in peace. We should clear out the trees around the body, however. We don't want to set the entire forest ablaze."

"Won't it take too much time to clear out all of these trees?" Anders asked looking around at the thick stand of pines surrounding them. "We don't have any tools with us other than our weapons. I don't know how long it would take me to fell a tree with my sword."

"Zahara can knock them over for us," Ivan said. "Can't you?" he asked.

Zahara took the opportunity as a chance to honor a fallen member of her race. *Of course, I can*, she said, positioning herself between a nearby tree and the body of the dragon. She pushed hard against the base of the tall tree with her shoulder. Anders watched as her talons dug deep into the soil as she heaved against the tree, pushing it to the ground with a crash.

As she continued to plow over the remaining trees near the dead dragon, Anders and Ivan carried the rider's lifeless body over and laid him next to the dragon. His neck was broken and his head had twisted around in an unnatural position.

"Who were they?" Anders asked Ivan when they lay the elf next to his dragon.

"The elf was a young rider named Keanu. He was a hundred and eight years old, which is fairly young for an elf. He wasn't a rider during The War of Magicians though, so I didn't train with him. He had since bonded with this dragon. I'm not sure the dragon and I have ever met before, but I was an acquaintance of Keanu. It's evident to me that he wasn't ready to engage in battle with Merglan. They needed more training," Ivan said.

As Zahara finished taking down the last of the trees surrounding the two bodies, Nadir caught up to them. Anders noticed that he was breathing heavily, apparently beginning to fatigue from running through the rugged mountains. His face scrunched with remorse when he joined them. A tear rolled down his cheek as he knelt next to his fallen kin. He spoke in his native tongue as he ran his hands over Keanu's face. Before he rose to his feet, he removed the sword and belt from Keanu's body. With his head held low, he walked over to Anders and handed him the blade, "Take this in his honor."

Anders held out his hand and took the blade, but before he accepted the transfer, he asked Nadir, "Are you sure?"

Nadir nodded, "This is what Keanu would have wanted, for Lazuran to go to another rider."

Anders stood, eyes wide and mouth slacked in awe. He'd never been given anything from someone who'd passed on before, especially not a bonded rider's sword. Nadir placed the sheathed sword into his hand. Before taking the generous gift, Anders glanced to Ivan for approval, who nodded, making it clear that he was to accept the gift.

Anders examined the ornate craftsmanship of the stunning blade. Starting at the hilt, Anders eyed the dark wooden grip. Its handle arched slightly providing the sword with a comfortable two-handed hilt. Several sapphire crystals had been embedded into the handle, the crystal in the pommel atop the grip being the largest by three times. The huge blue crystal would keep his hands from sliding off the grip in battle. As he wrapped his hand around the grip, he noted how little the crystals protruded into the flat of his hand. If he had not seen them first, Anders wouldn't have known they were there at all by the feel of the hilt.

Slowly he exposed the first several inches of Lazuran. The thinly crafted steel reflected what little light shone from the starry sky that night. He could make out Lazuran's elven name etched into the blade near the shortened guard. Anders paused before revealing more of the curved blade, rolling it slightly and watching the light glint off the blade's steel. With a final display of grandeur, Anders withdrew the elven sword from its scabbard. The steel rang as it came cleanly out of the leather sheath. For an instant, Anders felt the blade come to life. It sounded as though it was speaking to him. He nearly dropped it, but an unexpected surge of energy passed from the blade directly into his arm. He thought he saw a blueish hue emerge from the sapphire crystal in the pommel, but when it startled him, the hue vanished as suddenly as it had first shone.

Shaking off the unexpected sensation and chalking it up to the excitement of holding such a spectacular blade, Anders hefted it, letting the weight of it register with his grip. He thought a sword of such greatness would be heavier. To his surprise, Lazuran was light in his arm, lighter than his dagger that was less than a third the size of the elven blade.

Anders was about to test the sword's balance during a set of swings the Rolloan warriors had taught him when Zahara let them know she'd finished clearing the area of trees and was ready for the fire.

"How should we start the fire?" Anders asked. He'd never had to burn the bodies of the dead before. The few funerals he'd been to in Grandwood were burials.

"Can you do it?" Ivan asked Zahara.

Zahara shifted uncomfortably, her weight moving from side to side, *I haven't been able to produce a steady stream of fire on my own yet. My mother had just started teaching me when we were separated.*

"That's okay," Ivan said. "If you can initiate the flame, Anders and I can keep it going."

"We can?" Anders asked.

"I'll show you how," Ivan said rolling up his sleeves and preparing for the spell necessary to expand a flame.

Anders nodded. "Ready?" he asked Zahara. She gave him a look that told him she was nervous to begin. Groaning lightly, she pointed her snout toward the bodies, opening her massive jaws. For a moment nothing happened, then a thin spray of flame shot out of her mouth. It lightly spread over the bodies of the dead dragon and elf. It was enough of a spark to catch the elf's clothing and the duff on the forest floor beneath the dragon. Ivan showed Anders how to channel his energy into the flames.

As he followed suit, the smoldering and smoking turned into small flames. Anders focused his energy and reenacted Ivan's spell. With the two of them working to spread the flames, the fire quickly consumed the dead bodies. After the fire had caught sufficiently, they stood in silence and watched the dragon and rider turn to ash.

CHAPTER

FOUR

NATALIA

No one spoke as they watched the elf and dragon return to the elements through the flickering flames. Anders wasn't sure what to look for when the spirits of the two beings passed back into the energy force flowing within the very fabric of the forest around them. He stood in silence, slightly confused but reserved and respectful. The sword Nadir had passed on to him hung from the belt threaded through the scabbard and cinched tightly around his waist. There wasn't anywhere to place it while he rode on Zahara, so he decided to wear the belt, strapping the sword opposite the one he was already wearing.

When he placed the sword on the belt, he felt different somehow, more experienced or knowledgeable. It could have been his reaction to receiving the gift of such a fine blade from a rider he hardly knew and was now watching the rider's cremation process. The sensation he felt could have been his imagination, but he thought he could feel something slightly different.

"We need to find the other rider," Ivan said suddenly.

"What exactly did you see in your vision?" he asked, turning away from the flames and addressing Anders.

Ivan's expression was severe and Anders didn't dilly-dally with his response. Closing his eyes in an attempt to better recall precisely what happened during his dream, he said, "I was standing in darkness. The ground was dirt without grass. I heard the cries of a woman, faint at first, but as I ran closer, her cries became clearer. She was calling for help. When I found her, she was pinned under her dragon, lying in a pool of its blood. I couldn't see her face because her hair covered it, but I do remember that I found them at the base of a large oak tree." Anders opened his eyes. Ivan, Nadir and Zahara were all staring at him with jaws open as though he'd done something unexpected. He raised his eyebrow and asked them, "What?"

How did you do that? Zahara asked.

Do what? Speak? He replied growing increasingly more confused by their almost frightened looks.

You spoke in a strange tongue and the vision you were describing came to life in front of you in a blue expression of lights.

What do you mean? I closed my eyes and just told you what happened in my vision, in the tongue I am using now.

"Anders," Ivan interrupted their telepathic conversation. "Do you realize what you've said?"

Shaking his head, Anders replied, "Zahara just told me I was speaking in a different language and some blue lights showed you all the images I was describing?" As he said the words, he still didn't quite believe that he'd spoken any language other than Landish, the only language he spoke.

"You spoke in an ancient dialect, one that has not been used in hundreds of years. There's been only one individual I know of who could speak it and that person died long ago.

I can't tell you that I'm fluent, but I've heard enough of it to know what it is. As for the blue lights," he paused, narrowing his eyes. "I can't say I've ever seen anyone use them for depiction in such detail." Relaxing his gaze on Anders, he said, "Let's find our missing rider. If Anders' vision is correct, then the dragon may not recover, but the rider could still be alive."

Ivan started for Zahara, while Anders shook his head trying to make sense of what had just happened. As he placed his hand on Zahara, finding a scale to grip before hoisting himself onto her back, he heard a whisper.

Turning to Nadir, he asked, "What was that?"

Nadir furrowed his brow and answered, "I didn't say anything."

Anders turned back to Zahara and hesitated, straining his ears for the whisper he thought he'd heard.

"Come on. We haven't time to lose," Ivan called to Anders whose leg was halfway bent about to step up onto Zahara's thick leg.

He finished his ascent to the middle of her back between her shoulder blades and sat down. As soon as Anders' rear hit her scales, she was off, jumping up through the gap she'd created in the trees, flapping her mighty wings to quickly carry them over the mountains once more. Nadir continued his pursuit from below as they continued their search for the missing rider.

Searching with the magic sense powered through their minds, Ivan, Zahara and Anders scoured the topography for any sign of the second rider who had failed to return. As they searched, Anders experienced a wave of gratitude. He now had time to realize how lucky he and Zahara had been in managing to escape unscathed, while the others had suffered horrific attacks. With one of the rider pairs found dead and the second possibly pinned and dying under the weight of her slaughtered dragon, Anders worried about what would happen if they caught up with Merglan.

He lost track of how long they'd been searching. The mental and physical effort required to continually seek for the rider was beginning to take its toll. Ivan and Zahara were the first to notice a life form ahead of them. As Zahara landed in a nearby clearing, Anders hoped it wasn't another carcass being harvested by the carnivores of the forest. The grass that had once blanketed the clearing was gone, leaving behind a large patch of dirt. Anders' heart began to beat faster. He recognized this place from his vision.

Ivan led as Anders, Nadir and Zahara followed him quickly along a narrow ravine gradually sloping down toward a patch of trees. The broad leaves of the massive branching tree could only be one kind, oak. Suddenly they heard a woman's faint cries.

Anders and the others ran faster. Just as he'd seen, there at the base of a large oak tree lay a dead dragon on top of a woman in a way that pinned her in a shallow pool of crimson blood.

Anders slid onto his knees through the puddle of blood to the side of the woman trapped under the dragon. Her face was covered with her long brown hair. Anders swept her hair to the side. When her eyes met him, relief washed over her face. She whispered something that he couldn't hear clearly. Closing her eyes, the woman let her head fall limply to the side. She didn't make another noise.

Ivan bent down next to Anders and put his ear to the woman's chest making sure he could see the rise and fall of her breathing before telling Anders to search her body for life-threatening injuries. Following Ivan's instructions, Anders swept his hands over both of her arms as they were the only exposed limbs. He couldn't tell if she was bleeding because of the dragon blood covering the ground. As far as he could tell, she wasn't mortally injured on her upper body, though he and Nadir worried for the integrity of her spine.

"She probably passed out from the exhaustion of being pinned here for so long," Anders commented to Nadir, who'd joined him in his examination.

I could feel a sense of relief within her before she passed out, Zahara said. *She was hanging on with the hope that friends would find her. She's extraordinarily tough.*

"We need to get this dragon off her," Ivan said. "Her legs are most likely broken, so we'll need to take her back with us on Zahara."

The first glimpse of sunrise was beginning to show in the east, allowing them to see the scene more clearly. After Anders, Nadir and Ivan attempted to push the lifeless dragon off the rider, Anders gave in to asking Zahara the obvious. He could tell she didn't want to put her mouth around the giant dragon's body and lift it up so they could pull her out. She'd been avoiding eye contact with them while they attempted to move the body by hand, but after several stern looks from Ivan and Nadir, Anders gave in and asked for her help.

Zahara opened her massive jaws and slid her mouth around the side of the dragon's body, closing her eyes tightly. Anders could sense she'd separated her thoughts from his to protect him from the tragic event. She gently clamped down. Lifting her head, the dragon's body began to rise in the center where Zahara gripped it. The body came up off the ground slightly. Anders and Ivan were able to carefully slide the injured rider's body out to safety. The instant her body was in the clear, Zahara let go, the dead dragon splashing back into place. Zahara leapt back, revolted. Her gagging and hacking noises made Anders cringe as she vomited the fish dinner she'd eaten the previous afternoon.

Immediately attending to the injured woman, Ivan cut away the lower legs of her leather riding pants and began unstringing her boots. Once her skin was exposed, Anders could see instantly that she was in serious trouble. The lower half of her legs were bent at an unnatural angle. He helped Ivan remove her boots and began to address the broken leg when he noticed that her skin was incredibly cold to the touch. He reached up and felt the woman's forehead with the back of his hand. Also cold to the touch. Anders knew that wasn't good. He told Ivan, but neither could figure out how to warm her as they didn't have blankets or any dry clothing. Looking back at her legs, Anders decided to focus on something he could attempt to help with, healing her broken legs before flying her back to camp on Zahara.

Both legs were bent in zigzagging fashion, suggesting multiple breaks. He put his hand out to attempt to heal the injuries with the spell Ivan had shown him after the battle.

Ivan saw what he was doing and grabbed him by the shoulder, stopping him. "Her injuries are far beyond our skill to repair."

Anders looked at him confused and said, "We healed so many people yesterday. I mended broken bones and sealed deep wounds. What's different about her wounds that I can't heal them?"

"The breaks go well into her femur on both sides. Her knees are seriously damaged and both legs down to the heels are broken in many places. It's much simpler to heal an open wound or mend a bone cleanly broken in one place. If you try to heal her without the proper magic, you'll risk expending too much energy, which could kill you. Besides, if you did have the power to use the magic and miscast it in the slightest, she wouldn't heal properly and would likely never walk again. This injury needs to be mended by a skilled healer with excess available energy."

Anders nodded, lowering his hand to his side, slightly frustrated. "Okay. Well, what can we do?"

"You'll need to create a splint for her. Using the energy correctly you'll be able to form a splint where her legs won't be allowed to move. I no longer possess the ability to use this kind of magic. Ever since I lost," Ivan gulped, seeming to choke on his words. He glanced over to the dead dragon and Anders thought he could see Ivan's hands shaking before he regained his composure. "If you use the magic, I can tell you what to do and show you how to create the spell, but I can't do it for you," he said sternly and looked again to the dead dragon.

Anders took a deep breath readying himself for the new lesson, "Alright, tell me what to do."

Ivan walked Anders through the process of summoning the proper flow of energy to form a perfectly molded cast around the woman's legs, rendering them fixed in their current position. The splint of magical energy didn't repair her broken legs, but it merely protected them from further injury during transport.

"If the splint works as it should and everything you've just done is correct, she won't experience any further damage to her legs when you and Zahara fly her back to camp," Ivan said with a sense of trust in his tone.

Anders began to nod in agreement, but Ivan's choice of words confused him slightly. He cocked his head to the side and asked, "Why did you say, 'you and Zahara' and not us? You are coming back with us, aren't you?"

Ivan shook his head, "I doubt Zahara could carry all three of us over that distance. She's fatigued and still very young."

Don't tell me what I am, Zahara chimed in.

Ivan turned to address her, "I didn't mean to offend you, Zahara. I'm just thinking about the best way to get this rider back quickly. My extra weight would slow you down. Besides, I'll need time to dispose of the dragon's body. When we're finished, I'll start to walk back with Nadir."

Irritated that Ivan was right about trying to get the rider back as quickly as possible, Zahara and Anders relented, agreeing to fly back without him.

But we're coming back to get you after we deliver her safely to the medical tent, Zahara said, lowering her massive head to Ivan's level.

"Alright, you can come back to get me," Ivan agreed.

Together they lifted the woman's body up onto Zahara's back. With no way to strap her down, Anders had to make sure she didn't slide off during the flight. Zahara assured him that she'd fly smoothly.

The sun had fully risen by the time they took flight. Zahara flew as fast as she could back toward the fortress where the elven and Rollo armies had established camp. Unlike the many hours it took them to find the rider, this time their path was straight and direct, not meandering and full of dips and dives. Two hours after they'd left Ivan, Anders could see the white canvas tents of the army encampment.

When they touched down, a group of elves stood waiting. Somehow, they'd known this case was urgent, but by their shocked expressions and gasps, Anders understood the elves weren't prepared for the state of what he and the others had discovered. The elves helped Anders climb down cradling the injured rider.

As he passed her body off to the elves, one elf gasped upon seeing her face, "It's Natalia!"

The group of elven warriors carried her body carefully to the medical tent nearby. Once she'd been handed over to those trained in healing, several of the elves returned, asking Anders what had happened. He told them about finding the dead bodies of the young elf and his dragon. He also informed them that Natalia was still alive when they found her, but her dragon didn't survive. Before leaving the elves, Anders warned them of the splint he'd used on the rider's legs, and how Ivan was worried that he wasn't skilled enough to mend her.

Anders was relieved to hear one of the elves reply, "Don't worry, young rider, I will get the healer."

As the elves headed back into the tent to work their magic, Anders took a moment to reflect on the events of their search. He'd forgotten how haggard and beat up he was. His forehead was split open and his clothes were torn from the crash. On top of feeling thrashed and looking the part, his face was crusted in dried blood from the cut on his head and his clothes were saturated in dragon's blood.

"I'm tired," Anders said to Zahara, not bothering to switch to using mindspeak.

You look it, Zahara agreed.

Anders wavered in his two-legged stance, "I think I need rest. How are you doing?" he asked her.

I'm tired, too, but not as tired as you. I have enough in me to go back for Ivan.

"Oh yeah. I'll come with you," Anders insisted.

No, Anders, you need to stay here and rest. If you come

with me, I'll be too tired to make the return flight. I have never flown this much or this hard in such a short period, she told him.

Anders furrowed his brow, "Everyone seems to think I should be resting."

Have you seen yourself?

Anders looked himself over and attempted to brush the crusted blood off his clothes. When the stains didn't brush away after several swipes, he straightened up and said, *Well, I guess if you can't carry me, I'll have to find somewhere to lie down, but I don't like it when I'm away from you for too long. If anything happens, you'll let me know, won't you?*

Zahara nodded, *Go, get some sleep. I'll be joining you when I return.*

Anders did as she suggested. He stood back while she jumped into the air and flapped her wings, creating a rush of wind around him as she took flight. He placed his arm across his forehead, blocking the sun from his eyes as he watched her fly away.

Not feeling entirely comfortable in being away from Zahara for the first time since they'd bonded, Anders decided he should find Max, Maija and his cousins to let them know he'd made it back from the search safely.

He didn't have to go far from the medical tent before Maija, Kirsten, Max and Thomas came running toward him from the camp. Surrounding him, they bombarded him with questions.

"What happened to you? Did you find the missing riders? Is that your blood? Where's Zahara? Where's Ivan?" The questions seemed to be coming from all angles. In his exhaustion, he couldn't make sense of which questions to answer first, so he offered a short answer to each of their queries.

"Found one rider alive, injured, brought her back. Zahara is going back for Ivan. Yes, my blood," he pointed to his head, "and, yes, blood from others," he pointed to his stained pants. He finished by quickly adding, "Tired, headache and need rest." Anders swayed slightly as he spoke.

"Here, drink this," Maija said handing him a skin of water. He opened it and began gulping. The fresh water rushing down his dry throat felt amazing. He wiped away the dribble with his sleeve and raised his other arm over his brow to shield the late morning sun from his eyes.

He squinted and asked, "Is there somewhere quiet where I could lie down?"

"You can have my tent," Maija sprang at the opportunity before anyone else could respond.

"Thanks," Anders said. He followed them back to their side of the encampment.

"How did you get covered in blood?" Max asked, coming alongside him as they walked.

"Long story," Anders said. "Zahara crashed, that was part of it. Dead dragon was the rest." Everyone glanced at one another out of the corner of their eyes. Anders noticed their looks but was too tired to pay much attention. It was as if he'd just told them the world was going to end tomorrow. "I'll explain in more detail after I've gotten some rest," he said. "I need to sleep."

Maija led him over to her tent. It was pitched slightly away from the others in their group and bordered a beautiful grassy hill at the far edge of the camp. She pulled the flap aside and ushered him in.

"You can lie here," she pointed to several blankets that covered a cot.

Anders thanked her and laid down on top of the blankets, not wanting his dirty clothes to mess up her sleeping arrangements too much. Maija turned to walk back out of the tent as Anders called after her in a gentle tone, "Maija, wait."

She stopped and turned, coming back several steps to the side of the bed.

"What is it?" she asked.

He held out his arm from the side of the cot and extended his hand toward her. She took his hand in hers and smiled, bending down; she kissed him softly on the lips.

"You can tell me all about it after you've rested," she said.

He nodded, his eyes closing with the motion of his head. Maija took her hand and ran it through his hair several times, kissed him on the forehead, and left the tent. Anders was asleep before she'd closed the flap.

ANDERS STIRRED from his slumber twice before late the next morning. He woke the first time when Zahara returned. She'd dropped Ivan off at the medical tent where the elves were attempting to heal Natalia. He was glad she woke him, so he knew she'd made it back safely, but he fell right back to sleep as quickly as he'd awoken.

The second time was only for a moment and he wasn't entirely sure it happened. He thought Maija woke him when she entered her tent. When Anders opened his eyes, the inside of the tent's white canvas walls were brightly lit with the glow of the rising sun. He could hear the busyness of camp life bustling around them, muffled through the canvas walls. He turned his head to the side where he thought he heard Maija making some noise. He was surprised to see her lying next to him.

The cot wasn't designed to hold two people, so their bodies were snuggled closely together. Her eyes were closed and she had a small smile on her face. She looked like she was dreaming of something sweet. Anders enjoyed how beautiful she looked in that moment. Her wavy amber hair was slightly ruffled from the pillow, exposing her ear on one side. Quickly he realized that he had never fully seen her ears before; she always wore her hair down. Seeing her ear now, he noticed that it came to a subtle point at the top.

His eyes followed the curve of her neck, her caramel skin ran down into the top of the blanket they slept under just below her collar. Anders' eyes widened, she wasn't wearing any clothes, at least not a shirt from what Anders could tell. He'd never seen her bare skin before. His eyes wandered, only for a moment, as he gawked at her beauty.

Suddenly he wondered if he was still wearing his clothes. He moved his hands to his sides and felt the clothes he'd been wearing from the search. He sighed in relief as he would've felt embarrassed if Maija, or any of the others, had undressed him while he was asleep. Bringing his head back down to the pillow, Anders fell back to sleep, snuggling with Maija.

When Anders stirred for the third and final time, his movements woke her from her peaceful slumber. He smiled at her and she pulled her arms out from under the covers and stretched them high into the air letting out a long and drawn-out yawn.

"Good morning," she said, turning back onto her side, facing him and pulling the blanket a little higher up over her shoulder.

"It sure is," Anders replied. "And from the looks of it, a

late one, too." He looked around the tent at all the brightly lit walls.

"Not too late, I hope. I want to check on how the elf woman you found is healing. We tried last night, but Ivan told us it wasn't an appropriate time and to come back in the morning."

Anders nodded, remembering all that had happened the previous day.

"How'd you sleep? You were out cold for a long time. Zahara fell asleep outside the tent right after she got back."

"I slept hard," he said truthfully. "I even fell asleep with my clothes on," he added, looking down her neck to the edge of the blanket. "I hope that wasn't awkward for you."

"I tried sleeping on the floor, but I got cold, so I came into bed with you. I knew you were sound asleep and you wouldn't notice. And, well," she blushed, "I feel very uncomfortable sleeping with my clothes on. I hope I didn't offend you," she said biting gently at her lower lip.

"Oh no, not at all," Anders said trying to show her that he wasn't offended. "I hate sleeping in my clothes, too." He attempted to pull off his shirt but struggled since he was lying down. "I'm glad you decided to come into the bed with me. If anything, I should've been sleeping on the ground; this is your tent," he said with the shirt halfway off and his head stuck inside it. He jerked off the last bit that was giving him trouble. His head came out of the shirt with a bright smile, only to see that Maija had already gotten out of bed.

She stood facing away from him. His eyes widened as he caught the fleeting glimpse of her as she pulled up her pants, her exposed backside disappearing in a flash as she fastened them around her waist.

She could tell by the silence that he was watching her.

She turned her head slightly to the side, letting her hair swing across her back. She giggled playfully at the dumb-founded expression slapped across his face.

"Oh, sorry," he stammered, feeling like a kid that had just been caught with his hand in the cookie jar.

She bent down and picked up her shirt, sliding it on over her head, then turned around. With both hands, she pulled her long hair up and out of the neck of her shirt, flinging it lightly behind her.

"It's fine, Anders," she said looking away from him. "If I didn't want you to see me, I wouldn't have let you stay in here."

She walked to the cot and sat on the edge, "You're funny. Did you know that?" She kissed him twice, the second longer than the first, then stood up. She moved to the tent door and slid on her boots. Putting her arms through her jacket sleeves one at a time, she said, "We should wake Zahara if she isn't up already. And you need to clean yourself up. You're still pretty filthy."

Anders rubbed his cheeks with his palm. He'd forgotten he was in such haggard shape. He threw the covers aside and sat up, ready to get out of bed. He sat there with his hands on the edge of the bed slumped forward for a moment, sore from crashing off Zahara.

Maija looked at him, "Well, are you coming?"

"Give me a second. I'll be out in a minute."

When Anders stepped out of the tent, the first thing he noticed was Zahara sprawled out in the grass next to Maija's tent still sound asleep.

Maija stood, waiting. "Have you ever heard her snore before?" she asked.

Anders shook his head, realizing that even though they

were bonded he still didn't know everything about her, "No, has she been snoring?"

"Yes, she snores mostly when she rolls over onto her back," she said. "Let's wake her up."

Maija stepped toward her, but Anders said, "No. We've had a long couple of days. Let's let her be until she wakes on her own."

Returning to Anders' side, Maija said, "Okay," with a pleasant smile. He'd never seen her like this, the way she was acting the last couple of days. He liked it.

"I should go check in with Ivan and see how the elf woman we brought back is doing."

"They aren't in the medical tent anymore," Maija said, grabbing Anders by the hand before he could take a step. "I saw them move her last night. They're on the elven side of camp. Come on, I'll show you."

As they walked toward the elven encampment, Maija asked Anders about their search for the riders and dragons. Anders recounted looking for them using their newly formed magical abilities. He explained how they flew into an airmine and crashed along a mountaintop. "That's how I got this cut on my head," he said putting his hand up to his forehead to feel the hardened blood just below his hairline.

"That must have hurt," Maija said with concern.

Anders nodded. He continued to explain how they'd found the first dragon and rider. "Killed by magic," he said after seeing Maija's shocked expression. "And Nadir said I should take this," Anders pointed to the sword he had belted around his waist. "As a gift. He said the rider would've wanted me to use it in his honor."

Maija frowned and held his right arm as they walked, bringing him closer to her, "That sounds like a terrible thing to see."

"And that wasn't nearly as bad as the elf woman's dragon," Anders replied, the words spilling out before he could think fast enough to realize that telling her about the gory scene would possibly sour her unusually cheerful mood. He glanced down at the browned blood stains on his lower body. "Her dragon was cut and wounded badly. Probably a slow death. The elf woman was being crushed under its weight."

Maija shivered at the thought, "That is awful."

"Yeah, I can't imagine what I would do if that happened to Zahara, and I haven't been bonded with her for that long. The rider's going to be distraught when she wakes up."

Maija pointed to a large tent where a group of elves had gathered. She let go of Anders' arm and pointed to them, saying, "That's where Ivan and the others took her last night."

"Okay, thanks," Anders said and began walking toward the tent. Maija didn't continue walking with him. He stopped, looking back at her, "Aren't you coming with me?"

She shifted uncomfortably, "Wouldn't it be weird if I came?"

"I don't think so. I'm sure it's fine, come on," Anders motioned for her to join him. After a moment's hesitation, she relented.

As they approached the tent, the group of elves stopped their elvish chatter. One of them turned and bowed, saying, "Many thanks to you, young rider. Natalia has been taking to the healing better than expected. We are grateful for your efforts in returning her safely."

Anders glanced at Maija and then bowed slightly to the elf, "That's great to hear, and thank you for the update. It was Zahara's and my honor to help a fellow rider in need."

The elf bowed again as did Anders to show his respect. The elf separated from the others and led them into the tent.

Ivan and Nadir were standing next to a cot where the injured elf woman lay. They all looked tired, turning slowly toward the door as Anders and Maija entered. Nadir's face instantly lit up upon seeing them. Ivan's facial expression was harder to read, but he looked relieved to see them.

Anders and Maija came to the edge of Natalia's cot. Looking down at the resting rider, Anders asked, "How's she doing?"

"The healing was difficult, but the elves did a good job restoring her physical injuries. We have yet to see her awake. I would assume she'll be distraught over the death of her dragon and fellow rider," Ivan said.

"It's possible that Merglan injured her mind as well," Nadir said. "But based on the physical nature of the attack, it's likely that she was able to defend against him on that front. If her mental barriers were susceptible, she would have wound up like Keanu."

Anders peered down at the elf woman. She'd been cleaned up during her treatment in the medical tent and he could now see her features clearly. Her face bore hard lines, strong jaw and bold cheekbones. She was striking in appearance and shared the same color hair as Maija.

As they gazed at the elf woman, Natalia's body slowly shifted. Anders quickly looked up at Ivan and then to Nadir. She moved again, this time more quickly as though she was becoming restless. Slowly she opened her eyes. To Anders' surprise, they were bright green.

First, her eyes moved to Ivan and then to Nadir. Next,

she shifted her head, her gaze coming to rest on Anders and Maija. When Natalia saw Maija's face, her expression transformed from slightly confused to shocked.

With her eyes wide and mouth ajar, Natalia tilted her head slightly and said, "Maija?"

CHAPTER

FIVE

A HARD TRUTH AND A DIFFICULT GOODBYE

Maija stood alongside Anders at the injured rider's bedside, bewildered at the elf's joy upon seeing her.

How does she know my name? Maija thought to herself, not recognizing anything about the woman who clearly seemed to know her.

"Maija?" Natalia questioned again when Maija failed to show the same level of excitement upon seeing her. "Is it really you?"

Maija furrowed her brow, taken aback by the seeming familiarity with which the elf said her name. She glanced at Anders who responded with a quizzical look similar to her own. "Yes, my name is Maija, but how do you know who I am?"

The elf sat up in bed, wincing as she shuffled her back up against the headrest. "It's me. Natalia," she said, placing her hand on her chest.

Maija shot questioning looks at Ivan and Nadir who eyed her curiously in reply. Maija shifted uncomfortably, bringing her hand across her body and gripping her left elbow. She eyed the elf rider warily, shaking her head slightly.

"Don't you remember me?" the elf asked.

Maija cringed slightly, "I don't." Shrugging, she said, "I'm sorry."

Natalia moved gingerly to the side of the cot. Gritting her teeth and grunting through pain, the elf rider pulled the bedsheets off and swung her legs over the edge of the bedding. Anders moved to help Natalia, but before he could reach her, she held her arm out warding him off.

Anders wondered if the healing had gone as well as they thought.

Once on her feet, she faltered. For a moment, Anders thought she might fall, so he reached out to catch her. Waving him back again, she regained her balance. Natalia turned, using the side of the cot to steady herself as she moved on her recently healed legs. Natalia straightened and looked Maija over before she spoke. "It really is you," she said quietly. "I've been searching everywhere for you, but never knew what they did to you."

Anders watched Maija's expression change slightly. She seemed to be grasping for a memory long since forgotten.

Natalia smiled, hoping Maija had suddenly recognized her. Maija furrowed her brow, the memory she'd been searching for vanishing like a puff of smoke.

"Maija, I'm your sister," Natalia said with a smile.

Maija froze in shock, staring blankly at the elf.

Anders' eyes widened. He turned to Ivan and Nadir, who both looked at him as if he might have held a clue to this discovery since he'd spent more time with Maija than the rest of them. Anders shrugged, shaking his head to tell them he was just as surprised as they were.

Maija shook her head in disbelief, staggering backward

and muttering under her breath, "No, that's not possible. No."

"What? What do you mean she's your sister?" Ivan asked in surprise.

Natalia stepped toward Maija and Anders but stumbled under her weakness. As she fell, Maija instinctively surged forward in a flash, catching Natalia before she toppled to the floor. Anders had been closer to the elf, but Maija reacted before he could. Anders gaped in awe as Maija helped Natalia onto the bed. She smiled as Maija assisted her. Catching her gaze, Maija quickly shuffled away, affirming the awkwardness she felt toward Natalia's claims.

"Natalia, you should be resting. The healing process hasn't run its course," Nadir said coming swiftly to the bedside.

Natalia waved him aside saying, "I'll be fine."

Ivan interjected. "Please explain to us how you two could be sisters," he said glancing to Maija as she slid behind Anders, hiding somewhat from Natalia's view. "Maija doesn't even recognize you," Ivan said motioning toward the girl.

"That I can't explain, albeit we were separated at a young age. It's not likely, though, that Maija forgot for lack of being aware," Natalia paused, eyeing Ivan and Nadir curiously. She continued, "Is it possible someone tampered with her mind just after the separation?"

"Like a memory swipe?" Anders asked. "I didn't know that was possible."

"It can be done, but it's not something just anyone who possesses magic can accomplish. The mind is complicated, making it difficult to alter permanently with magic." Ivan said. "I don't know anyone living other than Merglan who could perform such a powerful spell."

Maija tapped Anders on the shoulder as they spoke.

Anders turned to address her, "What is it?" he asked, causing Ivan and Natalia to take notice.

"Oh, this is embarrassing," she whispered to Anders. Stepping out from behind him, Maija said loud enough for all of them to hear, "I can't really remember anything from my childhood."

Anders' eyes widened as the words registered with him, "Really?" he blurted out. Seeing the disapproving look she gave him, he fumbled to recover, "I mean, that's got to be hard. How far back does your memory go?"

Maija blushed, shying away from him slightly, "The first thing I can remember is the day I woke up in a bedroom that somehow felt foreign to me. I knew it wasn't mine, but the place looked lived in. Two older people lived in the house. They told me I was their granddaughter. I knew my name and who I was, but nothing about where I'd been or anything that had happened to me before that day. They told me I'd been in an accident that killed my parents and my memory was damaged."

"So, if Natalia's claims are true, then that means, Maija, you're an elf?" he said. He recalled seeing the slight points to her ears earlier that morning. Anders hadn't thought it strange at the time, just a unique attribute that made her that much more interesting.

"There's one simple way to check and see if Natalia's claims could be true," Nadir said, walking over to the side of the cot where Maija and Anders stood. Nadir moved, reaching toward Maija.

Maija jumped back in a defensive stance. She held her hands up ready to block herself from Nadir.

Nadir dropped his arms to his sides and backed away saying, "I don't intend to harm you."

Anders leaned toward Maija and said softly, "I think he just wants to see your ears?" Anders glanced to Nadir, who nodded.

Maija slackened in her stance slightly but remained on guard.

Anders stepped closer to Maija. He stopped, gesturing toward her and asked, "May I?"

She nodded.

Anders pulled back her hair to expose one of her ears. Maija leaned away awkwardly but let him hold his position.

Ivan leaned forward, placing his hand on the side of the cot. Nadir did the same. Before she pulled away, Anders saw her ear in its entirety. It was pointed like an elf's, but much shorter than others he'd seen. Even Natalia's protruded through her hair as it hung loose, where Maija's did not.

Maija moved toward the tent door. Flushed in the face, she said, "I, um, I need to go." She turned and left the tent before Anders or anyone else could stop her.

Anders moved to follow her, but Ivan called to him, "Let her be, Anders. She'll need space to think."

Anders stopped.

"He's right," Natalia said. "Let her be."

Anders turned and walked to the bedside where the others stood.

"They are pointed;" Nadir said bringing the focus back to the discussion and confirming Natalia's assertion, "however, I have never seen an elf with ears so small."

"Perhaps she's only half elf," Ivan suggested.

"No," Natalia said emphatically. "She's my sister, not half-sister. She's the little sister that my parents had to send away in the face of danger, to protect her life."

"Weren't you separated as well?" Anders asked.

"When we were young, our parents were powerful

sorcerers, bonded with the two most feared dragons among the five kingdoms. After Merglan began his conquest to rule Kartania, the elf king sent our parents to ride out and stop him from taking any more territory. Underestimating his power, they were unable to stop him. During one battle they became locked in combat with the dark sorcerer. Merglan broke through our father's mental wards and glimpsed into his mind, learning of his two daughters. I'd just been paired with a young dragon, bonding with her at a young age, but Maija was still a toddler at the time.

"Our father was able to force Merglan from his mind at that point, but before the channel was closed, he discovered Merglan's burning desire to stop a prophecy from coming to fruition. After our parents were forced to retreat, Merglan focused on hunting them down. They suspected Merglan believed one of us could become involved in the prophecy of his demise. Our parents didn't want to endanger other elves when Merglan came for them, so they went on the run, taking the two of us with them.

"He chased us for nearly a year; every time he came close we managed a narrow escape, until one day. On that day our parents sacrificed themselves, ensuring our survival. Our mother managed to free herself, but not before our father and his dragon were killed. Merglan fatally wounded both our mother and her dragon, but she survived long enough to hide us from the evil sorcerer.

"The spells our mother cast just before her death were so powerful not even Merglan could get around them. Before she separated Maija and me, she made me promise that I would not look for Maija until Merglan was gone forever. For sixteen years I kept that promise, struggling each and every day not to take up the search. A year ago, I thought Merglan had been defeated, so I began looking for her, but my mother's spells concealing Maija's location were much too strong, and, as is obvious today, I was unable to find her... until now," Natalia said, tears welling in her eyes.

Anders stood in silence, amazed by her story of their separation.

"Natalia," Ivan said after several long moments of silence. "There's something of importance we need to tell you. Something that's already been delayed for too long."

Natalia's expression hardened as she looked to Ivan. Anders suspected by Natalia's reaction she already knew what Ivan had to say.

"It's about your dragon. She, well, I'm sorry, but she didn't make it." As Ivan spoke, Anders could see tears trickling down her cheeks.

"And Keanu?" she asked in a shaky voice.

Ivan pursed his lips, shaking his head, "I'm sorry, but they didn't make it either."

Natalia looked away, sniffling. Anders knew he didn't need to be in the tent for her mourning. He nodded to Ivan and turned to exit the tent.

As soon as Anders stepped outside, he stopped. Maija was sitting on the ground next to the door, legs crossed and picking at the grass.

"Maija?" Anders said surprised to see her still at the tent. "Are you okay?"

Maija shivered as if to expel her transfixed stare at the ground. "Did that really just happen?" she asked reaching for Anders and grasping him by his forearm as he helped her to her feet. "She said I was her sister and our parents were dragonriders killed by Merglan?"

Anders nodded slowly, rubbing his hand up and down the small of her back comfortingly. "She did," he said softly.

"How can that be?" she said furrowing her brow and looking into Anders' eyes.

He saw her confusion and tried to comfort her by saying, "It may not make a whole lot of sense now, but perhaps Natalia can provide you with some answers about your past, about the early years of your life you can't remember, or about your heritage. I still don't know that much about my parents either and less now than I thought I did when I was younger. Theodor avoided telling me much about them, other than that my mother – his sister – was just like his mother: sweet, kind, caring and thoughtful. He never talked about my father at all. Ivan's told me more about him than Theodor ever did, and he's only told me one story about the guy. Try to look at this as a positive. If we find out that what she's saying is true, then you have a sister," he said, cautiously excited.

She cracked an awkward smile and began to chuckle, "It's really hard to take you seriously right now."

Anders furrowed his brow in confusion.

"It's just that you look like you went and rolled in a pig pen, then dunked your face in brown goo."

For all his efforts to comfort Maija on an emotional level, Anders appeared to be failing because he continued to wear the remnants of the previous night's events. "About time that I washed up?" he said looking at the filth caking his body.

Still giggling, Maija said, "Yeah, I think it's about time. I'll meet you back at the tent. Zahara's probably still sleeping, and I saw the others packing up. Judging by the movement in camp, we'll be leaving soon."

Anders noticed the bustle of camp for the first time. Rollo Island warriors were breaking down their campsites and hauling their belongings down to the beach. "Alright,

I'll see you back there after I clean up," he said and gave her a peck on the cheek.

Maija tried to dodge him, but his filthy lips were too close.

As ANDERS WALKED through the crowd toward the beach, he saw that they'd somehow acquired new ships. The vessels anchored near shore were not the same style as the shallow-hulled Rollo longships he'd sailed on before. These ships were much taller and looked to have several levels of cargo holds below the main deck. The masts were much taller with black sails. The sight of the black sails snapped like a piece to a puzzle in his mind. *Those are the ships Thargon attacked Grandwood with,* he thought to himself. It made perfect sense now that he thought about it.

During the attack at the fortress, the soldiers must not have had time to move them elsewhere. *At least now the warriors won't have to walk the long way back to civilization to get more ships,* Anders thought.

He walked down to a small stream flowing near the fortress walls and into the coast. He stripped off his clothes and tested the water. He'd walked far enough away from camp that nobody would be able to see him bathing. The water's chill shocked him at first, but with the heat of the sun bearing down, the frigid flow felt refreshing. He used the sand along the stream bottom in place of a sponge and scrubbed the dry blood and dirt off his skin.

When he finished, he put on his dirty clothes; he'd have to walk back to get clean ones. Before leaving the stream, Anders noticed a small mint plant growing on the bank. He smelled its pungent scent on the light breeze and remembered an old trick Theodor had taught him when he was younger.

"Take a handful of mint and rub it liberally in the crotch of your arm. The girl you're courting will appreciate it more than you think," Theodor had said with a laugh.

He had done it when Anders had a crush on the miller's daughter. They were relatively young, and she didn't seem impressed by the fragrance. Still, it was worth a try. He pulled up a handful of mint leaves and rubbed them in his armpits. *My clothes may be dirty, but at least I won't smell like a dead rabbit*, he thought to himself.

When he got back to their campsite, he quickly grabbed his one spare change of clothes and put them on and buckled Lazuran at his side. Somehow the blade already felt like a part of him, and he didn't want to let it out of his sight. After Anders was scrubbed and had changed into proper clothes, he saw that Kirsten and Thomas were rolling up their sleeping arrangements. Max and Bo struggled to do the same but had already started bickering over whose blankets were whose. Maija had packed up her tent and was sitting on the hill next to Zahara, who had awakened but lounged lazily.

He reached out with his mind, connecting with Zahara, *I'm glad to see you made it back safely.*

When she didn't respond immediately, he began to think he hadn't made the connection properly, but a moment later she answered, *The flights were good, but long. I'm talking with Maija right now about the recent events. She's an elf, you know, and has riders in her family.*

I know, I was there when she found out, he said through his thoughts. *I'll leave you two to chat awhile and get acquainted.*

Anders rolled up the blankets he'd used as a bed and

tied them in a bundle. Max walked over as he tossed his things onto the pile.

"Heard you found the missing riders," Max said sticking his hands into his pockets.

"Yeah," Anders replied. "Both dragons dead and one of the riders as well."

Max grimaced. Noticing the new sword Anders had acquired, he asked, "Is that where you got that? I didn't know you were a thief," Max joked, trying to make light of the conversation.

Anders moved his arm that was blocking it and looked at it saying, "Oh no, I didn't steal it. Nadir gave it to me. He said the rider would've wanted me to have it. It's crazy sharp and super light." Anders pulled the blade from the sheath and handed it to Max.

Max gripped it around the hilt and admired it. He stuck his finger to the blade and pulled it back instantly wincing with pain. Blood dripped from his fingertip. "You weren't kidding," he said, handing it back. "Why do you suppose it has sapphires?" he asked, pointing to the hilt.

Anders hadn't yet had enough time to think about how and why Lazuran was created. Shrugging, he said, "Not sure. Decoration, I guess."

"Maybe the rider was rich and liked his sword to look it?" Max suggested.

"Could've been," Anders said doubtfully.

"There's something I've been wanting to tell you," Max said, changing the subject.

"Oh?" Anders asked, curious about what his friend had to say.

Max fiddled with his belt buckle and glanced down as he spoke, "Well it's about what happens next. To us, I mean. I guess you'll be busy training with your dragon and learning how to use magic now, and well, Britt offered me and Bo spots as crewmen on her ship."

Anders hadn't really thought about his future and Zahara's; he hadn't even considered what Max's plan would be. They'd become very close since leaving Grandwood. He blushed as the silence before responding seemed to last too long. "Well, yeah. That's great that she wants you," Anders said. "And you're not one to say no to an adventure," he added with a smile, sheathing Lazuran.

Max half smiled and glanced up.

"I guess we were so focused on getting this far in our quest that I hadn't really thought about what's next. You're probably right though, Ivan will want us to go train now that Zahara and I have bonded," Anders sighed. "I was hoping to go back home. Get the farm going again, you know, but I'll bet Merglan would hunt us down as soon as he got a chance; stupid prophecy," he muttered under his breath.

Max chuckled, "Yeah. Well, I just wanted to thank you while I have you alone, you know so I don't miss the opportunity to be soppy in front of the others when we actually leave." He extended his open palm for a handshake.

Anders brushed his hand aside and pulled him in for a hug, "No, thank you, Max," he said wrapping him in a brotherly embrace. "I would've never gotten this far without your help. Seriously."

Max pulled away after allowing the hug to last longer than he would normally. Looking around to make sure nobody had seen their show of emotion, he cleared his throat and brushed the wrinkles out of his shirt. "Well, now that that's taken care of," Max gave up his macho act, breaking from his firm posture, and said with a tear in his eye, "I'll miss you, Anders."

"You say that like I'm going to die tomorrow," Anders replied, slugging him playfully in the shoulder.

"You probably will," Max said jokingly hitting him back.

"I'm sure I'll be seeing you sooner than you expect."

"I hope so," Max said. He picked up his packed bag, slung it over his shoulder and began walking toward the beach. Bo fell in behind him as he walked past their tent site.

Anders watched them walk into the crowd, then turned to join Maija who was still seated alongside Zahara. Thomas and Kirsten now sat with them looking out at the Rollo camp as the tents disappeared, collapsing to be packed for their journey home.

"That was awfully cute," Kirsten teased him as he approached.

"Max was really hoping nobody saw that," Anders said, taking a seat next to them.

"Why?" Thomas asked. "There's nothing wrong with two men embracing one another."

"I know," Anders said. "But Max is kind of embarrassed to wear his emotions on his sleeve. That's why he jokes so much. He uses his jokes as a shield, instead of saying how he really feels."

You, humans, are strange, Zahara said, projecting her thoughts into all of their minds. Everyone burst out laughing.

Ivan emerged from the crowd, walking toward them with purpose. They rose from their relaxing seats to address him.

"How's Natalia doing?" Anders asked as Ivan came to a stop before them, looking determined.

"She'll heal just fine. Her legs will work as they once

did, but the emotional toll from the loss of her dragon is much worse. She's asked to be left alone."

Anders noticed Maija seemed concerned about the mental status of her newly discovered sister.

"The elves are eager to leave now that she's been found and attended to, considering the looming threat of Merglan's return," Ivan said nodding toward the movements within the camp. The elves moved much faster than the human camp, making ready to leave in a hurry.

"Looks like the Rollo Island warriors will be ready to sail soon as well," Kirsten noted, as the others listened in on their conversation.

Ivan nodded curtly to her and, turning back to Anders said, "Which leads me to what I've come to talk with you about. You and Zahara must be properly trained in the ways of a rider, as I was. We'll be leaving with the elves and returning to the Everlight Kingdom once they're ready."

"What about my cousins?" Anders asked. "Can they come with us?" Thomas and Kirsten looked eagerly at Ivan, awaiting his reply. They were anxious to see the elf kingdom their father had spoken about but knew they would need to be invited or face the wrath of elvish justice.

"No," Ivan said shortly. "The elves will not allow anyone but elves or riders to stay with them for the amount of time we'll be there. Your family should return to Grandwood."

"How are we going to do that?" Kirsten asked. "You don't expect us to walk all that way do you?"

"You'll set sail with the Rollo people and they'll drop you off at Grandwood since it is on their way home."

"Oh," Thomas and Kirsten said simultaneously. They were not thrilled with the idea of going back on the ships where earlier they'd been held as prisoners, but at least this time they'd be able to leave their cabins to go to the bathroom.

"When will I see them again?" Anders asked strongly.

"You and Zahara will remain in hiding until your training is complete. We don't want Merglan to find out where you've gone. By now he'll know you've bonded. You've become a major target for him, which is why we need to leave as soon as we're ready. The magic embedded in the capital where we'll be training is ancient and powerful. It's protected them from evils like Merglan since its creation."

"How long will that take?" Kirsten asked, placing her hands on her hips and planting her feet.

"I can't be certain, but it took me two years to complete my training. Seeing as how our situation is dire, Anders and Zahara will be on an accelerated program," Ivan said.

"Can't Zahara and I fly back to Grandwood on the weekends to visit?" Anders said hopefully.

"And have Merglan waiting there for your arrival? No, you would be killed," Ivan stated.

"What about their safety?" Anders asked. "Won't Merglan come after them to get to us?"

"It's possible, but not likely. We'll make sure the Rollo warriors keep an eye out for that possibility. Merglan somehow missed that you two were Anders' kin," Ivan addressed Thomas and Kirsten. "It's possible that he still doesn't know, but we'll have to keep an eye out for that scenario."

"Okay," Anders said, unhappily but agreeing to the stipulations because he knew they were necessary for his duty. "And what about Maija? Will you send her away too?"

"No, Maija is coming with us. Natalia wants her to

come back to their childhood home in Cedarbridge. That is if you will agree to it?" Ivan asked, turning to Maija.

Maija raised her eyebrows, looking slightly surprised, "Yes, I'd like that. Maybe I'll find some much-needed answers about my past."

Anders smiled, glancing over at Maija. He was glad they'd be able to continue their relationship.

"Then it's settled," Ivan said, clapping his hands briefly. "The elves will be ready to leave by nightfall. And you two," Ivan pointed to Thomas and Kirsten. "The Rollo people will be ready to set sail in a matter of hours, so I suggest you find a ride."

With that, Ivan turned and walked back toward the elf camp.

"Come on, let's see if Britt will take you aboard her ship," Anders said.

Kirsten and Thomas nodded and grabbed their things.

I'm hungry, Zahara said to Anders. *I'm going to find something to eat.*

Okay, Anders replied. *Don't venture too far though; there could be more of those airmines nearby.*

Zahara nodded, leaping off the ground and taking flight.

"Where is she off to?" Kirsten asked.

"She needs to find something to eat," Anders said as he watched her rise into the sky.

"I'm glad it isn't us," Kirsten replied.

"She would never eat people," Anders said, casting her a scornful glance for thinking such a terrible thought.

"How do you know that?" Kirsten asked.

"I just do," he said defensively. "We're bonded now, so I can feel her emotions. She doesn't have the desire to eat people; especially my family."

Together they walked down to the beach where they found Max, Bo and Britt loading her ship. When Britt saw Anders, she ran to him, giving him a big hug and laughing.

"Anders, I'm so happy you're still alive," she said in accented Landish.

"What? You doubted I would be?" he asked with a smile.

"Last time I saw you, you were about to be slain by that evil beast, Thargon, and then a dragon came from nowhere and took you away," she said acting out the flight by moving her hand through the space in front of her.

"That was actually very terrifying," Anders said. *Wow, that seems like it was so long ago*, he thought. He knew it had only been a few days but so much had happened to him since then that it seemed like a lifetime.

"Will you be joining us on our voyage?" Britt asked. "I need a few more good warriors."

"Unfortunately I can't come along. Zahara and I need to be trained properly if we're going to have a chance at taking on Merglan and his dragon," he said.

"Aw, shoot. What about them?" she asked, pointing to the three behind him.

"That's what I'm here to talk to you about," Anders said. "My two cousins, Kirsten and Thomas, need a ride back to Grandwood. Ivan said you would be stopping by there on the way back to the Rollo Islands. Can you take them?"

"Of course, we can take them back. And if they're any good at fighting, they're welcome to stay on with me and the rest of the crew."

"I'm good with a bow," Kirsten piped in.

"I'm not too bad with a blade," Thomas added.

"Good. You'll fit right in with us then," Britt said. "Go

on then, find a place for your items and then get to work helping us load the rest of the boat," she ordered.

Kirsten and Thomas began to carry out what Britt told them to do before Anders called to them, "Wait! Aren't you going to say goodbye?"

They stopped short and Kirsten said, "Yes, we're just excited to join the crew. Besides, we'll be seeing you sooner than you think."

"I hope so," Anders said, hugging them one at a time and squeezing them tightly for several seconds each before letting them go. Maija did the same. "Don't do anything I wouldn't do," Anders called after them as they ran aboard the ship, joining Max and Bo in their duties.

"Thank you so much," Anders said to Britt. "I know they're in good hands with you."

"If you ever decide to trade out that dragon for a ship, let me know. I would be glad to have you," she said shaking his hand.

Max, Bo, Thomas and Kirsten ran to the ship's railing and shouted back to him, "See you soon!"

Anders and Maija both waved goodbye before walking back across camp to join the elves.

"What's going to happen to us now?" Maija asked.

Anders stroked several strands of her hair away from her face and said, "I'm not sure. We'll have to wait and see what lies in store for us among the elves."

"At least we're able to stay together," Maija said smiling at him.

"I know, we're lucky in that," he said and leaned in to kiss her. Their lips met with a soft and warm embrace. Anders didn't know how much time he would have to devote to her, but he knew he wanted to make it work no matter the cost.

CHAPTER
SIX
NEW LEADERSHIP

Kirsten and Thomas watched the Eastland coastline fade into the distance as they set sail into the Marauder's Sea once more. The warm afternoon breeze filled the ship's sails as seagulls flocked around the masts, squawking loudly. Kirsten recounted the last time she'd been above deck when Merglan hauled them out in the light of the full moon. The more she had struggled against the invisible force he had imposed on all of the captives onboard, the more strenuously the magical force required her to obey its will, so this time she made sure not to take the experience for granted. The wind washed across her face as she stood next to her brother gazing off the ship's stern, the scent of saltwater and fish tickled her nostrils. It reminded her of home back at Highborn Bay.

"Isn't it strange to think we're going home?" Kirsten asked turning slightly to address Thomas.

He took a breath, letting the sea breeze fill his lungs, and then exhaled heartily before responding, "I thought this day would never come. Back there at the fortress, I wasn't sure we were going to make it out alive."

Max and Bo joined them at the rear of the ship. Max placed his forearms on the deck railing and looked longingly at the fading coastline. "We shouldn't worry about him you know," he said, his gaze fixed to the east. "Anders is resilient and surprisingly quick-minded. He'll be just fine without us."

"I know," Kirsten said. "He'll be alright without us, at least he'll be with Maija."

"I can't believe she turned out to be an elf," Thomas said, running his hand through his hair.

"She was an elf?" Bo asked, surprised.

"Yeah," Kirsten said. "She had this crazy magical hearing while we were captive, but I would've never thought she was that rider's sister."

"Wow," Max said, eyes widening. "So that's why she stayed behind?"

"I guess," Thomas said.

"I knew there was something special about her from the moment I saw her," Kirsten said.

"Sure you did," Thomas said sarcastically.

"I did. And I like Maija, I'm glad she'll be with Anders, but it's hard for me to see him go after such a brief time together."

"Things are going to be different now, no doubt. We've just been reminiscing about what it'll be like once we get back to Grandwood," Thomas said.

"At least you've got a home to go back to," Max said pushing his black hair out of his eyes.

"You two aren't going home?" Kirsten asked.

Together Max and Bo shook their heads, "Even if we were welcome, I wouldn't want to stay there again," Max said.

"Not as long as Tony's alive anyway," Bo added.

"Yeah, besides Britt's offered us working positions among her crew," Max finished.

Kirsten felt a rush of disappointment when she heard the two boys would stay on with Britt, not because she didn't think them capable of the job, but because she realized her time with Bo would be ending soon. Nothing between them had been said, but Kirsten could feel that he was beginning to grow fond of her and she'd only recently warmed up to the idea.

It's probably for the best anyway, she told herself, trying to see reason. Kirsten suddenly became aware that she'd been staring at Bo while she was wrestling with her thoughts. His dark eyes were locked with hers as they gazed longingly at each other from opposite sides of their respective brothers.

"Have you two ever been to the Rollo Islands?" Thomas asked, abruptly changing the subject after noticing the look Bo and his sister were sharing. When he spoke, Kirsten snapped her head back forward, rosy-cheeked and flushed with embarrassment. Bo kept his eyes on her for a moment longer before he, too, looked back to the east.

"No, but I'm eager to see them. I've heard their beaches are like none other in the five nations. It could all be a rumor, but I intend to find out," Max said with a smile. He placed his hands on his hips and puffed out his chest, striking a pose for them, "I'm not one to turn down an adventure, you know."

Bo scoffed at his older brother, hitting him with the back of his hand directly in the belly and making Max double over.

"The only thing you're ever up for is talking someone's ear off and bragging about all of your wonderful accomplishments," Bo mocked while taking several steps backward and readying for Max's retaliation.

"I do not!" Max paused, crouching before he lunged after Bo while adding, "Unless it's a beautiful girl, of course." He sprang at Bo, tackling him onto the deck.

Kirsten rolled her eyes as she and Thomas watched the dark-haired brothers roll around on the wood decking. She crossed her arms and shifted her weight onto one leg, "I'm so glad we don't do that anymore."

Thomas shrugged, "I don't know, it looks like fun to me."

Kirsten uncrossed her arms and Thomas grinned and faced her. "Don't get any ideas," she said putting her hands up defensively. "I might be smaller than you, but I'll," she cut off as Thomas launched himself at her.

Over the following weeks, Kirsten and Thomas became very familiar with Britt and her crew. Britt ran a tight ship, well organized and regulated. The days passed quickly as most of their time was spent cleaning, cooking and rigging the sails onboard. Their experience on the journey homeward was vastly different than the trip over to Eastland; everyone seemed to be in high spirits as opposed to the oppression they had faced before. The Rollo fleet sailed two dozen of the ships they'd taken from Merglan's fortress. And with the extra passengers, Kirsten didn't mind the extra space.

As they sailed across the Marauder's Sea, the fleet stopped nearly once a week to replenish their supply of fresh water and fresh meat. The journey back west took much longer than it had when they'd been captured. Kirsten chalked it up to the lack of escape and pursuit. After sailing three days beyond their last stop along the

Bareback Peninsula, the ships turned inward making for shore.

"Why are we landing here?" Kirsten asked. "We resupplied a few days ago before reaching the Bareback Plains."

"From what I gathered last night, the clan leaders want to stop and have a ceremony to elect their new head chief," Thomas replied.

"It seems like a strange place to do that," Max said. He stood near a group of Rollo warriors listening in on their conversation.

Britt didn't skip a beat in her response, "The location isn't important to the ceremony. Unlike the other western kingdoms' traditions where a coronation would take place in a capital like Kingston, the Rollo leaders decide once the clans have come to a consensus on who the final candidates will be. The location often varies because all of the clan leaders must be present, and this is often difficult to facilitate. Since we're all together at this time and they've had several weeks to consider their options for a new leader, they've decided to call the meeting now."

The bow of the ship plowed through the rough water offshore as they cut in toward land. Like the other crew members, Britt assigned Thomas, Kirsten and the brothers positions on the oars. Kirsten was paired with Max; they sat directly behind Thomas and Bo. Max was older and had a slight advantage over Bo in strength, so Britt matched them to allow the most equal pull along the ship.

While the crew rowed the heavy ship inland, several of Britt's warriors were tasked with rolling up the mainsail to allow for the fastest mobility. Britt barked the rowing cadence as they pulled with all their might to bring the large ship across the rough waters and into the calmer waters within the reef.

Just as Kirsten's arms began to seize up and cramp from the exertion of rowing as hard as she could for an extended period, they finally crossed the threshold to calm water. Halting their strenuous rowing, the ship glided in, slowing just before Britt ordered the anchor to be dropped, bringing them to rest among the other ships that had already anchored offshore. Britt began sending her crew one skiff at a time to shore, leaving one person to ferry the small transporter boat back for the next group.

Thomas, Kirsten, Max and Bo all piled into the same skiff, crawling into the boat from the hanging rope ladder dropped over the side of the tall ship. Coming to sit on the firm wooden bench, Kirsten remained quiet as Britt leapt down into their boat, the last to leave the ship.

As they approached the shore, they could see several clan leaders searching for a place out of the wind where they could build a fire and begin their deliberation. Hopping out of the boat, Thomas, Max and Bo lightened the skiff once it hit the beach, adding some buoyancy to the boat before dragging it up onto the beach so the craft couldn't float away.

After securing the shuttle boat, Thomas asked, "How long will the ceremony take?"

"The fastest one I know of only lasted a few minutes. Usually, they take several hours, although it can go on for days," Britt said. "It all depends on what the various clan leaders think. A new head chief must be selected by unanimous vote."

"Are other people being considered in addition to Red?" Max asked.

"Two others are up for consideration," she said. "I am one of them."

The group gasped in surprise.

"Really?" Max asked.

Britt nodded, "Yes. I offered my name and enough of our people saw me as a fit candidate. Come on let's get this over with," Britt said heading toward the other Rollo Islanders across the sweeping shoreline. The windblown and crusted-in sand made the footing unsteady.

As Kirsten looked back at the ships, she noticed that not all of the Rollo army had come ashore. "Why aren't the others coming to participate in the ceremony?" she asked as she hurried to join the others following Britt.

"Only those who are seen as worthy are allowed to join," she said simply.

"Who decided we were worthy enough but not the other warriors?" Kirsten asked.

"I did," Britt replied. "Each captain is invited by the clan leaders, but it's up to each captain to decide who can observe the ceremony. Most captains do not bring their crew, some may bring their first in command, but I treat all members of my crew equally, so all are welcome to join."

Kirsten raised an eyebrow and whispered to Thomas, "I wish I were as strong-willed as she is."

Nearing the other Rollo leaders, Kirsten became acutely aware of how few people had been invited to witness this historic event. In addition to the twelve clan leaders, most of the other captains were present, only two of whom brought along another crewmember.

They'd gathered near several large boulders that sheltered them from the wind gusting steadily off the grassy plains. All of the warriors' eyes scrutinized Britt's crew as they joined the group. Kirsten immediately recognized Red's large bearded face among the others scowling at the arrival of Britt's whole crew.

Kirsten thought he looked more weathered since the

Grandwood Games, but his large frame and dark curly hair were just as recognizable.

Seeing Britt's crew arrive en masse, Red said in protest, "What is this? You can't bring your whole crew to such a sacred ceremony. This decision is for leaders only." Many of the others nodded, grumbling in agreement.

"A captain can allow those she or he sees fit to join in such an important decision for our people. I treat every member on my crew as an equal and so I gave them the option of whether to participate in this monumental decision or not," she said firmly, folding her arms across her chest in defiance. "Do you have a problem with the laws of our people?" she asked in a self-assured tone.

Red scowled. As the son of their people's previous leader, he knew the laws and knew she was right, she could bring any members of her crew that she wished. "This is something I mean to change when I become the next chief," he said, looking around to the other leaders with a boisterous grin. Many of them nodded in agreement.

"This way of thinking is cancer to our people's ways. If I'm elected chief, I intend to see these close-minded ideas eradicated from our culture," Britt said, firm in her beliefs.

Kirsten felt that this wasn't how most ceremonies started, but it seemed this one had turned political right away. Bo stood close to her and she nudged him with her elbow. He dropped his head close to hers ready to listen to what she had to say.

"Looks like this could take awhile," she whispered.

Bo raised his eyebrows and nodded.

He motioned his head to the side, mouthed the words, "Come on," but was careful not to say the words aloud. He backed carefully away from the group and walked around behind the boulders. Already standing near the outer edge of the group, Kirsten allowed Bo to leave first, then followed shortly after to avoid causing a scene in leaving the ceremony they'd obviously been privileged to witness.

The wind streamed steadily across her body as she left the shelter of the rocks.

"Let's check this place out a little bit," he said pointing to the grassy plains beyond the sandy borders of the beach.

"We shouldn't wander too far," Kirsten said. "If the ceremony ends quickly, I don't want to miss our ride back to the ships."

"We don't have to go far," he said. "I just want to check out the Barebacks a little. I've never been to this side of the plains."

"The what backs?" Kirsten asked.

"The Barebacks," Bo said, raising an eyebrow. "The Bareback Plains," he said again when she didn't respond. "This grassland is called the Bareback Plains. It's the largest grassland in Kartania."

Kirsten quickly tried to play along, nodding and agreeing, "Oh yeah, yeah. Sure, I know about them."

"Oh, you do, do you? Tell me something about them," Bo said calling her out.

"Well," Kirsten began, her eyes darting back and forth as she quickly tried to come up with something clever to say. "The plains are... grasslands and..."

"Home to the largest group of wild horses," Bo said as she fumbled to come up with something.

"That's right," she said unconvincingly.

"You don't know anything about them, do you?" he asked seeing right through her from the start.

Kirsten flushed and shook her head, "Sorry, I don't."

"Don't be sorry," Bo said. "I only know this stuff

because Max and I used to live on the edge of the plains near Brookside."

Kirsten raised her eyebrows impressed.

"Come on, let's walk a little and see if we can see any horses."

Kirsten joined Bo. They hiked up onto the top of the grassy hill that rose just beyond the edge of the beach. From this slightly higher viewpoint, Kirsten could take in the vast beauty of the plains. For as far as she could see, the green and yellow grass danced lightly in the wind. It looked as if waves of water were washing over the hills as the long grass lay flat from the wind.

The setting sun in the west highlighted the rolling hills scattered in the distance. The contrast of endless ocean with endless grass gave her a peaceful feeling as she examined her surroundings. She inhaled deeply, breathing in the sweetness of the spring grass. As she scanned the area for the horses Bo had mentioned, she noticed thin wispy columns of smoke rising far off in the distance.

She pointed, "Is that smoke? Should we be worried that fire's spreading this way?"

The wind slapped their faces as they looked out at the plains; it wasn't hard to imagine a wildfire running through the hills.

"It is smoke," Bo confirmed. "But I doubt it'll be coming this way." Kirsten eyed him warily, not sure if she believed in his confidence that the fire couldn't move toward them. "There's a vast city out there," he continued. "The City of Aquina. It's home to all who live among the plains and it's not that far from here."

Still somewhat skeptical, Kirsten relaxed a bit, feeling more at ease knowing that the columns of smoke likely were just trailing off from warming and cook fires. "Have you ever been there?" she asked peering into the distance.

Bo shook his head, "No, but I really want to go, someday."

They stood for awhile in silence, watching the sky turn different shades of orange, yellow and violet as the sun sank more profoundly in the west. Kirsten kept looking behind them and down to the beach in case the ceremony ended suddenly, but each time she saw no change – the clan leaders remained huddled within the protection of the boulders apparently deep in political discussion.

"Look," Bo said, nudging her and pointing.

Kirsten followed his finger and saw a herd of horses galloping across over the plains. "Wow!" she exclaimed. They watched the horses run through the tall grass navigating the ground like a large flock of birds moving across the sky.

"Isn't it beautiful?" Bo asked dreamily.

"Yeah, it is," Kirsten said looking directly at him. She hoped he would look at her.

Bo kept his eyes fixed on the herd, "They truly are free animals." He turned to see Kirsten staring starry-eyed at him. Taken by surprise, he jumped slightly.

"Oh, sorry," Kirsten said reaching for his arms when she realized she'd unintentionally scared him.

Bo laughed placing his hand on Kirsten's as she held his arm, "That's alright, you just caught me off guard is all." He wiped the corners of his mouth and asked, "Do I have something on my face or something?"

"No," Kirsten said. "I was just..."

"Oh look," Bo said pointing back at the horses. "They're coming right at us."

Kirsten, slightly frustrated and reluctant to look, turned

her head to see that the herd of horses was much closer now and was heading straight at them.

"Come on, let's get down the hill a ways, down to those flats and see how close we can get," he said starting down the other side of the hill.

Kirsten looked back at the beach. Still no change in the decision. "You really like horses, don't you?" she asked, following him.

"Come on," Bo urged as he ran down the hill.

She ran to catch up with him. Bo led them to a small depression at the base of the hill. He crouched inside and motioned for her to stay low as they leaned against the sink-hole's sloped walls.

They watched as the herd of wild horses galloped into their midst. Kirsten's instincts told her to get up and run, but Bo held her hand tightly making sure she didn't leave. She watched wide-eyed as the thundering horses came closer. In a rush, the herd galloped right past them. Kirsten could've reached out and touched one if she'd wanted to. She squeezed Bo's hand and looked at him, smiling from the thrill. He was smiling too, moving his head back and forth watching them as they flew by.

When the last of the horses ran on, Kirsten felt she could finally relax a bit. They watched as the horses slowed their pace and circled back toward them. They came to a trot before moving into a slow walk. The herd spread out in the tall grass around the base of the hill they'd been standing on moments before and began grazing. Kirsten breathed heavily from the adrenaline still pumping through her veins.

"That was incredible," Bo whispered, looking at Kirsten with a huge smile.

Kirsten hadn't felt that kind of rush since the attack at

the Grandwood Games. She squeezed his hand and exclaimed while still whispering, "Wow, that was awesome!"

"Look, they're grazing right here," Bo whispered.

Kirsten suddenly became more aware that she and Bo were still holding hands.

"Wild horses are incredibly hard to tame," he continued in a hushed tone. "I wouldn't be surprised to learn that most of these horses have never even seen a human."

"Really?" Kirsten asked. She didn't realize how wild horses could be. "What would they do if we stood up and tried to pet them?" she asked.

Bo looked at her as if she was crazy, "People have died trying to do that." Kirsten raised her eyebrows in disbelief. "How could a horse kill someone, they don't have claws or sharp teeth?"

"They can rear back and knock you down with their two front legs," he replied. "Once you're down, they can trample you to death. One kick to the head and you're a goner."

"Wow, I had no idea they could do that," she said, surprised at the potential ferocity of the wild creatures.

As if to exemplify what Bo had told her, she watched two horses grazing nearby bite one another on the shoulders and rear up on their hind legs. They kicked wildly at each other with their front hoofs. When they landed a blow, each thud boomed against their muscular bodies. Kirsten understood then how a wild horse could easily kill a human.

"I was going to suggest we try to pet them, but now I don't want to," Kirsten said.

"Come on, we should get back to the beach," Bo said letting go of her hand. "It's getting dark and I don't want them to come looking for us."

They snuck slowly out of the small sinkhole and crawled through the grass. Once they were far enough away to avoid startling the horses, they stood up and walked to the top of the hill overlooking the beach. The clan leaders remained in the same place, talking at length.

Kirsten turned back to watch the horses grazing below and asked, "Why don't you want to go home, back to your family?"

Bo pursed his lips, "It's kind of complicated. They're not really our family."

"How so?" she asked.

"They're our foster parents. Our real parents were taken when we were young."

"Taken?" she asked.

"Killed," Bo said frowning. "I was only a toddler, but Max told me we lived in a great big castle, somewhere in Southland. Our parents worked there or something. One day, toward the end of The War of the Magicians, our castle was attacked. Max never told me how we escaped without them, but all I know is that we were taken in by Tony and his wife. They took us to Brookside and brought us up."

"Don't you find it odd?" she asked.

"What do you mean?"

"That you and Max, Anders, Maija and now Thomas and I all find ourselves in the same sort of situation, our parents tragically taken or claimed by a war that started decades ago."

"It is odd, but it's the way it is. All we can do is continue on, making sure this world is a better place than it was before."

"I like that outlook," Kirsten said starting down to the beach.

BACK BEHIND THE BOULDERS, the Rolloan leaders continued to debate heavily about who should succeed Jorgen as the new their chief. From what Bo and Kirsten could tell, it sounded like the decision had been narrowed down to two candidates, Britt and Red. Most of the leaders sat in the sand as Kirsten and Bo joined in with the rest of Britt's crew.

"Where have you two been?" Thomas whispered to Kirsten when they sat down.

"We went for a walk."

"Oh, that's what they call it nowadays." Thomas teased.

"Thomas," she said hitting him in the arm. "I'm not that kind of girl."

Thomas giggled, "I know, I was just giving you a hard time."

"We were looking for wild horses," she said defensively.

"Really?" he asked truly surprised.

"We saw some," she nodded.

Bo leaned over Kirsten's lap and whispered to Thomas, "They stampeded right by us, just a couple of feet away."

Thomas' eyes bulged. "They did?"

Kirsten nodded, "It was terrifying."

"Wow, they can be pretty dangerous, you know," Thomas whispered to Kirsten.

She raised an eyebrow and asked, "Since when do you know about wild horses?"

"Father always told stories about the wild horses of the Bareback Plains and the rough and tumble natured people of Aquina. Don't you remember?"

Kirsten scoffed, "What? I never heard him talk about that."

"Well you were pretty young, I guess, but so was I and I remember," Thomas said.

"Tsk, tsk, Kirsten," Bo whispered waving a finger at her.

She exhaled a short harrumph and Max turned and put a finger to his lips, shushing them.

The three of them went silent and listened to the debate for another half hour before the Rollo leaders eventually came to a final vote. It was unanimous, all of the leaders voted for Red to succeed his father. Britt rose and walked across the circle of men, coming to stand directly in front of Red. Kirsten held her breath, wondering if Britt was going to challenge him, but instead, she extended her arm. Red didn't bother to rise but took her hand and shook it firmly.

"Your father would be proud," she said boldly. "Congratulations." Britt turned back and waved her hands ordering her crew to get back to the ship. As they walked away, they could hear the cheers of the men as the clan leaders chanted Red's name. Once Britt's crew got the boats back into the water and began rowing back out to the ship, Red's voice could be heard barking orders.

"Back to the ships!" he ordered them.

Aboard the ships, Britt ordered them to wait until the rest of the clan leaders and their new chief set out into the open ocean. Kirsten rowed alongside Max who remained silent along with the others. Their somber mood could be felt as a collective group. When they'd rowed out to open water, Max made his way to where Britt stood, steering the ship, a job she usually delegated to another member of the crew. "Taking control of the ship, I see," he said lightly.

She gave him a cold look and said, "At least I can control this."

"It seemed as though the clan leaders weren't quite

ready for a woman to be their leader," Max said, trying to get her to speak her mind about the ceremony.

"I was so close to convincing them that change was a good thing. They just weren't quite ready for that kind of forward-thinking," Britt said, wishing things had gone differently.

"Red is stubborn and a fool," Max said. "I never really did like him much. He's good when a battle breaks out, but as a leader of a group, I'm not convinced he'll do a good job."

"He's very stubborn and stuck in his ways. He has a closed-minded view of the way things should be and doesn't listen to suggestions from people who don't align with what he believes," Britt said, clearly frustrated.

"He really didn't like your view of treating your crew as equals," Max added.

"No, he thinks it weakens the role of the leader. But take a look at my crew," she swept her hand across the ship. "Every person here would not hesitate to put my needs before their own. It's their choice to do that. I don't make them. Everyone on Red's crew has to be ordered to do so; not one of his men would sacrifice themselves for him. Sure, they fear him, but they don't respect him."

"I couldn't agree more," Max said calmly.

Britt looked deeply into his eyes and Max felt his heart quicken. "Red will try to remove me from my command and perhaps banish me from the Navy for running against him."

"He wouldn't?" Max protested. "Surely he knows how much of an asset you are to the Rollo forces. He wouldn't be so blinded to relieve you of your duties."

Britt looked back down the length of the ship again, "I

feel it in my heart. He will try to get rid of me as soon as he can."

For the next several weeks the weather was superb for sailing and they rode a steady wind along the coastline. Max and Bo pointed out Brookside to Thomas and Kirsten as they passed by. Max recounted the shipwreck resulting from one of Red's decisions that set them on land for several days before they were able to reunite with the Rollo Navy.

At last, after six weeks at sea, they saw the town of Grandwood. Kirsten and Thomas took note of the wreckage that still scarred their hometown. People could be seen milling about the town. As they drew near in their shuttle boats, Thomas pointed to black and gold banners that hung from the buildings.

"What are the banners all about?" he asked Kirsten.

She shrugged, "I don't know? I've been gone just the same as you."

"They weren't here before?" Britt asked.

Thomas and Kirsten shook their heads and Britt groaned, making them feel uneasy.

When they arrived at the docks, the greeting they'd expected didn't come. The people passing by hardly turned their heads and quickened their pace as the people kidnapped from Grandwood stepped off the skiffs and onto the docks.

Thomas frowned slightly and said to his sister, "Not quite the welcome I was expecting."

They walked along the dock looking more closely at one of the black and gold banners hanging near the shore.

"Who is that man painted on them?" Thomas asked.

That's Merglan, Kirsten thought to herself.

CHAPTER

SEVEN

ELVEN SPEED AND SEEDS OF DOUBT

Anders and Maija sat together, looking out at the Marauder's Sea as the last of the Rollo Islander's fleet sailed toward the horizon. The late spring air blew steadily off the water, ruffling Maija's long amber hair. Anders could sense Zahara's presence as she flew toward camp along the Eastland Mountain front.

Anders turned, pausing to look at Maija's beautiful face. She saw him staring at her and said playfully, "What?"

"Oh, look," Anders said, pointing across her toward Zahara in flight. Her scales glinted different shades of green against forested backdrop behind her.

"What do you think your training will be like?" Maija asked, watching intently as Zahara approached.

"I hope it's not too much bookwork," he replied looking back out across the dark blue sea. "I never really liked to read things that I was forced to."

"But you do like to read?" she asked, twisting her head sharply to see his reply.

He nodded, "I like choosing the things I read about, and getting through them on my own schedule."

"I love reading. Anything my grandparents gave me or suggested that I read, I devoured."

"Kirsten's that way, too," Anders said holding Maija's gaze. "I was always jealous of her aptitude for learning from books," he paused, glancing at Zahara as she glided over camp. "I can get along with bookwork just fine if I need to, but I've always been more of a hands-on learner."

"Well, I'm sure your training will involve a lot of hands-on learning."

"I just hope I can absorb it all as quickly as they need me to," he said with a tinge of worry. "It doesn't seem like we'll have much time before Zahara and I will need to face Merglan head on."

"I don't envy you, Anders," Maija replied leaning back on her elbows against the grassy hill.

Anders laughed, "I don't either, Maija. I didn't ask for any of this to happen. It just has. I'm not sure the path I'm following is meant for me. I feel like I'm the least qualified person to have been handed this responsibility."

Zahara circled above them spiraling lower with each turn, eventually landing softly on the grass next to them.

In his peripheral vision, Anders could see Maija observing him as he did her earlier. She wrapped her arms around him, resting her head on his shoulder as she whispered, "I wish we could go back to the first time we met and stay there for a while longer."

Anders met her brown eyes, streaked with golden brown flares, and said, "Me, too. Me, too."

"Did you find something to eat?" Anders asked Zahara as she sat down behind them. He spoke aloud so Maija could hear their conversation.

Yes, I did, she replied, switching to their telepathic link.

There was this lovely flock of white furry creatures just down the mountain range. They were the most satisfying meal I've had in my life. She then let out a belch that included a puffed ring of smoke. Her forked tongue swiped across her razor-sharp teeth. Purring, she added, *They almost taste as good coming back out as they do going in.*

Anders and Maija rolled on the ground laughing.

"Oh, Zahara," Maija said. "You're so funny."

Zahara cocked her head sideways and looked at Anders, *Ivan's telling us to get ready to leave. The elves are about to begin their return home.*

Anders sat up, "I guess it's time to face reality."

"One more minute," Maija said pulling Anders back down to the ground.

"Okay," he said feeling the surprising strength of her grip.

They wrapped each other in their arms, holding one another close and feeling the warmth of their bodies against the oncoming evening.

Anders could see the elf horde beginning to move across the valley toward the mountains, "We'd better catch them. They're leaving now."

Anders and Maija ran down the hill toward Ivan and the others who'd remained behind waiting. Zahara glided low to the ground next to them as they ran. Maija seemed to be maintaining a faster pace than Anders with ease.

When they stopped, Anders could see that Ivan, Nadir and Natalia were still waiting for them. Ivan was the first to speak, "Anders, you and I will ride with Zahara. Maija, since you probably haven't figured out how to run like an elf during your years of living as a human, you will travel with Natalia and Nadir. Natalia's still recovering from her injuries and will be going much slower than the others. Nadir's agreed to stay behind and help. Anders, Zahara and I will follow along from the air. If anything should go wrong, Nadir and the three of us will be quick to come to your aid. Is that clear?" Ivan concluded in a commanding tone.

"You want me to run all the way to the Everlight Kingdom?" Maija half shouted in surprise.

"You're an elf," Natalia said. "It's in your blood to be able to sprint and for great distances. Since your memory was wiped and you were living with humans, you weren't taught the proper way to tap into this skill. I honed this skill as a young adult. Now that I must relearn it, we can go through the steps together."

Maija raised an eyebrow questioningly. She looked to Nadir, Ivan, and then to Zahara and Anders.

"You can do it," Ivan said. "You've always had the capability, you just need to learn how to use it."

Anders shrugged, "If you can't make it, Zahara and I will give you a ride."

"I would much rather do that," she said pointing to Anders and looking at Ivan.

"We don't have time for this," Ivan said, frustrated. "You're just going to have to trust in your abilities. Nadir and Natalia will show you the ropes. Come on Anders, let's get moving. We need to go over what you'll be learning once we arrive."

While Ivan climbed onto Zahara's back, Maija gave Anders a wide-eyed look. "I'm sorry," he mouthed to her.

With visibly clenched teeth she let out an 'ahhh.'

"You can do this," Anders said, taking her by the hand. "I believe in you." He smiled, trying to make her feel better, but the worried expression on her face didn't fade.

"Anders, come now!" Ivan shouted. "Time to go!"

Anders let go of her hands one at a time and said, "Good luck. I'll be close by if you need anything." He turned and climbed onto Zahara's back, sitting between her shoulders in front of Ivan. She pushed off the ground and let her wings carry them high into the cool evening air.

"Maija," Natalia said, tugging at her sleeve to get her attention as she continued to stare after Anders and Zahara.

Maija pointed to them, shaking her head, "That is so unfair."

"I know," Natalia said. "Flying on the back of a dragon is a great privilege, but tonight we'll be learning to run."

"Why don't we begin by seeing what you've got based on instincts," Nadir said, pointing to the group of elves fading into the distance as they ran together into the mountains. "Natalia, follow your sister but do not push it too hard. Your legs could still be susceptible to injury so soon after the healing."

Natalia nodded, bending into a running stance.

Maija saw her sister preparing to bolt and asked, "Now?"

Nadir nodded while closing his eyes, "Yes, now."

Maija mimicked her sister, crouching with one foot ahead of the other. She'd rarely tried to see how fast she could run, and even then, she'd only gone as fast as others her age. Even in situations where she could've tested her speed, such as when the thief at the Grandwood Games took off with the prize money, she had followed Anders. Perhaps subconsciously she knew that he would catch the man, so she didn't feel the need to push herself to her limit.

Maija inhaled slowly, drawing the evening air deep into her lungs. Exhaling slowly, she closed her eyes and bowed her head. Then she took off. At first, she took small steps, quickening as she ran forward with her chin still tucked. As she increased her speed, she began to lift her head, eventually looking straight ahead.

Maija ran faster than she'd ever felt she could, but she didn't think she was going at the speed of the elves. Natalia jogged up alongside her.

Maija glanced at her through the corner of her eye and asked through short gasping breaths, "How are, you? Not tired?"

Natalia replied calmly, "Don't worry about me, you're doing great. Just focus on breathing steadily, in and out. Bring the oxygen deep into your lungs, not your stomach, and extend your legs out, expanding your stride."

Maija faced forward with determination. She did exactly as Natalia suggested. She slowed her breathing with each breath and let her chest expand as the air filled her lungs. She exhaled calmly and slowly, in succinct repetition. Once Maija felt she'd developed a good breathing cadence, she began to focus on her stride. She let her legs extend farther between each stride, stretching them out one step at a time until she felt as though she was bounding like a deer through tall grass. She looked to her side, smiling at her sister, but Natalia was no longer beside her. She was now far behind. Surprised, Maija realized she was running much faster than she had been before.

The cool evening breeze flowing across her warm skin helped her relax into the run. Her heart pounded steadily, and she could feel her body temperature rise as elven blood coursed through her veins. She slowed slightly, letting her older sister catch up.

"That was excellent," Natalia said as she came alongside again.

"I can't believe it!" Maija shouted. "That was amazing! What a rush!"

Nadir caught up to them. He'd been watching them both from a distance to monitor their progress. "That was good, Maija," he said simply. "If you pick your knees up a bit higher, you'll lengthen your stride even more. Also, don't forget to push your arms back, raising your elbows behind your core as your run. This will drive your legs to move even faster."

Maija nodded at his advice.

"Natalia, you're looking very comfortable. I think you could increase your speed if it feels good. If you have any pain, however, any pain at all, you should slow back down to a more comfortable pace. Pushing yourself too hard could result in permanent injury," Nadir warned.

"Okay," Natalia said. "Hey Maija, let's see if you can keep up." Natalia took off in front of them at an alarming rate.

Maija attempted to match her sister's pace. She kept her breathing in control and used what Nadir had told her to drive her knees up. She turned her legs over faster using the pull of her arms. Soon she was right behind Natalia as they sprinted across the valley floor toward the Eastland Mountains.

Coming up on her right side, Maija asked, "How are your legs feeling?"

Natalia replied, "Just fine. I don't want to push it too hard though, so I'm going to slow down a bit." She short-ened her stride and returned to a fast run. Maija did the same.

Nadir caught up once again, "Natalia that looked great. Smart choice to hold back though. And Maija, nicely done, you seem to be a natural at this. As you run more, you'll find that there are countless fine details you can work on to improve your speed and stamina, but as a whole, for now, I wouldn't change a thing."

Maija smiled. She had been so worried about not being capable, but now she wondered why she'd been so nervous; it was just running after all.

They continued to follow the elf army. Due to the army's slower pace, Maija knew they wouldn't arrive at Cedarbridge at the same time as Anders. At least they wouldn't be days behind them, as they would've been if they'd had to walk like humans or dwarfs.

Anders had watched as Maija and Natalia started out across the valley. At first, they appeared to run relatively slowly, but suddenly Maija gained speed and was running much faster than Natalia and Nadir. Then Natalia who took off like a bolt of lightning, running as fast as any other elf. To his surprise, Maija responded to the challenge, catching up with Natalia in no time. He laughed seeing the long-lost sisters competing as they neared the mountains.

"It looks like Maija's figured it out," he said over his shoulder to Ivan.

Ivan glanced down, "I knew she would. She's an elf after all. It's in her blood."

"Hey, Ivan," Anders asked, no longer worried about Maija. "There's something I'd like to see while we're over here."

"What's that?" Ivan asked.

"Nadir told me about the kingdom of the dwarfs and their home within the mountain. He said it's not far from here. I was wondering if we could see it?"

Ivan didn't respond right away, pondering the question

for a moment. Then he answered, "Yes, Mount Orena is not far. I don't see why we couldn't make a few passes over it. That is, as long as Zahara doesn't mind the extra flight time?"

I don't mind. I would like to see the dwarf kingdom. That way I'll know what they look like and won't take them for enemies or food in the future, she said.

"We might find ourselves making a journey there anyway," Ivan said.

"What do you mean?" Anders asked.

"With Merglan openly launching attacks again, we're going to need all the help we can get, and the dwarfs are terribly fierce fighters. We'd be lucky to have them as allies in this war."

Anders fantasized about meeting dwarfs. He pictured their stone carving, unique masonry, and abundant riches mined from the depths of the earth.

How do I get there? Zahara asked.

Ivan pointed Zahara in the right direction using his mind. They flew farther east over the Eastland Mountains. Nestled among the craggy peaks was a large mountain, its apron spread wide at the base. Lush green fields wrapped around its base like a blanket.

"Is that it?" Anders said, pointing to the towering mountain.

Ivan nodded.

"It's beautiful," he said in awe of the majesties of the mountain. As they flew closer, Anders noticed livestock grazing along the mountain's base and felt something inside him, much like the stomach pain of an irresistible hunger. He took a closer look, squinting to see tiny white critters scattered along the hillside.

Zahara, Anders said.

Yes, Anders, Zahara replied, trying to make her thoughts feel innocent.

Are those the little white creatures you so blissfully enjoyed eating earlier? he asked. He didn't need to hear her response. He could feel it within her and knew these were the sheep she'd eaten earlier that day.

I don't think the dwarfs will appreciate you eating their sheep, Anders scolded her.

I didn't know they belonged to anyone, she said trying to come up with a good excuse.

We'll just have to hope they don't know it was a dragon that ate them, he said.

Zahara circled over the mountain several times. Anders noticed more than one walled entrance into the mountain. Even from the air, he could tell that they were designed and built with great skill and detail. He marveled at the masonry the dwarfs used to craft their city and kingdom under a mountain.

"What do they look like?" Anders asked, turning on his seat to address Ivan.

"You don't know what a dwarf looks like?" Ivan asked surprised.

"I know they're shorter than the average human, but that's about it," Anders said.

"They're indeed shorter than a human," Ivan replied. "They're stout people and many of the men have great beards," Ivan said, motioning a long extension below his chin. "Their women are stout as well, but fair nonetheless. I have seen many beautiful young dwarf women in my years. They come in all manner of race, just as humans or elves, and they're emotional creatures just like we are," he added.

"Have you spent much time with them?" Anders asked.

"I have," Ivan said. "You will, too, I expect."

"How so?" Anders asked.

"Oh, you'll see soon enough," Ivan said.

Once they'd circled Mount Orena a couple of times, Zahara headed back toward the pass through the mountains the elves would follow through the forest.

"So, when do I begin my training?" Anders asked later as they flew through the night sky.

"When we get back to Cedarbridge, we'll begin as soon as possible," Ivan said. "But first, we'll need to fit you with a proper saddle," he shifted uncomfortably on Zahara.

"They make saddles for dragons?" Anders asked, intrigued by the idea.

"Yes, the saddles allow the rider to stay on the dragon's back during aerial maneuvers. The fit is comfortable for both the dragon and the rider. You'll be crafted one once we land in the elven capital."

Anders thought in silence, wondering how the rigging of a dragon saddle would fit best around Zahara's body. He kept imagining the saddle sliding back as it often did on a horse when fitted too loosely.

Ivan broke the long silence, "Did you notice anything strange about any of the elves?"

The question caught Anders by surprise and his thoughts turned to curiosity, "What do you mean by strange? Like how you were acting before the orcs attacked in Glacial Melt Bays?" He didn't mean the words to come out as harshly as they sounded, but Anders was still feeling slighted by Ivan's secrecy about the orcs.

"No," Ivan said. "I mean, did you get any sort of feeling or vibe?"

"About betraying us before the battle and alerting Merglan of the riders' presence?" Anders asked.

"Yes," Ivan replied. "The reason I ask is that you had a vision of Natalia before we even went looking for her. I just thought you might have noticed one of the elves who leaked information about our planned attack."

Anders wracked his memory for anything strange from any of the elves. "No," he said eventually. "So, you think it was one of the elves who betrayed us?"

"Well, Merglan does have the ability to sense people coming. I know he's capable of using his abilities more powerfully than any sorcerer in history, so it's possible he was aware of our movements and always knew we were coming. However, I'm not convinced that's the case. I think someone was sending messages to him of our movements. I'm not sure who it could have been though since most of what we did was in privacy," Ivan said.

"You're not suggesting someone inside the fortress was leaking information to him, because if you are, Maija was taken prisoner just like the others. She was in Grandwood during the games and didn't have any knowledge of the attack. She didn't even know she was an elf, so how could she be the source?" Anders said defensively.

"I didn't mention anything about Maija. I know she was taken and held captive against her will and didn't know of her elven past until recently. I wasn't suggesting it could be her. All I'm saying is that it's strange how Merglan knew the elves were coming."

"Oh, sorry," Anders said slightly embarrassed. "I didn't notice anything odd, but I also didn't spend much time with any of them individually. The only one I actually spent any time with was Nadir. I feel he truly wants peace in Kartania, so it doesn't make sense that he would betray us. Besides, what could he possibly gain from giving Merglan information?" Anders spoke with conviction.

Ivan seemed to ponder the possibility of Nadir going to Merglan with the information. As Zahara flew above the mountain pass, Anders could see by starlight glimpses of Maija, Natalia and Nadir running at a rapid rate. Anders asked, "What will Maija be doing in Cedarbridge while we train?"

"Maija's family history is a complex one," Ivan said. "Natalia will be helping her to restore her memory if it's at all possible."

"What's so complex about her family? Is it because both her parents were riders? Does that mean she will become a rider, too?"

Ivan thought carefully about how to phrase his response, "If multiple family members become dragon-bonded, then it's likely other family members will become bonded too. It's mostly a testament to their character and moral values, not genetics. But since she was absent from her family for so long and for so much of her childhood, it's likely Maija's not much like her parents and more like the people she thought were her grandparents."

"That's very interesting," Anders thought. "Was anyone in my family bonded with dragons?" he asked, hoping Ivan could add to his scant knowledge of his ancestors and even his parents.

When Ivan didn't say anything for a moment, Anders began to think he hadn't heard him, so he opened his mouth to speak again just as Ivan responded, "I'm not sure, Anders."

He thought it slightly odd that Ivan took so long to answer, but brushed it off knowing that Ivan had the betrayal on his mind.

"I was hoping you could answer something else that has been bothering me," Anders asked.

"More about your family, I suppose?" Ivan mumbled.

"No. Actually, it's about how some of the elves could use magic, but they don't have dragons. Like the healers that helped heal Natalia's legs."

"Most sorcerers who are bonded with dragons develop a specialty in a style of magic they can do best. For me, it was sensing where people were in relation to myself. For some, it is battle magic and for others healing."

"Will I have a specialty?" Anders asked.

"You most likely will," Ivan replied. "Usually it will present itself when you've had more opportunities to use magic. You'll get a feel for which magic comes to you more easily."

"So all those elves had dragons they were bonded with at one point in their lives. I would assume if the dragons were still alive, they would've joined in the fight?" Anders asked.

"Yes," Ivan said. "Merglan caused a great deal of devastation in the population of those bonded with dragons. Likewise, there are solo dragons. Remember all those dragons we saw when Zahara was reunited with her family?" Ivan asked.

Anders nodded.

"Well, most of those dragons are solo, as in they have lost their bonded partner. Or they haven't bonded yet, as Zahara hadn't at that time."

Anders hadn't realized the extent of the destruction Merglan had caused on their kind and felt deep sorrow for those who were affected by him. As far as he knew, the only ones left that were still bonded were the two elves that came with the elf army, one of which lost her dragon and the other that had died alongside his dragon.

Anders thought of the importance of his bond with

Zahara and knew that many people depended on him to succeed in his mission. They flew the rest of the night in silence, making sure Maija and Natalia were able to return safely. Eventually, they landed just outside Cedarbridge and waited for Maija, Natalia and Nadir to catch up.

EIGHT

THE MOLE

Anders stretched his legs, shaking them out one at a time while also yawning. Shuddering, he attempted to ward off the sleepiness he felt. It took Zahara, Ivan and him the better part of the night to get within view of the elf city. They'd decided to stop short, as the ancient magic concealing the city within the forest made it particularly difficult to locate from the air, so they thought it best to walk the last half-mile with Maija, Natalia and Nadir. The bulk of the elf army had made it back hours before; otherwise, they would've entered with them. With Maija and Natalia pacing themselves at a slower rate, they lagged behind the army by a few hours.

Ivan turned to Anders as he slipped off Zahara's back. Seeing Anders' big yawn, he said, "Wake up, they're almost here."

Anders stood, but swayed with his eyes nearly closed. "I'm up, I'm up," he replied. Widening his eyes, Anders attempted to wake himself by slapping his cheeks with both hands.

Within seconds, the three elves were upon them, slowing their speed rapidly and coming to a halt in the path.

"It's a surprise seeing you two here," Nadir said. "Is everything alright?"

"Yes, everything is fine. We just thought we should join you in passing through the gates so King Asmond wouldn't worry that we abandoned our watch. It might look bad if we arrived ahead those we were tasked to keep an eye on," Ivan said.

"True," Nadir stated simply.

They walked the last half mile of forested trail to the outer gates of the Cedarbridge. With the sun absent for at least another hour, seeing through the dark forest proved difficult, but Anders was able to recognize the faint outline of the gates. Spellbound, the gates blended into the trees and brush, making it nearly impossible to see even with the advantage of the sun. Nadir spoke the magic words and the gate opened, allowing them to enter beyond the evergreen walls. Once inside Cedarbridge, Anders was surprised to see so many people up and moving about their morning duties already. As they walked down the main path toward the tree houses the elves called home, Zahara's head drooped with fatigue from the extended flight with passengers.

Before entering through a door at the bottom of a tree where Nadir had led them, Zahara said, *I'm going to sleep at my parents' dwelling. They'll want to know I'm alright. Just send me a thought when you're ready to begin training.*

Okay, Anders replied. He knew this was a safe enough place for her to be away from him for awhile.

Anders followed Nadir and Ivan into the tree house, closing the door behind Maija and Natalia as they entered. He could see the many dormitory doors lining the inside of the tree, going all the way to the top.

"This is the travelers' tree. We'll find more suitable accommodations for you later in the day," Nadir said. He turned sharply on his heels and exited the tree house.

"Alright then," Ivan said rubbing his hands together. "Pick a room and get some shut-eye. I'll be waking you in a few hours," he pointed to Anders, "so don't get too comfortable. Training starts soon." He walked into the closest room and closed the door behind him.

Anders raised his eyebrows and shrugged with a slight frown as he mouthed, "g'night" to Maija. He then walked into one of the rooms at ground level. Maija and Natalia did the same, each picking one.

Closing the door behind him, Anders examined his room. Two straight walls, mirroring the inside of the large tree's grain, ran the length of the small room and joined the cylindrical tree several inches inside the exterior bark. Only a single bed stood in the middle of the room. The frame appeared to have grown into place out of gnarled branches. It weaved together, bound with magic to shape the bed. One round window, crafted cleverly into a large knot, allowed some light from the city's early morning glow to creep into the dimly lit room. Anders immediately lay face down on the bed, not bothering to pull back the wool blankets. He closed his eyes, letting sleep take him.

A moment later, it seemed, he heard pounding on his door. Anders bolted upright, startled. The pounding stopped briefly, so Anders swung his legs over the edge, feet on the floor. When the pounding resumed, he stood up and shuffled to the door. Rubbing his eye with one hand, he used the other to pull the door open. Ivan stood in the hallway, looking away from Anders, glancing around the entrance to the tree house, his hand still raised in the pounding position.

"Come on, let's go," he said lowering his arm. "Tell Zahara to meet us at the cliff's edge in half an hour."

Anders nodded sleepily. He reached out to Zahara with his mind, sensing her distant presence. He sent her a message, *Zahara are you there?*

Yes, what is it? she asked.

Ivan wants us to meet at the cliff's edge in a half hour. You know, the spot where I left you with your parents on our last visit to Cedarbridge.

She acknowledged him and Anders told Ivan with a yawn, "Okay, she'll be there."

Closing the door behind him without changing from the clothes he'd slept in, he followed Ivan out of the tree house. The elf city was brightly lit by the morning sun. The blooming vegetation added to the city's vibrancy; the city felt much more alive than when they'd arrived a few hours ago under cover of darkness. Anders almost jumped out of his skin when he noticed Natalia and Maija rising to their feet in his peripheral vision. Seated on a root wad bench next to the door, they had been waiting for the two to exit.

Anders gasped, startled as he jumped back, fists up and ready to defend himself. It wasn't until he registered who it was that he relaxed and said, "You scared me half to death."

"A little jumpy, are we?" Natalia said mockingly.

Maija snickered, trying to hold back her outright laughter at Anders' rosy-cheeked embarrassment.

Ivan shook his head, "Come on, jumper, follow me. We need to meet with King Asmond and the high council before we can begin our training."

The three of them followed Ivan through the city. They wound their way between large trees spanning widths several times larger than his home in Grandwood. Finally, they approached a singularly wide tree with

ornately carved doors. Recognizing the doors, Anders realized he'd been to this place the last time he and Ivan were
in the elf capital. He marveled at the delicately carved
wood, wondering how long each door would have taken to
create.

Ivan swung the doors open, entering the building. Just
as before, Ivan led them up the stairs and out into the vast
tree's canopy. There on the treetop's large deck-like courtyard sat the elf king and his wife, Lageena, the queen. Nadir
stood straight and at attention near the table, one arm
tucked properly behind his back and the other resting on
the back of a chair. Upon seeing them enter, Nadir waved
them over and invited them to sit down. This pleasantry
wasn't offered to Anders the last time he was in the king's
presence, so he gladly accepted. Nadir then joined them at
the table.

"Natalia," the king said in a somber tone. "I was so
saddened to hear about your misfortune as of late. Your skill
and presence as one of our most important lines of defense
in this war will be greatly missed. I offer you my deepest
condolences for the tragedy that's befallen our people."
Asmond rested his hand over his heart and tilted his head,
bowing slightly.

Natalia clenched her jaw, pushing down her emotions
as she responded, "Thank you, your majesty. I will continue
my service to our people and offer what knowledge I can to
Anders in his training."

Asmond nodded, turning his attention to the others.

"I thought the high council was to be meeting with
us?" Ivan asked, a bit surprised.

"This is a delicate matter. One I want to keep between
us for now," the king said, raising an eyebrow toward Maija.

Natalia cleared her throat, understanding the king's

implication, "You may remember my sister, Maija." Natalia said motioning toward Maija.

The king and queen simultaneously gasped. "I thought she was in hiding! Your parents, Ormond and Isabella, used powerful magic to disguise her from ever being found?" Lageena said, leaning over the table and gawking at Maija.

"How did you possibly find her?" Asmond asked.

"She more or less found me," Natalia said.

"It's a long story, and we can fill you in later," Ivan said trying to gain control of the conversation. "Maija's been made aware of our situation and can be trusted. She's one of us."

Asmond hesitated, eyeing Maija for a breath before responding, "Very well. Like I was saying, this is a delicate matter. One you all have been directly affected by, so I've decided to include you in confiding this information. As it's been determined by those I trust, Nadir and my wife, the mole who betrayed us in our attack on Merglan's fortress is likely a member of the High Council, so no one else is privy to this meeting."

So that's what this is all about, Anders thought to himself.

"You trust that everyone in present company isn't involved?" Ivan asked.

"I know it is not me," the king began, placing his pale hand on his chest. "As for the rest of you, I have my own suspicions. But it is more likely that it is someone in the High Council."

"And if you're wrong?" Ivan asked bluntly.

The king cocked his head slightly and visibly exhaled before addressing Ivan. "If I'm wrong, and it is one of us here today that's been leaking sensitive information to our most formidable foe this world has ever seen," Asmond paused, drawing in a deep breath before continuing, "then the details of this meeting will be made known to him, and I'll have narrowed my search down to the six of you." He widened his eyes as he spoke.

"Good enough for me," Ivan said raising his hands in an open gesture. "Let's get down to business. After Merglan knew we were attacking, he sent his entire orc and kurr army out to meet us. Merglan and his dragon rode off to attack the elf army, which he did. I wasn't there, but from what I could gather, he changed his focus to Natalia and Keanu, who led him away from the elves, giving both the army and Zahara a chance to escape and help us win the battle. Once the battle was won, Anders, Zahara and I helped free the prisoners Merglan was using for slave labor. Maija here," Ivan pointed to Maija, "was one of those forced into labor. She was a chambermaid for his head officers and army commanders. It's my understanding that she found a secret room with crystals that were being guarded by his dragon, Killdoor."

"Can you describe what the crystals looked like?" Asmond asked Maija.

She cleared her throat, not realizing beforehand that she was going to have to speak during a meeting with the king and queen, "Um," she started slowly, "They were kind of blue in color and varied in size. He had people mining them inside the confines of his fortress."

"How large was the largest crystal he obtained that you saw? And how many would you estimate that his dragon was guarding?" Asmond asked, very interested in her observations.

"The largest crystal I saw was about this big," Maija said while making a circle with her arms out in front of her chest, her hands clutching her elbows to show the king the estimated diameter. "He had an entire wall filled with them. It was, oh, I don't know, about twice the length of this table and as wide this room?"

The king's jaw dropped, his mouth agape. He didn't say anything right away. The queen spoke first, "How do we know that what you are telling us is true? For all we know, she could be lying for her own personal gain."

"I know what I saw," Maija protested, raising her eyebrows at how aggressively she defended herself to the queen. She blushed with this realization.

Ivan raised his hands before Lageena had time to respond, "I believe that she's telling us the truth. She doesn't have any reason to mislead us."

"If what she said is true," the king interjected, "Then potentially Merglan has more power than he's ever had before."

"How is that possible? What do the crystals do?" Anders asked.

"There are crystals in this world known to have unparalleled powers," Natalia said.

Anders glanced down at his hip, looking at the small sapphire crystals worked into the handle of his recently acquired sword.

"The riders of old wrote of the secrets to using these crystals, but their writings were lost ages before they came into power. Rumors of the Norfolk..."

"That's enough," Asmond said, cutting her off. "I'll not have talk of those people in my presence."

"If I may, your majesty?" Ivan said.

The king nodded.

"Merglan has obviously invested heavily into acquiring crystals of all kinds and for some unknown reason he has chosen now as the time to come out of hiding."

"Is that how Thargon could use magic?" Anders blurted out. "I saw Thargon wearing a crystal necklace."

"It's possible," Ivan said. Although the king glared at them disapprovingly, Ivan continued, "I'm not entirely sure how Thargon was alive. Merglan must have found a way to restore his body after..." he paused, glancing at Anders. "After Theodor slew him."

"Not possible, it must have been another kurr," Asmond said.

Anders opened his mouth to dispute him, but Ivan gave him a stern look clearly warning him to hold his tongue.

"Really?" Maija asked unaware. "Because I heard Merglan speaking with him and calling him by name."

"An illusion," Asmond said, waving a hand. "He probably brought another devilish kurr into his employ and named him after that wretch. Besides, Merglan was probably harvesting those crystals to help sell swords to the orc armies. You know how they worship those sapphires."

"Regardless of his intentions," Ivan said. "It still begs the question as to why he's chosen now to come out of hiding."

"No one can be expected to understand the mental decisions of a mad man," Nadir said.

"Whatever the reason, it's safe to assume Merglan will attempt to take control of the five kingdoms," the queen said, bringing their conversation back to grounded ideas.

"Yes, I believe that's still his goal," Ivan said.

"Well then," King Asmond said. "We must get to work with your training." He looked to Anders. "You've got quite a lot of work to do if you're going to beat Merglan alone."

"I have to fight him alone?" Anders asked, looking to Ivan.

"Well, there aren't any more dragonriders on our side," Asmond said. "Merglan killed our youngest pair and Vieadore was taken from Natalia as well. You and Zahara are all we've got left."

Anders felt sick. He had no idea that he was the only rider left fighting for justice. He thought perhaps that with all the dragons still in the world more pairs would be out there somewhere. He wasn't ready to take on the most powerful sorcerer in the world. He didn't even know how to use magic properly yet.

Ivan took the opportunity to end the meeting, "We'll be using the training facilities outside the city if you need to reach us."

As Ivan rose from his seat, Asmond said, "Ivan, I think you'll appreciate the additions we've made to the training grounds."

Ivan furrowed his brow as the king continued, "Don't worry, it's nothing major." He waved him off before Ivan turned to leave the table. Ivan led them toward the exit when Lageena called, "Maija." She turned to address the queen. "It's good to have you back," the queen said with a smile.

Maija curtsied slightly and followed the others, leaving the room and descending through the stairwell.

Once outside earshot of the king, Ivan turned to Anders, still pale and absent-minded, "Are you alright? You looked like you were about to have a breakdown."

Anders shook his head, "I'm not ready for all this. I don't want to fulfill the prophecy."

"No one is ever ready to do things like this," Ivan said. "Try not to think about the end goal, just think about what we need to do next. Begin training. That's what we'll focus on now."

Anders nodded.

IVAN LED as they exited the large tree and walked to the cliff's edge where Anders had planned to meet Zahara. She stood waiting for them.

What are we going to do now? Zahara asked when she saw Anders.

We're going to begin training because that's what we need to do next. Just practice, not fighting yet, Anders said, still rattled by the immense task ahead of them.

Zahara eyed him strangely, then turned her attention to Ivan, who said, *Training is what comes next, so that's what we're going to do. Head to the training facilities.*

Where's that? Zahara asked.

Ivan pointed beyond the cliff to the far reaches of the valley below. *The training grounds are at the end of the valley. There will be lodging and food for us there.*

Anders and Ivan climbed onto Zahara's back and waved goodbye to Natalia and Maija, who'd followed before seeking out their parents' home along the cliff's edge. Zahara leapt off the edge of the tall cliff at the edge of Cedarbridge and let herself fall with her wings tucked for several seconds. Anders' adrenaline began to pump through his veins as they plummeted toward the ground. The air rushed through his wavy hair, pulling it straight back. Letting her wings extend out and catch the air within their leathery expanse, Zahara pulled herself out of the dive and used the momentum to climb and glide over the forested valley below.

See the tower at the far end of the valley, Ivan said to them. *That's where we're heading.*

Anders let himself become lost in the joy of flying. If only for a short distance, it gave him the chance to shed his worries and feel the freedom of the sky. Zahara brought them down in a clearing next to the training facilities.

A three-story tower made of stone stood at the far end of a grassy opening. The castle-like building bore a resemblance to the depictions of towers surrounding the castle keeps in several books Theodor had in his personal library. A long single-story hall extended out from the bottom floor, attached to the rounded stone building. The length of the room stretched several times that of the tallest trees in Cedarbridge and was built with an extensive roof crafted entirely of timbers. Next to the tower was a massive circular depression, digging deep into the ground and absent of grass near the base. The sloped sides rising out from the bottom of the pit were covered with grass and boulders.

Surrounding the stone building was the large grassy clearing they landed in. The clearing and training facility sat nestled near the base of rolling hills that rose up from the valley bottom. Looking up from the clearing, Anders could see several stone spires reaching high over the trees. These rock formations rose up from the forested hilltops, jutting high above the trees in magnificent fan-like spires, of varying heights.

"This is it," Ivan said, jumping down off Zahara. He pointed to the stone tower, "This will be our dormitory for the next several months. There's a large hall for dining and a library complete with every book ever written about magic and dragons. The fighting pit's a new addition and looks like it will be a great place to learn how to battle with magic. And the cliffs are used for flight training."

Anders and Zahara ogled at it all in wonder, drinking it all in. "Where do we begin?" Anders asked Ivan.

"In the library," Ivan said as he walked toward the tower.

Anders was eager to improve on his battle skills and learn battle magic and flight maneuvers with Zahara, but he was not excited to read about them.

"Shouldn't we start by working on my fighting skills?" he asked Ivan, jogging to catch up with him.

"We'll start every day by going to the library to study. After lunch you and Zahara will practice what you have learned that morning," he said.

When they entered the stone building, Anders looked around at the paintings and banners that covered the walls. They depicted dragons and sorcerers of the past. House banners with their slogans were interspersed among the paintings.

Ivan led them through the entryway, passing a large dining hall. Anders paused to admire the enormous room. Long tables ran the length of the hall. He marveled at the large doors and high ceilings, each big enough to accommodate all sizes of dragons.

"Follow me," Ivan said, opening a door that led down a set of stairs into a sizable cave-like basement.

He lit a torch on the wall and held it up as Anders and Zahara entered the cave. The light revealed hundreds of books on shelves that lined the walls of the enormous cavern. Anders was taken aback by the size of this hidden underground library.

"Will I have to read all of these?" he said, looking around.

Ivan chuckled, "No, but you will need to read quite a bit if you're going to gain enough information to take on Merglan."

"Where should I begin?" Anders asked.

"Here," Ivan said leading him to a row of books all stamped on their spines with a golden dragon wing. He pulled out one volume and said, "Start with this and let me know when you have completed it."

Anders sat down on one of the many chairs within the cave.

"Zahara, I have something for you to read as well," Ivan said, leading her across the cave.

But I can't read your language in writing, Zahara said.

"You don't have to," Ivan said. "There's a special kind of book created just for your kind." He showed her a large bookcase and pulled open the doors. The cabinet held stacks of stone tablets. He attempted to lift one off the shelf but set it back in its place after trying to pick it up. "These are a lot heavier than I remember," he said. "Why don't you start with that one," he pointed to the slab he'd attempted to lift.

Zahara grabbed it with her clawed hand and held it up, examining the front and back. *It's just a stone*, she said confused.

"Oh, it's much more than just a stone," Ivan said excitedly. He spoke an elfish word and the stone slab lit up, the strange light illuminating from within the tablet's core. "It's a book for dragons," he said, showing her how to use it. "You touch the side here to turn the images. Each image plays out the content of the story. The magic in the stone slab links with your mind and narrates what is happening. Pretty ingenious, wouldn't you say?"

Zahara's eyes widened as she held the stone.

For the next several hours they read separately about the workings of ancient magic written by the riders of old. When Anders finished reading the last line in his book, he closed it. He turned to Zahara, who was blowing out puffs of smoke. *What are you doing?* he asked.

I'm trying to breathe fire, she said.

I thought you already knew how to do that? Anders asked. *You did it when we needed a flame before,* he said referring to the sad burning of the bodies of the fallen dragon and rider.

That was the first time and I don't know how I did it, it just came.

Oh, well I'm finished with my reading, let's go see Ivan, Anders replied, standing up and stretching.

Zahara nodded and followed Anders out of the library. They found Ivan sitting on a bench near the entrance to the dining hall. "We're finished with our readings," Anders said. "What's next?"

"I guess that means it's lunchtime," Ivan said. "After lunch, we'll practice some of what you just learned."

Ivan had their meals prepared for them when they entered the large hall. They ate a mix of dried fruits and nuts, a small loaf of bread, and a pitcher of water completed their human meal. Ivan had somehow managed to get several legs of lamb for Zahara. As they ate, Anders wondered if anyone else were using the facility. Chewing through his food, he asked, "Are there any others who will be using this place?"

Ivan shook his head.

"What about the cooks?" he asked.

"No cooks," Ivan said.

Anders furrowed his brow and was about to ask where the lamb and bread came from but decided against it. Ivan was apparently not in a telling mood.

After they'd eaten and were back out in the heat of the day, Zahara and Anders were given separate physical tasks.

Anders and Ivan practiced the basics of understanding magic, while Zahara practiced flight maneuvers and creating fire from within.

"You won't have it this easy for long," Ivan told the two new students. "Starting tomorrow, Natalia will be helping train you. She's an excellent sword handler. In addition, we'll begin to have several dragons come and train with Zahara."

"Other dragons? Will we be getting hurt?" Anders asked.

"No, we place a magical buffer around the teeth and claws of the dragons so they won't damage themselves. It's much safer. I can teach you how to do the same with our swords. This way you can get used to fighting with the sword you'll use in battle and at the same time you'll avoid damaging the blade's sharp edges," Ivan said.

"I read this morning about how to close your thoughts off from someone who specializes in mind tricks," Anders said. "Will we be learning about that?"

"Yes, I can show you how to block a mental probe after we clear our heads with some physical activity," Ivan said.

"Excellent," Anders said. "Let's get to it." He clapped his hands together loudly and heard the echo reverberating back off the walls of the training building and the cliff walls above.

"Right," Ivan drew his sword out of the sheath that hung from his belt. Anders did the same. Ivan pointed to the cliffs and said to Zahara, "Why don't you go get acquainted with the spires. You will need to know every nook and cranny to use to your advantage during the bouts to come."

Zahara nodded and took flight, letting her large wings lift her body up to the spires.

"The spell was originally meant to create a seal around a person's body before going swimming. It allows the person to breathe the air trapped inside, allowing them to swim much greater distances underwater," Ivan said. He hovered his hand over the blade of the sword. Nothing happened. It seemed to Anders that the spell hadn't worked. With a look of frustration, Ivan said, "This is one of the downsides to losing your dragon. Spells that once were as easy as lifting a finger become impossible to complete."

"Maybe I could try?" Anders asked.

Ivan nodded, motioning him closer, "Here," he said showing Anders what to do. "Put your hand out over the sword like this." He placed his hand over his blade and Anders mimicked him. "There are two ways to cast a spell. First, with a word. Second, with an emotion. If you speak the correct word, the magic will come; likewise, if you emit the correct emotion, the magic will come. After years of using the speech, you'll know which emotion accompanies the word. Some sorcerers continue to use the words while others use emotions. It depends on the magician's preference."

Ivan told him the word in elfish and Anders spoke it. A spark of light shimmered from his hand and reverberated across the blade. He felt the energy flowing from him stop once the blade was covered entirely. He glanced at Ivan and said, "Wow, did that work?"

"See for yourself," Ivan said stepping back.

Anders took his sword, Lazuran, and brought it down toward the ground, half expecting it to slide into the dirt like it usually would've with such a motion. Anders was happily surprised to feel it bounce off like a stick hitting a rock. He smiled, "Neat!" he exclaimed, his mind racing with all of the possibilities magic could provide.

Ivan had Anders shield his sword in magic before they began to practice. While Ivan focused on Anders' footwork while Zahara flew and examined the entirety of the cliffs, occasionally blowing puffs of smoke as she tried to recreate the power she'd used once before. When she had finished searching the spires, Ivan instructed her to practice some evasive flying maneuvers. He showed Anders how to create an image of a dragon, he called it a shadow dragon, to chase after her while she worked. If it ever caught her, it would run into her and disappear in a puff, then reset itself, forming again right behind her, ready to pursue once more.

After spending most of the afternoon sparring and flying, they were too exhausted physically to continue. Offering them a rest from the physical activity, Ivan instructed them in the mental art of closing off one's mind. The task proved more difficult than Anders would've expected. He found it hard to know if they were sealing their minds correctly because Ivan couldn't launch a mental attack and Anders' link with Zahara was hard to differentiate.

By the day's end, Anders and Zahara could hardly walk to the dining hall. Luckily, Maija and Natalia had returned from their day's journey and helped them hobble inside.

Before they parted ways after dinner, Ivan said, "Get some well-deserved rest. Tomorrow's training will be longer and harder."

CHAPTER
NINE
MEMORIES

Maija followed as her older sister, Natalia, led her along a path at the cliff's edge. She marveled at its magnificence and the sheer size of the massive rock walls streaking down in a jumble of vertical blocks to the forested valley below. The belly of the valley was lined on either side with hills climbing their way upward from the base and plateauing about a quarter of the way up the total height of the cliffs where they now stood, on the edge of Cedarbridge. Maija watched in awe as dragons occasionally stepped out from the rocky ledges below and flew away like a bird when a person gets too close. Each time, she paused to marvel at the magnificent creatures as they soared away above the trees, wings outstretched catching the air.

"Why don't these dragons have riders?" Maija asked curious as to why there weren't more dragonriders.

"Bonding with a dragon is a complex equation and one that not even the brightest minds in Kartania have solved. Many of the dragons that haven't yet found a match do not want to be pressured into a situation where they would give themselves to another and live to regret it later in life. The bond lasts a lifetime and can only be given once. When the other half of the bond is gone, it's difficult for the other to move forward. Luckily for me, you came back into my life at a time when I needed something to live for," Natalia paused, scanning the expansive view from the cliff. "Many of the dragons that live in the Enlightened Forest have been bonded at one time, but Merglan and his dragon killed many of our kind."

"I hate what he is doing, has done and what he stands for," Maija said clenching her fists. She felt strongly toward the preservation of dragons and the use of magic for good. In her mind, a dragon's beauty was unlike anything she could imagine.

"I agree," Natalia said. "Dragons aren't rapid in their reproduction either. There have been several newborns in my lifetime that the elves know of, but most dragons take their time when selecting a mate and don't always have success when they've matched. And then there are the wild dragons of Nagano."

"There are more dragons?" Maija interrupted.

"Yes. There's a place to the northeast. A land we call Nagano, where the dragons first came to this world. They've survived there, mostly staying out of contact with humans, elves and dwarfs since the beginning of our world's existence. It wasn't until Merglan first attacked their lands and tried to take them captive, bending them to his will, that they agreed to send dragons willing to bond with skilled warriors of our choosing. That's how the dragons came to stay here in the Enlightened Forest. To this day many dragons still live in Nagano, but no one dares attempt to contact them."

"Why not?" Maija asked.

"Because wild dragons are very dangerous. Even if you were bonded with a dragon and went to see them, thanks to Merglan, they would likely view you as a threat and attack on sight." Natalia said.

"I would love to see them someday."

"Maybe once Merglan is dead and gone that would be possible, but now the closest anyone can get without being attacked is the dwarf kingdom at Mount Orena. They have tunnels that run through the mountains and places where you can look out at the vast valleys of Nagano. Unfortunately, at present our peoples are feuding politically; something to do with trade I've been told. Besides, the dwarfs hardly ever go to the overlooks anymore because wild dragons have a terrible thirst for wealth and the dwarfs mine gems, jewels and precious stones. They keep the overlooks heavily fortified so the dragons can't enter."

Dreaming up excuses for a reason to visit the dwarf kingdom, Maija was lost in thoughts of investigating Nagano when Natalia halted. Maija instinctively leaned around her sister, noticing an overgrown building, the vegetation appearing to suffocate any possible life within the dwelling.

"This is it," Natalia said, raising a hand toward the forested house. "Our childhood home."

Maija could see that the main structure of their parents' home was built into a cedar tree larger than any other around. The outer walls of the house extended out from the main tree, built right into smaller cedars on either side. The home was perched along the edge of the cliff. She also noticed two large decks extending out from the main level, overhanging a good fifteen feet past the rock wall's edge.

"Want to go inside?" Natalia asked.

Maija nodded. She followed as Natalia pulled back

branches grown over the path leading up to the front door in the large cedar. Maija and Natalia had to rip moss, vines and ferns away from the nearly concealed door to gain entry to the house. Maija wiped away the last of the dirt and moss on the ancient wood to expose a beautiful entrance. A dragon's head arched back, its forked tongue licking out past the open jaws of the carving adorning the door.

Natalia bobbed her head toward the rounded brass handle, suggesting Maija be the one to open it. She stepped forward, placing her hand on the knob and feeling the latch click as the mechanism opened. Still fighting the years of growth and neglect, Maija had to put her shoulder to the heavy door to force it open.

With a whoomph, the long-closed door cracked open. Together, Maija and Natalia pushed a second time, this time nearly falling into the entryway, now flooded with daylight, chasing away the shadows from their parents' beloved home. Maija glanced to Natalia, who smiled. Sweeping her arm out, she stepped inside their home for the first time that she could remember.

Once inside, Maija hesitated, almost losing her balance. She looked down to see if she'd miss-stepped or tripped on something that had seemed to throw her off balance when a sensation came over her. Like a hot wave of energy, she felt a force pulsing into her being and she was transported.

The years of abandonment and accumulation of dust vanished. A small girl with wavy amber hair and tan skin ran past her laughing. Another girl, older, was chasing her. She watched as they ran inside the house laughing. A man stepped into view from beyond the entryway; he was muscular and had hair similar to the two girls'.

He bent down and hoisted the younger girl into the air as she ran into his arms. She shouted playfully, "Save me

Daddy, she's gonna get me!" He laughed holding her with one arm wrapped around her waist and placing her snuggly on his hip.

"Give your sister a break," the man said to the older child.

"But we're just playing a game," the girl replied innocently.

"I think your mother needs help with the saddles," he said. "Why don't you see if you can help her. And when you're finished, you can continue this game, okay?"

The girl nodded, spinning on her heels and running off to find her mother. The man placed the amber-haired girl back down on the floor and said, "Maija, come with me. I must show you something."

Suddenly the scene Maija had been watching melted away. The abandoned walls muddled in moss came back into view. She looked around confused.

"Are you okay?" Natalia asked, placing a hand on her sister's shoulder. Maija saw a look of concern on her sister's face. "You look like you've seen a ghost."

Maija searched for words to explain what she'd seen, "I... I remember this place," she said. "I remember, Ormond, our father."

Natalia smiled, her concern vanishing, "That's great, Maija. Do you remember anything else?" she asked.

"I remember that we played here," she said looking across the entryway. "I ran into Father's arms and he told you to help Mother with the saddles; then he said he needed to show me something."

Natalia's eyes rolled upward as she searched for a memory of the exchange Maija described. "I think I remember that," she said questioningly. "That was right before we had to leave, I think. Before we were separated."

146

Maija stepped farther into the entryway. The space opened into a central living room and dining hall. Several doors lined the walls of the hallways leading off the entryway. Maija looked left and felt herself walking to the first door. She turned the knob and forced it open. This door opened much more easily than the front door but still required a push. A bed and a small table with two chairs filled the room. The same force of energy she'd felt upon entering the house rippled through her again, this time without the accompanying vision.

"I think I remember this room. I've got a feeling about it," she said.

"This was your bedroom," Natalia said calmly.

Maija gave her a weak smile and turned to walk out of the room.

"Do you want a tour of the rest of the house?" Natalia asked.

Maija nodded, "Yeah, I think that would be helpful."

Natalia led her into the next room, "This was my bedroom. Often, you would come in here during the middle of the night and want me to comfort you when you were scared." She smiled at the memory. Next, she gave Maija a tour of the living room and dining area, followed by the kitchen. "You might remember this," Natalia said running her hand along the surface of the dining table. "You and I had several food fights here. Mother and Father didn't like that very much," she chuckled.

Maija smiled but couldn't remember any of it.

"Come on, I'll show you Mother and Father's room," Natalia said gesturing for her to follow. Maija trailed her up a flight of stairs built into the side of the cedar tree, wrapping their way up to the second floor. The master bedroom was one large space with a balcony extending out beyond the tree. Their parents' bed sat in the middle of the room, facing the large windows and platform extending out from the side of the tree. A couple of desks and several dressers lined the walls of the circular room. Trunks overflowed with clothing and other items. Seeing them, Maija grew curious. She couldn't feel any pulse of energy as she had when they entered the house and her room. The two began rifling through their parents' belongings.

Pulling apart a pile of clothing, Maija discovered a leather-bound book. Several papers appeared to have been hastily tucked within its pages before it was thrust down within the stack of clothing. She opened the book carefully. The pages were filled with charcoal drawings.

Natalia noticed the book in Maija's hands and said, "That was Mother's. She drew all of those herself."

"Really?" Maija said looking closer. "I didn't know she was an artist." She realized after she'd spoken that she really didn't know anything about her mother, Isabella.

Landscapes she recognized from their walk along the cliff were dispersed throughout the journal along with drawings of dragons. The book also included human, elf and dwarf portraits. She found a face that she recognized. It was her father. Maija pulled out the free page and stared, studying the rough lines that defined his features.

"She was talented," Maija said gently placing them back in the book and closing the trunk.

"Come on, I'll show you the platforms where their dragons would land."

Maija nodded and followed her sister back down to the main level. Passing through a double-wide door, they went outside onto the deck over the cliff. Maija was impressed with the size and girth of logs used in the deck's construction. It felt solid, even after years of neglect.

"Their dragons landed right here," Natalia said, spreading her arms wide and looking to each side of the deck. "Mother and Father would climb off and the dragons would fly off to their nests." She smiled, remembering the events fondly, "Then Mother and Father would bring their gear into the tack room," she pointed to a small shed built on the edge of the deck separate from the main house.

When Maija saw the tack room, she was hit with the surge of energy again and immediately transported. In a swirl of melting colors, she was pulled into a memory long forgotten. On the deck in front of her, she saw herself following her father as he walked toward the tack room. He opened the door and let her inside. Maija suddenly felt herself being pulled back to reality. She snapped out of the vision with a burst of light. She then motioned to the shed and asked Natalia, "Can we go in there? I think I'm remembering something."

Natalia nodded, but Maija was already walking quickly toward the door. With something of a lunge, she pushed open the overgrown door as they had done on the main house. The small room revealed a space that felt foreign to her, yet somehow familiar. She eyed the large saddles explicitly designed for her parents' dragons. Draped over long wooden planks protruding from the wall, saddle blankets hung alongside the leather saddles. Long leather straps made for a riding purpose she shouldn't recall were slung from metal racks bolted to the walls. Along the length of an entire wall of the shed, swords, axes and delicately carved bows hung from hooks reinforcing the dangerous military duty dragonriders were forced to serve during the terror of Merglan and Killdoor. Folded neatly on a bench rested several suits of thick, leather-plated armor designed specifically for dragonriding. Helmets sat on the bench at their side. Long metal tools she'd never seen before leaned against one of the corners near the door. Maija drank in the uniqueness of the space trying to remember why this room seemed more familiar than the others.

Suddenly she recognized it. "This is where my memory is from!" she exclaimed excitedly.

Natalia furrowed her brow and said, "I thought you didn't remember anything from your childhood, at least until coming here?"

"There was one moment that's never left me," she said her eyebrows peaked. "It was Father, I think. He was standing right there," she pointed to the middle of the tack room. "He was doing some kind of magic," Maija was cut off by another memory rushing at her. She continued, "He was showing me something. Something he hid. Hidden here with his magic."

"What was he hiding?" Natalia asked.

"I don't remember," Maija said, "but it was," she took several steps forward, searching the floor before pointing, "right there."

"I don't see anything," Natalia said, looking at the wooden floorboards spanning the shed.

"It was under the floor," Maija said. "He hid it with magic so other magicians trying to find it wouldn't be able to. It's hidden from sight and from magical sensing."

"Hand me that tool," Maija said continued, pointing to strange metal tools in the corner by the door.

Natalia turned, gripping the metal bar shaped in a slopping J hook. She handed it to her sister. Maija placed the pointy end snuggly into the tight crack between the floorboards. Prying forcefully, the wooden plank lifted out from its tight fit. Natalia helped her pull apart the floor, prying up additional boards until there was a gap large enough to stick their heads in and see into the space under the floor.

Maija fell to all fours, plunging her head into the gap, looking around, side to side in the darkness. After several seconds, her eyes adjusted and she could begin to distinguish shapes in the darkened area between the floor and the ground.

"Can you see anything?" Natalia asked.

Maija couldn't see anything obvious to her right and left, but she still needed to search the area in front of her. She rotated her body so her head could bend in the direction it needed to see up under the floor.

"Yes," she said, her voice muffled through the floorboards. Pulling her head out of the hole, she reached her arm down through the gap to feel for the darkened rectangular shape she'd seen. As she felt around, she said to her sister who stared at her in disbelief, "I saw something just here." Her arm was through the floor stopping at her shoulder as she searched for the item she had seen. Her eyes widened when her hand bumped into the item. She carefully wrapped her hand around it, gripping it tightly. Not allowing her grasp to loosen she pulled her arm out of the hole in the floor.

Holding the item in front of her, she looked at the wooden box clasped tightly in her hand. She placed it carefully on the floor so Natalia could examine it with her. The wood was dark in color, unlike any tree she'd seen before. The box bore no design. It was simple, sanded smooth, so smooth it felt slick, like polished stone. The sharp, crisp edges of the rectangular box ended abruptly, cut neatly at right angles. The dark wood was held together by a small hinge, locked with a simple locket.

Natalia picked it up off the floor, examining it carefully

and asked, "I wonder what's in there? It isn't anything too large, clearly because of its size."

"Maybe it's a powerful weapon," Maija speculated.

"How are we going to open it? I can only guess that it's been protected, and spellbound. That means it won't break if we attempted to smash it. Besides, I think we should keep it intact. It has some sentimental value to us," Natalia said tilting her head as she held the box up to eye level.

Maija's face brightened, "I know where the key is!" She bolted up off the floor and ran back out onto the deck. At the cliffside edge of the deck, she laid down on her stomach, her arms dangling over the side of the overhang. She swallowed hard when she saw the open space between where she lay and the valley floor far below. She quickly realized there wasn't anything stopping her body from sliding over the edge and falling to her death. Regaining her composure, determined to find the key, she tilted her head to peer along the underside of the decking to see a nail tacked halfway into one of the columns supporting the deck. She looked closer and saw that the nail held a small key hanging an arm's length away. Maija reached out, teetering over the edge.

Natalia shouted, "Maija!" as she saw her sister's legs angle up off the floor slightly. Maija snatched the key from the nail and planted her other hand firmly on the deck, pulling her legs back down to the floor of the deck. She struggled slightly in backing herself up onto the deck's surface again.

Natalia rushed to Maija's side to help her, but Maija slid the center of her body mass back behind the edge of the deck. She rolled inward, lifting the key up to show her sister. Smiling, she said, "I remembered where he hid it."

"I would've never thought to look there," Natalia said,

panting with relief in seeing that her sister didn't fall over the edge of the cliff after all.

Together they rushed back to the small box in the tack room. Maija held the locket in her hands. She took a deep breath, glancing at her sister before she inserted the key into the slot. The key stopped as soon as it entered, and for a moment she was dumbfounded.

Feeling like a fool, she noticed the key was turned backward and tried it again. This time it slid into place with ease. She turned the key, and the locket sprung open. Sliding it out from the hinged latch, Maija lifted the lid. To their surprise, nestled inside was a thin leather-bound book with several loose papers sticking out.

Maija looked at her sister with a slight frown, "That's not what I was expecting," she said clearly disappointed.

"Well, should we open it and find out what it is first?" Natalia asked. She reached in and pulled out the book.

The cover was blank. It was bound by a thin black leather cover and was about an inch thick. Natalia opened it to the first page. A small piece of parchment was pinned to the top of the first page and in what she recognized as her father's writing were the words:

Merglan's Journal

Maija read these words at the same time as Natalia. They gave one another an exasperated look. Turning back to the book, they looked in awe at each as they flipped through. The book contained pages filled with writing and drawings.

"We should show this to Anders and Ivan," Maija said.

Natalia nodded. Quickly, they closed up their parents' house and the tack room and then ran as fast as they could down a winding trail in the woods and along the cliff to the valley below where Anders and Ivan were training.

TEN

A HOMECOMING TO REMEMBER

Thomas and Kirsten stopped in their tracks, jaws gaping wide. The black and gold banners fluttered in the breeze from either side of each post at the end of the dock, clearly on display. The length of cloth bore Merglan's face silhouetted by a golden dragon, wings spread upward at a forty-five-degree angle. Thomas and Kirsten scanned the surrounding buildings and, to their surprise, the banners adorned each building as well. Somehow, Grandwood had been compromised. Either the people were forced to place the banners, or they had been duped into supporting the evil mastermind. Whichever the case, Kirsten and Thomas had a mind to change it. After the ordeal of being captured, imprisoned and enslaved, there was no way they were going to walk right back into the hands of their captor, the one also responsible for their father's death.

"What's with the banners?" Britt asked. She could tell by the look on their faces that something was off.

Thomas turned to her, "Do you know whose banners these are?"

Britt stepped closer and squinted, examining the details more closely. She shook her head, "It's not Southland's, the elves or the dwarfs. Does Westland have a new army?"

Both Thomas and Kirsten looked at her as though she was going to sprout wings and fly away. Her eyes darted back and forth between them, realizing she'd somehow offended them. A bit defensively, she said, "What? Did I say something wrong?"

Max and Bo finished lashing the shuttle boat to the dock. "So, is it good to be back?" Max asked walking in sync with his brother to Kirsten and Thomas. Bo halted upon noticing the banners and slammed his arm across his brother's chest, stopping him mid-stride.

Max looked first at Bo's arm barring him from proceeding and then at his brother, "What gives?"

Freeing Max, Bo balled his fist and pointed to the banner.

"Yeah, look at all of these banners hanging around town. Wait, those weren't here the last time we were here for the Grandwood Games." Max brushed his hand through his hair, searching for an explanation. "I bet the people found some kind of protection and they've hung the banners to ward off any more attackers."

Bo, Kirsten and Thomas all looked at him in the same way they'd gawked at Britt, as though he'd just spoken ill of them. Max glanced to Britt who shook her head slightly and shrugged.

"What did I say?" he asked, as Britt had.

"That's no protection, it's much worse. That's Merglan," Kirsten said through clenched teeth.

Max and Britt's eyes widened realizing what this meant.

Kirsten furrowed her brow as she stared at the banner that hung from a post midway down the dock. Blinded by rage, she stormed down the wooden walkway. Reaching the banner, Kirsten gripped it midway up the cloth and yanked as hard as she could, pulling at the material. The thick fabric tore but didn't rip entirely as she'd intended. She tugged on it again, but the material wouldn't give way. Her actions caught the attention of others on ferryboats that were just landing at the dock.

Understanding his sister's frustration, Thomas was quick to help her. He ignored the murmurs and pointing from other townspeople returning home and together he and Kirsten pulled the banner down, tossing it into the water defiantly.

"How could our own people do something like this?" Kirsten asked angrily while motioning to the sinking cloth.

"It could be as Max said. Maybe they were tricked into thinking he would provide some form of protection?" Britt suggested as she joined them.

Kirsten groaned with frustration but held back the choice words she wanted to shout, realizing Britt wasn't the source of her anger.

Townspeople also returning to Grandwood for the first time since their capture at the games began gathering on the docks. They kept their voices low as they pointed first to the banners, then to Kirsten and Thomas. Kirsten could tell this was not the homecoming they'd expected either. Their journey had been a trying time, and not all who'd been taken from Grandwood had returned. All who'd survived the months of captivity were allowed passage home on board the Rolloan ships. Red hadn't been pleased about transporting extra people who weren't skilled sailors in the first place. He protested the suggestion, saying there would be too many extra mouths to feed, but when he heard the other leaders supporting the notion, he quickly changed his mind. No doubt, his revised response served as a political ploy to make himself look better. At that time, he'd still been vying for the position as chief. To Britt and the others' disgust, his dubious change of heart had worked.

"I don't like this," Britt said uneasily as more skiffs unloaded returnees. Britt had been the only captain to see her passengers safely home. She made more of an effort to befriend those on her ship than the other Rollo Island captains. She felt obligated to at least see her friends safely to shore. Noting the confused faces of those returning, however, left her eager to escape the situation and return to her ship.

Grandwood returnees waved and called to several of the townsfolk who passed hurriedly by the docks. The passersby hardly batted an eye as they continued with their heads down, carrying on as if nothing could distract them from where they were heading. Kirsten frowned, watching more of her fellow former prisoners pointing to the banners, then shaking their heads in confusion.

Most hadn't actually seen their captor up close. The night they'd first landed at the fortress was the only time Merglan showed himself to the entire group of prisoners. Even then, most couldn't get a clear view, as they weren't able to move a muscle on their own. Maija and Kirsten were chambermaids working on the same floor as Merglan's rooms, so they saw him often, but the only time Thomas and Bo would have seen him was the night of their arrival. Kirsten remembered when Merglan had stopped next to her to take a closer look at Thomas when Thargon had pointed him out. Thomas would have seen Merglan up close, but she wasn't sure how Bo knew who he was.

"We need to leave," Britt said, panic in her voice. "It's

no longer safe here." Bo and Max followed her, stepping toward the boat.

Kirsten made to follow but stopped. "No. We can't abandon these people. Not after what we've been through."

The others hesitated, seeing the pain in Kirsten's eyes.

"Go if you must, but I won't abandon my fellow townspeople at the sight of a depiction of Merglan's face. For all we know he's not even here."

As she finished speaking, Kirsten heard the steady thud of marching. She turned to see that the Grandwood watchmen had arrived. They marched toward the docks in lined formation. Spreading apart once they'd closed in on the harbor area, the armor-plated watchmen took positions, standing at the end of each wooden platform in pairs.

"What's this? Are they blocking us from entering?" Thomas asked angrily. "The watchmen are supposed to protect the citizens, not bar them from returning home."

Max, Bo, and Britt placed their hands on their weapons, anticipating the possibility of a fight. Kirsten bent her knees into an athletic position, ready to pounce at the armored men, even though she was unarmed. Thomas balled his fists, holding them up defensively and keeping a close eye on the watchmen's movements. Other people who were anticipating a warm homecoming huddled together taking similar defensive stances as the watchmen planted their speared staffs blocking access to the street off the docks.

"Are they going to try to arrest us?" Kirsten asked glancing to Thomas.

"Let them try," Britt said fiercely, drawing her sword and flexing her hand around its hilt.

The armored men remained motionless, locked in place at the end of the docks. It was as if they were ordered to prohibit anyone from entering the town. A group of men walked down the main street toward the piers. The seven all wore gold-trimmed, black, thickly-padded leather, with long black capes clasped at the throat with golden buckles. The leather was the same kind the elves and the Rollo Island warriors wore to battle. Each one of these men had a sword hanging from his hip. They held their heads high and puffed out their chests with pride. They walked in a militarized fashion, in unison and in formation. In the middle of this organized military group walked a tall gentleman with striking features. Kirsten thought she recognized six of them as Grandwood business owners, but she'd never seen the seventh before.

"Who the heck is that?" Thomas asked, both intrigued and irritated.

"I recognize the others around him, but not the one in the middle," Kirsten said still huddled close to the others.

The group of Grandwood men spread out in a line to either side of the man in the middle, facing those attempting to gain entry to their hometown. They halted and faced the docks, puffing out their chests and standing tall.

"Quite the display," Max said mockingly.

Bo laughed, "You always have to break the tension, don't you brother."

"I couldn't help myself," Max said. "I mean, come on, it was too easy." He chuckled at his own joke, then returned to his combat-ready position.

The man who seemed to oversee the cocky group put both hands out, spreading them wide to each side almost as though he was going to try to hug some invisible person in front of him. Kirsten and the others could see him much more clearly now that he was standing at the end of the dock. His long black cloak was embroidered with gold trim along its edges. He didn't carry any visible weapons, but the group on the dock couldn't see whether anything was concealed under the cloak. The man had ashen skin and a slender frame. His jet-black hair matched his attire. He also sported a hint of facial hair. He stood nearly half a foot taller than the rest of the men around him. His voice sounded attractive in tone when he spoke. It almost soothed them, nearly convincing them to relax to the point of dropping their weapons entirely.

"Welcome home, lost citizens of Mergwood," he said loud enough so that all of them could hear clearly.

Upon hearing the new name he'd given the town, Thomas shook himself from the seeming spell, "What did he just say? Mergwood?"

"I thought it was Grandwood?" Britt asked.

"It is," Thomas replied. "This idiot has gone and changed the name of our town." He gestured toward the tall man.

"I am your new governor and warden of Westland. You may call me Governor Rankstine," the man said, addressing them with his arms still outstretched.

The people of Grandwood murmured to each other. Kirsten could see that the others were also skeptical of him, not trusting what he had to say.

"You may be wondering why I'm here. After your city was attacked, the new emperor and ruler of Kartania sent me here to protect his lands from all future attacks. I have been directed to ensure the safety of Mergwood, to whatever end. In that prospect, you'll be allowed entry to this lovely city after a brief inspection. Once cleared, you may be reunited with your loved ones who've missed you so dearly," Rankstine said with a smile while motioning toward the few townspeople passing by who oddly continued about their daily business as if nothing special was happening. "If you would be so kind as to form a line, my men will ensure that there are no threats to Mergwood's safety."

"Threats?" Kirsten nearly shouted. "Who the heck does this guy think he is? This is Grandwood, our home. Not some Merglan-infested place called Mergwood. This can't happen," she said trembling with anger and, striding boldly toward shore.

As she drew near, the watchmen standing sentinel at the end of the dock crossed their spears, blocking her path. She halted, looking irritated. She didn't recognize them as anyone she knew. They must've been assigned to "protect" the town, along with Rankstine.

"Let me through," Kirsten said firmly. The watchmen didn't move an inch, holding their spear-like axes in place.

Kirsten clenched her fists and said more emphatically, "Let me through, now."

Thomas and the others had closed the gap and were now standing right behind Kirsten. Britt still had her sword drawn.

Governor Rankstine saw what was happening and, before they could cause more of a commotion, he quickly strode the short distance to the end of the dock.

"What seems to be the problem, my dear?" Rankstine asked in his calm, soothing voice.

Kirsten scowled at the man from behind the crossed spear shafts. She clenched her jaw at Rankstine's remark, losing her temper, "I was forcibly removed from my home-town, taken as a prisoner, put through hell for weeks on end. Now I come home to this, and you ask me what my problem is?" her voice rising to nearly shouting. As tensions on the dock rose, she somehow managed to rein in her emotions and lower her voice before she lost her temper completely.

"By the way, it's pronounced Grandwood, not Mergwood," Thomas added stepping alongside his sister.

Glancing at her brother, Kirsten smirked, feeling the urge to berate the man more due to Thomas' sudden outburst of enthusiasm, "And I'll tell you something else…" But before she could utter another word, Rankstine flicked his wrist and Kirsten's mouth snapped shut. She tried to open it to continue to berate him, but couldn't.

Rankstine held his hand near shoulder height, with his index finger pressed firmly against his thumb as though he was pinching something. The current position of his arm naturally spread the front of his cloak slightly. Kirsten noticed something glowing faintly blue, something secured around his neck. Her eyes widened when she realized what it was and she scowled.

"You will cooperate with my laws, or be banished," he said in a calm tone. "I have already informed the people of Mergwood that Merglan is the true sovereign and savior of our lands. They believe it to be true with all their hearts; I made sure of that," he said as for the first time his voice took on a maniacal tone. "You can try to warn them of whatever it is that you believe will help you, but their loyalty now lies with the emperor of Kartania." Rankstine unclasped his fingers and let his hand drop to his side. Kirsten felt her voice come back suddenly.

"You won't get away with this," she growled.

"I already have," Rankstine said, turning to walk away. He paused for a moment and spoke over his shoulder to them, "Oh, and don't bother trying to leave. I have orders to make sure you become settled in your home." He laughed to himself as he walked away.

The last of the Rollo Islanders' shuttlecrafts returned to their ships. Kirsten watched as the ships that had brought them home readied to depart. Britt's ship was the only one among the fleet that remained. Her crew wouldn't leave their captain behind, not even if ordered by their new chief.

One of the men dressed in black and gold warriors' leather approached the end of the dock. "Step forward one at a time and spread your arms and legs. If you have any weapons on your person, place them in the hands of the watchmen. We'll pat you down to make sure you aren't hiding anything. Once you've been cleared, you may enter Mergwood and return to your families.

"My family is dead," Kirsten said to the man with a stark expression. "Killed on orders by your new leader."

"That kind of talk will not be tolerated," the man said through clenched teeth. "Consider yourself warned, and the next time you speak such blasphemy, you'll hang for it."

Kirsten thought of talking back to the man but stopped herself. She believed that he really meant the threat. She glanced at Thomas and the others. "Okay Britt, let's get out of here," she said.

They walked swiftly along the wooden deck toward the small shuttle boat. Kirsten tried to get into the boat, but something blocked her. It was like hitting an invisible wall, caging her inside the confines of the wooden dock. Britt shoved Max and Thomas aside after seeing Kirsten's failed attempt to get into the boat. She stuck out her hand, reaching for the boat. Just as Kirsten had, Britt touched the hard plane blocking them in.

"What the?" she said and motioned for them to stand back.

She lifted her sword with both hands over her head and swung it down hard at the air in front of them. The steel struck the hard plane, shattering the blade as she recoiled from the blow. Britt looked down at the missing blade, hilt still clutched firmly in her hands. She faced Thomas, Kirsten, Max and Bo, her mouth agape, and her eyes wide with disbelief.

"We're trapped," she said.

AFTER SUBMITTING to the search and seizure of the remaining weapons in their possession, Kirsten, Thomas, Max, Bo and Britt were allowed to enter the city. They weren't the only members of the captured returnees to put up a struggle against Rankstine's men. Others had tried to force their way through the watchmen but were met with similar repercussions; they, too, were threatened with death for any further disobedience. Kirsten realized that the thought of being prevented from reuniting with their family members kept them from revolting. After all, they'd gone through, they'd been led right back into the arms of their captors. The thought made her sick to her stomach.

When they were allowed to pass the watchmen, the rest of the militant townsmen left, returning to the heart of Grandwood with their new governor. Kirsten and Thomas yearned to return to their home atop Highborn Bay. They desperately wanted to see if it was still standing or if the raiders had burned it to the ground as they had so many other homes in Grandwood.

"Come on, let's go to our farm," Thomas said.

"The ships are leaving without me," Britt said in disbelief as she saw the Rolloan Navy oaring out toward the open ocean. "My people are abandoning me. I need to get back to my ship."

"But we can't get past the barrier," Max said.

"Maybe it's only here?" Kirsten suggested. "You can try to get back to your ship from Highborn Bay, where our house is. We have a small boat you could use to reach them."

Britt glanced at the ships as they began rigging sails, continuing toward the Rollo Islands. All of the ships had abandoned her except for one, her loyal crew. At least she knew her crew would never leave her. She nodded, "Okay. How far is it? I want to get out of here quick."

"It's about four miles," Thomas said. "We can get there in about an hour if we hustle."

As they made their way to the edge of town, Britt kept looking back.

"What's up?" Max asked her as they neared the edge of town.

"Those two watchmen who barred us at the docks, they've been following us," she said in a hushed tone as she pointed discreetly at their position.

Max glanced over his shoulder, seeing them trailing slowly at a fair distance. "What are they doing that for?" he asked.

She shrugged, "They must see us as a threat; otherwise they would've gone back to their posts."

"Hmm," Max groaned, and they continued to follow Kirsten and Thomas.

At the northern edge of town, they found many towns-people hard at work, digging a large trench and constructing a wall along the outer edge of town proper.

"So, this is where everyone's been hiding," Thomas said upon seeing a substantial amount of Grandwood's citizens hard at work.

Thomas and Kirsten walked up to several people they

recognized. "Hey, Billson," Thomas called to one of the men who was working with his head down, digging furiously to expand the trench. The man looked up upon hearing his name. Seeing Thomas, he smiled.

"Thomas!" he exclaimed, throwing his shovel so the spade tip stuck in the freshly turned soil. Rubbing the dirt from his hands, he walked over to the side of the road to greet Thomas and the others. Reaching out with his large paw, he shook Thomas' hand firmly, saying, "Boy, it's good to have you back. Awful business that attack and your capture."

"Yeah, it was," Thomas said, a bit surprised by the casual way he mentioned the horror that happened in Grandwood and afterward. "What's going on here?" he asked Billson, motioning toward the trench and wall.

"Oh, this," Billson said turning around to glance at the other townsfolk working. "Yeah, you missed out on all that's happened recently. I'll gladly bring you up to speed." He shifted his weight and adjusted his stance as he launched into an explanation of the events that occurred while they'd been captured.

"Right after the attack, we were in an abysmal state. We'd lost so much," Billson said. "Businesses, lives and families all torn apart by that awful mess. Luckily this Rankstine character showed up just in the nick of time. Anyway, he told us about how an evil army of raiders has been venturing from Southland and sending their ships north along the Westland coast, attacking and plundering our lands as they please.

"This Rankstine guy told us about Merglan, that he is a direct descendant of an ancient royal line and that it's Merglan's duty to protect our world from foes like these raiders. So, he promised us Merglan's protection, along with a whole bunch of soldiers. Rankstine told us that we could be attacked by other raiders, which is why we're building this wall and trench around our town.

"The Governor told us that Merglan wants to lead the charge on Southland and take back the throne in Kingston. If we're going to see a just ruler back on the throne, we'll need to help the emperor with his military strength. Rankstine and the soldiers will begin training troops once the wall is finished."

After filling them in, Billson grinned widely and said, "So good to have you back, Thomas. I should be getting back to work now. Come on down and help out when you get a chance, alright?" He returned to the trench and continued digging.

Thomas turned around with one eyebrow raised. "What?" he asked, looking to Kirsten and the others.

They all shook their heads in disbelief, not knowing if they should respond to what Billson said.

"Let's go home," Kirsten said. "We can get Britt back to her ship and think about what to do next."

Kirsten led them along the road, pausing several yards later at the area where the wall had been erected on either side of the road. She hoped that whatever magic had stopped them from reentering their boat would not be present at the wall. Thomas shouldered up next to Kirsten. He gripped her hand tightly and together they drew in a deep breath, holding it as they stepped forward. Their feet landed firmly outside city limits. Kirsten exhaled happily and continued to walk up the road toward Highborn Bay.

A little over an hour later Kirsten felt her legs weaken as her childhood home came into view. The house she, her brother and Anders had grown up in remained standing, its stone walls unharmed by the attack. As the small group got closer, they could see that the rest of the farm remained intact, virtually unchanged since they'd left two months earlier. A breeze wafted down the road. Kirsten drew in a deep breath through her nose, longing for the familiar smell of sea breeze and fresh farm air

The comforting scent and tranquil sight of their home almost had Kirsten forgetting the battle that raged between Thargon's men and the Rollo Islanders as she, her brother and Max were taken away. Glancing just off the road, she could see the decaying bodies of dead soldiers, bones loosely fitted in armored shells and scattered among the trees. The sight was a harsh reminder of the horrors that had befallen their hometown.

Near the house, several crows pecked at something lying in the middle of the path leading up to the farm. Kirsten, Thomas and Max knew instantly what the crows were feeding on.

Kirsten rushed at the black birds screaming, "Get off! Get off! Get off him!" The scavengers fled at the sound of her voice and Kirsten slid onto her knees next to the corpse.

Thomas followed, wrapping his arms tightly around his sister as they stooped over their father's decomposed remains.

Max was the first to reach them. Amid the cries, he placed a gentle hand on both of their shoulders, "I'm so sorry for your loss. Bo, Britt and I will cover him and dig a grave."

Through a stream of tears, Kirsten sniffled, "No. We'll do it together." She looked at Thomas, her lips quivering. She opened her mouth to speak, but found she had nothing to say. Thomas nodded and helped her back to her feet as he looked down at Theodor's skeletal remains. Nearly all remnants of their father's physical attributes had been picked away over the months of exposure.

"I'll get a sheet and something to carry him on," Max said, motioning Bo and Britt to follow him.

Kirsten nodded, biting her lip to try to stop crying. She turned away, tears coursing down her cheeks.

Max, Bo and Britt ran the short distance to the house, stepping onto the covered porch out front. Before entering, Britt turned and looked out over the bay, longing to try and make her escape. Bo pushed past her, opening the door and entering the stone house.

Max noticed Britt's expression and hesitated in the doorway, "We'll understand if you need to go now. I can tell them afterward."

"That's their father?" Britt asked, nodding to where the dirt road from Grandwood tapered into a flagstone path leading up to the house.

"Yes," Max said, continuing in through the entrance to help his brother. "Thargon killed him with magic right before Thomas and Kirsten were taken captive."

Britt followed shaking her head, "Nobody should have to see a family member like that. My crew won't leave. Not even if Red orders them to. I can stay a little while longer, out of respect for them."

They grabbed a sheet from a bed and found a wide plank in a pile of lumber after expanding their search to the rest of the farm. The three rushed back to Thomas and Kirsten, who stood with their backs to their father's body. After covering his remains with the sheet, Britt, Max and Bo gently placed Theodor on the plank. Max and Bo carried the plank as Thomas and Kirsten led them toward the house. Once a sturdy, fit farmer, his body was now easy to lift. The two brothers set him down on the worn path in front of the house before asking Thomas where they could find a pair of shovels. Thomas escorted them toward the barn, a short distance beyond the house. Max and Bo pulled open the barn door and grabbed the tools they'd be using to dig Theodor's grave.

Once they'd returned, the others stood silent in front of the house gazing out at Highborn Bay.

Thomas came alongside Kirsten and said through the shakiness of his voice, "We should lay him to rest under Mother's maple tree."

Kirsten nodded, swiping her tears away with the backs of her hands, "That's what he would've wanted."

Thomas waved for Max and Bo to follow him around to the backside of the house. A short distance toward the east a narrow stream flowed down from some forested hills. The stream bypassed the farm, turning north before entering their property and spilling down the hillside to the bay below. A healthy young maple tree grew in the middle of an open grassy area along the edge of the stream. Near the base of the tree, they began digging.

When the brothers had finished, Thomas and Kirsten brought Theodor's body over. Max offered to lend a hand, but Thomas and Kirsten insisted that they be the ones to put their father in his final resting place. Afterward, Max and Bo filled the hole under the maple tree.

"After our mother died, Father planted this tree in her memory," Thomas began once they'd finished the burial. "He told me that when he died, he wanted to be placed here with her. He was a good father and raised us well. I will always keep a special place for him in my heart. You will be missed, Father." He put his hand over the freshly tilled earth and walked back to the front of the house.

Britt, Max and Bo looked to Kirsten, expecting her to

say something as Thomas had, but as hard as she tried, she couldn't muster words to say anything at her father's grave. Instead, she wept. Max and Britt left her to join Thomas inside the house. Bo offered Kirsten company in her time of grief, but she shook her head. Bo understood and joined the others as well. Kirsten stood under the maple tree, losing track of time. When at last she wiped away her tears and walked to the front of the house, she found Thomas sitting on the porch. She sat down next to him and shoulder-to-shoulder they watched the waves roll into Highborn Bay in silence. At last, they were home.

ELEVEN

HOPE FOR A POTENTIAL RIDER

Natalia and Maija arrived at the dragonrider training facilities just as Ivan, Anders and Zahara were finishing up with their first day. As the elf sisters approached them, Ivan sat cross-legged atop a boulder along the outer ring of the sparring pit. He looked comfortable, his back straightened and head tilted upward. In stark contrast to Anders and Zahara, who sat opposite him squirming uncomfortably with their eyes tightly shut, the old rider seemed relaxed and in a state of deep meditation.

"What are they doing?" Maija whispered, pointing to Anders and Zahara who wriggled on the grass several yards below Ivan's perch.

"They're attempting to block other sorcerers' minds from gaining access to their thoughts. Ivan's teaching them to build vaults for their thoughts," Natalia said, slowing as they drew close to the others. Halting, she said, "I remember when I first had to learn how to shield a sorcerer from my thoughts. Learning how to do it well saved my life. Not all battles are fought with steel and fire."

"How can you build a defense system for your thoughts?" Maija asked as she watched Anders wince in discomfort.

"Not everyone can do it. You must be strong mentally if you're going to master the art. If you're curious, the library in the training center has many books that explain the process step by step."

Ivan cracked one eye open, noticing the two elf sisters standing nearby. Anders and Zahara's faces relaxed nearly instantly as Ivan relented on his mental attack. "That will be all for the day; we'll try again tomorrow," he said, unfolding his legs and leaping down from the boulder. "Good evening, ladies," he said as he bent to brush the wrinkles out of his pants and shirt while approaching them. "I wasn't expecting you until tomorrow," he said furrowing his brow.

"I'm sorry to interrupt, Ivan, but Maija and I discovered something that was hidden at our parents' house. We thought you should be the first to know about it," Natalia held out the journal for Ivan to inspect.

He plucked it from her hand, eyeing the thin leather-bound book curiously. He examined it by flipping it over several times, clearly intrigued. "It looks like a journal," he said. He flipped it open to the first page. They watched as he noticed the small piece of parchment pinned to the top. Eyes widening, he read the inscription. "Where did you say you found this?" he asked, his face souring.

"As we were touring through our parents' house," Natalia said. "Maija kept having brief, but strong, clear memories, almost visions, wouldn't you say, Maija, as we entered certain rooms. We were admiring the tack room when she remembered our father showing her where he'd hidden this and the key to access it."

Ivan thumbed through the small book. As he reached the end, he carefully turned the journal over in his hands, handling it almost as a precious heirloom. "Thank you for bringing this to me. This could hold secrets that will help us discover how Merglan has cultivated his power."

"And how we can destroy him," Natalia said coldly, her expression hardening.

Ivan held the journal firmly in his grip, "Come, we're about to eat and tonight's dish will be a delicious vegetable gumbo with a side of trout if you care to eat some meat. I know most elves prefer a vegetarian diet, but I prefer to eat like a carnivore." Turning to lead them to the dining hall, Ivan called to Anders and Zahara, who had been cleaning and prepping the sparring grounds for the following day.

Ivan and Natalia lit the torches lining the walls of the dining hall as they entered. Despite Ivan's dwindling powers, he still managed to ignite several at once with a few words. Natalia's magic was still fresh; her access to magic had not yet dwindled with the loss of her dragon. She spoke a few words and the entire length of the dining hall on one side lit up at once. Ivan took notice. When she turned to finish his side, he waved his hand stopping her. He shook his head, "I've got this." They all watched patiently as Ivan lit the remaining twelve torches two-by-two.

Anders and Zahara led them to the kitchen facilities at the far end of the dining hall. Buffered by a large bar-top serving station, the kitchen seemed unused. The small group didn't see anyone preparing the meal Ivan had described. "Ivan, I thought you said we were having trout and gumbo for dinner?" Anders asked as Ivan lit the final two torches along the stone wall.

"Yes, we are, and it's going to be delicious. I love the cooking here," Ivan said rubbing his hands in anticipation.

He looked over the bar-top and then back to Anders, "What are you waiting for? Grab a plate and dish up."

"But Ivan, there isn't anything to dish up. There isn't even anyone to cook the meal," Anders almost whined looking around the empty kitchen.

"Here, I'll show you how it's done," Natalia said, shoving Anders out of the way.

Maija came to stand at his side, nudging Anders slightly and giving him a look of confusion, conveying that she, too, had no idea what Ivan and Natalia were excited about. Together they watched Natalia reach behind the bar, grab a plate with one hand and a bowl with the other. As soon as she had her dishes in hand a large pot of steaming gumbo and a skillet full of fried trout appeared on the bar-top. Anders, Maija and Zahara all jumped back in surprise, Zahara's hop shaking the ground slightly.

"Where did that come from?" Anders asked, startled by the sudden appearance of the freshly cooked food.

"It's part of the magic embedded in the training facilities," Ivan said. "When the riders who built this place created the kitchen, they used recipes from the best cooks in Kartania. All you have to do is look at the chart in the back and select what dish you want, and the magic does the rest. When you grab your dishes, the food appears on the bar-top, ready to eat."

"Wow!" Anders exclaimed. He shared an excited look with Maija at the magical kitchen.

"And likewise, for the beverages," Natalia said, grabbing a mug from the end of the bar. "They fill with your drink of choice. Tonight, I'll have a mug of hot chocolate." She took her food and drink to the closest rectangular table and sat down.

And what about me? Zahara asked. *These elf- and human-sized portions are not enough for me.*

"Luckily for you, Zahara, the riders thought of that as well. Do you see the extra tall serving window at the other end of the bar?" Ivan pointed to the opposite end of the counter. "If you go there and place your hand on the countertop, a meal of your choosing will appear."

Anders felt her fill with joy and excitement. He knew exactly what she wanted, more sheep, like the ones she'd eaten outside Mount Orena. He chuckled as he watched Zahara bounce over to the other end of the hall and collect her raw mutton.

After letting Ivan dish up next, Anders stepped back slightly from Maija's side. Spreading his arms and bowing forward somewhat in the same way he'd seen Theodor do with his aunt before the Grandwood formal dance, "After you, my lady."

Maija's cheeks reddened. She curtsied neatly before taking a plate and bowl in front of Anders. Anders followed, filling his dishes with trout and steaming vegetable gumbo. Everyone followed Natalia's lead and filled their mugs with hot chocolate, a delicacy in most parts of Kartania.

After practically inhaling their meals with little talk, they sat back in their chairs, sleepiness creeping into their bodies.

"So, Maija," Natalia said leaning back.

Maija looked expectantly, snapping out of her relaxed state.

"You're probably wondering what you're doing here?" Natalia said, grabbing her mug and swirling the remaining liquid.

Maija glanced to Anders.

Anders sat up in his chair a little and shrugged as he was eager to hear her response. He'd been wondering how Maija would spend her days now that Natalia was tasked with training him.

Maija turned her attention to her sister. Clearing her throat, she said, "Didn't you bring me here so I might remember more about my past?"

Natalia narrowed her eyes, picked the mug up and shot the remaining liquid down her throat. "That was part of it," she said bringing the mug back down to the table with a clang. "I wanted you to come home, not only for you to accept the truth of your past, but to see if you've got what it takes to become a rider."

Maija bolted upright, jaw-dropping. Her eyes darted between Anders and Natalia.

Anders grinned widely, nodding at the suggestion.

"You wouldn't be training directly with Anders," Ivan said, noticing Anders' excitement. "You come from a long line of riders, your parents being two of the best the elven race has ever seen. You were robbed of your chance to join our ranks when you were sent away, but now..." he paused.

"Now it's time we see if you're ready," Natalia finished.

Maija struggled to find her voice but nodded eagerly.

Natalia grinned, "I'll take that as a yes."

"Yes, a thousand times yes," Maija said, finally finding the right words.

"Excellent. Natalia will help show you the basics. She'll still need to allocate her time primarily with training Anders in the sword, but when she's not instructing him, she'll work with you."

"Thank you," Maija said still grinning.

"Now that we've got that settled, let's have a look at this

journal," Ivan said, pulling the leather book out of his pocket.

"What's this about a journal?" Anders asked.

Zahara also perked up, looking up from the spot on the floor where she had splayed out, clearly having enjoyed the sheep.

"It's Merglan's journal," Maija said, her eyes widening as she spoke the words.

"What?" Anders asked sharing Maija's wide-eyed expression. "What other surprises are you going to offer us tonight?"

Zahara rose to her feet and trotted over to the edge of the table.

"Our parents had hidden this in their house. It appears to be Merglan's personal journal," Maija said.

Natalia nodded as Anders and Zahara looked at them in disbelief.

"And now it's time for us to take a look at what secrets he's written down," Ivan said, placing the book on the table.

He turned to the second page and began reading out loud. It started with a personal entry from his days of living in the king's castle. He wrote mostly about his friend William and the games they had played that day. After reading aloud several similar entries, the group heard a creak at the training facility's front door followed by a pattering of footsteps echoing into the dining hall. Ivan closed the journal and tucked it under the table out of sight as they all turned to see who'd entered the facilities. Nadir walked swiftly past the entrance to the dining hall, glancing at them as he passed the doorway. They heard him turn suddenly and step back into view. He entered the hall.

As he approached their table, Ivan asked, "Nadir, it's

good to see you. Care to join us for dinner? We're just finishing up, but you're more than welcome to have a bowl of vegetable gumbo."

"Thank you for the offer, but that's not why I'm here. My father has requested your presence, at once. There's news of Merglan."

Ivan rose immediately, answering, "Take me to him."

Once Ivan and Nadir were well out of earshot, Anders looked to Natalia and Maija, "Should we keep reading?"

The sisters' heads bobbed in unison.

This story isn't very fascinating. Are all humans intrigued by these writings? Zahara asked, lying back down next to the table.

This isn't a story, it's a journal. We're hoping to gain some insight or advantage by understanding Merglan better before we have to confront him, Anders said.

But why does it have to be so dull? she asked.

"Should we even be reading through this without Ivan?" Natalia asked. "We decided to search through the readings as a group, so if the person reading misses something, the others can point it out."

"Ivan can catch up when he returns, or we can reread the passage if it's important enough," Maija suggested.

"Good enough for me," Anders said reaching over and lifting the journal from Ivan's chair. He opened to where they'd left off and began to read aloud.

Despite their droopy eyes, the four stayed up late into the night reading Merglan's journal. The writing continued much as before, with Merglan as a boy playing in the castle with the king's son, Prince William. He often mentioned how he wanted to rule alongside his best friend someday.

As they delved further into the journal, Anders was surprised to discover some striking similarities between his and Merglan's childhoods. Merglan grew up without a mother, just as Anders had. At least Merglan never mentioned his mother, or having her around in his life, so Anders thought it safe to assume she wasn't there. Despite the presence of Merglan's father, it sounded as though Merglan felt his father didn't take much notice of his existence. In fact, Merglan often spoke in his writing as though he had no parents.

More striking still was the fact that Merglan, too, was fascinated with competing in the Grandwood Games, which was a relatively recent event in Kartania's history. On its own, this wasn't such a compelling similarity between the two, but the fact that Merglan actually competed when he was only seventeen years old couldn't, in Anders' mind, be ignored. The prince had his father write a letter and send it with Merglan when he traveled to the games, compelling the judges to let him compete. The similarity became eerie when Anders read that Merglan had sustained an injury during the mountain race that forced him to withdraw before completing the course. He was disqualified just as Anders had been when he was pushed off a steep edge on the trail by another contestant. Anders had broken a leg in his fall. The anger with which Merglan described the event echoed Anders' feelings at the time. It wasn't necessarily rooted in the truth, as he hadn't seen who'd done it, but Merglan suspected a contestant from the Rollo Islands had pushed him off the trail because when he last glanced over his shoulder, a Rolloan was close on his heels.

Anders closed the journal after reading Merglan's rantings about those he suspected as having had a hand in making sure he didn't win the games at such a young age.

"This guy has some serious issues," Natalia said as Anders closed the journal.

"Well, I guess you'd have to end up as crazed as he has," Maija said.

"Yeah, what a nut," Anders said, recalling how he'd felt after the games when he'd been forced off the trail by an opponent, ruining his chance to be the youngest person to win. The words Merglan wrote after that experience struck a chord in Anders, but he hid his feelings so Natalia and Maija wouldn't notice.

"We should read more tomorrow, with Ivan here. He might be able to point out something in the story that we don't know about. He was, after all, in this fight from the beginning," Natalia said.

"So, you two are staying here, too?" Anders asked, changing the subject to distract the dark wanderings of his mind. He wanted to spend more time with Maija and hoped they wouldn't be returning to their parents' home.

"Yes," Natalia said. "We have a lot of work to do if we're going to train two of you now."

Anders turned as they heard Ivan open the door. He entered the dining hall and said, "What are you all still doing up? We have a big day of training tomorrow. Come on, I'll show you to your sleeping quarters."

They joined Ivan, Natalia extinguishing the torches as they left the hall. Ivan pointed to a large door near the base of the stairs, "Zahara, this is where the dragons' chambers are. You can have your pick of the rooms. They're all somewhat similar, but in my opinion, the third door on the left is the best."

Thanks, she said and pushed her way through the doors, her tail the last of her to disappear from view.

Ivan led them next up the stairs to the second floor. "This is where we'll be sleeping. Just as with the dragons' chambers, these are all very similar."

Natalia immediately pushed her way through them and walked to the end of the hallway, claiming the last bedroom on the right for herself. Ivan followed, taking the room opposite Natalia.

Anders stood in the darkened hallway with Maija; at last, they were together alone. He felt her hand reaching for his as their fingers entwined. Anders turned to face her. He placed his free hand around to the small of her back, gently pulling her in close. He placed his forehead against hers and could feel her warmth all around him. Simultaneously they tilted their heads slightly to the side and locked their lips, kissing with the vitality and yearning of having been apart for months. Anders took his hand from her grip and ran it along the curvature of her body as she wrapped her arms around him. Maija pulled him into her and they stumbled, thudding against one of the wooden doors in the hallway.

Hearing the noise, Natalia poked her head out and looked down the hallway. Upon seeing the two losing themselves in each other's embrace, she shouted, "Come on, you two! Get a room!" She slammed the door behind her.

Anders and Maija halted, looking down the hall toward Natalia's voice, but she'd already retreated into her room.

Placing their foreheads back together as they initially had, the two smiled, giggling at themselves. Anders searched for the doorknob on the wooden door they'd been pressed up against. Feeling its cold metal touch, he twisted it and they stumbled into the bedroom. Laughing, Maija placed her forearms on Anders' shoulders, locked her hands behind his head and brought his face closer toward her own. Kicking the door closed behind them, Anders let himself be pulled into Maija's embrace. Feeling the fullness of her lips on his, they once again became lost in each other's arms.

THE FOLLOWING morning Anders and Maija were the last to arrive for breakfast.

"You two look tired," Natalia said. "Get much sleep?" she asked through a bite of toasted bread.

Maija blushed and Anders smiled. "Mate," Anders mumbled to himself as he shuffled over to the kitchen, grabbing a mug and raising an eyebrow at the appearance of a hot teakettle steaming with his favorite caffeinated tea.

Good morning, Zahara, Anders said as he watched her rip apart the sheep's meat she was devouring.

Morning, she replied, somewhat distracted. *I tried to block my mind from what you two were doing last night, but it was hard to accomplish.*

Sorry, Anders blushed. *I should have realized I needed to block my emotions from our connection.*

Now you know, she said as she tossed a sheep leg up with her head and releasing it, letting it fling up into the air spinning several times before falling back down into her open jaws. Swallowing she hummed with joy and licked the outer edges of her mouth with her forked tongue.

"Eat quickly, Anders," Ivan said. "You need to join Zahara and me in the library in ten minutes. Got it?" he asked, pointing his steak knife in Anders' direction.

"Okay," he answered. He shuffled over to the counter and grabbed a plate. Freshly cooked eggs, bacon, sausage, and toasted bread appeared on the table. *I love it here,* he thought to himself.

Me too, Zahara agreed.

Natalia eyed Maija as she followed Anders' lead and sat down at the table with her food. "I've got something planned for you as well," she said, grinning slightly.

Maija raised an eyebrow.

"Take your time eating though. You're going to need your strength," Natalia said taking another bite of her toast.

After devouring his breakfast and quickly pounding down several cups of mate, Anders joined Zahara. The two walked down to the library. Ivan had already laid out the books they required for their studies.

"Read these and I'll be back before lunch," he said.

"Where are you going?" Anders asked.

"Natalia and I are going to set up the sword fighting stations for this afternoon."

"Isn't Natalia working with Maija?" he asked.

"Maija's training today is one she'll be doing on her own," he paused. "To test her and see how well she'll follow orders and complete a seemingly meaningless task. It's important you don't mention it to her until she's finished. Now get reading," Ivan said as he walked out of the cave.

Leaving them to their books, Ivan returned to the dining hall where Natalia and Maija sat discussing the parameters of Maija's training in the coming weeks. Joining them at the table, Natalia halted her conversation with her sister and asked him, "What did Asmond tell you regarding Merglan?"

Ivan looked over his shoulder, making sure there was absolutely nobody else in the dining hall before he spoke, "He mostly wanted to talk about the leak they have in the elven political party."

"Oh," Natalia said curiously.

"Somehow the details we discussed during the meeting after we returned from Eastland have been leaked to Merglan," he said.

"You mean our discussion of his crystals?" Maija asked.

Ivan nodded, "Someone in that room got word to

Merglan. He's retaliated by going on a path of destruction across Southland. He's destroying cities and taking on more slaves, claiming the elves and their spies are to blame. With each attack, he's sent several survivors to spread word of his actions. He's calling himself Emperor and all those who don't obey his orders are doomed for all eternity. One of the survivors was told to specially tell the elves that Merglan knows the riders are talking about his souls of sapphire, whatever that means."

"Maybe that's what he calls the crystals?" Maija suggested.

"How could Merglan know what we discussed? The only humans and elves privy to that conversation were all of us and Asmond's family," Natalia said.

"Asmond suspects Nadir," Ivan said bluntly.

Natalia shook her head, "He would never do such a thing."

"I know," Ivan said. "But the king will not listen to my counsel. He's determined to place Nadir on trial once he thinks he has enough proof of this betrayal."

"He would do that to his own son?" Maija asked.

Ivan nodded, "He thinks Nadir is power hungry and wants the throne for himself. I fear the king is under the influence of whoever is responsible for the information leak."

"Who do you suspect?" Natalia said.

"I have someone in mind, but it's too early to say. They obviously have a way to listen in on conversations they're not privy to," Ivan said.

Natalia raised her eyes to the ceiling.

Ivan joined her gaze, "Who knows how many spies they have and where they are lurking?"

Natalia lowered her voice to a whisper, "Whoever's

responsible for this betrayal, either way, it's a massive scandal that will scar the elf council's credibility for generations to come."

"I know," Ivan said. "I strongly believe that Nadir's not involved."

"How are we going to convince Asmond?" she asked.

"I don't know," he shrugged. "We'll have to catch whoever's responsible before it's too late for Nadir." Ivan sighed, running his hand through his hair. "In the meantime, we need to fast-track Anders and Zahara through this training before we face Merglan again. We're not prepared to fly out and meet him in open battle just yet."

"What's the plan then?" Natalia asked.

"Today we are going to work with the sword and battle strategies. I was going to talk with some of the dragons and see if any of them would help Zahara in her defensive and offensive flying," he said.

"Good idea, that will force her to cultivate practical experience quickly. Also, could you make inquiries about any dragons possibly being receptive to meeting Maija? Perhaps a dragon here in the Everlight Kingdom will be a good match for her?" Natalia suggested.

"I can check, although several months ago when Nadir inquired about the same thing, there weren't any who were keen on forming a bond. I'll have to be delicate about the matter, but I'll ask. Before I leave, would you and Maija help me set up the sword fighting station?" he asked.

"Of course," Natalia said. "It will be a good warm-up for Maija's training."

"You've got me awfully curious what I'll be doing," Maija said.

Natalia grinned and rose from the table, leading them out of the hall.

Ivan didn't stay for long before he set out to seek the help of ex-bonded dragons. The practice stations consisted of wooden platforms in a variety of heights, so setting them up took time. Anders and Zahara had set up the fighting pit the night before, so Maija and Natalia erected several wooden walls to mimic the city or fortress walls they might encounter during a battle or siege. It helped that Natalia's magical skills remained fresh, though she struggled with many of the placements of the heavy wooden structures.

Shortly after Ivan returned, an enormous dragon with dark green and reddish scales approached. The giant dragon was flanked by two slightly smaller dragons shimmering with green and purple hues.

"Excellent timing," Natalia, said. "It's almost lunchtime. After we eat, I'll set you on your task," she said turning to Maija.

"What will my task be? So far all we've done is set things up for Anders."

"Do you see this," Natalia said holding out her hand. A swirl of light formed in her palm, shaping itself into a small falcon. The magical bird glowed with bright light as it moved its head from side to side in a similar jerking motion she'd seen birds do as they tried to look at something in front of them.

"A bird?" Maija asked confused.

"Yes. This is Cora. I conjured her up for you. She exists only as long as I'm able to hold the spell to produce her," Natalia said.

"That's neat, but what's that got to do with me training to be a rider?" Maija asked.

"I want you to take her for the rest of the day after we eat."

"Okay, but," Maija began when Natalia suddenly cut her off.

"You want to be a rider?" she asked closing her hand and making Cora disappear in a puff of light.

Maija nodded.

"Then you start here, with this task," Natalia said. She eyed Maija waiting for another question, but none came.

Walking down into the library, Ivan gathered Anders and Zahara from their studies. Anders and Zahara halted in shock upon seeing the three large dragons in the dining hall. Anders felt Zahara swell with delight. He recognized the two dragons that matched her hue as her parents. Zahara hopped up and glided over to them, greeting them with loud purrs and the rubbing of necks.

"Let me introduce you," Ivan said as Anders approached the new dragons. "This is Gendavie, the red," Ivan pointed toward the large dark-colored dragon with reddish highlights. "He's agreed to help Zahara with her flight training."

"How do you do, Gendavie? My name is Anders," he said bowing to the massive dragon, not entirely sure how to address him properly.

Nice to make your acquaintance, the large dragon's voice sounded in his head. His mental tone was different than Zahara's light and youthful one. It was low and gravely, like an old man.

"And I believe you have met Sebar and Elebryss, Zahara's parents," Ivan said pointing to the other two dragons.

"Only for a moment," Anders said as he bowed to them. "It's nice to meet you again as well."

They bowed their heads slightly but did not acknowledge him with a response.

Anders watched as the four dragons ate a variety of animals on the floor in the corner of the dining hall. He was amazed at how large the red dragon was compared to the others. Gendavie ate nearly three times as much as Zahara. Anders could tell he was trying to act polite in front of them. He was sure if the dragon felt like it, he could devour twice the amount he'd taken and still have room for more.

Rising from the table, Anders followed the others out to the sword training facility they had set up for him. He wished Zahara and Maija good luck as the dragons took flight and Maija ran after the magically fabricated falcon, Cora, who glided from Natalia's palm to a nearby tree.

After receiving some basic training with the Rollo Islanders and fighting in a couple of battles already, Anders felt he was probably starting out ahead of most beginners, where Maija would soon be. The book he'd been reading before lunch covered many stances and ways to maneuver your body when attacking or to defend against an opponent. Though bookwork wasn't his favorite, he'd tried to absorb all he could from the literature.

Ivan and Natalia went to work explaining the basics to him again. When they had finished, Anders had Natalia show him how to place the protective layer on his blade so he wouldn't damage it during their practice.

Natalia and Anders had never sparred, but Natalia's injuries were still freshly healed so she would have to go easy at the start. They began slowly piecing their way through the stances. She would point out small tips to help him clean up his form as they worked. Gradually they picked up the pace as they began to feel more comfortable with one another. Natalia was far superior in both speed and maneuvering her blade. Her parries and advances were well timed and placed with high accuracy, whereas Anders' were made of desperation.

During one of their sparring sessions, Natalia was soundly beating Anders. He couldn't seem to place a single hit on her when suddenly he thought he felt the presence of someone else standing nearby.

Anders dropped his defense, glancing over his shoulder to see if anyone had unexpectedly entered the fight. Natalia slapped him hard in the side with the flat of her blade.

Anders winced, rubbing his shoulder and returning his attention to Natalia. "What was that?" she asked, stepping in for another attack. "You just let me have that one."

He blocked her jabs, looking behind quickly once more, "Um, I thought there was, ah, something there."

"Distractions can occur in the field of battle," she said raising her blade. "You must learn to stay on guard while observing your surroundings." She lunged at him and he blocked her swings.

Suddenly he felt the urge to attack by rotating to the left. He hadn't ever felt the sensation to perform a particular attack before, but as he fought Natalia, he could sense Lazuran somehow wanted him to attack in this way. At first, Anders hesitated, but then relented, moving left and advancing. She began to falter and he was able to hit her on the knee with the flat of his blade, following that with a score to her arm.

Hey, that actually worked, he thought to himself.

Natalia looked shocked at his sudden ability to gain an advantage over her. "How did you know to do that?" she demanded with a scowl.

Anders shrugged, "I'm not sure. I just had a feeling that it would work," he lied, not mentioning the sensation he felt from the sword.

She eyed him warily. Sheathing her blade, she said, "That's all for today. We'll pick up here again tomorrow. Report to Ivan."

"But," Anders called as she turned to leave.

"Report to Ivan," she demanded through clenched teeth.

Anders was left wondering what he'd done wrong. She was clearly agitated by something. *Did she know I lied about knowing to attack in the way I did?* he wondered. He quickly dismissed the notion as they didn't share a bond and he couldn't possibly figure out how she would know such a minor detail he'd left out of his explanation. Anders sheathed his blade and rushed off to find Ivan.

CHAPTER
TWELVE
MERGLAN'S PROPHECY AND A KING'S
REQUEST

When Anders found Ivan, he was sitting on the building's stoop thumbing through Merglan's journal. He quickly closed the book and tucked it into his pocket when Anders approached.

"Why aren't you training with Natalia?" he asked, clearly irritated that Anders would cut short on his duties.

"She dismissed me for the day. Told me to report to you."

"So, what did you do to make her want to quit early?" he asked.

Anders shrugged, "We were sparring, I got two hits in on her, and then she told me we were done for the day."

"Strange," Ivan said under his breath. "Her injuries weren't bothering her were they?"

Anders shook his head, "No, it was weird. She suddenly seemed offended and took off."

"And you didn't cheat, landing the blows on her?" Ivan asked skeptically.

"No, honestly, I didn't. We were practicing the forms

I'd read about and then I felt an urge to attack in a different way. I did, landing the blows, and she called it over for the day."

Ivan rose to his feet, eyeing Anders. From their practice during the previous day, Anders could feel Ivan probing him with his mind, gently but to ensure Anders wasn't hiding anything from him.

"You don't need to do that," he said.

Ivan retracted, "Well since you seem to suddenly have become master of the sword, we'd better go over some battle strategies. You'll need to study them if we're going to meet Merglan in battle."

Anders followed Ivan down to the library. At the center of the vast cave sat a large rectangular table. Anders had studied at the table the past couple of mornings. Ivan walked to the table and began to run his hands along the edges, searching for something.

Anders watched, intrigued, "What are you doing?"

"I'm looking for a trigger," Ivan said as he bent over to more closely examine the table's corners. "It has been awhile since I've used this."

"Why would a table have a trigger?" Anders asked as Ivan rose with a satisfied expression.

"Because of this," he said while pressing in on an acorn carved into one side of the table. With that the surface of the table vanished, revealing a box filled with sand.

"Wow!"

Anders stepped forward to take a closer look.

"It is used to explain visually how certain battles have played out throughout history. Using the table's index, we can select a battle that's been recorded and the sands will form the topographic layout of the battle's location. The events that took place during the conflict will unfold as quickly or slowly as we want. I'll take you through them step-by-step, using struggles from the past to help you recognize how and why decisions were made on the battle-field and, in some cases, how you might want to change your approach."

"This table can do all that?" Anders asked astonished.

"With a bit of magic, yes. This table can replay any recorded battle in the history of Kartania."

"When will we learn more magic?" he asked eagerly.

"After you've learned to create a decent mental block," Ivan said sharply. "Until then we'll hone other skills."

For the remainder of the afternoon, Ivan showed Anders several battles that had had defining outcomes in Kartania's history. The sand table's visual element was far more useful than any book in Anders' opinion. The magic even showed the armed forces rushing across hills, their numbers dwindling as the battle progressed. Ivan could pause the fight and explain to Anders why the commanders ordered their soldiers to move in certain ways depending on the circumstances. There weren't any dragons in the battles Ivan chose to show Anders, and when Anders asked if he could see one, Ivan explained that he must first learn the basics before adding such a transformative element to the field.

Before their meal, Anders and Zahara faced Ivan once more in their mental exercises. Hard as they tried, neither Anders nor Zahara could keep Ivan from breaching their walls. Though Ivan's magical abilities had dwindled, he held onto his specialties much better than Anders had anticipated.

That evening, seated around one of the dining hall's long rectangular tables, Anders and Zahara spoke about the progress they'd made that day. Zahara informed him about the maneuvers Gendavie had shown her and how she'd improved already. Anders filled her in about the sand table in the library and about his short lesson with Natalia. He eyed the door, wondering when they would return. Natalia had disappeared after their sparring came to an abrupt end and he hadn't seen Maija since right after lunch when she ran after Cora.

"Where are Natalia and Maija?" Anders asked Ivan between bites of seared salmon and roasted vegetables.

Ivan went silent for a moment, closing his eyes. He pointed his fork toward the door just as the two elf sisters entered the hall. "You know, you could use that gift Zahara gave you."

Anders slapped his hand on the table, "I can't believe I didn't think to do that." He felt foolish for not having tried searching for them with his mind before asking Ivan.

Anders smiled at them as they walked by to pick up their meal. Natalia kept her focus on the kitchen area, not acknowledging them as she passed. Maija, however, returned the smile and placed a hand on Anders' shoulder as she walked by. To Anders' surprise, Maija appeared to have gone rolling around in the dirt. Her clothes were stained and smudged with dirt and grass. Her hair was a mess, twigs and leaves sticking out from tangles. He chuckled as he watched her get her plate and mug and join them at the table.

"What did you do with her?" Anders asked Natalia as they sat down.

Natalia raised an eyebrow at him but didn't answer his question. She just stabbed her fork into a pile of crisp brussels sprouts and brought it to her mouth with gusto.

"Just some introductory lessons," Maija said, placing her hand on his knee under the table.

"Oh," Anders said, reaching around and pulling a twig from her hair.

Maija chuckled, "As I said, some introductory lessons."

They quickly recapped the day's events, Natalia continuing to remain uninterested in contributing to their discussion.

"What's going on with Nadir?" Anders asked, curious about the political status within the High Council.

Ivan spoke after swallowing a mouthful of salmon, "He's being watched now by his father's guard. He tells me that Asmond has been fooled into believing he was the one to send word to Merglan." Ivan shook his head. "I'm not sure who it is, but this is a dangerous game to play. It can only end in sorrow."

"I can't believe the king would think his own son, who fought in his name so bravely, would betray him so willingly," Anders said.

Ivan nodded, "He's under mounting stress."

"The king?" Maija chimed in, clarifying who Ivan was talking about.

"Yes, Asmond. Nadir informed me all these whispers of spies have the High Council paranoid and it's affecting their relationships with other nations," Ivan said.

"How so?" Natalia asked, speaking for the first time since she'd entered the dining hall.

"Trade with the dwarfs has decreased greatly. With the rising threat of Merglan's re-emergence, they're on the verge of ceasing all trade with the elves," Ivan replied, wiping his mouth with the underside of his sleeve.

"How would that affect the elves? Aren't they self-sufficient here in the Enlightened Forest?" Anders asked.

"We are as long as we don't go to war. The dwarfs mine the steel and other precious metals that our people rely on.

Sure, we can last without the ore, but we need the metal for weapons," Natalia said in a monotone.

"Don't the elves have enough weapons left over from The War of the Magicians?" Maija asked.

"They have steel and other metals from those days, but with nearly twenty years of peace, they've been scattered, traded, sold and lost. Besides, if the king wants to prepare his people properly for this war, he may have to place a sword into the hands of every man, woman and child old enough to fight. He'll need to forge new weapons regardless," Ivan said, turning his attention back to his food.

After everyone had finished, Ivan pulled the journal from his pocket and placed it on the table. "Who wants to read first?" he asked.

Anders had spent hours each day reading and didn't want to volunteer. When he used to read in Theodor's library, he would become lost in the story, but when Anders had to read particular books for study, he found himself disliking the task. He'd had some inkling of this realization when studying for the Grandwood Games, but it was never this bad. With all the excitement of training to be a rider, he merely wanted to absorb the material instead of having to read through it at a slower pace.

Anders assumed from the look Maija gave him, she felt out of place taking the responsibility, and he knew Natalia was still not in the best of moods to read to them.

"Don't all raise your hands at once," Ivan said mockingly. "I guess I'll do the honors." Ivan looked the journal over for awhile before opening it and beginning to read.

Listening to Ivan, Anders was again reminded of the similarities between himself and Merglan. As they pressed further into Merglan's writing, Anders found he was comparing himself to Merglan's every action, trying to justify how he would turn out differently. The words of Solomon, the wise little man they'd consulted while trying to track down his cousins' kidnappers, ventured back into Anders' mind and he wondered if he was staying on the right path. One distinct difference between himself and Merglan was Merglan's twisted thirst to strike back at any opposition. Young Merglan often described in detail in this journal how he'd dealt with those who sparred with him during the prince's training sessions. He always made sure to land twice as many hits as any of his opponents.

Ivan paused after reading an entry, "There's a long gap in time between entries here." He flipped through several pages, double-checking the dates of each entry. "I guess he stopped writing for awhile. Let's see what inspired him to pick it back up. It could be telling," Ivan continued.

The next entry described Merglan's first encounter with his dragon. For some unknown reason, Merglan had left the king's castle. From his choice of words, the group could tell that he'd had a falling out with his best friend, Prince William. Anders and the others were left to speculate what had happened as Merglan chose to avoid the events in his writing.

Instead, Merglan recounted meeting a young dragon alone in the woods. The lost dragon and Merglan quickly formed a tight connection over the coming days. Merglan kept his entries short, but they reflected that he was in good spirits, considering he only badmouthed the king and his son several times in each passage. The whole experience seemed eerily like Anders and Zahara's.

Over the next several pages, Merglan described the moment he and Killdoor bonded. Anders took comfort in the fact that at least he hadn't felt the need to immediately test the boundaries of his bonding with Zahara. Anders had always known when to stop pushing the limits of their strength, whereas Merglan described the urge to push harder. It wasn't clear why Merglan was wandering in the wilderness with his dragon, but he offered few entries again for an extended period.

When next he wrote, he'd come under the tutelage of a powerful sorceress. From the powers and teachings he wrote about, he'd learned to use magic exceptionally quickly. Anders found it strange that each time Merglan wrote about these teachings, he referred to them as religious teachings. The young sorcerer wrote of his longing for revenge and how he'd soon leave his instructor to exact revenge on those who'd wronged him. Merglan's last entry was a quote. They'd assumed he'd learned it from his instructor because of its warring nature.

The quote read:

"If you seek to destroy those you've held most dear in life, you'll enact this prophecy. A son of royalty and a daughter of the veiled huntress will rise and seal your fate. Dare to use the powers I've granted to you for evil and a day will come when those you've betrayed will exact their revenge. Fail to follow our ideals and justice will come on the backs of dragons wielding powers of old. Beware the sapphire soul."

Placing a thin strip of leather into the spine between pages, Ivan closed the book and looked up. Natalia jerked awake when the book snapped shut; she'd fallen asleep, but both Maija and Anders stared at him glassy-eyed.

"Was that last bit the prophecy?" Anders asked.

"I heard Merglan tell Thargon about the prophecy. He did mention that bit about the dragons and the son and daughter, but never mentioned anything about a sapphire soul," Maija said.

"Did you hear him say anything else about the prophecy?" Ivan asked intrigued.

Maija shook her head, "We had to return to our duties because the head maid had returned."

"Why didn't you mention this before?" Anders asked.

"With all that's been going on lately, I kind of forgot."

Ivan interrupted, steering the conversation back to what they'd read, "It's fine, this version is much more accurate than the whispers Maija would have overheard anyway." After a moment of silence, he continued, "I've heard of the ancient teachings of the North, but I didn't know Merglan was taught directly by a sorceress of their religion. There have been many who've sought the teachings of these riders. All those in recent history, excluding Merglan, have died in the attempt."

"It was pretty vague. I mean why does he think I'm the son who will come to destroy him? Sure, that's exactly what we're trying to do, but I'm not the only son who's bonded with a dragon. And besides, I don't have powers of old and I'm not of ancient nobility. My father was just a man, same as you," he pointed to Ivan.

Ivan paused, breathing in sharply and holding Anders' gaze, "He was more than just a man; he was a good husband, father and leader."

"But he wasn't a king or ruler of one of the five nations," Anders protested. "Is it possible that the prophecy isn't accurate?"

"I can count on my hand the number of times a prophecy foretold by a sorcerer or sorceress of the North wasn't accurate. In the entire history of the world, there have only been two prophecies that didn't come to fruition and that could very well be because they haven't happened yet. No, the prophecy isn't wrong," he said.

"Even if it were right that I was the son in the prophecy, it says a son and daughter. Who is the girl? Maija's in training, but we're going to face Merglan soon. Natalia was the last female rider and without her dragon, the prophecy can't be true. Besides, they aren't descendants of ancient lines either. So, when we ride out to defeat Merglan in battle, how can we do so with any hope of succeeding? If the prophecy is true, we can't win," Anders said folding his arms across his chest and sitting back in his chair.

"Not true," Ivan said. "We can stop Merglan and take away his grip on the world and still have the prophecy be intact."

"How's that?" Maija piped in.

"The prophecy foretells of his fate being sealed, not about his downfall from ruling Kartania. In any case, we don't have much choice. We're the only people who have any hope of stopping him. If we don't try, then we'll be giving up on the world."

Ivan rose quickly from his place at the table, the chair's legs squeaking against the stone floor as he pushed it back. "Good night," he growled, turning and marching the length of the hall.

Anders noticed that the dragons had already gone to bed. It was then that he realized Ivan had been reading from Merglan's journal for hours.

"Sleep tight love birds," Natalia said as she followed Ivan out of the long room.

After she'd left, Maija said to Anders, "Do you find anything familiar about the description of William from Merglan's journal?"

Anders yawned, stretching his arms high above his head, "No, why?"

"What do you know about the prince?" she asked.

Anders shook his head and said, "Not much. Ivan told me once the prince went on the run to avoid the deadly clutches of Merglan and his dragon, but after that, nobody's seen or heard of him since. I bet he died or changed his name and is now living in hiding somewhere far away. Maybe with the riders in the North?"

"Went into hiding," she repeated, trailing off while pondering the words.

"What did you mean by his description sounding familiar?" he asked.

She ignored him, "I wish I could still hear like I used to."

"Your hearing changed?" he asked.

"When we were in the fortress, Kirsten and I discovered I could hear things she and others couldn't. It's how we found out about Merglan's plans and were able to sneak into his chambers undetected. But suddenly, it's changed. As hard as I try, I can't hear anything more than anyone else. I didn't even know Nadir was coming until he entered the hall the other night."

"Strange," Anders said.

"Yeah," Maija said staring past Anders. She rose from the table, extended her hand and smiled, "I'm off to bed, are you going to join me?"

"My muscles ache and I need rest," he replied.

"I think I know a remedy for that," she said moving behind him and placing her hands on his shoulders, rubbing them firmly.

For a moment he melted, her fingers working the tense muscles in his neck. Opening his eyes, he rose and said, "After you."

OVER THE NEXT month and a half, Ivan and Natalia worked hard training Anders and Zahara in the ways of swordsmanship, battle strategy and magic. Maija continued her tutelage under Natalia, and though she met with several dragons residing in the Everlight Kingdom, she did not form a reliable connection with any of them. Despite this, Maija worked hard to master the basics of becoming a rider. Often, she joined Anders and Zahara in the library during their studies and was tasked with developing her mental barriers and fighting skills.

Anders was surprised to learn that he had a knack for the training and picked up their lessons quickly. Yet another thing he shared with Merglan. Anders felt his muscles grow stronger. He could wield Lazuran faster and with more ease than ever. Learning to block mental attacks from Ivan was more challenging. Though Ivan's powers weren't as strong as they once were, Anders had to work hard and finally was able to stop him from entering his thoughts. He and Zahara read countless books on spells and how to channel their magical energy into uses for battle. Zahara had even managed to breathe thin wisps of fire, though most often she could only muster smoke. With the intense training, Anders no longer felt scared to death at the thought of facing Merglan, hopeful he'd at least be able to escape.

Reports of their enemy's progress trickled into the Everlight Kingdom several times during their time at the training facilities. Merglan had been taking advantage of their absence from the battlefield and took control of most of Southland, converting humans to fight in his name. Placing himself in the capital as his headquarters, Merglan continued to refer to himself as Emperor. The elf scouts reported some groups of people resisting his grasp, but they were no match for Merglan and his dragon. The two of them often hid, only attacking small groups where they'd be able to escape quickly.

Nadir was spotlighted as a traitor and brought to trial as an informant. Ivan fought to try to prove Nadir's innocence to the King and those on the High Council. Unable to find concrete evidence that would absolve the elf prince, Ivan had to witness Nadir's arrest by the king's guard. He was placed in a cell in the elven prison.

Ivan and Anders continued to reread Merglan's journal every night, gaining more personal information and knowledge of his twisted mind than anything else. Anders hoped there would be some vital information about a weakness they could use to trick him when it came time to face him in battle, but to his disappointment, they'd not found anything. The closest thing Anders could find that could be seen as a weakness in his power was the last sentence of the prophecy, *Beware the sapphire soul.*

Anders didn't have much time to devote to his and Maija's relationship, but they made the most of the time they had alone together. She seemed almost more interested in magic and fighting than he was. She'd begun to join in on their sword fighting practices and was learning how to block her mind from a mental probe. Ivan mentioned how people who don't possess magical abilities can still learn to seal off their minds, but this was thought to be much more difficult for them and they couldn't hold anyone out for very long.

Before Nadir was arrested, he had confided in Anders about the political strength his people had once enjoyed as a free nation in Kartania. Nadir became distraught that his father and stepmother believed him to be the mole. In addition to the stress of the allegations, Nadir seemed genuinely saddened that their people's strength was slipping away in the wake of his family's scandal. The relationship with the dwarfs had gotten so bad that the dwarfs had halted all trade with the elves.

One day during their evening meal, Asmond came to the training facilities' dining hall. Anders watched as he strolled into the expansive room with several of his guards, velvet and silk cloak billowing around him, his boots clacking against the stones as he strode across the hall. Anders thought he looked ill, pale in complexion and missing his usual, noble glow.

"The King requests your audience," one of the guards said, planting himself squarely between the King and Ivan.

Pushing the guard aside, Asmond said, "Get out of my way, you idiot."

Natalia, Maija, Anders and Ivan immediately stood and bowed, offering the King their respect. Ivan asked, "What can we do for you, Your Majesty?"

The Elf King moved his upper lip, so the tip of his nose angled sideways for a moment, then he said, "I have to ask you a favor." His eyes wandered over to the dragons staring in his direction. Shifting his weight, he turned quickly to face Ivan, "The dwarfs have refused to trade with us. They say our lack of commitment to keeping the faith in our relationship is appalling and they will not conduct an ounce of trade between us anymore. My people need an ambassador to go to Mount Orena and convince them that we remain as faithful in our business dealings as ever. Given that our regular ambassador is incarcerated for heinous treason and the other members of our party are just as likely to commit treason, I need you and Anders to go in my stead. I would go myself, but I'm afraid if word got to Merglan that I had left the protection on the forest, he would hunt me down and kill me."

Ivan nodded toward his companions standing at the dining table and said, "I'll need to continue Anders and Zahara's training while we travel."

The King nodded.

"Natalia and Maija are to accompany us," he said calmly.

To this plan, the King showed a look of concern.

"Our training can't be properly performed without their help," Ivan added.

Asmond paused while mulling over the idea of the two elves accompanying them on their quest. Finally, he said, "Fair enough, the two young women can accompany you. You will leave tomorrow," he ordered and turned away with his guards.

Once the King was out of earshot, Ivan said, "Asmond isn't the same person he once was. Something about him has changed. Only a month ago he wouldn't have placed his own son under such an invasive investigation. I fear he's been affected by the real traitor's influence."

"I hope they don't do anything to Asmond or Nadir while we're gone," Anders said.

They returned to their evening ritual, reading from Merglan's journal. He often spoke of Prince William in his writing and it seemed he had a brotherly bond with the young man, until William's girlfriend and later in their story, his wife, drove Merglan insane with jealousy.

Closing the journal after reading the part in his story where he decided to leave the kingdom, his father and his best friend to find himself, Ivan said, "I'm off to bed. We need to pack for our trip and be ready to leave as soon as we're ready. Let's shoot for a midday departure." He carried the book off with him when he left, which Anders thought was odd. Ivan usually left the book with Anders. How Ivan slid the journal off the table and into his pocket was so subtle Anders almost didn't notice. By the time Anders realized Ivan was keeping the journal, he was already walking out the door.

I'll get it from him tomorrow, he thought.

"Good night, you two," Natalia said as she cleared her dishes and left the hall.

Anders and Maija walked out with Zahara and the other dragons.

Have a good sleep, Zahara said to them as she followed the others into their dormitory-style hallway.

"You, too," Anders said aloud.

Opening the door to the bedroom Maija and he shared, Anders asked, "Have you ever been jealous of anyone before?"

"You mean like Merglan is of William's girlfriend?" she asked.

Anders nodded.

"Well, only of myself," she said.

Anders leaned, taken aback by her seriousness.

Before he could ask, she explained, "I'm jealous of my past self for having the ability to hear things that others couldn't. It seems like I've lost that and replaced it with speed. You know, I always thought I was capable of running faster than I thought I could. It just took the right person to show me how."

"Maybe it's the same with your hearing?" Anders suggested.

"If it is, I would like to meet that person as soon as possible."

"So, you've never been jealous of anyone else?" he asked again.

"No. Why do you ask?" she replied, taking him by the hand and sitting on the bed.

"I've been worried that Merglan and I share a lot of similarities," he said, looking into her brown eyes. "He was raised without a mother and his father was so absorbed in his work that he basically wasn't there. I never knew my parents. He competed in the Grandwood Games at seventeen, so did I. He mentioned how he met his dragon, which was very similar to how I met Zahara. Do you think I'm like him?"

"You are nothing like him, Anders," Maija said emphatically. "You have so much love and compassion in your heart; love and compassion Merglan obviously never has experienced. In their place, he holds contempt and hatred."

"I hope you're right," he said. "I guess I've never been so jealous I wanted to leave for months and come back and take over the world just to prove a point that I was a better choice than the prince's girlfriend," he said with a smirk.

While Anders lay in bed that night, worry flooded his mind as he hoped he would never become as twisted and dark-minded as the madman they had to stop before he could take over Kartania.

THIRTEEN

THE SAPPHIRE NECKLACE

"**B**ritt, we've got this handled. Go to your crew if you can, before that new governor tries to stop you," Thomas said.

"I can stay a little while longer if Kirsten needs," she began, but Kirsten cut her off.

"No, Britt, I'm fine. Really. You should escape while you can."

"Are you sure?" she asked.

"Someone needs to go for help if we're going to take on Rankstine and his men," Kirsten said through sniffles.

Britt smiled, nodding her final farewell. She exited the house, walking down the hill to waves lapping at the shore-line. Grabbing the beached fishing boat, Britt pushed. Max and Bo were quick to follow her, jogging after to help.

"Looks like the tide's going out," she said, noting the receding highwater marked by wet ground. "You two coming with me?" she asked.

"I think we'll be more useful here," Max said. "They might need our help if they're going to try to hold out until you make it back with reinforcements."

"Yeah, and I imagine you owe it to Anders to stay," Britt said, nodding. She hugged Max and his brother, then climbed in the rocking boat as the brothers helped push her out into the bay.

As she made her way past the halfway point across the bay, Max called out to her from the shoreline, hoping for one final goodbye. Britt stood in the hull, her momentum carrying her through the calm water. As she turned to wave back, the fishing boat came to an abrupt halt, pitching her forward and almost sending her overboard. Catching herself on the boat's rim, she shouted in frustration.

Britt came down hard in her seat, burying her face with her hands. She sat defeated, her boat steadily knocking against the invisible barrier as the receding tide tried to carry her out into open water. After what seemed like hours, Britt began rowing her way back to shore. Suddenly she heard shouting. Britt whirled around assuming she'd see armed soldiers on land. With the sun setting and the light fading, Britt strained to see the source of the shouting onshore, but she couldn't see anything out of the ordinary. Max and Bo had joined Kirsten and Thomas in the house. The shouts came again. She whirled around to find the source, this time she could just see her ship rowing into view.

Before they could get too close, she warned them of the barrier and told the crew they should not cross it. Initially, they disagreed, but after ordering them to leave her behind and return with a more significant force to rescue her, they obeyed. Crestfallen, she watched them trail off in the distance before returning to shore and climbing the hill to the farmhouse. Max could tell that her decision to order her crew to leave them behind was a difficult one, but the risk of having all of them become trapped within the barrier was too significant.

Settling in at the farmhouse, Kirsten and Thomas spent the next several days venturing to town and interviewing townspeople about why they'd become so enthralled with the new governor. Rankstine had his watchmen placed throughout Grandwood, so they had to time their interviews when the workers were on their way to and from the wall's construction. Meanwhile, Max and Britt tasked themselves with searching for a way out of the invisible barrier that had barred them from leaving the docks. They wanted to know if it encircled the entire area or if there was a break or gateway of some sort. Bo went to town with Kirsten and Thomas but split up with them to buy food and supplies. He began observing the patterns of the newly appointed governor. Rankstine kept mostly to himself, staying in his guarded building in downtown Grandwood; none of them could bear to call the town 'Mergwood'.

Each time Kirsten asked one of the workers why he or she thought the wall was necessary, she'd hear, "I thank Rankstine and his new leadership on behalf of our community. Many blessings to him and the emperor for saving us."

One day after trekking back to the stone farmhouse, Kirsten left her muddy boots on the porch and entered through the front door. "The people in town are acting strangely. They seem different than before. They all think this Rankstine guy is a god or something. Everyone keeps saying things like, "blessings to him," and thanking him for saving the community. It's as though they're under a spell," Kirsten said as she helped Thomas pile kindling in the fireplace.

"Do you think Merglan could cast a spell so powerful from such a great distance?" Thomas asked.

"Assuming he's not here. For all we know, Rankstine is Merglan in disguise?" Max suggested, speaking across the room from the kitchen.

"I highly doubt it," Britt replied as she uncrossed her legs and sat up on the couch in front of the fireplace.

"Yeah," Thomas said, lighting the kindling, "He probably isn't Rankstine. I mean, seeing as how he hasn't killed us yet and the fact that he doesn't have a dragon."

Kirsten hummed lightly to herself while she thought of a reply to play devil's advocate. "Whoever he is, Rankstine is working for Merglan. I'm sure he's already talked with him about us and has orders to keep an eye on us or take us out and soon."

"Actually, I saw someone following us on our way home," Bo said as he cut up fresh vegetables while his brother cut cubes of lamb for a stew they were making. The others looked at him with burning curiosity.

Britt remarked, "Really? Someone's spying on us?" she rose from the couch and walked to the window on the front door, pushed the curtain aside, and peered into the darkening evening.

"No, the guy following us never made it all the way out here. I hid along the path about halfway here, waiting for him to walk by, but he suddenly stopped when he got close. I remained hidden, so he didn't see me, but I could see his expression turn to confusion. He was looking up, down and all around as though he'd just realized he was lost or something," Bo acted the part of the confused man with dramatic body movements. "It was weird, like he was trying to figure out where he was. And the strangest part of the whole deal was when I walked back out onto the path. He noticed me, waved with a smile and then turned back around, walking back toward town," Bo shook his head and shrugged. "It was the weirdest thing."

"That is strange," Thomas said as he sat back on his elbows on the floor next to the rising fire.

"Why would he just turn back?" Britt asked, turning back toward the living room and welcome warmth of the fire.

Kirsten shrugged and stretched out on the floor next to Thomas, "Maybe he was under one of the spells or whatever. He could've been affected by something like that and it just wore off or something?"

"The way you described how he just stopped following you and looked around like he didn't know where he was, does sound like he was affected by some kind of trance-like spell or something," Thomas said. "And we know that either Rankstine or someone with him can do some magic. Just look at the barrier that kept us from leaving from the docks and kept Britt from reaching her crew."

"Yeah, that's true," Bo said, pointing his chopping knife toward Thomas.

Suddenly alert, Kirsten asked, "I just remembered. Did any of you check to see if we could leave through the forest?"

Dropping onto the couch, Britt replied, "Yes, we tried that today. Max, Bo and I spent the whole day walking in different directions to see how far we could get before running into the invisible wall. Haven't found a breach in it yet," she said folding her arms and crossing her legs as she lay back into the couch. "We'll try again tomorrow."

"The bay isn't any different," Bo said. "You know what happened to Britt and her crew out there, but we actually saw what happened."

Britt shot Bo a menacing look, "I thought I made myself clear not to talk about that."

"That was actually pretty funny to watch," Max said.

"What are you guys talking about?" Kirsten asked.

"Well, Bo and I were watching from shore and we thought she'd found a way out because she'd made it pretty far beyond the shoreline. I called to her and waved, you know to say my heartfelt goodbye and all that. So she stands up as the boat is skidding through the water, raises her arm to wave back," Max thrust his hand into the air above his head. "Like a glass plate dropped on stone, reality came when the boat rammed into the invisible wall, knocking her almost overboard." Max slapped his hands together, "Wham! She went down hard, like a sack of potatoes."

After a breath of silence everyone looked at Britt, who didn't appear amused; then she cracked a smile and they all erupted in laughter, even Britt, though she was blushing, "Sure, sure. Laugh it up. We're all trapped here together, you know."

When the chuckles had subsided, Thomas said, "I think some of us should go to town tomorrow and spend more time spying on our new governor. Bo's not been able to gather much information because Rankstine keeps himself locked up out of sight."

"That's a good idea," Britt agreed. "I'd like to do some spying myself, but I think my time would be better spent searching for a way out of this barrier since Max and I already know the places we've searched."

"We should probably split up into groups. Thomas, you and I will see what Rankstine is up to since we know Grandwood the best. We'll be able to sneak through town more easily than the rest of you," Kirsten suggested.

Thomas nodded in agreement.

"Britt and Max can continue searching for the barrier's edge and any openings. Bo, what do you want to do?"

"Well, if you two want to be stealthy, I can help my brother and Britt," Bo said.

"If we finish early, we might do some digging into what the townspeople think about Rankstine, pick up where you two have left off?" Max suggested, gesturing to Kirsten and Thomas with a long wooden spoon.

"That's a good idea," Britt said. "The townspeople don't know us as well as Kirsten and Thomas. They actually might say more to us than they would to you."

"Sounds like a plan," Thomas said rising to help Max and Bo carry the large stew pot over to the wrought iron hook hanging over the fire. They relaxed as it cooked, their conversation turning to more light-hearted topics. Once they'd finished their meal, Thomas turned in for the night.

The first night they'd spent in the house, no one slept well. They were on edge, expecting an attack from Rankstine's men at any moment, never leaving the living room. The next few nights had been similar, though Max and Thomas had ventured into different rooms while the others huddled together on the floor near the fireplace. They were beginning to feel more comfortable in the house, gathering wood for the fire, checking on the overall condition of the farm after the Grandwood Games attack, and coming to terms with the idea that they'd most likely be using the farmhouse as a home base for a while.

"Goodnight," Thomas called as he headed up the stairs and closed the door to his bedroom.

"I'll take the couch again," Britt said, unbuckling her belt and tossing it onto the couch near the fireplace.

"Is that an official placeholder?" Max asked, walking

over to look down at her as she lay belly up on the living room floor.

"Yes," she said nodding. "You wouldn't take your captain's sleeping arrangements, would you?" she asked playfully.

Max stroked his smooth chin pretending to be deep in thought, "I... might be inclined." He raised his eyebrows.

"You wouldn't," Britt gasped, rising to a seated position.

Max made a jerking motion toward the couch and Britt leapt off the floor pouncing forward and beating Max to the couch.

With an exaggerated sigh of disappointment, Max began to laugh. Britt smiled and laughed, stretching out along the cushions.

"Too slow," she said through giggles.

"Darn," he said, snapping his fingers and crossing his arms over his chest. "Guess I'll take Anders' comfy bed again."

"What?" Britt asked surprised, "There's a bed in there? I thought it was a storage room."

Max laughed more heartily and nodded his head.

"I'm going to sleep in my father's room," Kirsten said. "Max or Britt, you are welcome to have Anders' room or the couch; Bo you can sleep in my old room upstairs."

Bo nodded and glanced to Britt and Max who gave him a look as if to say, get going or we will take it instead. He bid them goodnight and rushed up the stairs to Kirsten's room.

"I'm off to bed as well," Kirsten said to Max and Britt and walked across the room, closing the door to Theodor's bedroom behind her.

Still half chuckling Max said to Britt, "You can take the bed if you want."

"A true gentleman," Britt joked.

"No, really," Max said more seriously. "I've been sleeping on couches all my life; you take the bed."

Britt eyed him up and down and said with a raised eyebrow, "Or we could share it?" She rose from the couch, paused for a moment as she stood sideways in front of Max. She let out an exaggerated yawn, stretched her arms toward the ceiling and arched her back.

Max seemed to be seeing her for the first time. As she stretched, her shirt raised slightly exposing the dark smooth skin just above her waist. He felt his pulse quicken. His eyes grew wide.

Lowering her arms, but keeping her back slightly arched, Britt walked across the room slowly, glancing over her shoulder as she sauntered provocatively toward Anders' door. Stopping in the open doorway, she tilted her head to the side making sure Max was still watching, then slowly entered the shadowed room, leaving the door ajar. Max breathed deeply as he stood in the living room. He glanced down at the couch, then to the open doorway to Anders' room.

After entering Theodor's old room, Kirsten locked the door behind her. She didn't want Bo wandering down during the middle of the night and trying to see her. She thought he was cute and sweet enough, but she just wasn't in the right place in her life to start a romance, especially in her father's bedroom. She wasn't tired enough to go to sleep right away, so she spent the fleeting hours of the evening searching through her father's personal items. He'd kept all of their mother Lucy's possessions, just as she'd had them arranged before she passed away.

Kirsten remembered so vividly the beautiful summer day when they lost their mother. She'd been out gardening when she suddenly tipped over. Theodor, walking to the house from the barn, just happened to glance over witnessing his wife collapsing. He rushed to her aid, taking her in his arms as her body shook violently. Theodor shouted for help. Thomas and Anders were doing chores and came running when they heard Theodor's calls. The three carefully carried her inside. When her seizures stopped, she could no longer speak clearly and she could only move one side of her body. Theodor had sent Anders to get the doctor, but by the time he'd returned, Lucy had suffered another seizure, this one ending her life. Kirsten, Thomas and Theodor were all at her side in the end.

A tear rolled down Kirsten's face as she thought about the look on her mother's face as she passed away. She wiped it away with her shirtsleeve and continued searching through her mother's and father's desks, dressers and drawers. She pulled dresses out of her mother's closet and held them up to herself to see how they compared in size. It was when she was looking over a pretty blue flowered dress that she noticed something heavy in one of the pockets. Reaching inside, she felt the coolness of metal and a thin chain balled around it. She pulled it from the pocket and let the dress fall to the floor. She gasped at what she saw.

A pink-hued sapphire trimmed in gold formed the centerpiece of a magnificent necklace. Clasped onto a golden braided chain, the gem's beauty was captivating. Kirsten held it in her open palm, marveling at its size and weight. The sapphire covered half her palm and weighed more than any pouch of coins she'd ever held. Walking over to the mirror on top of the wooden dresser on her mother's side of the bedroom, she held the necklace up to her chest. Pushing her shoulder-length flaxen hair back, she clasped the golden chain around her neck. Half focused on the precious jewelry, she stared at the woman looking back at her in the mirror. The beautiful translucent pink crystal hung just below her collar. She was surprised at how it made her feel. She thought at first the large gem would make her feel silly, but it didn't. She felt strong, powerful even. Kirsten tried to remember if she'd ever seen her mother wearing this necklace.

It must have cost a small fortune, she thought as she sat on the edge of the bed.

Not wanting to tarnish the magnificent necklace, she took it off and placed on the nightstand. Kirsten blew out the candles she'd been using to see in the darkened room. She curled up in bed, imagining her mother wearing such a magnificent piece of jewelry.

THOMAS WAS WAITING for Kirsten at the kitchen table when she emerged from Theodor's bedroom the next morning. She rubbed her eyes and yawned as she sat down across from him.

"What time is it? Did the others already leave?" she asked.

Thomas stared at her wide-eyed; he didn't respond to her questions, he just looked at her in awe.

"What?" she asked, shaking her head. "Why are you looking at me like that?"

Thomas stood up from his chair, sliding it out from under him with the back of his knees, and walked over to her. Kirsten pulled away when he approached her so suddenly. He bent down and grabbed onto the sapphire hanging from her neck. Still wild-eyed he asked, "Where did you get this?"

Remembering she'd put the necklace on in her sleepy state, Kirsten said, "Oh yeah, I found this in mother's things last night."

Thomas let go and said, "It's absolutely gorgeous. I would never take it off if I were you."

Kirsten blushed a little at the compliment and looked down at the large necklace, "You don't think it's too much?" she asked.

Raising his eyebrows and frowning slightly, he answered, "No. It's just perfect. You look stunning."

Kirsten smiled, "Thank you, Thomas."

"Can I have it?" he asked her immediately.

Slightly taken aback by this comment, she said, "No. I'm surprised you didn't take it from me as soon as you saw it. It's not like you to be this nice to me."

Thomas walked back to his chair and fell into the seat, "You're right, I should've just taken it from you. Oh well, maybe I'll steal it later when you're not looking," he smiled at her.

"That sounds more like the Thomas I know," she said while tucking the crystal under her shirt collar.

"Yeah, Max, Bo and Britt left pretty early. They were walking out the door by the time I got up," Thomas informed her.

"I guess we'd better get going then, too," Kirsten said.

As the two siblings set out for Grandwood, they discussed their plan. Kirsten suggested they not draw too much attention to themselves and try to follow Rankstine's guards. The guards would eventually be called to his side and then the two could attempt to spy on what he was doing. Their plan settled, they walked the path to town in high spirits, hopeful of discovering more information on the intruding minion Merglan had sent to Grandwood.

Cresting the last hill before town, they looked down at the once peaceful burg and watched as the many townspeople exerted great effort to construct a wall around Grandwood. Thomas waved Kirsten over to the side of the trail and stood behind the shelter of a large tree.

"It's a good spot to search for Rankstine's guards," Thomas said peering down at the city. They could see the townspeople hard at work. Construction was underway in two places: at the northern edge of Grandwood near the docks and port and around the southern end of town. The wall and trench on the opposite side of town emerged from the woods, cutting across the bombed-out fields where the vendors set up for the Grandwood Games before the invasion several months earlier. The new wall headed across the beach and would eventually wrap around to tie into the section ending at the docks.

After some silent observing, Kirsten pointed toward a street along the eastern edge of town away from the beach and port, "There they are."

Thomas strained, but despite his efforts, he couldn't see exactly where she was pointing. "Where? I don't see them," he asked.

"Between the bakery and the grain mill," Kirsten said. "I see a group of men wearing Merglan's colors walking down the street."

Taking a moment to locate the windmill, Thomas nodded, "Ah, yeah, I see them now. It looks like they're heading down to the gateway where our road enters the town's limits."

"Come on. Let's go," Kirsten said, rushing forward to get closer to town.

Reaching some bushes on the leeward side of the wall, the townspeople could be seen digging the trench and constructing the wall. Kirsten and Thomas hid quietly, waiting for the guards' arrival. In short order, four men clad in black and gold surrounded a small group of those laboring. The workers looked up at them, pausing from their efforts.

"Billson," one of the guards called out to the group. "Come with us. The governor would like a word with you."

Billson, who Thomas had spoken with shortly after their arrival several days earlier, looked around at his fellow workers and with a compliant gesture stuck his spade into the ground, and walked toward the guard who'd called his name.

The guard grabbed his arm as he approached and attempted to pull him along, but Billson pulled his arm away quickly and said, "I'm a-gettin', aren't I?"

The guard glared at him, curling his lip in disgust, "Go on then," the guard barked, "Get!"

Billson led the two closest guards away from the workers, passing through the streets. Two of the guards lagged behind, eyeing the workers who'd stopped to watch them take Billson away. "Get back to work!" one of them shouted before they hurried off to catch up with the others.

"Now's our chance," Kirsten said.

Thomas nodded and they ran out onto the road, following the guards and Billson.

Sliding up to the edge of a building and peeking her head around the corner to catch a glimpse of the group, Kirsten asked, "I wonder what they want with Billson?"

"I'm not sure," Thomas said. "I wonder if he's in some kind of trouble for speaking with us earlier?"

Kirsten shrugged, "Could be, but why would that irritate Rankstine?"

"Just a guess, but he seems to have the whole town

scared into doing what he wants. He probably feels the need to silence Billson if he spoke ill of him," Thomas suggested.

"It's possible. Or, maybe he's going to give Billson orders to try to sabotage us since he might've heard that he spoke to us."

"There's only one way to find out," Thomas said and the two left the wall they were pressed against and continued to follow the guards.

They took a winding path through the cobblestone streets of Grandwood, past the central courtyard where markets were held and up near the temple where those who worshipped could honor their gods. They watched as the armed guards forced Billson through the back door of the large stone temple.

"So that's where he's hiding," Thomas said. "I bet he thinks he's some kind of god or something and is forcing people to pray to him in there."

Kirsten nodded, "Yeah, I wouldn't put it past him."

They waited until the guards closed the door before emerging from their hiding place. Approaching the door with caution, Thomas carefully reached forward and grabbed the doorknob. He twisted but felt it stop almost instantly when the locking mechanism engaged.

"It's locked," he said with a snort.

Kirsten pursed her lips as she thought. Raising her eyebrows, "I've got it. There's another way in. Come on," she said motioning him to follow. She led them around to the front of the building.

Thomas grabbed her by the shoulder, "Don't you think they'll be watching the front entrance?"

She nodded and pointed up toward the top of the building.

Thomas followed her finger to the peak of a spire

reaching skyward from the roof. "The bell tower?" he asked.

Again, she nodded, "This way." He watched as his sister began to climb the overlapping bricks running up the corner of the building.

"How many times have you done this?" he asked as he placed his hands on the bricks below her.

Looking down at him, she smiled, "A few."

"Lost a bet I suppose," he mumbled, pulling himself off the ground.

"No," she replied. "Actually, Becca Henderson and I used to climb up here during choir practice and make haunting sounds to scare them."

"Ah, so you're one of the ghosts all the choir kids whispered about," Thomas chuckled. "That's pretty funny."

Reaching the top of the spire, Kirsten led her brother through the gap where the bell hung. They crawled their way inside the tower and stood on the wooden walkway. Kirsten placed an index finger over her mouth to shush her brother as they pinned their ears to the edge of the walk, listening for any voices.

"Ahh!" their eyes widened upon hearing Billson's shouts.

"We have to help him," Kirsten whispered with a worried look.

Thomas nodded, "But how do we do that? Is there another way down?"

Kirsten opened a hatch in the walkway. It revealed a wooden staircase leading down the circular tower to the lower level of walkway inside of the tower. Following her down, Thomas was surprised when they emerged into the balcony area inside the place of worship.

Treading as quietly as possible, the two crouched low,

staying hidden behind the balcony's railing and creeping toward the edge. Peeking down onto the worship hall's vast expanse, Kirsten and Thomas scanned the area for any sign of Billson or the guards.

"I don't see them," Thomas whispered.

Kirsten shrugged a hushed reply, "Maybe they have him in another room?"

"How do we get down to the main floor?" Thomas asked.

"There's a set of stairs near the back," she pointed to the back of the balcony behind the pews.

"Let's do it," Thomas said, reassuring his sister that he was not afraid to continue.

She gave him a half smile in return. When Kirsten's foot landed on the first step leading down to the main worship hall, they heard the cries of their friend, Billson. Pausing and looking wide-eyed at her brother, Kirsten waited until the shouts faded.

"That sounded close," Thomas whispered.

Kirsten nodded and continued slowly, placing her feet carefully on each step to make sure no unwanted noise sounded from the wooden boards. Upon reaching the end of the narrow staircase, Kirsten pressed her back against the wall and tried to look around the room. As she did so, they heard a door swing open. The voices of two men echoed into the hall. She made herself as thin as possible, stretching her body against the wall of the stairwell and hoping her brother was doing the same.

Breathing slowly, fully aware of how much noise her breathing was making; she remained still. Suddenly two men walked out into the worship hall, nearing their hiding place in the stairwell. The guards' shadows ran the length of the floor directly in front of the stairwell entrance.

Kirsten held her breath and watched the shadows as they stopped.

"That's what happens to those who can't keep their mouths shut around here," one of the guards said in a gravelly voice.

"Yeah," the other responded. "The governor don't tolerate any sneaky business from the townsfolk."

"I wonder what their secret meeting was about?" the first guard asked, then Kirsten heard Rankstine's rough bark ordering the guards to return into the room.

She let out her breath as she listened to their footsteps echo across the floor. It wasn't until she heard the door close that she turned to Thomas.

"That was so close," Thomas said.

"Did you hear what they were saying?" Kirsten asked him.

"Yeah, they said something about Billson having a secret meeting. I wonder what that was all about?"

"We should try to get a closer look at what they're doing in there," Kirsten whispered.

She began to step out into the worship hall when Thomas stopped her with a hand on her shoulder. "Look," he whispered pointing to the balcony that wrapped around the rim of the worship hall. "If we go back up on the balcony, we can get right above that room. Maybe there's a vent up there that we could peek through."

"Good idea," Kirsten agreed. They quickly snuck back up the stairs and onto the balcony. Quietly, they worked their way around the horseshoe-shaped balcony to the opposite side of the building.

Kirsten leaned over the edge of the railing to see if there might be a better way to spy on the room where Rankstine and his guards were keeping Billson. The room stuck out slightly from the base of the balcony. Thomas rolled his leg over the edge of the railing and gently placed one foot at a time on the lip of the room's ceiling. He noticed a gap between the room's roof and the balcony's base. Lying on his stomach, Thomas shuffled partially under the balcony and motioned for Kirsten to join him.

Once inside the gap between the balcony and the room, Thomas and Kirsten searched for a ventilation duct or some other way to peer into the room. Not seeing anything on the top, Kirsten maneuvered her body to the front of the room, just above the doorway. She hung her head over the edge and was pleased to see a half-inch gap between the door and the doorframe. She placed her eye in line with the crack and saw Billson tied to a chair. Rankstine was standing in front of him with the two guards standing on either side of Billson, their arms folded over their chests.

Next to Rankstine, she could see something round and glassy like an orb. She shifted, trying to get a better visual. To her surprise, the orb reflected a small replica of Grand-wood, from a bird's eye view. She could even see little dots moving about the city, and she realized suddenly that the dots were the people of Grandwood.

That must be what he's using to keep everyone trapped, Kirsten thought.

She caught a glimpse the width of the area that the orb enveloped before Rankstine shifted, blocking her view. The orb seemed to cover an area that stretched just beyond Highborn Bay. She thought it extended well into the woods around the town, but couldn't see it clearly enough to be sure before her view was blocked.

I wonder if the orb's powers are related to his control over the people as well as his control of the barrier, she thought.

As she hung over the doorway, she felt her mother's

necklace begin to slide up around her chin, dangling in front of her face.

Oh, no, she thought as the necklace's chain rolled over her ears. She couldn't let her hands come off where she held herself or her weight would carry her over the edge and she'd fall head first onto the floor below. She tried to move one of her hands to catch the necklace before it slid all the way off her head, but her body began to slide off as soon as she'd let go of the roof, forcing her to return her grip.

Crap, she thought as she watched the chain roll over her eyes and slide over her head. It fell loose through the air, momentarily weightless, before landing hard on the wood floor in front of the door. The large gemstone cracked loudly as it collided with the ground. She looked through the gap in the doorway to see Rankstine's head turn sharply at the sound.

Looking at the dumbfounded guards, Rankstine said, "Well," he spread his arms out and shook his head slightly. "Don't just stand there, go check it out."

Kirsten pulled herself back up into the safety of the gap between the balcony and the room's roof. Thomas met her with wide eyes and a concerned look.

He mouthed, "What the heck?!"

She mouthed back, "Sorry!" and cringed.

The door swung open and the two guards emerged, looking down on the floor in front of the door. One of them noticed the pink-hued sapphire necklace. He bent down to pick it up. Showing it to the other guard, they shrugged confused and looked directly up. Not seeing anything out of the ordinary, the two began to search the worship hall. Kirsten and Thomas remained still. She could see the guards' movements and watched as they searched the large open room. Moving up the stairs, she listened to their footsteps as they made their way around the balcony and came to stand directly over them. After several long breaths, they moved back along the balcony and down the stairs. The guards exited the main worship area, in a hurry, obviously thinking they'd catch whoever had left the necklace behind. Thomas and Kirsten carefully crawled back out of their hiding place and onto the balcony. Tiptoeing, they were already beginning their climb up the bell tower when the two guards returned.

By the time they'd reported their unsuccessful search to Rankstine, Kirsten and Thomas were at the top of the bell tower. Before they emerged onto the side of the building to climb down, Kirsten heard Rankstine enter the large sanctuary.

"Get him back to the others," he said. "I'll deal with the spies."

Kirsten and Thomas hurried down the spire and were on the ground running by the time the guards emerged from the temple to escort Billson back to the wall project. The two sprinted as fast as their feet would carry them. They didn't stop until they were back outside Grandwood's limits.

"What the heck was that?" Thomas asked, exhaling heavily.

Bending over with her hands on her knees next to her brother, Kirsten nearly sobbed, "I'm sorry. I couldn't. Take my hands. Off the edge. Or else I'd fall." She waited until she'd caught her breath to speak again. "The necklace slid off my head."

Thomas shook his head, "You lost mother's necklace. Now Rankstine has it. He doesn't deserve such a nice piece of jewelry."

"I was able to see through the gap in the doorway," she

said. "Rankstine had some kind of orb in that room. Inside the orb was a mini version of Grandwood. The whole town, including Highborn Bay, and I could see small people walking around inside it."

"Wow, really?" Thomas asked astonished.

"Yeah, but I didn't see anyone beyond the city limits," she added.

"I wonder if that's how he's keeping everyone trapped inside Grandwood?" Thomas asked.

"That was exactly my first thought. And maybe that's what he's using to control people and make them follow us. But it must have limits to its power, and for some reason, his manipulation over people doesn't work very far beyond the city's limits."

"That would explain why that guy following Bo suddenly acted like he was lost and turned back," Thomas said.

Kirsten nodded.

"Wait," Thomas said, "so if Rankstine knows where everyone is in the city at all times, he knew we were in there with him, right?"

"I'm hoping he didn't look until we were already gone, but yeah, it's probably safe to assume he knew we were spying on him."

"What do you think he'll do?"

Kirsten shrugged, "I'm not sure, but the best place for us to go is outside the city limits."

"Okay, let's go home and look for the others. We should warn them that Rankstine might be searching for us."

CHAPTER
FOURTEEN
FEASTING WITH DWARFS

*N*o! Zahara snarled, rearing back.

Zahara, Anders said in frustration.

"If she keeps doing that every time we try to put it on we're going to be here all day," Maija said.

Come on, Zahara. The saddle was designed to be comfortable for you and me both. We'll need to get used to it sooner or later, why not when we're not flying into battle? Anders urged.

Zahara stepped forward, *It looks like it will be constraining. Are you sure that's supposed to be comfortable?*

Yes, it's what dragonriders have used throughout history, Anders said holding up the complicated webbing of straps.

Zahara raised her lip, but lowered her head, letting them know she was finally willing to give it a try.

Ivan says it will take some time getting used to it, but it will make it easier for me to hang on during flight. I don't want to hit an airmine and fall off again, Anders said as he and Maija gently placed the leather seat on her.

Zahara shuddered for an instant when the saddle came to rest on her back. Maija and Anders stepped away, expecting her to rear again, but she didn't. Zahara bent her neck around and examined the unstrapped saddle.

It's, soft, she said after straightening herself.

See, I told you it felt comfy, Anders said.

"She seems to like it," Maija said.

"Now we just need to figure out how these connect," Anders said as he stooped to pick up one of the leather straps that hung from the saddle.

After several confusing attempts to fit the saddle properly, Maija said, "Maybe we should get Ivan or Natalia to help with this?"

Anders watched Zahara walk a few paces, feeling the fit of the saddle. It slipped off her back and hung around her stomach. Running his hand through his hair, he conceded, "Yeah. I don't think that's how it goes on."

Maija summoned Ivan to help Anders with the saddle. The troll-skin saddle Ivan commissioned for Anders and Zahara proved to be less complicated to cinch up once the experienced rider showed Anders how to work the strapping.

The large bags didn't attach directly to the rear of the saddle as Anders had expected. Each time he'd tried to affix them, Zahara couldn't properly lift her arms because they came to rest over top the middle of her leathery wings. Instead, the bags hung over her haunches, folding comfortably behind the crook of her wing where the backsides met before her tail. The bags were large enough to hold an additional rider if one wished. They were connected by long straps fitting off the backside of the saddle and extending down the length of her back connecting with the bags. The back end of the strap wrapped around Zahara's tail, so the bags wouldn't come flying forward if Zahara had to take a steep dive while in flight. A third set of straps ran around her underside, connecting at the base of each bag, ensuring they wouldn't come loose if she flew upside down.

Zahara complained of the discomfort of the tail strap but gradually accepted it, for safety reasons, so the bags wouldn't knock Anders off during flight. They wouldn't have needed the extra bags if they were going alone. The smaller bags that attached at the front of the saddle near the handles were large enough to fit a change of clothes and several other supplies. In traveling with Natalia, Maija and Ivan, however, they'd need to carry all of the group's clothing as well. Given that speed was necessary for their arrival, the elves would need to be unencumbered by luggage when running through the forests and over the mountain trails. Zahara would be slowed by the extra weight from Ivan, Anders and the packed bags, but Ivan assured her if she climbed high enough, the winds would carry her much faster than when she'd flown lower to the ground in the past.

As Anders packed for their ambassadorial mission to Hardstone, he realized the clothing he owned was less than acceptable for an audience with a king and queen. When he'd visited the High Council in the past, he'd been wearing the leather battle armor Britt had given him. Though the armor wasn't suitable to wear for such an audience, at least it told a story and served a purpose, one appropriate for the dreary task they were setting out to complete. This time, however, the purpose and story were different; the political and diplomatic visit demanded more fashionable attire. As Anders looked at the clothes he owned, he quickly realized he'd need something more fitting to the tastes of nobility.

Anders walked down the stone corridor of the second-floor dormitory. He entered Ivan's room to find Maija and Natalia standing inside.

"Let me guess," Ivan said, addressing Anders, "you don't have anything presentable to wear for the mission either?"

Anders glanced to Maija and Natalia, who looked at him impatiently, "Well, yes. That's just what I was coming to ask you about."

"Very well," Ivan said, turning to the desk behind him against the wall of his room. He opened a drawer and pulled out a pouch. Digging into it, he rattled among the coins. He then handed some money to Natalia, "Take him with you and make sure he gets something suitable for the occasion."

Natalia thanked Ivan and pushed her way past Anders as she left Ivan's room. Maija took Anders by the arm and they followed her sister as she led them down to the front of the building.

"I know a few places where we can find something for all of us," Natalia said when they'd stepped out onto the grass. "Can Zahara give us a ride since you'll need to come along?" she asked, giving Anders a pointed look.

Anders nodded. Moments later, Zahara walked around the side of the training facilities. She was wearing the travel harness, trying to get used to the extra bulk before they flew. When Anders asked her to carry them to Cedarbridge, she gladly accepted. It would allow her the chance to feel how the saddle handled with multiple people on her back.

As THEY APPROACHED CEDARBRIDGE, Anders realized that it was a larger city than he'd thought while on the ground. Maybe it was because they spent so much time outside it, or because all of the homes and buildings were incorporated into the living forest, but the place seemed more woodland than urban sprawl and dramatically different from the cobblestone streets and brick storefronts that were standard in the cities of Westland. The elven city was much more livable than any human settlement, he thought. The elves seemed to coexist with the ancient forest, harnessing the resources as opposed to harvesting them. Anders had read in his studies that the magic imbued within the elven forest allowed them to utilize the trees, coaxing them to grow in whichever way served their architectural needs best.

After Zahara landed atop the cliff edge, Natalia led the way, Anders and Maija bumping shoulders as they strolled together down the capital's trail system. Like any city, Cedarbridge had a business district, which in Westland was generally referred to as 'downtown.' In Cedarbridge, the downtown area was widely referred to as 'shoptop.' The elves named it so since all of the highest quality shops were located in the tops of the trees. The higher the quality of a shop's merchandise, the higher up the tree the store would be.

The three passed several lesser-known businesses as they entered Cedarbridge's shoptop area. The market-style shops selling produce, trinkets and utilitarian clothing lined the ground level. Anders speculated that even the least desirable of the shops they passed was of higher quality and standard than that of its human counterpart in Westland.

Anders and Maija followed Natalia as she led them up a staircase of toadstool conks spiraling the outside of a large cedar tree. Conks seen growing from a tree were typically a sign of decay, but here in the elf city, it was an implicit design choice, using a natural element for a functional purpose. Each level of the tree housed a business, which displayed samples of its wares on a balcony-style landing. As they climbed the tree, the stairs entered and exited each floor's balcony, forcing shoppers to walk past each business as they rose, a clever way for the lower-end businesses to attract more attention to their products.

Anders and Maija frequently stopped, lingering longer than Natalia wished on each platform. The first balcony they walked through was a pottery store, displaying the most exquisite plates, bowls and vases Anders had ever laid eyes on. The third floor was a smith's shop with works of silver, gold and other metals he and Maija hadn't known existed. The fourth floor of the tree housed an elegant eatery. Despite the lack of meat on the menu, Anders had to be dragged away from the pungent smell wafting from the kitchen. The fifth and final floor of the tree was their destination – a clothing shop Natalia knew of.

Racks of woven silk shirts, pants, robes and dresses lined the landing outside the store. Anders couldn't help but touch the soft fabric as they began looking through the articles for something suitable to wear in a diplomatic setting. Anders rubbed the thin fabric between his fingers, occasionally lifting the silk up to his cheek. Maija saw him and slapped his hand playfully, raising her eyebrows, saying through her tight-lipped smile and giggling slightly, "Stop that, you'll get us kicked out of here."

A slender elf dressed in the regal silks of the upper class approached them, standing tall and looking down his nose at Anders as he blissfully felt the silks. "What can I help you with?" he said melodramatically while gently placing a hand on the material and sharply pulling it away from Anders.

"We require of a set of clothing fit for a meeting with a royal council," Natalia said politely.

"All three of you?" the elf eyed them suspiciously.

Natalia nodded.

"Really? May I ask with whom?" he asked clearly having difficulty believing they were important enough to be seen by anyone of noble standing.

"King Asmond has asked us to reason with dwarfs on matters of diplomatic trade," Natalia said, her voice now more forceful than polite.

"You?" the man spat, peering down his nose at them. "Ambassadors for the elven race?"

Maija stepped toward the elf before Natalia could speak and said, "Your business depends on a healthy economy, right?"

The elf looked taken aback by Maija's question and stuttered a response.

"And you do understand how important the dwarfs are to the trades of Kartania?" Before the elf could answer Maija continued, her voice remaining calm, but authoritative, "If you did, you wouldn't be standing here questioning our integrity, you'd be rushing off to find the finest clothing you've got so that we can secure our kingdom's fruitful future."

A long breath passed before he straightened and said, "My apologies." He bowed slightly, "Please, follow me to the dressing rooms. I'll find you something suitable for such an occasion."

"Thank you," Maija said, pulling at the hem of her shirt and entering the store.

Anders grabbed Maija by the hand, squeezed it and whispered in her ear, "That was amazing."

Maija smiled. She'd never acted in such a way before, but the elf's apparent rudeness got her goat, especially since they were telling the truth.

"Wait here," the elf said and disappeared into the back of the store.

"Wow, Maija," Natalia said. "You really put him in his place."

Maija shrugged, her cheeks flushing as the elf returned with several ensembles for them to try on.

Holding a flowing jade dress out for the young women to examine, the elf said, "For the ladies, I have found several of our finest silk dresses spun from the very silkworms of the mulberry trees in our ancient city," he paused for a reaction. Failing to get the impressed response he'd expected, he continued, "It's the oldest and most rare silk ever produced. Fit for a queen," he bobbed his head enthusiastically as he held out the dress.

Maija and Natalia's faces lit up with the explanation. Clearly, neither of them knew much about sophisticated dresses. The elf handed each of them four dresses: the jade, a blood red, a black darker than any black Anders had ever seen, and a sleek moonlight silver flowing gown. Starry-eyed and astonished, they scampered into the fitting rooms.

"For the human," the elf started, holding out three suits. "I have selected three of our most exotic brocade suits."

Anders took a darkly colored suit jacket with a decorative floral pattern. "Brocade," he said under his breath, feeling the fabric between his fingertips.

"Yes, it's a soft weave," the tall elf said. "Woven from silkworm silk and wool off our elven sheep. It's the most desirable material among those in high society."

"It's nice," Anders said, taking the three suits selected for him.

The elf exhaled shortly, "Nice is an understatement."

Anders walked into the fitting room and tried on each of the suits. He liked the charcoal one more so than the green or tan suits. Before making his final decision though, Anders thought he should get the girls' opinion.

When he emerged from the dressing room, Maija and Natalia were showing one another the dresses they'd each picked. Natalia had chosen the silver and Maija was wearing a long black dress with an open back. Anders gulped when he saw her. She skipped slightly as she came over to him, smiling brightly. Anders couldn't take his eyes off her. The dress formed perfectly to her figure, highlighting her beauty and confidence.

"Wow, Maija, you look absolutely stunning," Anders said, his eyes widening and mouth gaping.

"You look dashing yourself," she replied, twisting on the balls of her feet as she half turned.

Anders mimicked her, "You like this one?"

She nodded vigorously, "And we'll match."

Natalia joined them, stopping alongside Maija. Wrapping her arm around her sister, she looked to Anders and asked, "What do you think?"

"Lovely," Anders said with a smile.

Natalia turned to the elf and said, "We'll take them."

"Wonderful," the elf replied in a monotone that slightly dampened their enthusiasm.

Once back in their everyday clothes, the elf packaged up their formal wear and asked, "How do you plan to pay for these, through a series of payments?"

Anders knew they didn't appear to be the wealthiest people, but the way the elf assumed they weren't of importance or means irritated him.

Natalia reached into her pocket and practically threw the coins on the counter, "No. We'll be paying in full."

Anders and Maija chuckled as the elf scrambled to retrieve the coins strewn about the counter.

"It was nice doing business with," the elf cut off looking up to see them leaving the store. Natalia hadn't given him the chance to thank them for their purchase before leaving.

"We'd better get back to Ivan," Natalia said. "He'll be cross if we're late."

They rushed down to the trail below, not stopping to look at any other shops as they descended. Anders called to Zahara as they left the shoptop area. Landing softly near the edge of the cliff, she picked them up where she'd dropped them off. They climbed onto her back and she soared across the forested valley to the training facilities.

On the short flight, Anders noticed that Zahara had grown since he had first met her more than two months earlier. She was several feet longer from head to tail and stood half a foot higher. Her muscles were developing more rapidly than he could have imagined and she was beginning to resemble a more full-grown dragon. She could easily carry three of them for a considerable distance if she desired.

IVAN WAS WAITING for them at the training facilities. Natalia and Maija quickly loaded their things into Zahara's saddlebags. Anders strapped Keanu's sword to his side and nodded to Ivan that he, too, was ready to depart. Ivan climbed onto Zahara's back, settling on a pad he'd lashed to her saddle. Anders hugged Maija as she and Natalia prepared to make the run from Cedarbridge to Hardstone.

"See you in a bit," Anders said, running to join Ivan on Zahara's back.

Natalia and Maija took off at a sprint, running in the direction of the trail system that would lead them to the Eastland Mountains. Zahara took several steps and leapt into the air, letting her wings extend out and cup the air beneath them, lifting them off the ground in two powerful pulls. She continued to climb until they were high above the forest. Using the air funneling upward from the cliff's edge, Zahara rose above the clouds in a matter of minutes.

"Did you bring Merglan's journal?" Anders asked Ivan.

"Yes, I put it in the bags," Ivan said.

"I saw you take it last night when we were finished reading. You usually leave it for us to study."

"I must have had my mind elsewhere and forgotten."

Anders opened his mouth to pry more into the matter but paused, deciding it best if they didn't argue during the long flight. Instead, he asked, "What's the plan once we reach Hardstone?"

"The dwarfs will likely have us escorted to our accommodations. Then I assume we'll be introduced and a feast will be held in our honor. Tomorrow morning we'll begin our negotiations. The dwarfs will receive us well if we don't discuss politics immediately after our arrival. They prefer to get acquainted with those they deal with before such talks can begin."

""I've always wanted to see the dwarfs; it'd be nice to see their kingdom and how they live before we get thrown out for pushing the elves' political agenda on them," Anders said.

"They won't throw us out; we'll be asked to leave and if we don't then we'll be thrown out," Ivan said with a chuckle. "Whatever stories you've heard about the dwarfs are most likely wrong," Ivan said suddenly serious.

"What do you mean?" Anders asked.

"Only a handful of humans have ever spent a lengthy amount of time with the dwarfs. None has ever written about their experiences. The stories you grew up hearing about the dwarfs may have elements of truth to them, as in they do mine the riches of the earth and they are short in stature, but all of the stories I've ever read in books are no more accurate than fairytales."

"Nadir told me some history of the dwarfs," Anders reminded him.

"His accounts are much more accurate. You'd be wise not to bring up anything you've been told about them though. They're a proud race and will easily take offense from any misinformed foreigner who rambles on about the fantasies he was told about them."

"So, I'm not allowed to talk about dwarfs to the dwarfs; got it," Anders said sarcastically.

"Avoid the subject unless directly asked about it," Ivan replied sharply.

"Who rules the dwarfs? Do they have a king?" Anders asked.

"Yes," Ivan said. "Their king's name is Remli Madhammer."

"That's quite a name," Anders interjected.

"In dwarf culture, their last names are given to them by major events in their lives."

"So, Madhammer was given to him because he goes mad when he's got a hammer?"

"Sort of. Remli was given the name after his father was killed in a battle with the goblins. He avenged his father's death by slaying his foes wildly with his warhammer. Witnesses of the battle saw him become mad with rage after his father fell. After the battle was over everyone began to call him Remli Madhammer and it stuck."

"Does he have a queen? Are there dwarf women?" Anders asked seriously. The stories he'd heard growing up only described male dwarves with full beards.

"They have to reproduce, don't they?" Ivan said disapproving of the question. "Yes, of course, there are female dwarfs. His queen is called Joslina Rubyshield. Before you guess at her last name's origin, she was given a warshield from her father when she became queen. It had a large ruby embedded in the center of the shield."

"Okay," Anders nodded.

"They have one daughter. She's younger than you, I'm not sure how much, but her name is Maylox."

"No last name?" Anders asked.

"Not yet," Ivan replied. "There will be others, but Remli and Joslina are the names you need to know before we meet them."

Anders and Ivan rode in silence the rest of the way. To keep his mind occupied, Anders played a game of sense-and-seek with Zahara. One of them would reach out and sense a creature in the forest and the other would have to guess what it was. The game helped them learn to read the feelings they shared through their bond.

The setting sun dropped beyond the western horizon as they approached the Eastland Mountains. Anders couldn't see where Maija and Natalia were, but often reached out with his senses to make sure they were still making progress. Darkness had consumed the Eastland Mountains when they reached Mount Orena. Zahara spiraled as she circled in lower around the mountain, searching for a place to land. Locating the main entrance to the city, with help from Ivan, Zahara landed softly at the stone entryway.

I hope they don't bring up that I ate some of their sheep, Zahara said to Anders as he climbed down from her saddle.

I hope so, too. They're very close to Nagano and could have thought it was a wild dragon that flew in to snatch their sheep, he replied.

They didn't have to wait long before Maija and Natalia came running up the stairs to the city's large carved-stone doors. Approaching the arched stoop, Ivan asked Zahara if she would do them the honor of knocking on the large stone doors. Zahara balled her claws up into a fist and rapped her knuckles against the front of the stone door. The pounding echoed into the mountain and reverberated through the stones at their feet.

She pulled her paw away and cringed, *Whoops, was that too hard?*

Just right, Ivan said as the doors swung inward and a host of small, stocky people emerged. They were dressed in beautiful clothes woven in delicate geometric patterns. Anders quickly identified the king and queen by their crowns. Those around the king and queen admired Zahara. Anders could tell they didn't know whether to trust her enough to bring her into their city.

"Welcome, Ivan," the short king bellowed in a voice more powerful than that of a man twice his size. "It has been too long." Remli strode forward and held out a stout hand to Ivan.

Taking it firmly, Ivan replied, "Remli, your majesty. It's wonderful to see you in such good spirits. And you as well, Queen Joslina." He bowed elegantly after shaking Remli's hand. "I'm honored to be in your radiant presence."

Wow, Ivan sure knows how to greet royalty, Anders said to Zahara.

She chuckled in response, causing the dwarfs around the king and queen to jump at the sudden noise.

"Allow me to introduce my student, Anders, and his dragon, Zahara," Ivan swept his arm to Anders who stood alongside Zahara. Anders bowed and Zahara did the same, her neck lowering toward the floor.

"We're honored to meet you," Anders said, returning to his full height.

"Thank you for coming," Remli replied. "And who are these two lovelies," he asked pointing to Maija and Natalia.

"They're elf sisters, long lost and recently reunited. They've been helping us in our training exercises," Ivan said.

"Ah," the king said, raising a bushy eyebrow. "And their names are?"

"Natalia and Maija," Ivan said pointing to each as they stepped forward and curtsied politely.

"Lovely names, indeed," the queen said.

"Well come in, come in," Remli said waving them in. "Watch your head," he called back to Zahara as she ducked to enter through the doors.

The entrance to Hardstone rose high after they passed through the doorway, the ceiling following along the slope of the mountain. Once inside, they walked along a wide marble hall with stone pillars extending up to the ceiling high above.

"Welcome to Hardstone," the king said, his voice echoing off the walls as they advanced.

At the end of the long hallway, the room opened, exposing an entire city under the mountain. Buildings rose up along the interior walls of the mountainside. Stone stairs climbed high into the mountain's peak, rising higher than Anders thought possible. The enormity of the place blew Anders away. Hardstone was so large Zahara could fly freely around the city if she wished. Compared to Grandwood, the dwarf capital was much more magnificent and inspiring to view. Masonry crafted the dwarfish buildings and shops. Carvings in the stone were unlike any he'd seen before. In the way the elves were masters of nature, the dwarfs were masters of minerals. At the edges of the city, Anders noticed tunnels leading out to what he assumed were the mines.

"Come, I'll show you to your inn," the king said as he walked down steps leading into the city.

Anders smiled and waved at all those who stopped to stare at them as they walked through the stone city. Zahara followed, stepping delicately, careful not to stomp or squish anything or anyone under her feet. After passing many suitable looking inns, they came to a building carved into the side of the mountain. The sign on the front read, The Rocking Pebble.

Anders smiled at the name as he stood outside the small doorway. The king told the owner that his guests of honor would be staying the night in their rooms. Zahara waited patiently outside.

Stepping back outside and addressing Anders and Zahara, Remli said, "I'm sorry we don't have any rooms large enough for your dragon. She's welcome to stay in the entrance hall. It is plenty large enough."

Zahara nodded, showing him that she understood and accepted his offer.

"I would welcome you to stay outside if you liked, but recently a dragon has been tempted to eat several of our sheep," he tilted his head toward her knowingly.

After a moment of silence, he burst out laughing, "It's only a joke. Dragons have to eat, too."

"Very funny, your highness," Anders said chuckling with him. He was relieved Remli wasn't enraged by Zahara's past transgression the last time they were near Mount Orena.

"I'll give you some time to get situated, then you are to join us in the great hall for our feast. Ivan knows how to get there. We'll see you soon," Remli said and walked down the street with his wife.

Zahara waited patiently outside the hotel, staring at the new species of people as they passed by. Anders could feel her emotions as they gawked at her. Some just stared in disbelief that a dragon could sit idly by not eating them or destroying their walls. Others ran in fear upon seeing her tall body perched next to the hotel. Realizing that Zahara wasn't chasing after them, many slowed down, looking over their shoulders warily at her before scuttling off quickly, disappearing down an alley or street.

To Anders' surprise, Zahara was happily amused by their reactions. She liked being respected for her power. Anders only felt her mood change once, when a dwarf man stood across the street from her, looking her over. He wasn't afraid at all and examined her like a statue. She was about to let out a low growl at the dwarf, but Anders stopped her, *I wouldn't do that if I were you.*

Why not? This little creature is eyeing me like I'm his next meal. He should show some respect.

We're here to negotiate with the dwarfs on the elves' behalf. If Remli hears you're growling at the dwarfs, he might think twice about our credibility. We need to be on our best behavior while we're here, Anders said as he pulled his suit jacket on. Before leaving his room, Anders combed his unkempt hair, pulling the long wavy strands back similar to Ivan's combed-back style. He hadn't realized how long his hair had gotten. He was able to tuck it behind his ears as it folded down the back of his neck. Looking in the mirror, he noticed his facial hair was beginning to look unruly as well, so he decided to shave it down to his bare skin. It made him look younger than he felt, but as was the Westland fashion of the time, clean-shaven men were regarded as the most handsome.

Walking to the window, he could see Zahara's head close to his second-story room as she looked down at the dwarf. Anders watched as the dwarf came closer and began examining her scales. He reached out and tapped on one near her foot. Zahara wiggled her claws rapping them in succession on the cobblestone street. Startled by the sudden movement, he leapt back, straightened his beard and resumed walking down the busy street. Anders laughed, and Zahara moved her head to look in the window.

Did you see that? she asked.

Still chuckling, Anders said, *Yes, you scared him good.*

Was that too disrespectful?

No, Anders replied. *You handled that splendidly.*

Zahara purred with delight and resumed her pose at the side of the hotel.

Once appropriately dressed, Anders made his way down to the lobby where he waited alongside Ivan. Like him, Ivan was wearing a brocade suit with a floral design, his suit a dark olive. Ivan had trimmed his beard, cutting out stray hairs and combed his shaggy hair neatly, slicking it back to expose more of his face. If he didn't know him, Anders would have mistaken him for a wealthy elf lord from Cedarbridge, the only things missing were pointed ears.

"I see Natalia and Maija chose well," Ivan said when Anders came to stand at his side.

Looking down at the dark suit, Anders said, "They did, didn't they?" He smiled knowing he was the most well-dressed he'd ever been in his life. He couldn't wait for Maija to see him in the full suit. She was with him when they bought it, but he had only tried on the jacket for her. It was much more regal with the pants and boots.

Anders' jaw nearly hit the floor when he saw Maija walk down the stone stairs and into the main lobby. Her black dress fell around her body perfectly; he couldn't believe how stunning she was. Her hair had been braided in a way he'd never seen before. She'd cleaned up much better than Ivan or Anders had. Ivan nudged Anders, noticing he was practically drooling like a dog being teased with a bone. Anders cleared his throat and smiled. Natalia followed Maija; her dress also was stunning and fit her body to perfection. As they stopped in front of the men, Anders stood speechless.

"Well? What do you think?" Maija asked.

Anders fumbled for words to describe how he felt. He'd never seen anyone more beautiful. He stood gawking as the dwarfs had done to Zahara just moments earlier. His mouth opened and closed, but nothing recognizable came out, only a mumbling noise. For a moment, Maija looked worried until Anders managed to sputter, "I'm speechless. I can't even find the words to tell you how pretty you are. You're amazing!"

Maija blushed and glanced shyly to the ground.

"Well that wasn't awkward," Natalia said, rolling her eyes at them.

"You look as lovely as the star-filled sky on a moonless night," Ivan said, holding his arm out to Natalia.

Natalia curtsied and grabbed his arm with both of hers, "At least one of you knows what to say to a lady."

Anders stammered and gestured the same bent arm toward Maija. Wrapping her arm into his, Maija pulled Anders in and kissed him on the cheek. "You look dashing," she said as they followed Ivan and Natalia out of the inn and onto the street.

They found that Zahara had accumulated a mass of curious dwarfs. They had huddled in a half circle around her, pointing and whispering. She rose off her haunches, glad to see she could leave with her group. The gaggle of dwarfs scattered as she moved, pausing to watch her go from a safe distance. She walked behind the others as Ivan led them across the city toward the king and queen's castle.

Located at the edge of the sprawling city under the mountain, Remli and Joslina's castle was built with towering spires and expansive halls. The gates and doors were large enough to accommodate a dragon much larger than Zahara. Ivan showed them through a large archway, across a large courtyard and into an expansive dining hall, where the dinner party awaited them.

A long rectangular table stood adorned with vegetable platters and baked goods ranging from many different types of bread to tantalizing dessert pastries and pies. Roasted pheasants on silver platters were placed between every two place-settings. Candelabras ran the length of the table lighting the seating area. Large stone chairs were fixed neatly along the length of the table. Skilled musicians played lutes, harps and flutes while a dwarf woman sang a song so sweet it felt like warm butter melting over a freshly baked roll.

Upon seeing Zahara enter and noticing his guests had arrived, Remli clapped his hands loudly and raised his voice, calling for silence. He held out his hand to his wife as they approached Ivan, the first of the guests to enter. The three-dozen other dwarfs in the room watched intently as their king and queen stopped in front of Ivan and bowed their heads in greeting. Ivan, Anders and Zahara mimicked him while Natalia and Maija curtsied politely.

Remli spoke loud enough so all in the room could hear him clearly, "I'm humbled to have such notoriously honorable company here tonight. Ivan has been a friend to our people for a great many years. We fought together to overthrow the evil sorcerer, Merglan, nearly twenty years ago. Tonight, he joins us with his student in training, Anders, and his dragon, Zahara. Natalia and Maija, the lovely elven goddesses have joined them in gracing us with their presence. Thank you for coming on behalf of the elven people in hopes of mending our recently broken relations. Tonight, however, we'll not talk of business. Tonight, we'll feast and speak of happier things. Welcome!" he held up his hand gripped tightly with his wife's. Everyone in the room clapped in accord with the king's speech, their cheers echoing off the stone walls.

Remli and Joslina led them to the table and seated them near the head, where the king and queen sat, side-by-side. Zahara stood behind Anders as he took a seat in the stone chair next to Maija. Ivan and Natalia took their places directly across from them. Several dwarf men and women sat between where they had chosen to sit and the king and queen at the head of the table. While sipping from goblets, the king introduced his guests to the members of his protectorate. To Anders' left sat Metlarm Brightstone, a dwarf with a full gray beard and a weathered face wrinkled with experience. Sitting between Brightstone and the king was Windminer Roarhorn whose thick red beard was braided, concealing most of his face. On Ivan's right sat Josack Furyaxe, a stout dwarf woman whose brown hair was tangled in thick curls. Seated between them and the queen was Gilcrest Sharpstone, a clean-shaven male dwarf with a strong jawline. His distinction wasn't mottled by the years on his face.

Remli spoke of how these four lead members of his protectorate had guarded them through times of war, rebellion and skirmishes with the goblins in the mines. Anders found it surprising how well they seemed to know Ivan, holding him in high regard. He realized that he still knew very little about the man.

As Anders and Maija ate in silence, they listened to the many jokes and stories the dwarfs of the protectorate told. Every so often one of the dwarfs would ask Anders a question, mostly regarding Zahara and their training with Ivan. He kept his answers polite and short, not wanting to draw attention away from the fun discussion.

By the time all of the food had been eaten and the pitchers had run dry, it was late in the evening. Remli rose from his chair. "My friends. My heart is full of joy as my wife and I depart from this feast. We've been so lucky to surround ourselves with such good company."

Everyone at the table cheered, slamming their fists into the table. They'd grown much rowdier with a few drinks.

Motioning for quiet, Remli continued, "After tonight I think it's been shown that our guests of honor can be relied upon to enter into the negotiations planned for tomorrow morning." He turned to Ivan, "We'll begin after morning tea in the court."

Ivan nodded.

Remli turned to address his guests again, "I thank you for coming to this feast. Now enjoy yourselves and be well." He backed away from his chair and Joslina followed him.

Anders and Maija were about to do the same when Ivan gave them a knowing shake of this head. They settled back into their chairs and waited until the king and queen had departed the hall. Once gone, everyone at the table excused themselves. Ivan escorted them out of the hall; Zahara followed.

"It's rude to leave with the king and queen," Ivan told them once they'd exited the castle gates.

"Thank you for catching us before we embarrassed ourselves," Maija said.

"You two did wonderfully tonight," Ivan said. "The king was very pleased with our behavior, even you Zahara."

She purred in response.

Anders wished her goodnight as she went off to sleep in the entrance hall and the four of them returned to the inn.

Once back at the inn, Anders lay awake, his mind wandering. Unable to sleep in the bustling dwarf city, he sat up and reached for the saddle packs. Fumbling, Anders found what he was looking for, Merglan's journal. Through the glowing light of thousands of lanterns burning throughout the dwarf city of Mount Orena, Anders opened the pages of the leather-bound journal and began to read once more. He'd read through the entire book several times but felt he was missing a key element hidden in its pages.

Anders opened to Merglan's description of the crumbling of his friendship with Prince William. After skipping through ten pages of remarks about betrayal and thoughts of how to kill William's fiancé, the words came to a sudden halt. His heart skipped a beat. He'd read this part before; many pages followed before Merglan had stopped writing, yet tonight Anders found himself staring at a blank page.

He blinked several times and rubbed his eyes, flipping back and forth through the blank pages now found in the center of Merglan's journal. Suddenly he saw something, a crude drawing of a stone, no, at second glance it was a crystal. It looked like a diagram. He struggled to read the little scribblings labeling the crystal through the dim light of the dwarf city. Anders didn't recognize them as Landish, though the handwriting was hard to read.

Anders knew powerful magic had been woven into the journal. He'd guessed that it contained something valuable if Maija's father had hidden it so well. He grabbed the quill and ink on the stand next to his bed, tore a blank page from the back of the book and copied the drawing exactly. He knew the book might not show him this diagram again. When he finished, he tucked the piece of paper into the saddle bag, closed the book and placed it on the nightstand

He fell asleep wondering what the diagram meant and how it could be used to defeat Merglan.

FIFTEEN

A VISITOR FROM NAGANO

Aknock came at the door. Anders bolted to an upright position, sheets falling to cover his midsection. He looked to his left to see Maija already up and nearly fully dressed. She walked gracefully to the door, opening it slightly.

"Yes," Anders heard her say through the crack.

A low murmuring floated through the opening in the door.

Maija nodded and closed the door. She turned to face him as he sat half-awake in an early morning fog. "Ivan says we were to meet him downstairs in the lobby five minutes ago, so you'd better get dressed." She walked to the side of the bed and handed him a shirt from his strewn travel bags.

"I thought we weren't going to have our meeting with the dwarfs until after morning tea?" he asked, pulling the shirt over his head and crossing the small room to look out the window at the dimly lit city. "I can't tell if it's daytime or nighttime down here," he said over his shoulder.

"It's just before sunrise," she informed him casually.

Anders raised an eyebrow, "And Ivan wants to meet now?"

"Five, no six minutes ago," she smirked.

Anders gave her a half-cocked smile as he pulled his boots on, "What's he want to do before our meeting?"

"Training. Come on, you're late," she said as she opened the door and stood expectantly.

"One second," Anders reached down under the bed, his hand wrapping around the prized sword that Nadir had given him. He hadn't worn it to their dinner party with the dwarfs the night before. Ivan had made sure they all knew the proper attire.

Anders sprang to his feet and jogged to the doorway to accompany Maija, blade in hand. As he reached back to close the door he recalled the diagram he'd copied from Merglan's journal.

"One second, I forgot to grab something. I'll meet you down there," he called to Maija who was already on her way down to the lobby. He turned and rushed back to the saddlebags, quickly swiping the journal from inside. As he placed his hand on the leather-bound book, he thought he heard someone mumble at him from the hallway. Gripping the journal in one hand and his elven sword in the other, Anders rushed into the hall expecting to see Maija, Natalia or Ivan waiting for him, but no one was there. He glanced left, then right to be sure, but the hallway was empty.

That's weird, he thought. *I could've sworn I heard someone say something to me.* He popped his head back into his room to make sure no one had entered while his back was turned in rummaging through the saddlebags.

Nope, no one here. Weird, he tucked the journal into the waist of his pants and closed the door, rushing down to meet Ivan and Maija.

Ivan, Maija and Natalia were waiting impatiently as he scuttled down the stairs and into the lobby. Both Natalia and Ivan had their sword belts on, blades hanging at their sides. Stepping away from the front desk as Anders jogged across the room, they exited the inn. Anders thought about mentioning what he'd found in the journal to Ivan, but based on Ivan's silence and stern expression, he decided it best to wait until they'd had more time to wake up.

When they reached the top of the stairs leading into the entrance hall, they found Zahara waiting for them.

Ivan must have already informed her of our training, Anders thought to himself.

Yes, he did, Zahara's voice came into his thoughts. *And you're late*.

Was I the only one who didn't know about this morning's plan? he asked.

Yes, Zahara said shortly as she pulled open the stone door for them.

Together they exited the city and stepped out into the fresh Eastland Mountain air. The breeze rushed up the mountainside as the early morning sun warmed the ground. Settling near the center of the large stone patio they'd landed on when approaching the mountain the day before, Ivan and Natalia drew their swords and crouched into fighting stances as they faced Anders. Slightly taken by surprise, Anders hesitated, then drew his sword. He spoke the words to create a barrier around the edge of the blade, then placed his right foot behind him at a slight angle, bent his knees and held the sword at the ready.

Ivan and Natalia simultaneously rushed at Anders. He blocked and dodged their attacks, avoiding the painful blows from their guarded blades. Anders felt at peace with Lazuran in his hands. Over the course of their training, it had become a part of him, so much so that Anders often thought he could feel the sword guiding him through the sparring matches.

As Anders blocked a set of Ivan's powerful swings, the mental connection he felt with the sword suddenly disappeared. He glanced at the blade. Somehow it felt different, just folded steel, cold and hollow. Brushing off the sudden change in how he felt about the sword, he attacked Ivan and drove him back using the speed of the light sword to his advantage.

Maybe that chill I felt was from the cool morning breeze, he thought. *The sword seems to be working fine.*

Natalia came in from the side, sweeping in broad strokes, while Anders continued to strike quickly at Ivan, keeping him pinned in the corner. Amid the distraction of Natalia's movement, Anders saw an opening on Ivan and took it. He was able to claim a crippling blow on Ivan, stabbing him in the kidney; yet he had let down his guard to Natalia, who took full advantage of the opportunity. Bringing her sword down in an arcing motion, she struck Anders between the neck and shoulder. His arm hummed with pain. His lack of anticipation of her attack infuriated Anders and he whipped his blade in a backhanded slash against Natalia. She dodged his retaliation and met him in kind, winding up as she bent away from his sword. As he slashed at her, Anders exposed himself, completely opening his front. Again, she took advantage, punching him squarely in the nose. He dropped his sword as he rocked back. His hand shot up to his face, feeling for his nose. Natalia held her sword at his throat, making sure he didn't continue his attack.

"You should've known better than to retaliate after a killing blow," she scolded.

Anders let his hand down and examined the blood covering his face, "I think you broke my nose," he said with a nasal whine.

"Why did you expose yourself in such a reckless way?" she asked, still holding her sword to Anders' throat.

He pinched his nostrils, blood dripping steadily from his hand, "I didn't let you do that. You got lucky while I was busy killing Ivan."

"No," she said adamantly. "We've done this exercise time and time again. Every time I've had the opportunity to strike you in that blind position, you've been able to block it. What was different this time?"

Anders continued to pinch his nose trying to get the blood to clot. He answered reluctantly, "I don't know. The sword, it felt different somehow, almost like it was empty."

"What do you mean?" Natalia lowered her sword, concern on her face.

Anders shrugged, "Just a few moments ago. The blade felt like it changed somehow. It usually feels a part of me, guiding me, but all of a sudden that connection broke," he glanced at the sword as it lay on the stone slab. "I suddenly realized it's just a piece of steel."

Natalia's expression changed to anger and she said, "You should be able to defend yourself during any distraction, emotional or physical."

"I'm sorry. I'll try harder," Anders said still holding his nostrils together. He glanced over to where Maija had been watching and noticed she was no longer sitting there.

He turned to Ivan, preparing to ask if he or Zahara knew where she'd gone when he noticed Ivan crouching low and slowly walking to the edge of a large boulder rising above the half-wall at the entrance to Hardstone. Zahara crawled, wings tucked tightly to her sides as she and Ivan stalked to the edge of the entryway.

Anders formed his connection with Zahara's mind, *What are you two doing?*

"*You need to see this for yourself,*" she replied. "*But move slowly and remain hidden.*"

Concerned, his heart suddenly raced, *Has Merglan left Southland and returned to Eastland?* He hoped he wasn't about to see Merglan and his dragon searching for them.

Anders dropped low and worked his way over to the others along the edge of the half wall behind the large rock. They peered over the ledge and down the slope. There he saw Maija walking down the boulder-strewn slope. Her hands splayed wide; she held them away from her body, seeming to display that she wasn't armed.

MAIJA HAD WATCHED INTENTLY as Anders battled with Ivan and her sister. The twang of steel hitting against steel was somewhat muffled by the protective barriers they placed on the edges of their blades. She enjoyed watching them spar. She paid close attention to the forms, stances and body language of swordplay.

Back in the Everlight Kingdom, Ivan would often watch with her, explaining what her sister was doing when instructing Anders with his sword. Maija asked questions, trying to absorb as much of what they were teaching Anders as possible. She'd even talked Ivan into showing her how to create mental barriers, preventing sorcerers from invading her mind. In the dwarf kingdom, however, she didn't want to bother them with her questions, not until they returned from this trip and everyone was a little less on edge.

So, she sat on a small stone wall, a wall built to keep the rocks from rolling down onto the city entrance, at least that's what it appeared to be. Suddenly Maija thought she heard something moving behind her. She turned, looking out at the field of boulders running down the length of the mountain slope beside the city doorway. She searched among the rocks for the source of the noise. A breeze wafted up, blowing her hair into her eyes and she turned back to watch the sparring session.

As Maija watched Anders move with expert precision, blocking and dodging Ivan and Natalia's blades, she noticed Zahara's eyes transfixed on her, unmoving as her bonded partner danced between swords. The dragon stared intently, gazing directly through the sparring match. Having the large predator watching her so earnestly made her feel a bit on edge. Suddenly she heard the same sound of something moving over the rocks. This time, she thought she could pinpoint where it came from. She whipped around more quickly than before, but as soon as she turned the sound stopped. Staring toward the general area where she was sure the noise came from, Maija waited several long breaths before turning her back to the rocky slope. Across the stone floor, she met Zahara's eyes once more. Maija suddenly became aware that Zahara could sense whatever she'd been hearing. Maija cocked her head and gave the dragon a questioning look. Zahara nodded, confirming her suspicion.

Did she just tell me to check it out? she thought.

Maija slowly spun on her seat, bringing her legs to the leeward side of the wall. Planting her feet on the slope, she stood, glancing back at Zahara while Anders continued to be consumed by the sparring. Zahara nodded, moving her muzzle forward, almost coaxing her to venture out. As she moved across the boulder field, she stopped, pausing mid-stride at the faint sound of rocks shifting under the weight of something heavy.

The movement didn't last, and she continued inching toward its location. Three more times she paused, pinpointing which of the large boulders scattered along the slope hid whatever was making the noise. Keeping her eyes fixed on its location, she advanced carefully through the rocks.

When she started pursuing the noise, she hadn't put much thought into what it could be, but as she approached the large boulder, her imagination began to wander. As she neared the boulder, the rock seemed to have grown since she first saw it. The possibilities of what a rock that size could hide combined with the shifting sounds of rocks caused her to pause.

What am I doing? she asked herself. *What if there's something dangerous lurking behind that boulder?* She began to panic and started to turn back. As she stepped away from the rock, she remembered the encouragement from Zahara.

No, she told herself turning to face the large rock. *I need to know.*

Taking several deep breaths and summoning her courage, Maija strode toward the rock. Suddenly she caught a glimpse of something red flickering out from the boulder's side, then retreating in a flash. Halting abruptly, she shook herself, *Was that... no, it couldn't be. But on the other hand, we are close to Nagano.*

Changing the angle at which she'd been approaching, Maija's eyes widened as she saw what rested behind the large boulder.

She watched in awe as a dragon's head emerged into full view. Its scales were streaked with shades of red. The colors on its face varied from a red so bright it almost seemed to glow like hot coals in a blazing fire, to a scarlet so dark it neared a lava black. She watched in wonder as the dragon stepped out from the boulder, revealing its entire body. Maija's brown eyes met the glowing eyes of the dragon. In a flash of heat overwhelming her body, she felt the dragon's mind probe into her consciousness. The fierceness with which its mind entered hers could've only come from something truly powerful, and she could do nothing to block it. Within seconds her mind was entirely enveloped by the dragon.

WHAT'S SHE DOING? Anders asked as he watched Maija standing arms splayed to the sides facing down a gigantic red dragon. He moved to hop the wall they were crouching behind and rush after her.

No, Anders, wait. She's not in any danger, Zahara replied quickly before Anders could act. *Let's just wait and see what happens,* she urged him.

Anders gritted his teeth, clenched his fists and sighed, *Fine, but as soon as she's in danger, I'm going after her.*

He watched in suspense as Maija stepped closer to the dragon. The red dragon was much larger than Zahara, which made Anders' stomach turn with anxiety. To his surprise, however, the large dragon acted hesitant in Maija's presence, like a squirrel when offered some nuts from a human hand.

The dragon's head rocked from side to side, eyeing Maija like it didn't know what to think of her. Anders thought the dragon would attack her, but it didn't. It moved closer and then backed away shyly as Maija stepped toward it. Maija slowed her gait, moving closer as the dragon stood still, letting her come within arm's reach. Anders watched in disbelief as she carefully raised her arm up, attempting to touch the dragon. Anders held his breath. Just as her hand came to rest on the dragon's snout, something startled the creature. The dragon reared back on its hind legs, snapping its jaws as it thrashed its head wildly in the air. Maija stumbled back in surprise. Anders leapt onto the wall sword in hand. The dragon opened its wings and jumped into the air, flying vigorously to get away.

Anders ran several steps along the wall and jumped onto Zahara's back, but Maija had already run the short distance up the hill, her elven legs giving her speed to move quickly to safety.

"What were you doing?" Ivan asked sternly, though he'd been watching patiently with the others.

"Yeah. You could've been killed. Have you no regard for your own safety?" Natalia pestered.

Seeing that the dragon wasn't going to attack and had frantically flown farther away from the mountain, Anders stepped down from Zahara. Only moments before Ivan and Natalia had watched in silence as Maija closed in on the dragon. Now they badgered her as though she'd done something wrong.

Before Maija could answer and Anders could defend her, both Ivan and Natalia went off on tangents about how dangerous it is to confront a wild dragon, especially in this political climate. As they scolded her, Anders became increasingly aware that Zahara held different emotions about the situation.

He reached out to her, *Zahara, you knew the dragon was down there the whole time, didn't you?*

She didn't respond, but Anders could sense how she felt. He knew she'd been aware of the dragon's presence.

Did you encourage her to confront the dragon? he asked more earnestly.

In a way, she replied.

Anders directed his attention to Maija once more, "What was it like?" he shouted over Ivan and Natalia's ranting.

They halted their lecturing and turned to face Anders, bewildered.

"It was," she began, then hesitated to find the right words, "like an uncontrollable urge to be seen; to be known. Up front, its mind felt like fire and anger, but gentle and curious underneath."

"You felt its mind?" Ivan asked in disbelief.

She nodded, "When I drew close it took over mine. I couldn't stop it from happening. It was so powerful."

"Do you remember what you were doing after it took over?" Natalia asked.

She shook her head, "I can only remember feeling its mind and an electric pulse of energy coursing through my veins. Then like that," she snapped her fingers, "I was back to me, standing there as it reared back."

Ivan raised an eyebrow at this and looked questioningly to Natalia. She nodded, and they didn't say anything further on the matter.

"It's nearly time for our meeting with the dwarfs," Ivan said, walking back toward the large stone doors. Natalia was quick to follow.

Anders lagged behind with Zahara and Maija.

"How did you know there was a dragon down there?"

Anders asked in a hushed tone as they walked back into the city.

She shrugged, "I didn't really know. I heard something moving down in the rocks and when I looked to Zahara, she gave me a nod, like it would be okay to check it out."

He paused for a moment, glancing at Zahara. "She knew the dragon didn't mean you any harm?"

Maija shrugged and Zahara snorted.

"Do you think it means anything?" he asked. "The way Ivan and Natalia suddenly stopped their lecturing and how they just watched, seemingly indifferent when it was happening, makes me wonder if they know something."

She opened her mouth, then hesitated, closing it until she could find the right words, "I'm not sure. I feel like I need to meet him again."

"So, it was a male?"

She nodded.

"Let me ask you. Do you feel like there's an uncontrollable urge to have that electrifying pulse again? The one you described when you touched it?"

"I touched it?"

"Yeah. You held out your hand and touched it on the muzzle. Then it spooked and took off."

"Wow, I had no idea," she said amazed. "But yeah, it was amazing. I want that feeling again."

Anders gave Zahara a sideways glance.

She nodded.

"You should try to find him again. Maybe after the meeting, or later tonight?" Anders suggested.

"Really?" Maija asked.

He nodded, "I felt that same thing when I touched Zahara for the first time."

Maija paused, thinking about what Anders said. "We'll see," she said finally.

WHEN THEY RETURNED to the inn, Anders put on his charcoal grey suit from the night before and joined Ivan and Natalia in the lobby. Maija followed them, but Anders could tell her mind was elsewhere, thinking about the dragon encounter. They made their way across the bustling city to the king and queen's castle. When they arrived, the dwarf guards led them past where they'd dined the night before and into a throne room.

The stone throne at the head of the room shared the same craftsmanship as the rest of the dwarf masonry. It was carved with intricate knots and symbols depicting the dwarfish culture. Carvings of a battle axe and war hammer formed the armrests. At its center, resting on the seat, was a regal crown, fit for any king or queen.

Near the center of the room, in line with the throne, stood a long rectangular table constructed in the same gothic style as the rest of the room. Its intricately carved dragon-claw legs rested solidly on the stone floor. Five dwarfs emerged from a side door in the far corner, their steps echoing loudly as they walked across the silent room.

King Remli led them as they approached the table. They took a seat at the table, Remli sitting at the head. The dwarf king's chair resembled a large war hammer for a backrest, representative to the king's namesake, Madhammer. To his left, Queen Joslina took a seat at Remli's side, her chair adorned with a scarlet red ruby, displaying her namesake. Following her to the left, farther down the table, sat Metlarm Brightstone of the royal protectorate. Beside him sat Baylynn Coinhart of the royal court, and lastly, Korvir Richvien, the dwarf's delegated ambassador and chief negotiator for their work with the elves.

Clearing his throat loudly, Remli rose from his seat. Ushering them in with his thick arm, "Please, honored guests, sit down so we may begin our discussion."

Ivan stepped forward and pulled out the chair closest to Remli's right. He took a seat, folding back his coattails before sitting down. Natalia and Anders followed, with Maija taking a seat farthest from Remli on the right. Zahara sat back on her haunches opposite the dwarf king.

As soon as she did so, Remli smiled and said with a laugh, "Today the mighty Zahara and I will head this discussion. What say you, dragon?"

Zahara tilted her head and spat a small lick of fire into the air above her head. Anders said in his most embarrassing mental tone, *Zahara, that wasn't polite.*

She replied, *Tell him this is how dragons begin a negotiation.*

Before Remli could make up his mind whether Zahara meant him harm with her spout of flame, Ivan spoke up, "That is a sign of respect among dragons. To show that they are willing to discuss the terms of a negotiation."

Remli let loose a deep laugh. To his left, the dwarfs Korvir, Baylynn and Metlarm joined in after a short silence. Queen Joslina smiled and folded her hands, setting them on the table in front of her.

Wiping a tear from the corner of his eye, Remli took several long breaths, sighing as he regained his composure. "Let's begin with why you're here," he said now gazing seriously at his guests, "King Asmond and his wife have continued to be unbearable to work with on trade agreements. In the past, our people have bickered and taken shots at one another, but never to the degree they've reached this time. The king in the forest demands too much for us to make our trades profitable."

Ivan replied, "To my knowledge, Asmond is willing to discuss prices of certain goods, but isn't willing to be robbed blind."

Remli scoffed, exhaling audibly, "Well, if that pompous prig thinks we'll be taking anything less than what he's paying now for our ores, he's barking mad. We're hardly breaking even as it is. This kingdom can't continue to give its precious metals away so cheaply."

"I understand that there are rates of inflation, but I've seen the letters myself; you are asking far more than the metals are worth at present. I don't see how you can tell us that you're hardly breaking even at these rates," Ivan said splaying his hands on the table.

Remli slammed his fists on the table, his face burning a deep red. His full cheeks shook as he prepared to begin a verbal assault, when Joslina grabbed his wrist, wrapping her fingers around it tightly. As she squeezed harder, Anders saw Remli's eyes glance toward her. The queen's expression remained stern; she raised an eyebrow at him, tilting slightly forward and giving him an unspoken warning to calm himself. The whites of Remli's knuckles flushed as he loosened his clenched fists, color returning to his skin. He took several more deep breaths, drawing in through his nostrils and exhaling through his mouth, eyes closed, trying to calm himself.

While he did this, Joslina took his place in the conversation, "What rates exactly are you referring to?" she asked Ivan, a hint of polite formality in her soothing tone.

"The price of steel, iron, copper and silver specifically," Ivan said opening his hand to Natalia, who placed a small bag onto the table. Opening its drawstrings and carefully removing a scroll of parchment, she unrolled the scroll and read aloud the written prices for the metals and silver.

Remli and Joslina each looked confused. They whispered to one another and then Remli straightened, "May I ask what you were paying for them a year ago?"

Natalia dug through the pouch, pulled out a second piece of parchment, and read the prices aloud. The rates were five times lower than the current demand.

"Baylynn," Remli said, leaning across the table, "bring me the registry of coin." Baylynn pushed back her seat and walked swiftly out of the room. Remli and the others sat stone-faced while she exited.

After several long moments of awkward silence, Metlarm was the first to speak, "How is it that the elves ask a king's ransom for silk and cloth, made from naturally replenishing resources, mind you, yet during these hard times, shouldn't they see to kindly lowering their prices?"

Natalia replied before Ivan could, "The price of our silk hasn't risen. On the contrary, it has lowered as the volume of resources continues to grow. We recognize that your resources have a limit and it's wise to re-forge any metal that's lost its purpose, but our prices have stayed consistent with the growth of our production, where yours have not."

"Why is it then, that you say one thing and your king demands another?" Metlarm posed.

"Why is it that your king says one thing and the letters we've received in his name say another?" Natalia replied in kind.

Remli raised his hands commanding a stop to their bickering, "We'll resolve this matter as soon as Baylynn returns with the registry of coin. The records account for what's been mined and the prices the ores are set at."

Anders watched the disgruntled faces of the dwarfs as they awaited Baylynn's return. He settled his gaze on Korvir Richvien, the dwarf responsible for dealings in trade with the elves. Anders fixed his eyes on the dwarf, wondering why he hadn't contributed to the conversation. The topic was, after all, his job. As he examined the dwarf, he saw the glistening of sweat beginning to form on his brow. His eyes darted between the corner of the room where Baylynn had left and the king, then back to the corner of the room again.

Zahara, Anders said to her, *do you find anything odd about Korvir?*

Which one is he again? she asked.

He's the one sitting across from me. I think he might be hiding something, Anders said.

With no subtlety or nuance whatsoever, Zahara turned her head to look at the dwarf sitting across from Anders. Anders could tell she was trying to read the dwarf's thoughts. Keeping her gaze on him, she said, *His mind is sealed off from me. He's had training in how to keep magical beings from reading his mind.*

Anders leaned back in his chair, turned toward Ivan and coughed, covering his mouth with a closed fist. As he did, Ivan gave him a disapproving look, but Anders widened his eyes and moved them to his right several times. Ivan furrowed his brow and said with his mind, *Just use your thoughts if you need to tell me something.*

I think Korvir is hiding something from us. Don't you think it's odd he hasn't said anything and he's the one in charge of negotiations with the elves?

Of course, he's hiding something. He's the one sabotaging Remli's relationship with the elves. We just need Remli to discover it on his own, which he's about to do once Baylynn returns. Just keep an eye on that sweaty dwarf and don't let him slip away from us when he tries to run.

Anders felt a little foolish in receiving Ivan's scorn. Brushing it off, he focused his gaze back on Korvir. The dwarf had one hand under the table when just a moment before both hands had been folded on top in the same way Joslina's were. Anders didn't like not being able to see what his hand was doing, especially now that he knew Remli was about to learn the truth of his ambassador's dealings.

Baylynn returned with a large book bound in thick leather. As she walked across the hall, Anders said to Zahara, *Korvir's going to try to run. Make sure he doesn't escape.*

Zahara shifted her weight, her thick corded muscles tensing under her scales.

Baylynn placed the registry of coin in front of Remli. She returned to her seat alongside Korvir and Joslina. Remli flipped through the large pages of the book. Landing on the page he'd been searching for, he ran his finger across the width of the page at several different elevations.

With deeply furrowed brow, Remli said in a low tone, "The prices of our goods have not changed over the last year. I delegate the management of such agreements with the elves to a trusted member of the court. That means the fault lies with Korvir." Remli stood from his chair, balled his fists and leaned on his knuckles as he gave Korvir a look of disdain. "Korvir, why do the elves believe we need five times more money than our records show?"

Korvir shifted uncomfortably in his seat. Anders kept his gaze fixed on his arm, still under the table.

The ambassador dwarf stuttered for a moment before saying, "P-p-pardon me, your majesty. The prices I wrote were what I'd been told to."

"Lies!" Remli shouted, slamming his fist on the table, his cheeks returning to deep red in anger. "Tell me the truth, or so help me, I'll beat seven shades of beard out of you."

Korvir's eyes darted from the king to Ivan, to Zahara, and back to the king again. "I... I... I."

"Out with it you, half-wit!" Remli bellowed in a furious rage.

"Ahh!" Korvir shouted as he leapt up from his chair and released something shiny from under the table in a flash, throwing it directly at Remli's head.

Anders had been ready for this and simultaneously released a burst of energy from his palm, deflecting the projectile and sending it flying over Remli's head, lodging itself deep into the top of Remli's chair nearly two feet over his head where he stood leaning over the table.

Remli looked up as the handle of the dagger Korvir had thrown at him wobbled, sticking out from the top of his backrest. "Catch him!" the dwarf king shouted, but both Anders and Zahara were already after the dwarf at the other end of the table.

Korvir tried to run to the left, but Zahara blocked him with her large body. He tried to hurry right, but Anders stood with his arms spread wide making his escape on their side of the table nearly impossible. Korvir turned around, but the four dwarfs had already trapped him. Accepting that he had no escape, Korvir reached into his pocket. Anders flung up his hands ready to deflect any object he might release. Instead of drawing a weapon, the dwarf pulled out something small. Anders couldn't even see what he was holding. Korvir quickly put it into his mouth and bit down, falling instantly to the floor.

"No!" Remli shouted, rushing to his side. Kneeling over

him, Remli slapped the dwarf in the face and shook him violently, shouting, "Who are you working for! Who put you up to this?!"

Anders saw the dwarf king's efforts were useless. Korvir's eyes had already rolled to the back of his head and a fizzing foam poured from his mouth, seeping out through his clenched teeth. The dwarf had poisoned himself.

Remli rose to his feet still hunched over the dead dwarf's body. Turning to his wife, he commanded, "Korvir's quarters are to be sealed off from anyone or anything until we've completed a thorough investigation of his personal items."

Joslina ran from the room and began shouting orders to the guards standing near the doors. Metlarm followed her. It was his duty as head of Remli's guard to see that no one disturbed the dwarf's chambers until they'd searched them.

"It would seem our negotiations were compromised," Remli said to Ivan. "Rest assured, we'll get to the bottom of this. Do you have any more of the letters Korvir sent to Asmond on my behalf?" he asked.

Natalia handed him the bag of scrolls she'd placed on the table, "All of the transcriptions since the tension between our people began are in this bag. If you don't mind, we'd like to observe the letters sent from our ambassador as well. If what Metlarm told us was true, more than one person is tampering with the negotiations between our people."

Remli nodded, "Of course. We shall go to Korvir's chambers at once and search for the letters." He turned to Anders, "Thank you for deflecting the dagger meant for my head. The kingdom of the dwarfs is in your debt." He turned back to Ivan and waved him along as he led them out of the throne room.

A dozen dwarf guards awaited them in the corridor outside the hall, armed and ready to escort the king. Anders recognized two of them as members of the royal protectorate; he'd met them at the dinner party the night before but couldn't recall their names.

Remli and the guards stormed through the castle and into a separate tower. Winding their way up a long flight of stairs, they came to a small round door. Metlarm was standing guard with his battle axe in hand. Putting his arm before they crowded his space, Metlarm said, "The door is locked. I've made sure no one has entered or exited. Please stand back." He wielded his axe and hacked several times at the round door. After the third swing of his mighty weapon, the door flung open. The guards marched in and cleared the room to make sure there wasn't any danger.

Remli and the other dwarfs tore through Korvir's personal items. They dumped out the contents of his desk and dressers. Several chests were in his closet but revealed nothing they were searching for. Finally, Metlarm called Remli over to a corner of the room, pointing to a space in the floor where he'd pulled up two loose bricks. Hidden within the space in the floor were dozens of scrolls, stuffed tightly into the hole.

Remli plucked one from the top and opened it, his eyes widening as he read. After several long moments of silence, he handed the scroll to Ivan, "You'll want to read this."

Ivan read the scroll and turned to face Anders, Natalia and Maija, "We need to inform Asmond right away."

"Of what? What does it say?" Anders asked.

Ivan's lips pursed, then he said, "Merglan's spy. It's the queen."

SIXTEEN

MERGLAN'S MOLE REVEALED

Ivan clutched the parchment in his hand. His face grim, he stared past his companions into the wall.

"What do you mean? It's the queen?" Anders asked, deeply concerned.

Ivan handed him the letter, which Anders read aloud:

K,

I hope this letter finds you well. I've reported the time and departure to our lord, Merglan. He and Killdoor will ride out to squash the riders who fly among our elven troops. If the battle goes in his favor, we will no longer have to hide our true allegiance. I'll force the will of my husband as king to see the greatness in the plan Merglan's set out for us all.

I was instructed to tell you that if the battle doesn't go in the favor of our lord, we are to escalate the quarrels between our people. We'll need to keep our kingdoms distracted while he conquers the nations of humans. Once back in his prominent position, our lord will take us into the fold and assimilate all who will follow his plan.

Keep up the good work,

Signed Merglan's humble servant, Lageena.

ANDERS RAISED his eyes in dismay, the parchment in his hand shaking.

"We need to inform Asmond as soon as possible," Ivan said. "Get back to your rooms and gather your bags; we leave at once."

"Wait," Natalia said. "Can't we just send word to him via the mirror?"

"No," Ivan replied quickly. "Last I saw of the pair's other half, Nadir had it. So, it's probably among his possessions with the guards or in the queen's possession. Besides, now that we know Merglan's got the queen spying for him, who knows how many others she's recruited. Anything said to the king via the mirror could be overheard by traitors' ears. No, using the mirror is too risky. We must deliver the news ourselves."

Remli butted in on their conversation, his voice commanding, "You were sent here to negotiate with us on the terms of our commerce. Seeing as how it was tampered with by two of our people's highest ambassadors, we must forgive the damage they've caused to our relationship. I offer my sincerest apologies to King Asmond. May his wife burn eternally for what she's done. If there's anything my people or I can do to help, don't hesitate to ask."

Ivan looked off to the corner of the room, an idea forming in his mind, "Actually, there is something you could do," he trailed off.

"Anything," Remli said, stepping forward.

"After we deal with the spy, Lageena," Ivan started, "we'll be launching an attack on Merglan's location in

Southland. We can't afford to let him take control of the human nations again. Our reports last placed him near Kingston. I expect he'll attack the capital soon. Meet us in two days' time where the mountains approach the sea. Bring as many able fighters as you can muster and sail with us to Southland. We're going to war."

Remli's face went as stone as the castle walls themselves. Slowly nodding he said, "I will bring a host of dwarfs to fight with you, Ivan. It will be like the days of old when we fought side-by-side among the goblin pits." He held out his hand and Ivan gripped it firmly, nodding in reply. "Go now. I'll see you in two days where the mountains meet the sea."

Ivan led Anders, Zahara, Maija and Natalia back across Hardstone and into the inn. He rushed them into their rooms, ordering them to gather their things quickly. Anders and Maija stuffed their clothes into their travel packs, not caring to pack them neatly.

"I can't believe it was Lageena this whole time," Maija said as she gripped one of the large saddlebags and held the door open for Anders.

Shaking his head in disbelief, Anders said "I know. It's hard to believe she could do such a thing to her own people. And lead everyone to think it was her own son. It's terrible!"

As they spoke, they dragged the large bags into the stairwell, where Natalia rushed to catch up with them. "Nadir isn't Lageena's son," she said as she came alongside the pair.

"What? Of course he is. He's the prince," Anders said, hoisting the saddlebag onto his shoulder and crossing the lobby.

"Yes, he's the prince because he's Asmond's son, but Nadir isn't the son of Lageena. Asmond was married once before

Lageena and he bore several children with his first queen. They were long dead, all but Nadir, by the time Maija and I were born, but my father would often tell stories about them."

"What happened to them?" Maija asked while helping ready Zahara's saddle outside the inn.

"One day Asmond found his wife dead in the throne room and all of his children except Nadir missing. It was tragic and the mystery went unsolved. Nothing in the known world can penetrate the elven city without granted access, not even Merglan and his dragon could do it," Natalia said as they lifted the saddle onto Zahara's back and began arranging the straps.

"Maybe it was Lageena?" Anders suggested.

Natalia shrugged, "I doubt it. She had no reason to. It was before all of this Merglan nonsense. Why would she do such a thing if she wasn't working with him?"

Anders nodded as he cinched the second saddlebag onto Zahara's saddle. He watched Ivan exit the inn, holding a piece of parchment in hand. "What's that?" he asked looking at the letter in Ivan's hand.

"It's word from the elves. Asmond requests our imme-diate return for the execution of Merglan's spy," he said coldly.

"How did they figure that out so quickly?" Anders asked.

"Not Lageena," Natalia said. "Nadir. They think he's the one who's been spying. While we were gone, Lageena must have faked evidence to convince the council to prove him guilty."

"All the more reason to return at once," Ivan said.

"Do you have the letters from Lageena to Korvir?" Anders asked.

Ivan patted his breast pocket, "Tucked safely against my chest."

They rushed through the dwarf city and up the steps to the great entrance hall. Exiting through the massive stone doors where hours before they'd been training, they emerged into the open air. Zahara crouched for Ivan and Anders to climb on. Anders made to get on her, but glanced at Maija, noticing she hadn't rushed out as her sister had. The look on her face was unlike anything he'd seen from her before. He knew something wasn't right. Stepping over to her, he took her gently by the hand and asked, "What's wrong?"

Tears welled in her eyes as she met Anders' gaze, "I'm not coming with you."

Anders stammered in surprise, "Wha, what are you talking about?" he said shaking his head and half smiling. The half-smile faded when he realized she was serious.

"I need to stay here," she said the quiver in her voice disappearing. She wiped the tears forming in her eyes and stood firmly at the entrance to Hardstone.

"Why?" Anders asked.

"The dragon is calling to me. I can feel its draw pulling at me even now as I stand here. If I leave now, with you, the opportunity to discover what could be will be lost. I may never find him again. I need to go to him before he's gone too far from here," she said looking directly into Anders' eyes.

Anders could hardly believe his ears, yet he understood what she meant.

"What's taking so long?" Ivan shouted. "Whatever it is, you can discuss it when we get back to Cedarbridge."

Anders smiled at Maija, knowing he wouldn't see her again for a long time. Because of his bond with Zahara, his duty was to Kartania and stopping Merglan from taking control of their world. He was the chosen one. Maija's fate lay in the hands of a dragon, roaming the wilds of Nagano. He knew she had to answer its call.

He pulled her in close and embraced her as he'd never done before. He held her tight as tears welled in his eyes, too. "I'll miss you," he whispered.

"I'll miss you more," she replied.

"Come on you two; someone's life is at stake here!" Ivan shouted.

When Anders pulled away from their embrace, tears flowed down Maija's face. Anders kissed her through their tears of separation. He pulled himself away from her soft lips, his beginning to quiver as he choked out a quiet, "Goodbye."

She held his hand until he climbed onto Zahara's saddle, tears streaming down her face.

Zahara rose from the ground, lifting Anders and Ivan high into the air. Anders looked back and saw the two elven sisters holding each other in a long embrace before Natalia turned and ran down the mountainside.

Anders rode in silence on Zahara's back, trying to hide his tears from Ivan. Zahara felt the emotional toll Maija's sudden departure had on him. She shielded his mind from Ivan, granting him the silence he needed.

After several long hours of flying, Anders began to feel more like himself again, though he already missed Maija greatly. The time they'd spent together, although brief, was some of the happiest of his life. Attempting to distract himself, Anders asked Ivan, "Do you think I'm ready to fight Merglan and his dragon?"

Anders was beginning to think Ivan hadn't heard him when the older sorcerer responded, "You have to be ready.

The time has come. There isn't anything more we can do to prepare."

"That doesn't mean I'm ready," he said.

"No. But you will have help from Natalia and me. Our strengths combined with the skills you've learned with that sword you carry will certainly be a match for Merglan and his dragon."

Hearing this gave him confidence when suddenly Anders recalled the entry he'd read in Merglan's diary. "I discovered something in Merglan's diary, something that wasn't there before," he said.

Ivan paused again before responding; Anders once again felt as though he was going unheard. He repeated more loudly over the rushing wind of flight, "I found something interesting in Merglan's diary."

"Is it about William?" Ivan asked.

Taken by surprise, Anders said, "No, it was a diagram. Why did you assume it was about William?"

"Oh, it's nothing, not important. So, what about this diagram? It wasn't there before?" Ivan asked steering the conversation away from his comment.

"Yeah, anyway I was reading through the journal again and while I was flipping through the pages, they suddenly went blank, except for one. It was a drawing."

"A drawing of a diagram?" Ivan asked.

"Of a crystal," Anders said.

Ivan paused, clearly mulling over the information before responding. "Was there anything written about it?" he asked.

"Yes," Anders continued. "Aside from the labeling, which I couldn't read because it was in a different language, there was a message written at the bottom of the page."

"What did it say?"

"It read like a warning, but spoke like the prophecy," he said.

"Did you happen to save this diagram?" Ivan asked.

"I thought it might disappear if I ripped the page out, so I drew it on one of the blanks in the back of the journal."

"Good. We'll take a look at it after we land," Ivan said.

After a time, Anders asked, "What was it that you were wondering about William?"

"It was nothing, forget I said anything about it," Ivan said quickly rejecting the attempt at a conversation.

Anders opened his mouth to ask him what he knew about him but thought it better to keep his thoughts to himself. When Maija, Kirsten and Thomas told him of the prophecy they'd heard Merglan speak of, the chosen one to defeat him was the son of a king. Anders didn't know who his father was, but he was beginning to think William fit the bill, and Ivan did speak very highly of his father. That would explain Merglan's hatred for him and desire to kill him, well that and the prophecy, of course.

ZAHARA FLEW until nightfall before they saw the lights of the elven city glowing in the forest. Landing softly in the grassy area outside the dragonrider training facility, Ivan hopped off.

"Why did we stop here again?" Anders asked, following Ivan as he rushed inside the building.

"I need to grab something I left behind. After we tell Asmond about his wife's betrayal, we may need to capture Lageena. If things really go south, we'll need to break Nadir out of his cell."

"After he sees the letter, I'm sure Asmond will at least

hold his wife in contempt until he digs deeper to reveal the truth," Anders said.

"We don't know how Asmond will react. And we don't know how deep this conspiracy goes. For all we know, Asmond is in on it as well," Ivan said as he reached the door to his room.

Pulling the door open, Ivan began to rummage through his personal items. Anders wasn't able to see what he grabbed, but Ivan hastily pocketed it. Turning to leave he said, "I got it. Let's go."

Anders hesitated for a half second before Ivan nodded toward the door. He led them back out into the hall and down the stairs. Exiting the building, Anders saw Natalia waiting with Zahara.

"What are we doing here?" she asked.

"Ivan needed to get something before we confront Lageena," Anders said, quickly unhooking the saddlebag straps on Zahara's saddle, freeing her from some of the awkward weight.

"There's something else we'll need to do before we go into Cedarbridge," Ivan said.

"What's that?" Anders asked.

"We'd better get some backup. Just in case." He moved close to Zahara and asked, "Can you call on your parents?"

Zahara nodded and took to the sky. Moments later she returned, her parents close behind. Once they'd landed, Ivan addressed the small group, "I've called on you because we're in an urgent situation. What we're about to do may be considered treason and the elves could turn on us. If we're going to ensure our way out of here, we'll need help. That's where you come in."

What exactly are you trying to tell us, human? Zahara's father said cautiously.

"While we were in Hardstone, we discovered some very revealing information."

In what way?

"King Asmond's wife, the queen, has been a spy for Merglan and was working to undermine his every move. She's betrayed him and everything we've been fighting for these long years. Tonight, we'll reveal her true identity to the king. He might not take this well, so we need to plan for the worst. I'm not sure how much control Lageena has over the king, but she could turn on us and we're not sure what she's fully capable of. I'm hoping you can spread the word to the other dragons here and back us up in case something goes wrong."

I have not stuck my snout into human or elf business before, but seeing as my only daughter is swept up in this fight, I'll back you up. For her sake. That is the only reason why I will agree to help you, Zahara's father said. *As for my mate, I cannot make this decision for her.*

Ivan's attention turned to Zahara's mother, "Will you do this for us?"

She looked at Zahara, then to her mate, *I'll spread the word to other dragons, and stand by to see if anything befalls my daughter. I'll not get involved directly until I need to. I'll protect my daughter with my life if need be, but I'll not help save you humans or elves.*

"That is more than I could have hoped. Thank you for everything you can do," Ivan said.

Together Zahara's parents took flight, soaring to spread the word of Ivan's plan.

Ivan motioned for Anders and Natalia to come close. "I expect Asmond doesn't know of our return and Lageena is likely unsuspecting of our knowledge of her transgressions. I'd like to keep it that way if at all possible. We'll go into the city. Once we've arrived at Asmond's home, Zahara," Ivan pointed at her. "You'll be our eyes on the outside. Make sure no one escapes from the home or enters without our approval."

Got it, she replied.

"Natalia, I'll want you posted at the door, block Lageena's escape. Anders, you'll be with me. Stand back slightly and spread out, we'll be more effective if anything happens with a wider spread. Keep your weapons at the ready but try not to seem too threatening. We can't afford for the queen to become wise to our plan until Asmond knows the truth. If at all possible, I'll try to show Asmond the letter without Lageena present. This may be difficult, however. Sound like a plan?" Ivan asked looking a bit wild-eyed.

They nodded in unison glancing at each other to confirm everyone was onboard.

"Alright," Ivan said, taking a deep breath. Exhaling, he said, "Let's do this."

Ivan and Anders climbed atop Zahara while Natalia started toward the cliff. Zahara ran down the field, spreading her large wings as she did so. Anders noticed she'd grown since they first came to the training facility. Zahara's body rippled with muscle, and her wingspan had more than doubled.

You flatter me, Zahara said as they took flight.

Laughing at himself for assuming Zahara wouldn't notice his examination of her, he said, *You've grown! I hadn't noticed it lately. We've been so busy, but you're looking fierce.* He felt a warming sensation rising within her. At first, Anders thought something might be wrong, but he quickly realized that she was blushing.

Soon Ivan and Anders were dropping down off

Zahara's back outside the King's tree house. This style of living once again seemed strange to Anders after spending time with the dwarfs. Natalia was quick to follow.

"We're all clear on how we're handling this?" Ivan clarified before going any further.

"Yes," they said in unison.

Ivan rounded the corner of the large cedar tree house. Two armed guards stood sentinel outside the door. Recognizing Ivan, the guards weren't hostile.

"Ivan," one of them said as he came near. "You're back from your trip to Hardstone. How did it go? I hope Remli wasn't too headstrong with his negotiations. That old codger can be quite stubborn sometimes."

Ivan smiled, somehow summoning a calm and friendly demeanor as if nothing were the matter. "Right you are, Ray. I almost forgot you've spent time in Hardstone. They went well. Better than expected, I would say."

"Well, that's about all you can hope for. I'm glad to hear the delegation went well. I'd hate to see our people fighting in this dark time."

"You and me both," Ivan said. "We'd like to speak with Asmond."

"No problem. Let me make sure he's ready for you. One moment please." Ray opened the door and leaned inside. He grabbed a mirror, much like the one Ivan had used to talk with Asmond when they were traveling to Eastland. Holding it up to his face, he spoke. "Hello, Asmond, are you there?"

For a moment the mirror remained as a reflection of Ray's tan face. Suddenly the glass began to shimmer, and the scene depicted on the reflection changed. King Asmond appeared, his top half displayed in royal blue silk. He reclined against quilted pillows nestled against a sprawling headboard at his back. "Yes, what is it?" the king asked.

"Ivan and the others have returned from Hardstone," Ray said, moving the mirror to show who waited at his front door. "They wish to speak with you," he said returning the mirror to his face.

"Ah, yes, send them in," Asmond said.

"Wait," they heard the queen's voice before Ray set the mirror down. "Give us a moment to prepare," she said.

Anders' heart raced. *Does she know that we've figured out her relationship with Merglan? Why else would she need to get ready, before we enter?*

Ivan turned and glanced at Anders and the others. He raised his eyebrow and turned back to the guards.

"One moment," Ray said holding his finger up to indicate they needed to stand by.

They'd been waiting nearly ten minutes and Anders was beginning to sweat when Asmond's voice sounded through the mirror. "Send them in."

Ray opened the door and stepped out of the way, letting them enter. The king and queen's house was regal, but not as fantastic as Anders had imagined it would be. Embroidered silks hung from the tree's walls. Each one depicted a scene of elven history. Beautifully crafted stained glass windows glowed with the light of the moon. Twin chandeliers hung in the large open room. Cashmere rugs on the polished wood floor brought warmth to the room. A set of stairs with delicately carved banisters led up to Asmond and Lageena's master bedroom.

"Wait here," Ray said and left the room, closing the door to the outside behind him.

Asmond and Lageena emerged from the second floor.

They glided down the steps. Asmond bore a broad smile across his face while Lageena remained stoic.

"Ivan," Asmond said as he stepped onto the main floor. "How was your trip? Do give me good news."

"Don't get your hopes up," Lageena said dismissively.

"Oh, pish posh," the king said waving a hand at her. "Don't mind her. She's been in a mood all afternoon. So...?"

Ivan glanced at Lageena who returned his look with a glare. "The negotiations went," he hesitated for a moment while the king held his breath. "Better than expected. There is, however, a matter which we should discuss in private."

"I knew I was right to count on you," the king said, waving a finger at him. "Whatever you want to talk about can be said with my wife present. I'll just end up telling her what you've told me. We don't hide anything from each other," he looked to his wife lovingly, "do we, darling?"

A look of forced enthusiasm crossed her face, "No. We don't."

Anders let a hand come to rest on his sword at his hip. He didn't know what the queen was capable of. He noticed Natalia had positioned herself directly in front of the door and stood legs splayed, ready for action. To his surprise, the queen turned her attention to Anders when he let his hand come to rest on the hilt of Lazuran.

Eying him suspiciously, she said, "Why do you come so heavily armed into our home?"

The king seemed taken aback by her comment. "What do you mean? These people just traveled from Hardstone. Need I remind you we are at war with Merglan? He could have a host of enemies set upon them nearly anywhere from the outer edges of the forest to Eastland."

The queen remained unconvinced as Anders put his

hand back to his side, regretting his preemptive motion. "But there is no threat here; Merglan can't spread his reach within our city. Our magic forbids it, so I ask again. Why come so heavily armed into our home?"

The king shook his head, "Fine," he motioned for them to give up their weapons. "Take your swords off and hand them to the guards."

"Is that really necessary?" Ivan asked. "This matter I wish to speak with you about is urgent and will only take a moment."

"You will do as the king commands," Lageena said before Asmond had a chance to reply.

Sighing deeply, he muttered, "Damn her sometimes. Well you'd better do as she says, or I'll be in for it."

To Anders' surprise, Ivan began to untie the belt holding his scabbard. He nodded to the other to do the same. Hesitating, Anders did as Ivan and took off his sword. Ivan walked them to the door. Opening it, he handed their swords to Ray, who took them and closed the door.

"There," he said, looking to Lageena. "Asmond, can we talk now?"

"Out with it then. Like I said before, whatever you say to me, you can say to her."

Hesitating, Ivan said, "I really wish to convey this information to you in private."

"Nonsense, Ivan. Let's hear it."

Ivan swayed awkwardly trying to find the words to begin. "I... we, discovered something disturbing while at Hardstone. Something about why the negotiations had soured between your peoples."

"What is it?" Asmond said this time with concern.

Lageena remained calm as Ivan continued, "As we began discussing how things had gone wrong with the trade agreements, the dwarf ambassador to the elves attempted to kill Remli. After we captured him, he poisoned himself, leaving us wondering why he'd intentionally radically increased prices without King Remli's knowledge or permission."

"He must have been betraying the king to make money on the side. Typical dwarfish backstabbing," Lageena said. "Well, I'm glad you were able to cut this trouble off at the source and put an end to our squabbling."

"Does that mean Nadir is innocent?" Asmond asked.

"I'd bet he had an equal hand in this as much as Korvir," she said.

"I never identified the dwarf," Ivan said, emphasizing that he hadn't mentioned Korvir's name.

Asmond eyed his wife with suspicion for the first time, "What do you think; I'm stupid? I'm aware of who is communicating with our people." The king seemed satisfied with the answer she gave and returned to look at Ivan.

"You may know who's communicating with the elves, Lageena, but your husband does not," Ivan stated.

"What do you mean? I know who Korvir was?" Asmond said.

"I'm not referring to Korvir, your majesty," Ivan said. "After an examination of Korvir's quarters, we discovered letters."

"What kind of letters?" Asmond asked intrigued.

"Dangerous and revealing," Ivan said as he turned his gaze on Lageena. She began to fidget.

Asmond followed Ivan's steady gaze. Upon realizing what Ivan was suggesting, Asmond said in protest, "You mean to tell me that my wife is responsible for the trade agreements going sour and jeopardizing our relations with the dwarfs? How dare you accuse the queen with such slander!" he shouted. "You'd better have some explanation for this or I'll throw you in the cells to rot!"

"I knew there was a reason why they arrived so heavily armed," Lageena nearly snarled.

"This is nonsense! Guards!" Asmond shouted.

As Ray and the other guard came through the door, Ivan pulled the letter from his breast pocket brandishing it like a weapon. "I have proof, written in her hand," he pointed the parchment at the queen. "She's been working with Merglan to undermine our every move. She was the one who made our march on Merglan's fortress known to him. She's been spying for him this whole time!"

Both guards stopped dead in their tracks, staring at the queen. Asmond struggled to find the words to speak. He stared at his wife then back to Ivan who came to his side with the letter.

"Before you arrest us, read it!" he said, thrusting the parchment at the king.

As Asmond's eyes scanned the letter, a look crossed his face that showed he knew what Ivan was telling him to be true. Meanwhile, the queen, now uncovered as a traitor, rushed up the stairs. Before anyone could react, the king was hot on her heels. Ivan and Anders followed. Much slower to reach the master bedroom than the elves, they arrived just in time to witness the queen slinking through the curtained window.

"Stop her!" Ivan shouted to Asmond, who stood with his back to them, watching his wife escape. "Asmond, don't let her get away!"

The elf king slumped to his knees, falling back against the floor, a dagger protruding from his chest. Natalia and the guards pushed past them to the king's side.

"Where'd she go?" Natalia asked, seeing the king's body on the floor.

Ivan pointed to the window and Natalia leapt out in pursuit. Ivan and Anders knelt at Asmond's side as he took his last breath. Pure disbelief crossed his face as he met his end. The elf king was dead, and the queen had vanished.

SEVENTEEN

T he early afternoon sun slid slightly from its highest point in the sky, heating the air and causing beads of sweat to run down Kirsten and Thomas' faces as they jogged into their childhood home. They quickly searched the house for signs of Britt, Max, or Bo, but didn't find anything suggesting they'd returned from their search. Grabbing several strips of jerky and a half loaf of bread, Thomas stuffed the food into a pack before following his sister back out the front door. He found Kirsten searching the ground for signs of the direction in which Max, Bo and Britt had set out earlier that morning.

Thomas called to her, remembering that Britt had said she was going to continue working her way around the eastern border of the barrier. Turning east, Thomas led his sister beyond the edge of their property and into the Grandwood forest. They'd been hiking uphill for nearly a half-hour when they slammed into the invisible barrier, wincing as they bounced off the solid wall.

"Ouch," Thomas said rubbing his nose to see if it was bleeding.

Kirsten massaged a reddening spot on her forehead. "Ahh," she grunted in frustration. "I knew that was going to happen. Come on, let's head farther east," she said as Thomas continued to check his nose, sure that blood was going to start dripping out of his nostrils from the blow.

He wiped his nose one more time, at last satisfied with the clean result, and began searching the forest floor for signs of their companions. "Here," he said after a few minutes, pointing to a patch of newly trampled grass. "It looks like they've been here recently."

Kirsten flattened her hand on the smooth surface of the barrier and began to walk, not trusting that she wouldn't smash into it again unless she knew where it was the whole time. As they moved through the forest, she noticed tree branches cut cleanly, scattered along the edge of the barrier. Each downed log they'd seen along the strange barrier was cleaved neatly as though it had been sliced with a sharp blade.

"It's like someone placed a dome over our city," Kirsten said looking at another cleanly cut tree branch.

"Yeah. You wouldn't want to have been standing here when that happened," he joked.

Suddenly Kirsten thought she heard a noise. Stopping abruptly, she motioned for Thomas to do the same. "Did you hear that?"

Thomas shook his head, "No, hear what?"

"It was like a," she began to say, then the hissing noise sounded again, louder than before, 'Pssst.'

Thomas looked to Kirsten quizzically, "Oh, you mean that noise. It sounded like someone saying, 'pssst'."

Kirsten scanned the group of trees where she believed the strange noise originated. She nearly shouted when she saw Britt's dark arms sticking out from behind the trees, waving them down. Kirsten struck Thomas on the shoulder and said, "Look over there!" She pointed to Britt waving.

"Why doesn't she just come to us?" Thomas asked as he waved back.

He opened his mouth and inhaled preparing to shout at her. Acting quickly, Kirsten tackled him onto the forest floor, placing her hand tightly over his mouth. As he started to wriggle to get free, she brought her finger to her lips and bulged her eyes at him, indicating for him to keep silent. She released her grip when she could tell he was taking her seriously.

Thomas rolled onto his stomach and looked around the edge of the bush in front of his face. Two large kurr, clad in plated battle armor walked in from beyond the barrier and made their way downhill toward Grandwood. The two beastly creatures hammered the ground with their large feet as they jogged by. Luckily they had failed to notice the humans hiding in the bushes.

As soon as they were out of earshot, Thomas whispered to Kirsten, "That's why she wasn't shouting at us."

Kirsten slapped him on the shoulder, shaking her head at the poorly timed joke. "You're starting to sound like Max," she said as she shuffled on her hands and knees over to Britt's hiding place. Thomas was quick to follow. Max and Bo huddled together, tucked out of sight in the bushes next to Britt.

"I thought you two were going to be seen for sure," Britt said softly.

"Yeah, that was close. Good thing we didn't call you guys out," Kirsten said pointing her thumb over her shoulder.

"I was not expecting that," Thomas shrugged.

Britt lifted her finger to her lips, shushing them both, "Keep your voices down," she whispered.

"What are those things doing here anyway?" Kirsten asked in a hushed tone.

Britt shrugged, "There've been close to a dozen that have walked in just before you showed up. The two you saw were stragglers; I'm guessing."

"They must've been sent to Westland by Merglan to support Rankstine in Grandwood," Thomas suggested.

"What are you guys doing out here?" Max asked. "I thought you were going to spy on Rankstine."

Kirsten bobbed her head, "Oh, we did."

"But we might have been seen," Thomas cringed.

"When we got to town some guards came and escorted Billson away," Kirsten began to explain.

"The guy who talked with us the other day," Thomas added.

"Right, anyway they said the governor wanted to see him, so we followed them to the church. They took him inside through a side door. It was locked so we had to sneak in."

"Through the bell tower," Thomas interrupted again, nodding excitedly.

Britt raised her eyebrows, "Impressive."

Kirsten smirked, "An old trick. Anyway, they took Billson into a small room. To get a closer look, I leaned over to peek through the crack in the top of the door."

"That's when her necklace fell off," Thomas interrupted again.

"Right, that's when my necklace fell off," she said slightly annoyed by Thomas' interruptions.

"You wear a necklace?" Bo asked, questioning why he hadn't noticed it before.

"Well, not usually, but I found it in my mother's things last night and it was so beautiful, I wanted to wear it. I didn't know it was going to slide off."

"So, they found out you were spying on him?" Britt asked.

"Yes. Well, no," Kirsten trailed off.

"Which one is it, yes or no?" Britt asked irritated by Kirsten's confusion.

"So, right before the necklace slid off my head, I saw Rankstine standing in front of Billson. The strange thing was Rankstine had this orb. It was held in a sort of stand next to him," she said.

"An orb?" Max asked. "Were they using it to do something to Billson?"

"No," Kirsten continued, "I'm not sure what they were doing to Billson, but it didn't sound nice. But inside the orb was an exact replica of Grandwood, an alive replica complete with townspeople walking about inside it."

"That must be how he's trapping us in," Britt said.

Kirsten snapped her fingers and said, "That's what Thomas and I thought, too. I caught a glimpse of Highborn Bay before he moved and blocked my view."

"How long ago did that happen?" Britt asked.

"Just over an hour and a half, maybe two?" Kirsten said shrugging, looking to Thomas who nodded in agreement.

"Did you see any of us near the house?" Britt asked.

"Well, no. But that's because you guys weren't there, right?"

A smile slowly spread across Britt's face.

"Why are you smiling?" Thomas asked.

"We did return to the house for lunch. We were there for over an hour before coming here. We only arrived here maybe fifteen minutes before you two."

"So, the orb's powers don't recognize us?" Max suggested.

Kirsten nodded, "Or the orb's control diminishes the farther away you are from it?"

"So Rankstine doesn't know we can see the kurr coming into the bubble?" Bo asked.

Kirsten shook her head, "Probably not. But he might have seen us leaving the church," she said with a cringe.

"Hmmm," Max said. "That's not good."

"Wait a second," Thomas said. "If Rankstine's using the orb to create this barrier, and it's working pretty strongly, why would his powers diminish outside the city?"

Kirsten shrugged, "Maybe the orb's only designed for one task and he's exceeding its limits? How else can you explain the man who followed Bo and turned around halfway, seemingly confused?"

"That's true. Well, however it works, it's beyond my comprehension. I just hope you're right that he can't see us or influence us in the way he's been managing the townspeople," Thomas said.

"Either way, Rankstine's probably sending his guards out to the house right now to look for us," Kirsten said.

"And when he doesn't find you there, he'll post scouts to watch the place until we return," Britt said.

"You think he'll do that?" Kirsten asked.

"I would if I were him," Britt said.

"Shoot," Kirsten said. "I was afraid of that."

"What if we wait until dark and find the guards or guard left behind to watch the place, then take him out ourselves?" Bo suggested.

Britt's eyes searched the ground, thinking that option over for a moment. "You know, that might be a good idea."

"Really?" Bo said, straightening up and smiling at Kirsten.

"Yeah, I don't want to sleep outside any more than the rest of you. If we can locate the guard before he can find us, Rankstine won't be able to tell if his guard is still watching the place or tied up in a chair in your house," Britt said. "We might even be able to get some information out of him."

"This is all assuming the orb's use for observing people ends just outside town and that there's only one guard," Max said. "What if there are multiple guards or he can see us. What if he sends a kurr to do the guarding?"

"We can handle his men," Britt said confidently. "The kurr on the other hand..." she trailed off. "We can reassess later if that is the case."

"Sounds good to me," Kirsten said, Thomas and Bo nodding in agreement.

Britt turned to Max.

"I'm not one to turn down a challenge," he said shortly. "What are we waiting for? Let's get going."

Together the five ran quietly through the woods toward the farm. Nearing the point where they'd have to begin their descent down the forested hillside behind the house, Britt slowed her pace and then stopped, waving at them to gather round.

"Since we don't have a good way to communicate, we have a few things to consider," Britt said. "If we stay together as a group, we'll all know what happens once we're down there searching for Rankstine's spy, but we'll be a larger target and surely make more noise. If we split up, we'll be able to cover more ground quickly and quietly, but we'll need to rendezvous back here to discuss what we've found. What sounds best to you?" she asked.

"I vote we split up," Max said, then looked to the others.

"Yeah, that makes the most sense to me," Thomas agreed.

Bo nodded in agreement.

"I guess we're splitting up," Kirsten said.

"Okay. Max, you and I will sweep the road and the entrance to the farm, which will cover the southern perimeter. Kirsten and Bo, you two take the east side of the property bordering the woods. Thomas, you take the northern side. It's less likely there'll be anyone lurking that way because the most-used access points to the farm are accessible from the south and east, but keep your head on a swivel. We'll meet back here in one hour," she looked to each in the group and everyone nodded.

Without another word, Britt and Max split off down the slope toward the roadside. Thomas wished his sister and Bo good luck and then ran alongside the slope before descending toward the north side of the farm.

"After you," Bo said, extending his arm out in front of them.

"Very kind of you. Really," Kirsten said sarcastically as she walked past him.

Bo chuckled and followed closely behind. They slowed when Kirsten recognized they were nearing the forest's edge. Stopping behind a large tree, she said, "If someone's watching the house, they'll definitely be hiding along the edge of the forest."

"I agree," Bo said.

"Let's get a little closer and then begin to search the edge, skirting around to the right, then back this way again. If we don't see anything along the edge, then we'll take a closer look."

"Let's do it," Bo agreed, following Kirsten as they crept closer to the end of tree cover and toward the meadow.

They searched through the trees working north along the eastern slope behind the property. Not seeing anyone or anything unusual at the far end of the woods behind the house, they reversed direction. Kirsten and Bo back-tracked their way across the hill. Keeping their eyes peeled for anything strange, they stalked slowly through the trees. The afternoon sun had dropped lower and the shadows among the trees had grown longer. Kirsten kept thinking she saw something moving, but upon closer examination found it wasn't anything of note.

Bo suddenly dropped down, crouching behind a tree. He started to wave to Kirsten, but she'd reacted nearly simultaneously and was already backed up against a tree. Bo put his fingers to his eyes and then pointed in the direction they'd been heading. Kirsten nodded holding up one finger to indicate she'd only seen one person.

Bo nodded and mouthed, "Only one," holding up one finger as well.

Kirsten slowly peeked around the tree toward Rankstine's guard. In the long afternoon shadows of the forest, she watched as the man stepped in and out of the strips of light, illuminated from time to time. He was looking downhill toward the quiet farm. He crept to the edge of the forest; just as Kirsten would've suspected someone would do if they were spying on their house.

Comfortable that the guard was far enough away to allow them to move without being heard, Kirsten stepped out from behind the tree. Quickly and carefully she strode over to Bo.

"It looks like he's found his hiding place," Kirsten said as she knelt beside him.

Bo nodded, "What do you want to do?"

"You think we should take him out now?" Kirsten asked.

Bo shrugged, "If we leave to meet back with the others and he moves to a different location, we'll have missed our chance."

Kirsten looked around for something to use as a weapon. Finding a large stick at the base of a tree she said, "We'd better take care of it while we've got our eyes on him." She bent down and picked up the club-like stick, gripping it firmly in her hand.

"One sec," Bo said while searching for a stout stick of his own. Finding one below a neighboring tree, he picked it up and nodded, "Okay, now I'm ready."

Together they prowled through the forest, creeping toward the spy. Kirsten tried to stay hidden in the trees' long shadows, in case the man turned around while they were still too far away to catch him. Making sure to avoid anything that might snap under her weight, she drew ever closer to the unsuspecting man.

Coming within striking distance, she raised the club high above her head. She glanced to Bo at her side, his stick at the ready just in case Kirsten's blow didn't knock the man unconscious. Gripping the club tightly, she let out a 'humph' noise as she brought her weapon down toward the spy's head. Hearing the noise, the man turned, but he was too slow to avoid the blow. Kirsten thumped him hard on the top of the head and he toppled over, unconscious.

Kirsten looked back to Bo, her mouth open at what she'd done. "It worked," she said surprised.

"Yeah, it did," Bo said smiling. "Come on, let's tie him up with something."

"Crap," Kirsten said. "I didn't think about what we were going to do once he was out. I don't have any rope."

"Me either," Bo said. "Let's search his pockets. He might have something on him."

"Good idea," Kirsten said. She bent down and prodded the man's shoulder, making sure he wasn't going to suddenly move, then removed his sword from its sheath. "We could use his belt?" Kirsten suggested, pointing to it after she'd removed the sword.

"Perfect," Bo said and helped her remove the man's belt.

They quickly searched the rest of his pockets for anything else that might be useful in tying him up. Kirsten found a small balled up piece of cord about five feet long. Showing it to Bo she said, "I bet he was planning to use this on us."

Bo cringed. They used the sword to cut the cord into several pieces. Rolling him over onto his stomach, they tied his hands and feet, then strung them together so that if he woke up, he wouldn't be able to move.

"That ought to do it," Bo said taking a step back to admire their work.

"Just one more thing," Kirsten said, removing the man's handkerchief from his pocket and stuffing it securely into this mouth yet being careful to make sure he could breathe. "Now he won't shout if he wakes up," she said.

Bo smiled. They left the man propped up against a tree and made their way back up the hill toward the designated meeting place. They were the first to arrive. Still shaking with adrenaline from the capture, Bo asked, "Do you think it was okay to leave that guy all tied up like that?"

Kirsten looked at him, concern flooding her face, "Maybe we should've brought him with us?"

"Yeah, what if he wakes up and has some way to call to Rankstine?"

"We'd better go back and get him."

They walked the short distance back down to the location just outside the house where they'd left the man tied up. Kirsten sighed with relief upon seeing him still unconscious and bound in the same position. The limp man felt surprisingly heavy as they heaved him up the hill. She didn't think he was unusually large, but the bottom half of his body was nearly too heavy for her to carry. Kirsten had to set his legs down several times on the short way up the hill. Bo gripped the man under the armpits and seemed to welcome the short breaks, breathing deeply as they stopped to rest.

Britt and Max were waiting for them when they neared the meeting area. Rushing down, they helped Bo and Kirsten carry the man the last bit.

"What happened?" Max asked.

"We found him crouching just inside the tree line by the house," Bo began. "Thought it would be safer if we took care of him then while we knew where he was."

"We were just supposed to observe. Now Rankstine's going to know one of his men didn't come back," Max said disapprovingly.

"That's not entirely true," Britt countered.

"How do you know he wasn't the only one?" Kirsten asked. "Did you see anyone else?"

Britt and Max both shook their heads.

"If he was the only one out here spying on us, and Rankstine really can't see where we are on his little magic map, then Rankstine might just think he's still out here doing his job," Britt said.

"Where's Thomas?" Kirsten asked.

"Haven't seen him yet," Max said.

"You two were first to return since we've been here," Britt added.

"Maybe he went out a little farther than the rest of us," Bo said, trying to comfort her. "He'll be here soon."

Kirsten nodded, "Yeah, he's probably just taking longer than the rest of us."

"So what are we going to do with this guy?" Max asked.

Kirsten and Bo shrugged, "Find out more about the situation in Grandwood when he wakes up?"

"We could get some information about Rankstine and why the kurr have come," Britt said.

"Hey, is that a two-way door? Where we saw the kurr entering the wall?" Kirsten asked.

"I believe it's a one-way kind of set-up," Britt said. "I ran my hand by the spot where they came through just before we saw them walk in."

Kirsten kicked at the ground with her boot. "Maybe this guy will know something about it," she said.

They waited until nightfall for Thomas to return, but he never arrived. Kirsten was the first to offer a suggestion, "Maybe there were more guards out there and Thomas was captured?"

"Or he could've gotten lost?" Britt half-asked.

Kirsten shook her head, "No way, my brother and I have spent our whole lives playing in the woods around the house. He wouldn't get lost so close to home."

"We'd better go check to see if he's still in the area or if he's gone. He should've been back by now," Max said.

Britt, Max, Bo and Kirsten all took a limb of the man who remained unconscious on the ground next to them.

"How hard did you hit this guy?" Max asked as they carried him through the darkened woods.

"Maybe too hard," Kirsten replied looking at the man who still flopped in their arms.

Reaching the tree line before the farm, Britt said, "We'll sneak him down to the barn, drop him off, then go searching for Thomas together."

Nodding, they scanned the area for signs of movement. After determining that it was safe to continue, they carried the man through the dark to the barn. Kirsten slunk around to the door and pulled it open. They tossed the man inside and locked the door behind them. Searching around and not seeing any sign of movement in the trees, they headed back toward the woods.

Once in the cover of the forest, Britt asked Kirsten, "Where did you last see your brother?"

"We split off from him back here, where we began to search the east side of the farm. He was going to look around to the north," she pointed.

"We'll follow you," Britt said.

Kirsten led them around to the side of the farm where Thomas was going to be searching for Rankstine's potential spies. "We should fan out here," she said.

They settled on a grid arrangement, searching through the darkened forest. No one dared call for Thomas in case any guards remained in the area. They searched throughout the north side of the farm and woods, not finding any sign of Thomas. Kirsten, at last, heard a loud whistle and ran toward it.

Britt knelt in the dirt and waved them over. Pointing to the ground in front of her, she said, "Look, footprints."

Kirsten strained her eyes to see through the dark, but as she focused on the patch of bare ground, she saw the outline of several boots scuffing the dirt. "How did you see that?" she asked Britt.

"Freshly broken branches on the ground, disturbed duff, matted down grass," she said examining the greater area.

Once Britt pointed out these notable differences, she could see them through the darkness, but how she found them in the first place impressed Kirsten. It was hard to tell which way they were headed because they seemed to have been standing in all directions. "It's got to be Rankstine's men," she said.

Britt and the others nodded, "They must've gotten him first," Britt said.

"Either that or he took off running and is still hiding in the woods somewhere?" Max suggested.

"Maybe," Britt said. "If so, he'll come back tonight. If he's not back by dawn, we'll know he's probably been taken by them."

"Let's go back to the house," Kirsten said. "If there are any more guards, we can use the one we've got as a bargaining chip. If there aren't any and Thomas is still out here, he'll know it's safe to come to the house if the lights are on, at least safe enough to investigate who's there."

The four made their way back to the farmhouse. Kirsten went inside to gather some lanterns and start a fire while Bo, Max and Britt went to the barn to wait for the spy to awaken.

Max opened the door to the barn. Britt entered first reaching down to grab hold of the man's constraints and drag him outside. She halted when the man wasn't laying where they'd left him. She looked up and peered into the darkness of the barn. At first, she couldn't see very far.

"What's up?" Max said peeking over her shoulder.

Britt turned, "We left him right here, right?" She pointed to the ground next to the door.

Max opened his mouth to respond but then lunged forward through the door when he saw the silhouette of someone advancing toward Britt with his hands holding something high above his head. Max plowed through the door, knocking Britt out of the way with his right arm and reaching up to stop the downward swing of the assailant with his left. Grabbing the assailant's arms, still bound together, Max blocked the downward swing and tackled the man to the ground.

Britt was so surprised by the sudden action she stood in awe at the sudden commotion. Bo saw Max dive into the barn and instinctively followed him, pouncing on the man just after Max tackled him to the ground.

The guard's hands were still bound together, but he'd managed to get them in front of his body. The cord binding his legs had been cut and he must have heard them approaching the barn door before hiding in the shadows. Max and Bo wrestled the man to the ground. They struggled to hold him still when Britt finally came to her senses and helped them.

Once again, they tied his legs together and moved his arms behind his body. This time they made sure the arm and leg restraints were bound tightly together so he couldn't move his arms in front of his body. Max and Bo gripped his arms firmly behind his back, forcing him to obey their commands and sit still.

Kirsten came out to the barn to see what was taking them so long. Carrying a lit lantern, she discovered what events had transpired. A pipe lay on the ground near the door. The dirt of the barn floor was scuffed and their prisoner sat bloodied and dirty in a chair, lashed by the arms and feet. Max was holding the man still while Bo and Britt tied him to a chair they'd found in the corner of the barn.

"So this is what you've been up to?" Kirsten said.

"Our captive almost made a run for it," Max said through gritted teeth.

"Yeah, he nearly knocked Britt out with that pipe there," Bo said, tying the last knot to secure the man tightly to the chair.

"Now that he's awake, we can question him," Britt said running a hand over her thick, curly black hair.

CHAPTER
EIGHTEEN
BARRIER BREACH

Kirsten watched as the spy sent by Rankstine squirmed violently against his restraints. This time the cords held him firmly in place, locking him down to the chair in the barn.

"You going to talk to us?" Max asked darkly while raising the man's chin with his index finger.

The guard responded with muffled shouts, trying to speak through the rag stuffed in his mouth.

"What's that? I can't hear you?" Max said pulling the gag from the man's jaws.

"Just wait until the governor hears about this. You'll be hanged for kidnapping," the man spat at Max.

Max raised his hand, balled it into a fist, and was about to bring it down on their prisoner's face when Kirsten shouted, "Wait!"

Max half hopped forward to stop his momentum from carrying the punch all the way through. Everyone looked at Kirsten in confusion. They saw this man as an extension of Rankstine and wondered what reason she could possibly have to stop Max from striking him.

Shaking his head furiously, Max said, "What?!"

"Come here for a second. All of you," she motioned her group to the barn door and stepped out into the cool night air.

Once they'd circled in closely, Kirsten looked at each of them individually as she spoke, "I don't know how many people you've tried to beat into talking in the past, but from what I've heard, the men loyal to Merglan are trained to take a dagger to the gut before talking. We could beat at him all night and he probably wouldn't tell us what we need to know."

"What do you suggest we do then?" Max asked.

Kirsten held her breath for a moment waiting for anyone else to make a suggestion. When no one spoke up, she said, "I'm assuming he thinks like an average soldier."

"What's that got to do with it?" Bo asked.

"My father didn't talk much about his time in the war, but he sometimes spoke about the people he trained and worked with. He mentioned they were trained to follow orders and remain focused on their mission objectives. This guy is probably concentrating on what not to tell us, as he was most likely trained to do in this kind of scenario. If we could distract him in some way we might be able to trick him into telling us what we need to know," she said, now getting excited.

"How exactly are we going to do that?" Bo asked.

Pointing at Kirsten, Britt turned to Bo and said, "I think she's onto something. All we need to do is make him think we know more than we do. He might slip up and correct us on something, giving us the information we need."

"And I'd wager that you don't have to be a genius to

join up with Rankstine. He could be simpler than most soldiers, if he came from rural Westland," Kirsten added.

"Okay, so what is it that we need to know more about?" Max said, getting on board with the plan.

"When Thomas and I were spying on Rankstine, we saw the orb. We don't know exactly how it works, but maybe he does," she said, pointing her thumb in the direction of the barn door beside her. "We also know that kurr are walking in through a secret door in the bubble shield, but we don't know what he's planning to do with them."

"And if there's a way to escape the bubble," Bo chimed in enthusiastically.

Kirsten nodded, "Good, what else?"

"Oh, how Rankstine seems to have some kind of manipulative mind control over the townsfolk, making them build his wall," Max said.

"Great. Let's try to let him think we already know exactly what Rankstine's plans are. Maybe he'll give us clues or hints that will allow us to piece together what we need to know," Kirsten said.

Britt, Max and Bo nodded as they pulled the barn door open. Kirsten held the lantern up near her face as they entered the room. The guard eyed them warily as they formed a half circle around him.

"You can beat me all you want, I'm not telling you nothing," the guard stated firmly.

"You don't really need to tell us anything," Kirsten replied in a knowing tone. "We already know everything."

"Impossible," the guard spat.

"You're a smart person, aren't you?" Kirsten said, kneeling to meet his gaze. "You'd have to be in order to be granted such a prestigious role, to guard an important person like Rankstine."

The man raised an eyebrow and said, "Yes, I am. And pre-stiggus too, like you said." He fumbled through the word as he spoke.

"So, a smart person like you will know we aren't lying when we tell you we know how the governor's been able to track us while we're in the city," Kirsten said.

The guard's eyes darted from Kirsten to Britt, Max and Bo one at a time, their expressions firm and unchanging.

"He's in possession of a powerful orb," Kirsten continued. "It shows him where everyone is throughout the whole city. He would know if we went to Grandwood and where he could find us, even if we were trying to hide from him." She paused letting their knowledge of the orb settle into the guard's mind. "But the orb doesn't show him where we are right now. For all your governor knows, you're still doing your duty, spying on us," Kirsten held her breath, hoping she was right in guessing how far the orb's reach stretched.

The guard's face went pale, but he responded quickly saying, "You know if he decides to take the orb with him and come closer to this place, he'll see where we are and what you're doing to me. The orb has a limited distance of projection but he can easily move it."

Kirsten glanced at the others, now sure of the orb's limited scope. "But he wouldn't do that. He needs to keep an eye on the townspeople and make sure none of them are disobeying him."

"But they won't disobey him. They're caught under a spell. Merglan himself helped cast it. Rankstine uses the crystal around his neck to keep the spell's hold on them. The crystal's so powerful that it works on everyone in the whole city," the guard bragged.

"Not everyone," Kirsten said.

The guard looked confused.

"Billson directly disobeyed his orders. He was disciplined earlier today," she said.

The man flushed red with irritation. "The effects may be fading, but it still works. Those stupid people are building us a fortress, aren't they," the spy said through gritted teeth.

"For the kurr?" It was the first time Kirsten asked him a question, but the man was so worked up she didn't think he'd notice.

"Not just the kurr," the guard continued. "A northern stronghold for Merglan's growing army. It will be the first time in history the kurr, orc and humans have banded together to fight against the evil monarchy controlling the five nations."

"Merglan would richly reward a governor and his men for accomplishing such an important task," Kirsten said trying to keep the man talking.

He nodded, "I've been promised my own castle and title as a baron. I asked the others just this evening what they'd been promised," he smiled. "I was the only one who'd been promised baron papers."

"No doubt Rankstine would stay in Grandwood," she said.

"Someone loyal to Merglan will need to stay in command of the north."

"Did he tell you where you'd be given a castle?" Kirsten asked.

"Brookside," the man said.

"How would you get there? By boat or by horse?" she asked.

The man opened his mouth to respond but suddenly held his tongue when he realized what Kirsten was doing. "Hey, you're just trying to get me to tell you how to escape the barriers." He shook his head and started to laugh, "You thought you could trick me into telling you, but I'm not that stupid. I said before; I won't be telling you nothing."

Kirsten rose to her feet and said, "Very well. That's all we needed to know. Sleep tight." She turned and led the others out of the barn closing the door behind them. As they walked back to the house, they could hear their prisoner shouting for them to come back and let him go.

As they entered the house, Max laughed, "That couldn't have gone any better! He literally told us everything we needed to know, and not once did he notice he was doing it."

"I honestly thought he might tell us how to escape the barriers," Kirsten said kicking the wood floor with her heel as she halfway skipped with joy.

"He told us everything else," Britt said.

"Yeah, he told us the orb has a limited scope," Max began counting the information on his fingers. "The crystal was used to cast a mind control spell on everyone,"

"That's fading," Bo added.

"That's fading," Max repeated. Holding up a third finger, he continued, "Why the townspeople are building a wall and why the kurr are assembling here. He even let it slip that there were other guards with him earlier tonight. They must have captured Thomas and taken him to the church as a prisoner."

"Yeah. It was almost too easy," Kirsten said.

"You know you could have a future in interrogation," Bo said. "When this is all over, you could be a valuable asset to the Watch. The watchmen could use more watchwomen in every town."

Kirsten's cheeks reddened, "Thanks, but I'll focus on this first."

Bo smiled, nodding, "Yeah, getting rid of Rankstine is much more pressing."

"How are we going to do it?" Britt asked. "We need to come up with a solid plan to get Thomas back and thwart Rankstine's ambitions for creating a stronghold in Grandwood."

"Maybe we can sneak back into the church?" Bo suggested

"If we try to sneak into town, Rankstine will know where we are. He's got the orb and he's searching for us, remember?" Max said.

"That's just it," Kirsten said enthusiastically.

"What's just it? That Rankstine will know our every move as soon as we get within the city's limits?" Max asked.

"Yes."

They all looked confused.

"If we could get a horse and cart, we could go back to town with the guard. One of us could use his clothing as a disguise. While it's night maybe one of us can pass for him long enough to get inside the church. The rest of us will be tied up in the back of the cart, but the only one of us who will be properly bound and gagged will be the guard. With Rankstine's orb, it will look like the guard is hauling us in as prisoners."

"That might just work," Britt said. "Who looks the most like the guard, height and body type?" she asked eyeing at Max, Bo and Kirsten.

"Max is too thin," Kirsten said. Max scowled at her and she said, "What? Your frame isn't as bad as his. Get over it."

Max was slightly taken aback by her demeanor.

"I'm too short," she continued.

"That leaves us with you," Britt said facing Bo. Despite

his younger age, Bo had a bulkier frame than his older brother.

"What do I need to do?" he asked.

"Let's start by getting you dressed," Britt said as she grabbed his arm and led him out the front door. Max and Kirsten followed.

The guard's clothes were slightly baggy on Bo, but once he rolled up the pant legs and shirtsleeves, he looked the part. The cloak the man had worn was adorned with a deep hood that Bo pulled over his head. Even in the light of the lantern, his shadowed face was unrecognizable.

"Great," Bo said, placing his hands on his hips and striking a pose. "What's our plan from here?"

"We'll need a horse and cart," Britt said. "Then we will pretend to be bound and gagged while you bring us into the church. The other guards will probably help you unload us and take us into the holding area where Rankstine will no doubt want to question us. As soon as the opportunity arises, we'll turn on the guards, take their weapons and deal with Rankstine."

"Perfect. What could go wrong?" Max said sarcastically.

"Where are we going to get the horse and cart?" Bo asked.

"There's a cart just down the road," Britt said. "I saw it when we were looking for spies earlier."

"What about a horse?" Bo asked again.

"I bet he's got one tied up not far from here," Kirsten said thumbing toward their stripped prisoner.

After clothing the spy in Bo's clothes, they carried the man by the armpits and feet down the road to the cart Britt had seen. The cart had been flipped onto its side during the attack several months earlier and had settled into the brush near the side of the road.

They set the guard down in the middle of the dirt road and, with concerted effort, they hoisted the cart over onto its wooden wheels. Swinging the guard by his bound extremities, they chucked him up into the air above the flatbed of the cart. His body hung in the air for an instant before coming down hard onto the wood surface. He groaned through the gag tied around his head.

It didn't take long for them to find the guard's horse tied to a tree just off the road. Lashing the cart to the horse's saddle, Britt, Max and Kirsten joined the guard in the back of the cart. They tied their limbs loosely so they'd appear to be bound but could remove them with ease. Bo tied rags to their necks so they could give the appearance of being gagged as well. Climbing into the driver's seat, Bo steered them down the road toward Grandwood.

They were halfway to town when Bo wrangled the horse into a stop. Looking around concerned, Kirsten asked, "What's wrong? Why have we stopped?"

"I thought I saw something run across the road," Bo said squinting into the night.

"What did it look like?" Britt asked. "Was it an animal?"

Bo shook his head and spoke to them over his shoulder, not letting his eyes leave the road in front of him, "It looked like a person, but it was small and moved so fast, I'm not sure. Maybe it was an animal?" he said trying to reassure himself. "I think it was hunched over like a bear or something."

"There are plenty of black bears around here," Kirsten said. "I thought one was a person once, out of the corner of my eye, but when I saw it clearly, I knew it was a bear."

"Yeah, maybe it was a bear," Bo said not sounding entirely convinced as he urged the horse on.

Almost as quickly as they'd crossed through the town's steadily rising walls, several guards met them on horseback. Stopping Bo and his cart, they dismounted, walking to his side.

"What happened to you? When we left, we couldn't find you, so we thought you were taken prisoner," one of the guards said.

Grunting as he turned in his seat to face the passengers in the back of the cart, Bo lowered his voice to match the guard's tone, "I had an opportunity to catch them all at once," he said pointing to the four people bound and gagged in the back of the cart.

The guards peered at the prisoners he was transporting. "You're just trying to secure your place as the Baron of Brookside, aren't you?" the guard on Bo's left said, shaking his head. "Always trying to one-up us." They turned and mounted their horses once more. "Come on, Rankstine's got some questions for you," the guard on the right said, pulling his horse around and leading them into the streets.

The spy they'd captured wriggled in the back of the cart, attempting to alert the other guards with muffled shouts, but they didn't pay any attention. Kirsten joined him in his pleas for help and the other guards turned their backs, scoffing in disgust. Kirsten looked up at the tops of the buildings as they passed by, tracking their progress toward the church.

Once at the church, Rankstine's men dismounted. Bo acted as if he knew precisely what to do. He hopped down off the cart and waved the guards over. Bo dragged the bound guard out first, pulling the hood of his own jacket down over the bound guard's head so they wouldn't recognize their comrade. One of the guards walked up to help Bo while the others pounded on the side door of the large stone building. Two more men cloaked in Merglan's colors emerged from behind the door. One accompanied the other to help haul the prisoners inside while the other held the door open.

Bo kept his hood up so they couldn't look at him too closely as he worked with Rankstine's guard. Kirsten, Max and Britt wriggled and resisted and tried to protest through their gags the way Bo's actual prisoner had. After struggling through the side door with the prisoners, one of the men led them through the narrow hallway and out into the main worship area.

"We'll take the prisoners into the holding room with the other one," the man in the lead said.

Bo didn't speak but dutifully followed him down a hall off the main sanctuary. The man in the lead halted in front of a door. He turned the knob to the makeshift holding room where the group believed Thomas was being held when a guard arriving at the rear placed a hand on Bo's shoulder.

Stopping him and moving around Bo, the guard said, "Rankstine wants a word with," he stopped as he noticed Bo's shadowed face hidden deep within the hood. "Wait a second," he said loudly. All of the guards halted, their attention turning to Bo.

Before any of them could react, Bo shouted, "Now!" and slammed his fist into the man standing with his hand on his shoulder. His punch landed squarely on his chin, knocking him to the floor. Bo pushed their bound guard to the floor and drew the blade lashed to his belt as Kirsten, Max and Britt pushed their captors away, threw off their loose ties, and jumped each one.

Knocking them to the floor, they wrestled the men for their swords. Bo engaged the remaining guard who stood by the doorway in combat. Raising his blade, Bo suddenly felt his body tighten. He became stiff and rigid. Frozen in place, Bo found he could only move his eyes. He looked to the floor where the others had been. They too were locked in place, gripping the guards' swords, pulled halfway from their belts.

A door suddenly swung open, candlelight pouring into the shadowed hallway. Rankstine stood in the doorway, his hand gripping something that hung from his neck, bright blue light emanating between his fingers. Straining their eyes, they knew instantly what kept them from moving. The crystal. Rankstine used the powerful crystal to hold them in place, frozen, while his guards regained their composure.

Kirsten and Bo had experienced this feeling once before, when Merglan forced them off the ship at his fortress, but this was different. They could still look around. When Merglan had held them in place, they had been forced to look straight ahead. She strained against the hold Rankstine had on them and to her surprise, she began to move. The movements were languid, so slow it would have taken her an hour to move her foot one step, but she could move.

This magic isn't as strong, she thought.

"Well, well, well," Rankstine began, stepping out into the hallway, his hand still holding his crystal out around his neck. "Thought you could trick me, did you?"

As he stepped closer, Kirsten noticed a large pinkish-red stone clasped against his collar. Her mother's necklace, Rankstine was wearing it as though it was his own. As hard as she tried to move faster, she could still only move at a hauntingly slow pace.

He walked right up to her and said, "I know you were here with your brother earlier today." He bent down over her as she crouched on the floor attempting to move. He grabbed the pink sapphire necklace with his free hand and showed it to her, "You left something behind." Examining it with his dark eyes, Rankstine said, "I quite like it. I think I'll keep it." He straightened. "Take them into the holding room," he commanded his guards. They grabbed them by the armpits and drug each of them into the room where they'd been initially headed.

Once all four of them were locked inside the room, the spell controlling their movement was released; they could move freely again. Thomas was already in the room. He rushed to his sister the moment the guards closed the door.

"Kirsten," Thomas said. "You shouldn't have come here."

Kirsten held her brother in a tight embrace, "We came to rescue you."

"Nice job," he said sarcastically.

"Our plan would've worked if Rankstine hadn't come out waving that crystal and freezing us in place," she said.

"Like Merglan did on the ship?" Thomas asked.

"Kind of," Bo chimed in. "But this time I could move my eyes."

"Yeah, and I was able to move against it, just slightly. Not fast enough to do anything productive though," Kirsten said.

"What do we do now?" Max asked irritated.

"We need to break out of here," Britt said, beginning to search the room for a way out.

"I've been looking all night and haven't found anything," Thomas said.

"What happened to you after we left you?" Kirsten asked.

"I went over to the north side of the farm and was searching for anything unusual," Thomas began. "I heard a group of men approaching. Their whispers were growing louder so I tried to hide. There wasn't much cover over there, unfortunately, and they found me straight away. I tried to run but they tackled me and hauled me off. Next thing I knew, I was thrown in here. What about you guys?"

"Bo and I found one of the guards in the woods and knocked him out. After we met up and you didn't show, we went looking for you. We found signs of the scuffle in the dirt and figured you'd been taken. We tied the guard up in the barn and questioned him."

"It was amazing," Bo added. "She tricked that dummy into telling us almost everything," he laughed.

"I got him to tell us Rankstine's plans," Kirsten said.

"What are they?" Thomas asked.

"He's trying to turn Grandwood into a fortress, a stronghold for Merglan's forces. They plan to conduct operations from here as a northern base."

"That's why the kurr were arriving," Thomas snapped his fingers.

"We also found out a little more about the orb and Rankstine's ability to use magic. The guard let it slip that other guards were also at our farm, confirming our suspicion that you'd been captured," she said.

"What about the force field surrounding the area? Did he tell you how to escape?" Thomas asked.

Kirsten shook her head, "Unfortunately he caught onto us and didn't tell us how it works."

Kirsten turned to face the door when she heard shouts

coming from the guards. "Did you hear that?" she asked the others.

All of them remained silent. The screams were coming from the men inside the church. Max, Thomas and Kirsten began pounding on the door shouting, "Let us out of here! Hey! Let us out!" A moment later Kirsten saw the door handle jiggle. She looked down and watched as the doorknob turned partway. A loud bang sounded as the person attempting to open the door was slammed violently into it. Unable to turn the knob entirely, the door barricaded them from entry. Kirsten heard the terrible sounds of gnawing and biting, as though some creature was feasting on whoever had tried to open the door.

They all stood back from the door, listening in horror to someone being eaten alive. Suddenly the chewing stopped and claws scratched at the door. The knob twisted slightly once more. Britt ran to the door and pressed against it with her body waving the others over to help. They piled against the door. With some fumbling, the creature on the other side of the door managed to turn the knob and began pushing, trying to get into the room. The door opened as the creature pushed but slammed shut each time they rallied against it.

Kirsten's eyes widened as she saw a set of long claw-like nails pry their way into the crack of the door. "What the heck is that thing?" she cried out. Shortly after she shouted, she could hear the thing on the other side sniffing along the crack that its claws held open. "Eeew!" She shouted and pressed harder against the door trying to close it once more. Kirsten thought she'd rather be locked in the safety of the room than face whatever was killing off the guards outside.

With a heave, the creature forced its body against the door. Despite the combined force of the five of them, the creature opened the door slightly. Kirsten watched in disbe-lief as a single leg and arm worked their way through the opening. The creature shrieked shrilly as they heaved the door against its limbs, pushing harder now out of fear. The gray textured skin and thin wiry hairs covering the limbs helped them identify their attacker at last.

"Goblin!" Max said, realizing what the arm and leg were attached to.

"Where did they come from?" Kirsten shouted through grunts as she pressed firmly against the door.

"They must have found the way in where the kurr were entering," Max said.

"That's what I saw on the road," Bo said realizing what he'd seen.

"They must've followed us into town," Britt shouted over the goblin's screams.

"We need to shut this one up before it attracts more of them," Kirsten said.

"How are we going to do that?" Bo asked, leaning against the door.

"I've got an idea," Britt said. "On the count of three, we'll open the door."

"Are you crazy?!" Max shouted, "Then it'll be trapped in here with us."

"Let me finish," Britt said. "When we open the door, it'll come tumbling through. One of us will push it further in and very quickly we'll all hop out of here and close the door behind us, locking it in here."

They grew silent for a moment, thinking the plan over.

"I think it could work," Kirsten was the first to say.

"Okay, let's try it," Max said.

"Who's going to push it farther into the room when we open the door?" Bo asked.

"Whoever's closest to the crack," Thomas said.

"You're just saying that because I'm closest to the crack," Kirsten said.

"No. It makes the most sense," Britt said. "When we pull the door open, you'll be the closest one to it. You can quickly push it past us, and we'll run out together."

Thinking it over briefly Kirsten said, "Okay, fine. I'll do it."

"Okay. I'll count down from three. We open the door together on one. Is that clear?" Britt asked.

Everyone nodded.

"Three, two, one," together they pulled open the door and the goblin came barging into the room.

Kirsten stepped back and pushed the creature hard as it came stumbling through the doorway, sending it headlong to the far end of the room. Thomas led them out of the room and Britt grabbed Kirsten by the arm as they dove out of the room, slamming the door behind them.

Falling to the floor, Kirsten heard the clawing and muffled cries of the goblin from the other side of the room. Breathing rapidly and shaking with fear, she said, "Don't ever ask me to do that again." She shivered thinking about the goblin's gray skin, wiry hairs and bloodstained teeth.

"Thanks," Max and Bo said in unison reaching down and helping her up.

Looking around, Britt said, "Come on, we need to move. We don't know how many goblins are in here." She reached down and removed the sword from the dead guard at the foot of the door.

"After you," Max made a sweeping gesture with his arm.

Britt led them to the end of the hall and the edge of the church's cavernous sanctuary. She checked to see if the coast was clear before leading them across the short opening, into the hallway where they'd first arrived.

Before following them across, Kirsten looked over to see the room where Rankstine had been with the orb. The door was slightly ajar. Instead of following Britt and the others, she slid over to the doorway. The others didn't notice her slip away.

Kirsten placed her back against the wall next to the door. She could hear someone or something rummaging around. She leaned over and peeked into the room. Rankstine was lying face down on the ground and a goblin was searching through the shelves, pocketing anything that looked valuable. Kirsten pulled back to stand flat against the wall. She took several deep breaths; she knew what she had to do.

She gathered her strength and stepped out from the wall. She stood in the doorway, yet to her surprise, the goblin didn't turn around to see her. Instead, it continued to rummage through the shelves, climbing as it searched, pulling books and papers down off the walls. Kirsten quickly and quietly tiptoed into the room, stopping over Rankstine's body. Keeping her eyes on the goblin, she reached down and fingered the back of his neck for her mother's necklace. Her fingertips felt the cool chain around his neck. She slipped the chain over his head, pulling the pink sapphire out from under Rankstine's body. As she took a step back, she froze. The goblin had stopped pulling things off the shelves. It sniffed the air, then turned around laying its eyes on Kirsten.

Kirsten squeaked upon seeing the goblin's ugly gnarled features. She searched the area around her feet for something to defend herself with. The goblin hopped down from the shelves and stared at her for a moment. Her eyes caught sight of something glinting at Rankstine's feet. She bolted down for it and the goblin lunged forward at her, arms outstretched ready to grab her. Kirsten's hands landed on the crystal at Rankstine's feet and she used it like a sword, lashing its light out at the goblin. To her surprise, the crystal sent a wave of energy out, colliding with the advancing goblin and sending it flying across the room. It splattered against the wall, slumping to the ground unconscious.

Kirsten looked down at the crystal in her hand, *Wow. I can't believe that actually worked.*

She pocketed the crystal and before leaving the room grabbed the orb Rankstine had displayed in the corner on the desk. Tucking it under her arm as she exited the room, Kirsten heard her friends calling her.

"Over here," she answered as she rushed to join them near the side door.

Thomas asked, "What were you doing in there?"

"I went back for mother's necklace," she said.

"Did you find it?" he asked.

"I did," she said. They stopped at the door to exit the church and she pulled the pink-hued sapphire from her pocket. "Rankstine was lying on the ground face down, so I took it off him. I also got these," she placed the necklace back into her pocket and pulled out the crystal.

Seeing the orb under her arm and the crystal in her other hand, Thomas shook his head smiling, "You're crazy. You know that?"

She nodded and pocketed the crystal. As they stepped outside to join the others, Kirsten heard shouts of people and roars of kurr. Near the front of the church, they watched a large kurr as it backed its way out into the street, fighting off five goblins with massive swings of its sword.

"We need to get out of here, and fast," Britt said.

"Follow me," Kirsten said. "I know a back way out of town."

They followed Kirsten as she led them down the alley away from the main street. She stopped near the center.

"What are you doing? We need to keep moving," Britt urged.

Bending over, Kirsten pulled up on a metal lid in the center of the cobblestone alley. "Hurry," she said motioning them to climb down into the hole she'd uncovered.

"Seriously?" Max asked, "Isn't there another way?"

"Not if you don't want to be mauled by goblins and kurr," Kirsten said. "Now come on, let's go." She hopped into the hole. The others followed.

"Eew," Bo gasped once they'd landed. "What's that smell?"

"Human excrement," Max said pinching his nose closed with his fingers.

Kirsten pulled the crystal from her pocket. Its light-blue light brightened the tunnel so they could see. A steady flow of ankle-deep sludge ran along the tunnel floor.

"Aw, man," Bo said disappointedly upon seeing where they were standing. "We're in the sewer."

"It's safe down here," Kirsten said.

"How are we going to navigate?" Thomas asked her. "I've never been down here before, have you?"

Kirsten shook her head, "But we have this." She held up the orb she'd taken from Rankstine's room. "Using the crystal for light and this map, we should be able to navigate our way to the edge of town."

"Brilliant," Britt commented wide-eyed. "And where'd you get those?"

"No time to explain," Kirsten said, leading them

through the maze of tunnels winding under Grandwood. After ten minutes she noticed the smell wasn't burning her nostrils as severely as it had at first. She stopped when they had reached the edge of town. Kirsten looked up and saw a faint ring of light encircling another street cover. This was their exit.

She held the orb out and said to the group, "It doesn't look like anyone's near. It should be safe."

"Wait," Max said, holding out his hand. "That thing probably doesn't show goblins."

"What do you mean?" Kirsten said.

"Goblins are magical creatures. They can conceal themselves from being sensed. They did it to Ivan once on our journey to Brookside and that must be why Rankstine didn't see them coming. Just because it doesn't show people out there, doesn't mean there aren't any goblins."

Kirsten thought for a moment and said, "I'm going to risk it. I'll let you know if it's safe."

"Kirsten, wait," Thomas said. "I'll go with you."

"Let me go first. If there are goblins that pop out at us, I have the crystal and can wave it at them," she said.

"Will that work?" Thomas asked.

"It did on the goblin in Rankstine's room," she said with a smile.

"Okay, you first," Thomas said.

Kirsten slowly pushed open the heavy metal disc covering the hole to the sewer. She waited a moment with the crystal at the ready. Nothing attacked the hole, so she popped her head just above ground level and scanned the area. Not seeing anything, she climbed out. Thomas followed her. Searching the area quickly to make sure no goblins were close, they motioned to the others to join them.

With no trouble, the five of them made it back to the road to Highborn Bay. They jogged as they left the sounds of the goblin attack far behind. Kirsten kept checking the orb to make sure no one was following them.

Reaching the house, Britt said, "We need to take this opportunity to try to escape."

"We've searched nearly the entire perimeter and haven't found a two-way portal," Max said discouraged.

Kirsten held out the crystal in her hand and said, "What if the crystal is the key?"

They looked at her. She continued, "What if you need to have the crystal to get in and out of the barrier?"

"It's worth a try," Thomas said.

Britt and Bo nodded. They looked at Max.

"What? I'm always up for something new," he said.

Kirsten and Thomas quickly filled travel packs with extra clothes, food and some camping supplies. Setting off on foot, they hiked their way through the forest to the place where they'd seen the kurr entering.

"This is the only place, other than the docks, where we know things have come through. If the crystal is the key, then we should be able to leave through here," Kirsten said. "Who wants to go first?"

When nobody jumped at the offer, Britt took the crystal and said, "I'll do it."

They watched from a distance as Britt walked up to the edge of the barrier, stopped in front of it, took several deep breaths, and walked right at it. She wasn't blocked as they had been before. She passed through without effort. Waving them over, the others came close. Still holding the crystal, Britt stuck her arm through the invisible barrier and began to pull them through one at a time.

Thomas went first, then Max and Bo. When it was

Kirsten's turn, she held her breath as she grabbed hold of Britt's. Just as she was being pulled through the barrier, something grabbed hold of her other side, stopping her. She looked back to see a goblin grabbing her arm and clawing at the orb she held. Kirsten began to scream and kick at the creature that had taken hold of her.

Britt and the others pulled at Kirsten, but the goblin held onto her arm, keeping her halfway in and halfway out of the barrier. In a desperate effort to free herself from the goblin's grip, Kirsten tried to hit the goblin in the head with the orb. Before she could make contact with the creature, it saw what she was trying to do and bit down on her shoulder. Kirsten let out a cry as the goblin's teeth sunk deep into her shoulder. She dropped the orb. The creature had given way to their pulling when it bit down on her. They managed to pull Kirsten through the barrier. As soon as she'd made it all the way through, Britt let go of her. The goblin's teeth still sunk deep onto Kirsten's muscles. When Britt released Kirsten, the crystal's connection holding the barrier open was severed. The invisible barrier closed on the goblin, splitting it in two as it was dragged through. Its upper body fell to the ground on the outside of the barrier and its lower half remained trapped on the inside next to the orb.

Kirsten writhed in pain as she rolled on the ground gripping her shoulder where the goblin had bitten her. Britt and Thomas rushed to her side. They attempted to hold her still and examine the wound.

"The bastard bit me!" Kirsten shouted, looking down at her bloodied shoulder.

Thomas and Britt struggled to hold her still. "Damn it, Kirsten, let us see how bad it is!" Thomas shouted.

Kirsten stopped rolling around on the ground. Thomas

looked at the teeth marks in her shoulder. He watched as red streaks extended out from the center of the bite running out along Kirsten's skin. He stared horrified as Kirsten let out a blood-curdling scream, then fainted into silence. Thomas shook his sister shouting, "Kirsten! What's happening? Kirsten!"

Kirsten fell limp, turning deathly pale. Thomas looked to Britt who expressed the same horrified look. He turned back to his sister who lay still on the forest floor.

NINETEEN

FROM PRISON TO THRONE

A nders reached out to Zahara with his mind, but she had already seen Natalia chasing after the queen.

Did you see her? Anders asked as he watched her rush off into the night.

I sensed something terrible just before she came crashing through the window. Before I could make sense of what had happened, I saw Natalia rush out after her. I can see them both, but they're running faster than I can. I'll take flight and see if I can cut the queen off, she said.

Okay. Don't let her escape the city; she killed the king, Anders' mental voice rang with sorrow as he told her.

For a moment Zahara didn't reply, but suddenly her voice thundered into his head, so much so that he almost fell over with the pain in her voice, *I will not let her leave this place.* Anders could feel that in the moments she'd hesitated to respond, Zahara had taken flight. He saw her dark silhouette soar over the treetops in the distance.

Anders turned his attention back to Ivan, who stood sorrowfully over Asmond's body. Ray and the other guard had entered the room shortly after Natalia. They were as shocked at what the queen had done as any of them. Ivan lifted his gaze with an angst Anders hadn't seen before. "The city guards must be alerted of Lageena's betrayal at once. They must not let her leave the city gates. If she does, there will be no stopping her from getting to Merglan."

"We're on it," Ray said, nodding to his partner.

"Anders and I will inform the gate guards, while you two spread the word to the city watch," Ivan clarified before Ray and his partner left the home. "Anders, do you remember how to focus your mind and seek out others' minds individually?" Ivan asked.

"Yes, I've been practicing with Zahara," Anders reassured him of his training.

"We need to make a connection with the city gate guards. I only have the ability to connect with one at a time, but we'll need to alert them all at once. Can you make a connection with all of the gate guards simultaneously?"

Anders had never attempted to communicate with so many specific individuals spread out over such a large area but knew he must try. If he couldn't complete this task, how was he going to defeat Merglan? "I can," he told Ivan and focused his mental energy, closing his eyes as he felt across the city to its enchanted outer walls. Sweeping in all directions, he located the four gateways.

"Have you got them?" Ivan asked.

"One moment," Anders said as he narrowed his search to select the guards standing watch at each city gate. "Got them," he said still closing his eyes tightly in concentration.

"Okay, now let me in," Ivan said in a more calm voice than he'd used moments before.

Anders allowed Ivan to enter his thoughts while he kept hold of the gatekeepers' minds.

Sentinels of Cedarbridge, Ivan's voice boomed commandingly through Anders' mind into the collective thoughts of the guards at the gates. *This is Ivan, dragonrider and loyal friend to the Everlight Kingdom. I bring urgent news. The queen has betrayed the king and is not permitted to leave the city. Bar her and hold her in contempt until she can be brought to trial for her treason. I say again, do not under any circumstances allow the queen to leave the city.*

Ivan removed himself from Anders' mind and he instantly contacted Zahara, *Do you still have eyes on the queen?* he asked her.

She slipped my gaze. I'm watching the forest floor, but it's hard to see through the thick treetops. I'm scanning the area with my mind for any sign of her consciousness, but haven't located it yet.

Is Natalia still in pursuit? he asked.

I can sense her running, but I don't know if she's still on her trail or has lost it. I'll check and see.

"Anders," Ivan said as Anders broke the connection between himself and his dragon.

"Yes," he replied, ready to perform whatever Ivan needed next.

"Come with me," he said as he exited Asmond's room.

"Where are we going?" he said as he stepped in stride with Ivan.

"To get the king," Ivan said.

"But the king is dead?" Anders said pointing a wary hand back to the room they'd just left.

"Not Asmond, the new king," he said, opening the main door and leaving the tree house of the former elf king.

Anders followed Ivan as they quickly walked to the center of the elf city. Ivan stopped outside a large tree structure. The front of the building stood ten large cedar trees wide, grown tightly together to form the outside walls of the elven courts. The prisoners' chambers were built below the courts. They'd come to find Nadir, who'd been held here at the accusation of the queen.

As they entered the large building, Anders saw no guards or anyone who would be in charge of keeping the prisoners locked up below.

"Where are the guards?" Anders asked as they strode to the far corner of the room.

"The elves don't use their guards to watch the prisoners," Ivan said.

"Wouldn't it be easy for them to escape?" Anders asked. Ivan gave him a glance that made him feel foolish for asking, so he added, "Or for someone to break in?"

"The same ancient magic that runs within the walls of the city, protecting it from the evils of people like Merglan, runs within this building as well. Below this ground level are many levels of security designed to house criminals with magic and non-magic capabilities."

"Which level is Nadir in?" Anders asked.

"I'm not sure," Ivan replied. "But I would bet he is not too far down there. Once we are in the secure area, your ability to sense or locate him will diminish the deeper into the cellblock we go. I would expect that since we have entered this building your powers have already diminished, yet you have not noticed."

Anders tried to feel for Zahara but couldn't quite reach her; he only felt her with his emotions. "You're right. They are reduced. Is this what it's like for you?" Anders asked, wondering about Ivan's decreased powers and how that must feel since the death of his dragon.

Ivan nodded. "Here we are," he said as they reached the back corner of the room.

Anders looked around; he saw only the back wall at his side and floor beneath his feet. "Is this some invisible portal?" he asked still searching for a doorway or hatch in the floor.

"Sort of," Ivan said. He held a hand up feeling the well-worn bark walls until his fingers hit upon the crack he was seeking. Following it down, he reached to where the wall met the floor and knocked on it three times. Each knock sounded more hollow than the one previous. A section of the floor popped open slightly and Anders swore he thought he heard the floor exhale softly as it did so. Ivan reached his hand under the slab that protruded from the floor and lifted a hatch door, exposing a stone staircase descending under the building.

Ivan took the first step down into the darkness when Anders said, "Wait."

Ivan looked up at him curiously, "What? You are not scared of the dark, are you?"

Anders shook his head furiously, "No, it's not that."

"What then?"

"How will the magical prison cell that's holding Nadir know to release him into our custody?" he asked.

"That's a good question," Ivan said as he continued to descend into the hole in the floor.

Anders half expected more to follow, but Ivan disappeared beneath the floor. Shrugging, Anders followed his mentor, assuming he had a plan to get Nadir out of prison. As the light from the room above faded, the hatch door that they entered through closed with a loud 'BANG' making Anders jump slightly. He stood motionless on the stone staircase.

"Ivan?" he said, his voice echoing into the darkness.

He expected Ivan's response to come from a distance since he'd entered with haste before him, but it didn't. Instead, Ivan's reply came from almost right next to his face.

"One moment, Anders. Bear with me," he said. Anders could hear Ivan fiddling around with something.

Just as Anders was about to ask him what he was doing, a spark emanated from his fingertip. That single spark ran in a line straight up, sharply turning to the left, then coming to rest behind a round object dimly lit by the blue spark that had protruded from Ivan's finger. A half breath later blue flames burst forth from basins built along the walls. Anders watched as the fire spread from bowl to bowl, first lighting the small room in which they stood and then running down several long corridors leading off the room in five different directions.

Anders whirled as he gawked at the enormity of the chamber they'd entered. "Is this the first level?" he asked.

Ivan nodded, "We'll start here. It's probably best if we don't split up. You might get lost. Each corridor twists and turns the farther down you go."

"How are we supposed to find Nadir in this maze?" Anders asked, daunted by the cavern.

"Can you sense his presence?" Ivan asked.

Anders tried to feel for someone or something that might be out there, but as hard as he tried, he could only feel cold darkness. It chilled his head the farther he extended his reach. "Ah," he winced, clutching his head.

"You must try harder," Ivan said firmly. "He should be here on the first floor."

"It hurts, but I'll keep trying," Anders said.

He continued reaching out with his thoughts several

more times until the icy chill of emptiness consumed his mind, numbing his brain to the point of tingling.

"Put your tongue to the roof of your mouth," Ivan said.

"What?" Anders winced and continued to squeeze his head.

"When the chill comes, try sticking your tongue to the roof of your mouth."

Anders looked at Ivan like he was crazy, but Ivan said, "Trust me. It works."

Once more Anders let his mind extend into the chilled empty underground of the elf prison. As the cold crept into Anders' brain, he raised his tongue to the roof of his mouth, not expecting anything to change. To his surprise, however, the chill grip on his mind began to slip away. The heat from his tongue spread from the top of the inside of his mouth up into his brain. He reached further until suddenly he felt the faint hint of life. The chill began to come back, harder now than ever before. Anders pushed harder with his tongue against the roof of his mouth and shot out to the glow of life. The pain of the cold was too much to bear and he broke his connection, shouting in pain as he did so.

"Did you find him?" Ivan asked catching Anders before he could fall to the floor.

"Ahhh," Anders groaned through clenched teeth. He gathered himself and gained some control over his mind again. "Yes," he said half gasping and out of breath. "I've located him."

Ivan laughed, "Aha! That's my boy!" he shouted, shaking Anders by the shoulders.

Anders rattled like a rag doll in Ivan's hands. Ivan realized his overexcitement and restrained himself from roughing Anders up any further.

"Are you alright Anders?" he asked.

Anders felt his strength returning, slowly bringing warmth to his blood and pulsing through his veins. He took a deep breath, steadying himself with his feet squarely on the stone floor. Nodding, he said, "Yeah, I'm alright."

"Take your time, then we'll go after Nadir," Ivan said. "Where did you sense him?"

Anders took a moment to recall down which of the five corridors he'd sensed Nadir's presence. As he identified the hallway, they heard a brutish bellow come from within one of the corridors. Anders' eyes bulged and Ivan jumped as he turned to face the source of the noise.

"What was that?" Anders asked, worry melting the rest of the chill from his face.

"I'm not sure what kind of creatures they keep down here, but everything is locked up behind impenetrable bars," Ivan said, attempting to reassure them.

They heard the bellowing once more, this time, though, it sounded closer.

"I hope you're right," Anders said. "Because that time it sounded closer."

"Let's move. Where did you sense Nadir?" Ivan asked, hoping it wasn't the corridor where the boorish bellows continued to echo.

Anders pointed down the hallway directly to the left of the terrible noises.

Ivan looked down the darkened hall, then back to Anders. His expression serious, "Are you sure?"

Anders nodded, "I'm sure."

They took off in a hurry down the dark corridor, Ivan grabbing a lit torch from the wall as they entered. Three times they heard the bellows of the unknown beast. It faded slightly the farther down the hallway they went. Anders was convinced that whatever it was had broken free from its cell and was roaming the first floor of the dungeon.

Nadir's cell was farther than Anders recalled and both he and Ivan were beginning to heave exhaustedly by the time they arrived at the cage door. Nadir must have heard them coming because he stood with his hands wrapped around the bars of the iron-caged door.

"Ivan?" Nadir said with surprise as the old dragonrider and Anders came to a halt outside his cell.

Anders took a quick look at the surrounding cells; they were all empty, except for one. A small elf girl who looked to be no more than ten years old lay curled in a ball on the stone floor. Anders wondered what she possibly could have done to end up in there. His attention returned to Nadir as he heard his name.

"And Anders. How did you two find me? And why are you here?" he asked sounding slightly suspicious that their reasons for being there may not be honest or lawful.

Ivan read the changing expression on Nadir's face and quieted his suspicions, "Nadir, we've come here in the name of your father to set you free. We've discovered proof that will exonerate you of the crimes for which you are being held a prisoner."

"That's wonderful news!" Nadir exclaimed. When neither Anders nor Ivan's expressions turned to joy, Nadir asked, "Why do I get the feeling there's something terrible you're not telling me?"

Ivan turned to face Nadir and took a deep breath before continuing, "This will not be easy for you to hear," he began. "Shortly after you became imprisoned, your father sent Anders, Maija, Natalia and me on a diplomatic mission to Mount Orena. We were sent, in your stead, to restore the faith of good trade between your peoples. While counseling with the dwarf king, Remli, we discovered that Merglan had corrupted the dwarf delegated to be ambassador to the elves. He was sabotaging the relationship between the elves and dwarfs. His goal was to disrupt your alliance so Merglan would be able to strike while the feud between your two kingdoms escalated."

"That's terrible news," Nadir spat. "What kind of hateful person attempts to destroy such a just and noble cause?"

Ivan winced as though he'd been pricked with a needle as Nadir spoke.

Nadir noticed his reaction and asked, "Was that not the terrible news?"

Ivan continued, "It's the beginning to what terrible events came to unfold after our discovery."

Nadir clenched his jaw and steadied his stance as if he were about to be dealt a terrible blow. He nodded once to let Ivan know he was ready for him to continue.

"Once the dwarf traitor was rooted out and captured, he poisoned himself to avoid giving away his secrets. After a thorough search of his personal effects, we found letters."

"What kind of letters?" Nadir asked.

"Incriminating letters," Ivan replied. "Not only was the dwarf in cahoots with Merglan, but he'd been conspiring with someone high in the elven ranks."

"A member of the High Council?" Nadir suggested.

Ivan nodded slowly.

"Who?" Nadir demanded.

"It was the queen," Ivan said shortly.

Nadir spat a slur of elvish Anders didn't understand but assumed to be curses.

"Does my father know?" Nadir asked. "Is that why you're here in his place?"

Ivan hesitated to answer.

"Come on then, tell me."

"We tried to get the king alone to tell him the news. Lageena was present and the king insisted on her being in the room for whatever it was we needed to tell him. I underestimated her."

Nadir inhaled shortly and took a step back as if someone had pushed him. "What's happened to my father?" he asked in a shaky voice.

"Upon our revealing her false identity to the king, she attempted to flee. The king went after her. Before she leapt from their bedroom window, she delivered a fatal blow. I'm sorry, Nadir, but your father is dead."

A silence deeper than Anders had ever known befell the prison corridor. Nadir's face flushed a ghostly white as if all his blood had been drained. He stood staring into the darkened hallway, tears welling in his eyes. Anders couldn't gauge how much time passed during the lengthy silence.

Nadir was first to speak. "Where is she?" he asked coldly.

"Before we came down here to free you, Natalia and Zahara were hunting her down. All of the city watch had been made aware of her treason. All gates were sealed. She couldn't have left the city. Now we just need to smoke her out of whichever hole she has slunk away to," Ivan said.

"Good," Nadir said shortly.

"We need to get you out of here. Your people are in need of a leader. If we let this go too long without a firm commander, a coup could arise to try to take control of the crown. Nadir, you are the king now," Ivan let the words settle.

Wiping away tears, Nadir said, "You're right. I must

take command and see that this traitor is put to justice. Now how do you propose to get me out of here?"

"The magical bonds holding you here are designed to process and judge evidence that could convict you or set you free," Ivan said reaching into his pocket. He pulled out the letter he'd brought back from Mount Orena.

"What are we going to do with that?" Anders asked. "I don't see a judge or even a prison guard to read that."

"I just need to call on the jail keep," Ivan said calmly. He inhaled slowly and let out a slur of elvish words. In a matter of moments a blue light, much the same as those that spread like lightning when they lit the place, emerged in the hallway wall near Nadir's cell.

The blue light emanating from within the wall formed into a person, an elf. Anders didn't understand the elvish language, but he could understand the situation occurring. Ivan held out the letter to the blue elf in the wall, placing it in the elf's hands. He let go and the light held the paper in place as it read. Ivan spoke to the figure and when he finished, the blue-light elf vanished, taking the letter with it.

"What happened? Did it work?" Anders asked.

Before Ivan could answer, Nadir's cell door sprung open with an echoing pop. Anders smiled as Nadir stepped freely from his prison cell. Nadir's expression remained cold and Anders quickly hid his joy in seeing him set free.

"Let's go," Ivan said.

As Nadir and Ivan took their first steps toward the exit, Anders hesitated to follow when he heard a familiar sound. The boorish bellowing returned. This time it sounded directly in front of them. Whatever it was, it had broken free and was roaming the halls. And from what Anders could tell, it had sniffed them out.

Anders' hand shot to the sword hanging from his hip.

Keanu's blade, Nadir had given him. Somehow the blade no longer felt empty as it had that morning. The steel once again felt whole as he gripped its hilt. Anders came alongside Ivan and Nadir, whispering, "It's found us, whatever it is."

Ivan nodded, his jaw clenched and eyes burning a mean glare into the dimly lit corridor. "Get behind us," he said to Nadir, motioning him to take cover behind them.

Ivan and Anders stood at the ready, blades drawn for whatever evil monster headed their way. Suddenly Anders heard the clacking of claws on the stone floor. The deep, steady breathing of something large edged its way closer into the light. Anders held his breath as the beast came into view. At first, all he could see were two scarlet eyes glowing in the darkness.

Please don't let it be a dragon, please don't let it be a dragon, Anders thought to himself. It was bad enough that there was already one evil dragon in the world that he'd soon have to face. He didn't want to have to face another down here in the dungeon and without Zahara.

A set of gleaming fangs came into view, glinting in the dull blue light as they hung fiercely under the glowing red eyes. Anders held his breath and gripped his sword tightly, bracing himself for an attack. A dark snout, covered in black and gray fur came into the blue light. An enormous head and large pointed ears followed the glinting white fangs and glowing red eyes. The dark hair of a fairnheir came fully into view. It roared a vicious bark.

In a flash, the giant hound bolted into a full sprint at them. Anders raised his sword prepared to deliver a deadly swing once the beast was upon them. He hardly noticed that Ivan was still standing next to him when the fairnheir leapt off its large paws and into the air.

Anders brought down his sword, swinging ferociously at the assailing beast. Lazuran cut effortlessly through the air as it swung. Where he'd normally expected his sword to dig into flesh and bone, it didn't. His blade continued to swing through the air and he nearly toppled over frontward as he followed through. Ivan's swing was almost identically timed with Anders' and he, too, went stumbling into the empty space between them and the attacking fairnheir.

Anders quickly tried to make sense of the situation. He saw the beast, locked motionless in the air before them, midway on its descending pounce. Anders and Ivan's defensive sword swings would have hit their mark, but the beast failed to complete its advance. Something was blocking it from reaching them, holding the creature frozen in the air.

To his surprise, Anders could see a halo of red light encapsulating the fairnheir. He followed the source of red light down to the hilt of his sword. The large sapphire crystal embedded into the pommel of Keanu's sword shone brilliantly as the beam of light advanced from Lazuran. Anders clutched the hilt tightly; it seemed to be humming with energy and he thought he could hear a faint whisper.

"Anders! What, how are you...?" Ivan exclaimed, and stopped when he too heard the whispers floating through the quiet corridor.

Anders looked to his left meeting Ivan's concerned gaze when suddenly he noticed the girl in the cell behind them. She glowed a faint red, as she hung, floating several feet above the stone slab in her cell. Anders gasped as he saw the girl's dark black eyes transfixed on the sword, her tattooed hands held open out in front of her. She whispered in a dialect he didn't recognize.

The girl's face angled slightly as she cocked her head to

face Anders. "Go," she said in a voice much too low for a child of her age.

Anders hesitated, but Ivan grabbed him by the scruff of his collar and forced him on as Nadir followed them safely around the encapsulated fairnheir.

They returned down the corridor twice as fast as they had come. Nadir remained unfazed by the physical exertion it took to hurry back such a great distance, while Anders and Ivan panted heavily when they reached the room at the base of the stairs.

"This. Way," Ivan said between breaths as he pointed to the stairs that led out of the prison.

Anders looked down at the hilt of his sword, no longer glowing. He could hear the pounding of the fairnheir's paws sprinting through the corridor after them. Rushing through the trap door, Ivan stomped the door closed with his boot as Anders was the last to exit.

"Who was that?" Anders asked as he bent over, hands on his knees, gasping for air.

Ivan shrugged, "Someone or something very powerful to be able to use magic while placed under guard in the elvish prison."

Nadir nodded, "I've only heard rumors of her existence. She's of the Norfolk people in the north and it's said she's been locked down there for hundreds of years."

"How did she do that with my sword?" Anders asked, looking at Lazuran as he spoke.

Ivan stared at Anders for a moment, then turned to Nadir, "How much did Keanu know about that sword?"

Nadir shook his head, "I'm not sure. I wasn't present when he was given the blade. I do know that he wasn't aware of the sapphire's power. To my knowledge, nobody was."

Ivan paused, thinking over the possibility of the blade's powers, "Come on, we must hurry if we're going to find Lageena.".

Anders wanted to say, *But what about the girl? Isn't there something we can do to help her?* But he knew they wouldn't know how to help her. He didn't even know what she'd been locked up for. All he knew was that she'd helped them escape and she was most likely going to be punished for it. He wished there was something he could do, but he knew he'd have to return another time if he was going to be effective at rescuing her.

As Anders followed Nadir and Ivan to the door of the elven court building he realized the darkness of night had begun to fade. Dawn had started to peak in through the cracks in the doorway. *How long were we down there?* he wondered.

Ivan pushed open the doors and saw the sun rising to the east, "Dang," he spat. "We've been gone too long."

Anders reached out to Zahara. She'd already been searching for him so their connection was quick.

Where have you been? she asked, sounding worried.

Ivan and I were in the elven prison, freeing Nadir. We were down there much longer than we thought, he said. *What's been happing up here? Did you find Lageena?"*

An uncommonly long silence occurred between his question and her answer. Finally she said, *No. She's escaped.*

TWENTY

GROWTH, DISPLACEMENT, EXPEL

"What do you mean she's escaped?!" Nadir shouted when Anders relayed the message Zahara had given him.

Anders shrugged, "I'm not sure how, but that's what Zahara's told me."

"That's impossible. With the gates closed, there's no way she could've escaped, even if she could use magic, but she's never bonded with a dragon, so she can't use magic!" he shouted in frustration.

"Anders, go meet with Zahara and conduct an aerial sweep of the city. Nadir and I will summon the city watch and see if anything of use has turned up," Ivan said, trying to make Nadir see reason.

Anders nodded while he relayed their objective to Zahara. Before she'd come to circle overhead, Nadir and Ivan had rushed off to meet with the city watch. Zahara landed softly near the outside of the elven court building.

Why couldn't I sense where you'd gone? Zahara asked when he came to her side. Nuzzling her snout, Anders attempted to console his worried dragon, *I'm not exactly sure how it works, but the prison has ancient magic that prevents others from using magic. I nearly strained myself to death trying to locate Nadir once we'd gone down below the court building to the holding cells.*

Why do I sense a great relief and concern in you? she asked as he climbed into the saddle.

Something bizarre happened when we were down there. Ivan told me that the magic secured the prisoners entirely within their cells, but we were confronted by a fairnheir running loose.

Did you have to face it? Zahara asked concerned.

We nearly did, but there was this elf girl. At least she looked like a child, but when she spoke her voice was deep, making her sound older than she appeared. And she saved us. When the fairnheir was about to pounce on us, she trapped it in energy. Energy she used from my sword, Anders said as he glanced quizzically at the sword sheathed at his waist.

How is that possible, even with a decreased ability to use magic down there? How could she have used energy from your sword; it's just metal?

That's what we all thought, but the crystal in the hilt must be the key. Somehow, she used energy from the crystal.

Strange things are happening, Zahara replied. *I can't sense the elf queen anywhere. It's like she vanished into thin air. Natalia was chasing her but said the queen turned around a corner and was gone. Natalia swears she had nowhere to hide; yet now she's gone.*

Maybe Merglan's figured out a way to disrupt the magic embedded into Cedarbridge's walls. Up until now, the elves have managed to keep this place a sanctuary safe from his magic, but perhaps with Lageena's help, they discovered a way to unravel that safety net? Anders suggested.

You could be right. Whatever it is, it's not good, she said.

After several passes over the city without discovering a hint of Lageena's presence within or near Cedarbridge, Zahara asked, *How did Nadir take the news?*

About as well as anyone who's been told that his father has been murdered by his stepmother, who is a traitor operating in concert with our world's most evil sorcerer. Her escape from what he'd believed was a place incapable of being broken into or out of made it all the worse, Anders said.

It's a tragedy.

I only hope Nadir can lead his people amid all this chaos. We'll need the elven army if we're going to defeat Merglan, Anders said.

Are we ready for that? Zahara asked.

Whether we're ready or not, the time has come. We'll have to face Merglan soon or he'll take over the five nations. Look at the chaos he's caused already. He nearly destroyed the elven and dwarf relationship, the elven leadership is now in question, and he's taking control of Southland. We need to try to stop him before he grows stronger, Anders urged.

It will take a miracle.

According to Merglan, we're the closest things to that miracle that he knows of. Merglan tried to stop us from becoming bonded nearly our entire lives, yet we still managed to meet and recognize the bond. Maybe we are who he thinks we are? Maybe we were born to stop him?

Perhaps, she replied.

They'd been searching for any sign of Lageena for hours after exiting the prisons when Ivan called Zahara and Anders off the hunt. Flying toward the heart of the capital, Zahara landed near a group of armor-plated elves huddled in front of the elven court. Anders unbound himself from the saddle and hopped down from Zahara, striding hastily through the crowd. All the members of the High Council, leaders of the army and city watch, and many citizens huddled in the square in front of the cedar tree building where Nadir stood.

Shortly after Anders and Zahara joined the group, Nadir drew everyone's attention, speaking loudly and addressing them in a firm voice. "Friends, comrades and subjects. I stand before you no longer as your loyal prince, but as your leader in this fight for justice. My father was murdered late last night, killed by the hand of his wife, Lageena. When confronted with crimes of conspiracy with Merglan and plotting to destroy the free elf nation, she fled, only stopping to kill her husband and our former king before fleeing. Upon my father's death by her traitorous deed, the duty of leading the elven race falls to me. I will take full responsibility as the new elf king and will lead all of you, all of our people to do what is necessary.

"In my first act as your king, I hereby name the former queen a traitor and sentence her to death for the crimes of conspiring with Merglan's cause and murder. She may have fled the city, but we'll put her to justice before this war is over. As your new king, I'll lead an army to the gates of Kingston and tear out the infected evil that has so recently taken root in the human nation's capital."

The crowd burst into applause, but Anders saw many elves shaking their heads, disagreeing or not believing Nadir's words, several of whom were members of the High Council.

"I know some will not support my decision to fight in a war so far from our kingdom's borders," Nadir continued. "But I say to you, if we don't fight now, who will? Merglan's power has grown and will continue to grow. With each passing day, we lessen our odds of defeating him. I say we stop cowering behind our woven walls and take the fight to him before he shows up at our doors. He's already shown that he can reach his evil hand into our lives and strike at us from within. I'll not stand by and let this continue.

"Those of you who share my opinion are invited to join me in our march to the Glacial Melt Bays. There we'll make ready our naval fleet, sail along the Eastland shores and rendezvous with the dwarf kingdom's King Remli, who is in support of our cause. Together we'll take this fight to Merglan's front door."

Elf soldiers whooped and hooted, displaying their support. More members of the High Council shook their heads in disapproval of a plan to leave the kingdom at such a vulnerable time.

"Spread the word and all those who will join me are to gather at the city's south gate come nightfall. From there we'll begin our campaign," Nadir said and then he stepped away from the center of attention.

Anders watched as Nadir, Ivan and Natalia entered the royal court, out of sight of the host of elves gathered out front. He and Zahara waited for the crowd to disperse before approaching the towering wall of cedars where Nadir and the others had entered.

Before entering, Zahara stopped, *I must bring this news to my family and the other dragons.*

Anders nodded and watched her take flight, climbing rapidly out above the trees and disappearing into the blue sky beyond. He drew in a deep breath before stepping up to the large court's door and pulling it open. At the back wall of the entrance hall, Ivan, Nadir and Natalia stood hunched over a desk. As Anders approached, he saw they were examining maps and planning their route.

"So, she's left the city?" Anders asked, announcing his presence.

Ivan spoke without looking up from the map he and Nadir were examining, "We've spent nearly ten hours searching the city, combing with our eyes and our minds. With multiple sorcerers using our senses to root out the queen, we would have found something by now." He lifted his head to look at Anders and continued, "Natalia was right on her tail when it happened, she vanished."

"One moment she was there, then poof," Natalia snapped her fingers. "She rounded a corner and vanished into thin air. I've never seen anything like it. Not even trained sorcerers like Ivan and myself have mastered that kind of magic. I'm not sure how they did it, but Merglan must have gotten her out of here."

"That's impossible," Nadir interrupted, leaning heavily over the maps spread wide before them.

"Not necessarily," Anders began. He thought he might know how Merglan could have reached Lageena with magic, regardless of the magical barriers protecting everyone and everything within the city.

"What do you mean?" Nadir snapped. It was the first time Anders had seen him so impatient. Until now, the elf had remained in control of his emotions, but the stress of it all was beginning to show. The outburst was uncharacteristic. Anders wondered if he was fit to lead the elves into battle on such short notice.

Ivan eyed him suspiciously as Anders reached into his pocket and pulled out the piece of folded paper.

"What about crystals," Anders said, unfolding the paper and placing it on the desk.

"What's this?" Natalia asked, sliding the parchment closer and getting a better view.

"I discovered it in Merglan's journal," Anders said.

"But we read it cover to cover," Natalia said, meeting his eyes. "This wasn't in there."

"It appeared to Anders when we were in Hardstone," Ivan said.

Natalia shot Ivan a look of confusion, "You knew about this and didn't tell me?"

"I only found out about it when we were riding back to Cedarbridge. At the time, there seemed to be more pressing matters than discussing a drawing of a crystal," Ivan said defensively while motioning toward Nadir.

Natalia held the diagram Anders had traced closer as she tried to make sense of it. "I don't recognize the language, aside from the inscription at the bottom." She handed the paper to Ivan.

Ivan eyed the paper and asked Anders, "You're sure you got the wording, exactly right?"

Anders nodded, "I made sure to check it three times before I put it away."

"And the original?" Ivan asked, glancing up at him from across the desk.

"It vanished. The journal is as it was."

"Strange," Ivan said glancing down at the diagram again. "The words appear to be in Norfolk."

"Let me see," Nadir said, holding out his hand.

Ivan raised an eyebrow at him as he handed him the paper.

"Father made me learn it when I was in school," Nadir said taking the parchment. He examined it closely and said, "It's an ancient dialect. The Norfolk didn't write much down so their language varied greatly over time and region, but I think I can translate most of the words." Nadir picked up a quill from the desk, dipped it into a jar of ink and began to translate.

"What do you make of it?" Ivan asked.

"It appears to be some sort of instructions for the crystal," Nadir said. "The words are descriptive in nature I believe. This one at the top translates to inhabitance. Lower on the page the lines pointing inward say, 'energy in.'"

"That refers to the crystals' ability to store energy," Ivan said. "We've known they have that capability. Does it say how to identify which crystals possess the ability to harness energy?"

Nadir examined the words and shook his head, "No. None of the words I can identify say anything relating to the powerful crystals' identifying attributes. There is a curious phrase though. This line pointing out from the center of the crystal includes the words 'growth,' 'displacement' and 'expel'," Nadir looked to Ivan. "What do you think that means?"

Ivan took the paper back from Nadir. "The arrow pointing out in combination with expel probably refers to the energy out."

"Isn't that what the girl in the prison did?" Anders blurted out.

Ivan nodded, "Yes, like that. But these uses are already known to have been in existence. We're looking for clues as to whether and how Merglan is using them now."

"Like bringing Thargon back and transporting Lageena out of Cedarbridge?" Natalia added.

"Exactly," Ivan said. "So, what do the other words mean? They must also relate to things that can come from within the crystal."

"Well, if expel refers to energy out, the displacement

must mean the crystal can be used to displace objects," Anders said.

"And growth would explain re-animation of a dead kurr," Natalia said.

"Lageena must have had a crystal," Nadir said.

"And we know Thargon had one," Anders said. "He wore it."

Ivan nodded, "But this still doesn't tell us how we can defeat Merglan. Even if we knew how to identify which crystals could be used in this way."

"Well, we know we have one," Anders palmed his sword.

"True, but we don't know how to use it. It could be dangerous. My knowledge of them is minimal. No rider I've ever known has successfully used them, except for Merglan," Ivan said.

"Well, we do have his notes on how it works," Anders urged. "Translating *all* of the words on this diagram could help us discover what the crystals are capable of."

"It's too dangerous," Ivan said. "We need to know more about them before trying to use it. What if the crystal draws energy directly from you to create its power? You and Zahara have some training in using magic but not enough to stop it if the crystal used all your strength in one go. It could kill you both."

"But this is our chance to see if we can," Anders halted when Ivan slammed his fist into the desk.

"I said no!" Ivan shouted. "These are powers that the most evil human in history is playing with. Do you really want to follow in his footsteps?"

Anders was about to speak in protest but stopped when he saw Natalia shaking her head at him. He dropped his argument as the four stood in silence around the desk.

What Ivan said struck a chord in him. He spoke of a fear he'd been trying to suppress since he'd started reading Merglan's journal for the first time. Was he too similar to Merglan at his age? Their lives ran parallel in more ways than he would've liked to imagine.

Nadir was the first to break the uncomfortable silence, "I'll have to do some research, but I'll try to translate the rest of this diagram." He folded the paper and stuffed it into his pocket. Returning his attention to the maps, he and Ivan began to discuss strategies of how to best approach Southland.

Natalia motioned for Anders to step aside from the desk.

He followed her into the center of the room. Pulling him close, she whispered, "I know it appears like he's being hard on you, but he's just trying to protect you. You and Zahara are the last hope we have right now. You're the only rider pair in our arsenal and we can't risk your lives by experimenting with the crystals right now."

Anders nodded and replied, matching her hushed tone, "I know, but does he have to be so mean about it?"

"Hang in there, kid, he'll come around," Natalia said with a smirk and they returned to the desk.

"So, we'll meet the dwarf reinforcements here," Ivan said putting his finger down on the first exposed map.

"And Remli is certain about backing us up with this cause?" Nadir questioned.

"You should've seen how eager he was to get back to the glories of the battlefield before that whole business with his ambassador traitor. He'll be there, with a host of dwarfs ready to wage war," Ivan assured him.

"Good. I have a feeling we'll need them," Nadir said. "I

didn't get the feeling that everyone outside was onboard with the plan to set sail to Southland."

"There will be some backlash, and many elves will oppose a war so far from the kingdom's borders, but we must do what we must to keep Merglan from rising further in power over Kartania. If we don't, who will?" Ivan stated.

"What about the Rollo warriors?" Anders suggested. "And the human armies? Surely we can gather an army of men from Westland and Southland to oppose him?"

"With Red commanding the Rollo warriors, it's less likely that they'll support the elves in this. I got the feeling from his most recent letter that now that his people are back on their islands, he'll be staying put until he's directly attacked. With his father dead and gone, he'll not help the elves any more than he would the rest of Kartania," Ivan said.

"What about other human nations?" Anders asked.

"Forming an army large enough to face Merglan would take months, maybe years. We can't afford to wait that long. Our scouts say Merglan's taken control of most of Southland since we've been here in the Everlight Kingdom. Scouts have informed us that his orc forces are gathering in the Goblin's Grove. From there they'll sail across the narrows to Southland. Merglan's somehow gathered a large following of humans in Southland. The Lumbapi tribes, however, will never follow him. They've managed to evade his influences and have begun gathering in the Ramhorn and Drakeshead provinces in Southland. They're our only hope of recruiting allies in Southland," Ivan said.

"That's our plan then," Nadir nodded. "We'll gather as many elves as we can, rendezvous with the dwarfs and sail toward the Drakeshead in Southland. That way we'll be close to the Goblin's Grove and we might pick up some help from the Lumbapi who've congregated there. We'll attack Merglan's forces as they attempt to come across the narrows into Southland and hopefully drive him out, forcing him back to the Eastland territories and dividing his forces."

"That's as good a plan as any," Natalia added, glancing to them.

"Zahara and I can fly ahead to the Rollo Islands and try to convince Red to set sail for our cause," Anders suggested.

"You'll have a hard time prying him loose from the islands to help the elves, but it's worth a shot. Their warriors are such strong fighters, I agree we should try to convince them to join us," Ivan agreed.

"Well, what are we still standing around here for?" Nadir said, pulling the maps in and rolling them up. "We've got an army to assemble."

Nadir led Ivan, Natalia and Anders out of the building. To their surprise, a host of elves had already assembled outside the door, armed and ready for war.

As the elves marched through the city, Anders rushed off to find Zahara. She sent him a mental image of her location. He knew the place well; she was speaking with her parents near the cliff's edge where they entered and exited the city. As Anders approached, he could sense worry and angst in Zahara's parents. Their child was about to fly off to yet another war with her bonded human. Anders couldn't help but feel embarrassed and guilty for their worry. Despite his feelings, he knew Kartania needed them as a pair.

Anders didn't have to announce his arrival; Zahara and her parents sensed him when he approached in the distance.

He stopped when he drew near, patiently waiting for them to finish their conversation. He felt the burning of her father's glare just before he and his partner took flight.

I'm sorry about that, she said as Anders stepped into view.

No, I'm sorry. I feel terrible that I'm taking you away from them again, he said.

It's not your fault. I picked you. I knew exactly what came with it when I chose to bond with you. Someone must be strong and face this evil or it will consume everything we're fighting for. They don't see it that way, but I've seen what Merglan can do. He'll destroy everything that's good in this world unless we stop him.

I know. I've been having difficulty coming to grips with that reality, but it seems like we're Kartania's best hope right now.

We'd better get busy then, Zahara said lowering her shoulder for Anders to climb on.

He shared the discussion she missed in the royal court as they returned to the training grounds. Anders gathered their bags and communicated with Ivan via their minds to grab any items he thought they might need for their journey. Anders hoped Maija would be waiting for them there, back from her adventure to find the red dragon. As he approached his room, he held his breath and closed his eyes. Slowly he opened the door. He peeked through a crack at first, slowly opening his eyes and the door to see the room, which was just as empty as when they'd left. Sighing with disappointment, he joined Zahara in the dining hall for one last hearty meal before their long flight.

She'll come back, Zahara said as they chewed in silence.

I know. I just miss her, Anders said and returned to his

meal. His thoughts bounced between the workings of the sapphire crystal in his sword and the desire to see Maija.

The evening sky chilled him as Anders and Zahara flew toward the southern gate of Cedarbridge's fortified wall. The elves stood ready at the gate, waiting for their leader to advance toward the Glacial Melt Bays. Anders had hoped their numbers would have been greater. The host appeared to be half the size of the army that had come to Merglan's fortress several months prior.

Touching down near the gate, Anders stayed mounted on Zahara, knowing they were meant to leave at a moment's notice. Nadir didn't waste any time. Once the trickle of arrivals slowed, he opened the gates and led the army out into the forest. Anders and Zahara carried Ivan as they took to the sky, flying over the militant force running to the innermost bay.

The journey to the bay didn't take the elves long. Though they were weighed down with protective plate and steel, they advanced quickly through the forest. Zahara landed near the water as Ivan climbed down and rushed to join the elves. Nadir spoke of a naval fleet, but Anders didn't see any ships in the bay. It wasn't until he saw them climbing on the many cliff-like protrusions from the bay's coast that he realized the disguise. The ships had been cloaked by vegetation, appearing as natural landmasses. Anders watched wide-eyed as the vessels slid out from the forested shoreline into the open water.

As Ivan helped Anders offload Zahara's saddlebags to make her saddle as light as possible for their long flight to the Rollo Islands, Ivan spoke to them with his mind, *We'll be on a course to meet Remli and the dwarf army at the base of the Eastland Mountains, near Black Water Bay. From there we'll sail across the Marauder's Sea and around the easternmost reaches of Southland. You two should have just enough time to fly to the Rollo Islands, try to convince Red to join our cause, and join us as we near Southland. If Red does decide to sail, arrange a meeting time along the Ramhorn of Southland. We'll be attacking from near the Drakeshead, but the Ramhorn is not more than half a week's sail from there. If the winds are in our favor, we'll make landfall in just over a week's time. It should take you three days to fly to the Rollo Islands, one day of negotiations and three days south to Southland. That's one week. Plan to meet us near the Drakeshead. You'll probably have an easier time finding us, than us trying to locate you. Good luck and make haste. We're counting on you two in the battle to come.*

Anders nodded, settling into his seat on Zahara as she took flight. They veered to the west, following the coastline as they flew. Anders hoped Merglan wasn't wise to their plan. If he wanted to, he could ride out and intercept Anders and Zahara on their solo mission as he'd done to Natalia and Keanu. They didn't have much choice, however. They would have to hope they could fly under his radar for now.

During the following days, Anders and Zahara slept little, keeping to the sky. They flew low to the ground and bypassed any town or sign of civilization along the way. Anders didn't know how many disciples Merglan had in Westland, but he didn't want to take the chance of being seen by anyone. During one stop they camped near the place where they had first met, recalling how scared they were of one another, yet also intrigued. Anders and Zahara shared these memories. Though actually only months ago, it seemed like years to both of them.

After their rest, they began their last day of flying as they ventured out over open water. It was the most direct route to the islands from the Bareback Plains. They would cross the ocean rich with pelagic life and fly straight to the islands. If circumstances were different, they could lessen the distance over open water by continuing north along the coast. If they did that now, they'd increase the risk of being seen and alerting Merglan to their vulnerability. Most of Westland's major cities were built along the coast north of the plains. Anders desperately wanted to see his cousins and considered the risk. But he was sure that they had made it back to Grandwood. If they hadn't, Red's message would've mentioned it. He couldn't risk being seen, not when there was so much riding on his return before the fighting began.

The third day of flying was long. The travel over the open water for such a great distance made them uneasy. Having never been to the islands, they worried they would miss the small landmasses amidst the vast ocean. So, it was a great relief when they first saw the volcano island rising from the blue horizon. Anders was just beginning to wonder if they'd flown past it when islands appeared in the distance. And now came the hard part, convincing Red to fight for the elves.

TWENTY-ONE

A DRAGON IN THE ROLLO ISLANDS

The Rollo Islands shone brilliant green and indigo as Zahara and Anders flew over the island chain. Argon, the capital city of the Rollo nation, sat nestled below an actively smoking volcano rising from the largest of the islands. Dispersed around the main island, smaller islands scattered the waters. Anders marveled at the changing color of the ocean water as it turned from a dark blue out at sea to brilliant indigo with light blue edging at the base of each island. White sand skirted much of the islands and the Rollo's famous long-ships could be seen anchored or moving among the islands. Argon's port, however, hosted the most extensive collection of ships Anders had ever seen in his life.

As they circled above the city, Anders saw masses of mahogany-toned warriors gathering on the beaches. His mission was to negotiate with Red, but he was looking forward to seeing Britt and Max the most; if Max had stayed on with her crew. Anders missed Britt's strong will and determined demeanor and Max's light-hearted attitude and joy for adventure. The time he'd spent with them was brief, but they both had made a lasting impression on him that he couldn't ignore.

Zahara swooped low over the shallow water, bringing them in close to shore and preparing to land. The crowd of people that had gathered along Argon's white sand beach cleared an area of them to touch down. Anders had worried about the warriors' reaction to their unannounced arrival. As soon as he and Zahara came into view of the city, he felt a lot of worry rising collectively from the island people. The closer they flew, the less they could sense that feeling. The tension was replaced with familiarity and relief as the Islanders prepared to welcome these allies.

Many of the dark-haired Rolloans on the beach smiled when Anders climbed down from his perch on Zahara's back. Anders could still pick up some hostility from older warriors who'd been around to partake in The War of the Magicians, but their feelings were mostly drowned out by the joy of the others upon seeing a friendly rider.

Anders politely smiled and waved as he led Zahara along the beach through the crowd of Islanders gathered to greet them. Soon he heard a commotion arising among one section of the group. Suddenly Anders heard Red's voice booming from deep within the crowd.

"Make way, make way," Red called out to his people.

Anders waited for Red to approach him. The crowd parted as he walked, making a path for their new chief to come and greet their surprise guest and dragon.

Once Red could see Anders and Zahara, he quickened his pace. Anders smiled, but the newly elected leader of the Rollo people maintained his predictable scowl. Red came to a halt in a circle cleared around Anders and Zahara and stood, legs spread past shoulder width. Folding his muscular, tattooed arms, he said, "Anders, to what do I owe the pleasure of this unannounced visit?"

The irritation in his voice was palpable and Anders quickly recalled why he didn't have fond memories of the warrior brute. "Can't an old friend come to visit every once in a while?" Anders responded with just a hint of sarcasm. Anders thought Red to be less intelligent than he was, but even Red could recognize the Anders' slight.

"A friend, no. I don't mind when a friend comes to visit. So, I ask you again; what are you doing here?"

"Ivan sent me. There's a matter of urgency we must discuss." When Red didn't show any sign of allowing their conversation to be moved to a more secluded location, Anders added, "In private, if possible."

Red uncrossed his arms and shifted his feet closer to stand slightly taller. Puffing his chest out to emphasize his large stature in front of his people, he declared loudly, "I'll gladly hear what you've to say in my great hall. Tonight, we shall feast, not because of your arrival, but because it's the festival of the blood moon. We can discuss what Ivan wants you to tell me then." Red didn't invite Anders to follow him; he merely turned his back and walked steadily through the sand back toward the city.

That was rude, Zahara said to Anders.

We can't spend much time here. We really need to convince him to help us by tonight. We'll have to leave again tomorrow.

If we didn't need his support so badly, I'd not be opposed to leaving now. He's a jackass of a man. Did I use that term correctly? she asked.

Anders chuckled, *Yes, you nailed that one on the head.*

What's a nail?

369

It's a..., never mind. I'll explain it later. You used that term in the right way, he said.

Anders quickly scanned the crowd for Britt. He expected that she would've come forth through the gathering as Red had.

Maybe she's not on this island or off sailing somewhere else? Zahara said, attempting to comfort him.

I've tried to find both her and Max, but I can't. Maybe you're right. She's probably just on a different island. Well, we'd better follow Red and start these negotiations.

Anders and Zahara didn't need to force their way through the crowd. The people parted like grasshoppers in late summer, jumping out of their way as they advanced into the city.

Argon was the capital city of the Rollo Islands. As such, the city was structured around the chief's lodge. For more than a thousand years, the Rollo people had claimed the islands as their home. The main lodge at the center of the city was built of stone with wooden shingles gripping a steeply pitched roof. Sprawling around the main lodge, Argon consisted of many wooden houses covered with thickly layered leaves. The thatched roofs were made from the robust leaves on the tropical trees growing abundantly throughout the islands. Since the islands saw heavy amounts of annual precipitation, their buildings were built upon stilts slightly off the ground to avoid regular flooding.

Anders and Zahara trailed in Red's wake into the heart of the city. The dirt roads were lined with these houses. Many people had boats tied to their homes so when the rains came and flooded the city, they would have a means of transportation. As they ventured deeper into Argon, the crowd began to dissipate rapidly. Most of the warrior people spent their days on the water or by the water's edge.

Red approached the main lodge built for the Rollo people's head chieftain. The large doors to his home were decorated with a carving of two Rolloan long-ships. Red pulled open a door using the large brass-ringed handle. Anders wanted Zahara to come inside with him, but the lodge was not quite large enough for her to fit in comfortably. When he opened the large door, Zahara came as far as the entrance. Anders walked into the lodge and Zahara stuck her long neck through the doorway after him.

Inside the lodge was one large room. Several long tables filled the otherwise empty space. A stone hearth rose from the center of the room and out through the wooden ceiling. Red was searching through a chest near the throne-like chairs perched atop a raised platform at the far end of the hall.

His eyes didn't wander from the contents of the chest as he pulled aside parchment and other objects Anders didn't recognize. It wasn't until Anders cleared his throat loudly that Red acknowledged his presence.

"Yes. What do you want?" he said, barely looking up to see who it was. Once he caught a glimpse of Zahara's large head in the entrance, he straightened up. "Anders, the feast will not begin until later tonight. I'm sure you two would like to see all that the islands have to offer. Go and explore. Come back later and we'll talk."

"Red, this is an urgent matter and demands your attention now. I didn't want to discuss it in front of the whole city, but it's about Merglan."

"I thought we sent that old peacock running scared."

"We did defeat a portion of his orc and kurr army, yes, but if you recall, we never actually saw him."

"Because he was frightened by our fierceness," Red said,

stepping away from the chest and coming several paces closer.

"No. Other dragonriders were there that night. They led him away from the battle. He destroyed them while we defeated his host at the fortress. We don't know exactly why he didn't return after defeating the riders, but he could've fought us with ease."

"What's all this got to do with me?" Red said, crossing his thick arms again.

"Merglan's invaded Southland. He holds his position in Kingston's castle. A large portion of the forces sworn to defend it have been tricked or forced into serving him. The only people who've shown any resistance to him are the Lumbapi who've been forced to fight Merglan's growing army with guerilla warfare. They've managed to hole up in the Drakeshead and Ramhorn provinces."

"I still don't see what this has to do with me or my people," Red interrupted.

Anders let out a long breath, trying not to let his emotions toward Red get in the way of his plight. "Orcs have been reported to be gathering in the Goblin's Grove. Merglan's going to bring them across the narrows and into Southland."

"Still don't see," Red began, but Anders cut him off this time.

"What it's got to do with you, Red, is that you're now the leader of one of the three nations of humanity. Southland rules over the Rollo Islands. They have been just and kind over the years. You owe them your allegiance to fight for the fate of humanity. On top of that, Merglan will not stop once he's taken Southland. He means to rule all of Kartania. He'll come to these islands eventually and take them and your people for his own."

"Impossible!" Red shouted. "He'll never take down the might of my warriors. We're far stronger than anything he can bring. Our navy is the fastest and strongest in the world."

"He's the most powerful sorcerer the world has ever known! He doesn't need a navy to beat you! He could probably do it by himself with his dragon."

"Puh," Red exhaled. "Doubt it."

"Ivan and Nadir are leading the elves to rendezvous with King Remli and his dwarf force. They're sailing to the Drakeshead from there. We're going to bring the fight to Merglan and stop him from taking over Southland by force."

"Oh, and you expect me to help those freaks!?" Red bellowed. "No, not on my orders."

"Had it not been for Nadir and the elves, we would've been overwhelmed under Merglan's fortress. You owe them a debt of gratitude. Gather your warriors and sail for Southland."

Red's complexion turned a dark red as he stomped across the wooden floor to face Anders. Anders thought he might strike him. Zahara must have thought the same thing because when he drew close, she lifted her upper lip and growled low, warning him not to move any closer to Anders.

Red stopped when he heard Zahara's snarl and saw her exposed fangs. He stuck an accusing finger toward the two of them and said harshly, "I'll never help those bastard freaks and I'll never let these islands fall prey to some pompous sorcerer who thinks shining a flash of light will scare me away from my kingdom. I owe no allegiance to Southland or Westland either. We're our own independent nation and don't answer the calls of the elves or any of the other kingdoms."

"Red, you must be reasonable. We can't defeat Merglan alone."

"You'll have to. I'm not involved in this fight anymore, and my word is final." He strode back across the lodge to the chest he'd been digging through. Before returning to his search, he said, "I want you and your dragon gone by nightfall. You're not welcome here."

Anders had had enough of trying to reason with the childish chieftain. He turned and hastily exited the building. Zahara withdrew her neck and Anders slammed the door behind them. *Come on*, he said to Zahara. *Let's get out of here.*

Anders, we must try harder. He needs to see that he can't best Merglan on his own. I'm sure if he can see that it will be best for his people, he might agree to help us.

It's like reasoning with a spoiled child. He's never going to help us as long as we're working with the elves.

We should give him some time to clear his head and try to talk with him again, she suggested.

Alright, but for now I need to clear my own head. Let's see if we can find Britt. Perhaps she can speak reason to him, Anders hopped on Zahara's back and she took flight, rising high above the island.

ZAHARA COULD FEEL THAT ANDERS' mind was a jumble of anger and frustration, so she did something that she knew he loved. Flying freely through the open sky, she rose high into the air above the islands. Flapping her wings to slow her climb and then coming to a halt, she hovered for a moment, then dove down head first. She tucked her wings against her sides and they sped straight down toward the ocean. She could feel the adrenaline rushing through his body as they plummeted toward the blue water, coming closer as they dropped.

Zahara felt the fear building in Anders as they rapidly neared the sandy shoreline. Just as he began to panic, she spread her wings and pulled up. The gravity of the world pulled down on them hard as she banked out of her dive. The force was almost too much for her to keep her head upright; she had to fight hard to be able to look ahead. She could feel Anders being pressed tightly onto her neck as he gripped the saddle handles, working to hold on. The force pushed him down hard against her scales, but the magic lashing him to the leather saddle kept him in his seat. Soaring low along the main island's shoreline, Anders sat upright again, letting out a cry of pure joy.

"Yew!" he shouted as he let go of the handles, pumping his fists into the air.

Zahara smiled and angled herself up and to the right. She climbed, this time making herself corkscrew twice as she rose. When she was several hundred feet up, she angled backward and let herself fall, spiraling and folding as they dropped. She could sense, even with the saddle's connection, it was all that Anders could do to hold on. He dug his heels hard into the pits of her wings and clutched the handles. She spread her wings when they neared the ocean and dipped out of their tumble just as she'd done the dive before. Anders again shouted with joy.

Zahara, I want to try something, Anders said to her. He showed her a mental image of what he wanted to do and Zahara smiled.

She climbed again, higher than they'd gone before.

When she reached the point at which they were going to fall once more, Anders broke the connection with his saddle and lifted himself out of his seated position. Balancing awkwardly, he rested his feet on her shoulders where her wings came out of her back, he crouched. Still holding onto the saddle, he was standing almost unassisted. He signaled to her to fall and he let go.

Zahara angled herself so she wasn't dropping straight down at first. Anders stood on her back as they flew, he leaned hard into the rushing wind almost floating as they fell. He leaned harder forward as Zahara tilted more aggressively downward. Soon Zahara was pointing straight down and she could feel Anders' feet leaving her body. Anders shouted with joy as he came unglued from her back. He fell freely through the air. Zahara rolled herself to face him. Anders mirrored Zahara as they plunged head first toward the ocean. For what seemed like a minute Zahara watched as Anders rolled and spun himself, giggling as he fell through the sky.

When they drew near the point where Anders had to remount Zahara to avoid crashing into the ocean below, she dipped lightly under him. She angled slightly so when Anders caught her neck, he could place himself properly in the saddle and re-establish the bond with the saddle before she pulled up. After they'd finished their little stunt, they soared peacefully over the islands. Zahara could sense that the frustration and anger had left him entirely. He emanated pure joy and happiness at being with her in the sky. She purred as they flew and Anders hugged her tightly around the neck.

Anders looked on in awe as Zahara flew him around each of the eleven islands that made up the Rollo chain. Thatched houses were scattered throughout the tranquil forests below. People in boats paddled between the islands, some fishing, some just paddling for the fun of it. Anders imagined what it would be like to live there. Other than having Red as your leader, it seemed that it would be a happy life. The ocean would provide much of your needs and the tropical forest on the islands would supply the rest. Since it rained often and heavily, fresh water was plentiful. He wondered why their culture felt the need to venture away from that place and raid other nations.

After Zahara had helped Anders clear his head and find his sanity once more, he opened his mind to search for Britt. Anders wasn't the most experienced sorcerer, but he'd been polishing his ability to use his mind to find signatures of people, animals and plants. Each living being had its own signature. The signatures between species varied; each species had its own similar feel, but each signature was unique. Anders recalled Britt's as being interesting. She expelled certain confidence that he rarely found in others.

Anders searched each island individually as they flew over. As island after island came and went, Anders began to worry when he didn't sense her presence. She'd been on the same ship as Max and his cousins. He hoped they'd made it back to Grandwood.

Surely Red would have told us if Britt's ship didn't make it to Grandwood, Zahara comforted him, sensing this fear.

Yes, you would think he would've mentioned it if something terrible had happened to them.

After Anders and Zahara had searched each of the eleven islands and found no trace of Britt or Max, the possibilities of what might have become of her began to overwhelm Anders.

Let's see if we can find anyone from her crew and ask them where she is, Anders suggested.

Zahara agreed and they flew back to the beaches of Argon. Landing softly on the white sand, the once bustling crowd that had gathered for their arrival had gone. People had returned to their work, though several younger Rolloans remained huddled together grinning at Anders and Zahara.

The young islanders rushed up to Anders before he had a chance to search the area for any of Britt's crew. The youngsters pawed at him, jumping with joy while speaking in Rolloan. Anders couldn't understand them, but from their joy at seeing him return, he assumed they'd been watching when he and Zahara had been flying.

Anders shook his head and shrugged, "I don't speak Rolloan. I can't understand you."

One of the little girls among them spoke some Landish. She said, "We watched when you and dragon flying. Amazing!" She mimicked their free-falling with her hand and made several whooshing noises as she did so.

Anders laughed, "Oh you did, did you? Well, flying isn't always that much fun. Sometimes it's hard work and we must focus hard to accomplish our task."

"I wish I can fly. You go again? Please, please, please," she pleaded, clutching her hands together and hopping up and down excitedly.

"I can't," he said and watched the girl's expression sour. "I need to speak with someone. You might know her. Will you help me?"

A glimmer of hope returned to the girl's face. Anders felt she wasn't quite convinced, so he said, "You can sit on Zahara if you want."

Her face lit up and she began hopping up and down again, clapping her hands. "Can we?" she asked excitedly.

Anders didn't need to look at Zahara to know she

wasn't thrilled about the idea of a bunch of little kids climbing all over her. He brought his hand to his chin, rubbing it in thought, then said, "If you help me find who I'm looking for, each one of you can sit on Zahara." The little girl squealed with joy. "But you have to go one at a time, and if Zahara says you must get off, then you must listen to her. I'm not responsible if she decides to eat you for a snack." The girl's face went ghostly white and she stopped looking at Zahara with loving eyes. Realizing he'd frightened her to death, Anders said, "I'm joking! It was only a joke. I promise she won't eat you. She doesn't eat people; I promise."

The girl looked at him with kind eyes again. She cracked a smile and nodded vigorously. "Okay. Deal, deal." She held out her hand and Anders shook it.

The other children were unaware of the deal she'd struck so when they saw her actions turn from excited to scared then back to joyful once more, they shouted and pleaded with her in Rolloan. Anders couldn't understand what they said but the girl spoke quickly in their native tongue. The children's attention was all hers for a matter of moments. Then they erupted in screams and cries of happiness.

Once Anders figured she'd finished relaying the deal, he asked her, "Okay, will you help me now?"

"Yes. Who you look for?" she asked.

"I'm looking for a Capitan in the Rollo Navy. She's dark and has thick hair. She's a fierce warrior and her crew holds her in high regard. Her name is Britt. Do you know her?"

The girl's face lit up as she heard him say Britt's name. "I know, I know! She friend." The girls face soured once more, "But she no here."

Anders felt a sinking feeling in the pit of his stomach. "What happened to her?"

"Mother talk of her. She say, Britt and chief no like." The girl made a smashing motion with her fist into her palm. "Chief tell us, Britt no respect and leave."

"What?"

"He say Britt stay. Mainland, she stay."

"So, they made it to Grandwood, but Britt stayed there?" Anders asked hopeful.

The girl nodded, "Yes."

"Did any of her crew come back?"

The girl seemed to think hard about it, then she shrugged, making it obvious that she didn't know for certain.

"Do any of your friends know?"

The girl spoke to the group. Most of the kids shook their heads as she had, but two boys responded excitedly. When they'd gone quiet again Anders looked to the girl, his eyes wide and eager to hear what they had said. "He say father take her ship. Many new men. They sail far."

"Can they show me to their father's crew?" he asked.

The girl relayed the question. "He gone, sail far. No back soon."

Anders cursed under his breath so the girl wouldn't hear him. *There isn't enough time for me to track them down,* he thought.

"Ride dragon?" the girl asked, smiling brightly.

Anders turned to face Zahara. He could tell she was reluctant to let the little Rolloans onto her back.

As she knelt forward so the small humans could climb onto her, she said, *You owe me a huge favor.*

Sorry, Anders shrugged.

The things I do for you.

Anders looked to the girl again and said, "Who's first?"

Once the last of the children had scrambled down from Zahara's back, she shook herself like a dog ridding itself of water.

Don't ever make me do that again, Zahara said.

I'm sorry. I needed to know if Britt's ship went down or if they made it safely to Grandwood.

I know, but there are other ways of gathering that information.

Are you suggesting I read their minds?

Perhaps, Zahara said.

That's not very ethical, Anders protested.

Neither is me eating a bunch of small humans, but I might be tempted to if you ever make me go through that again.

Come on. Was it that bad?

She snorted a puff of smoke in response.

So what do we do now? Anders asked.

We need to make Red see reason.

It sounded like at least some of the people know that Red might be hiding something from them about what happened to Britt. I don't see her crew leaving her willingly. I think it's possible she tried to force Red out of leadership and he left her in Westland with no ship or crew, Anders suggested.

That does sound like something he would do. And if he timed it with the drop off of Max and your cousins, he may have been able to convince the other warriors that she opted to stay with them.

Do you think if we exposed that information to the warriors, they might oppose his decision to stay here and come with us? Anders asked.

It's risky, but it might work, Zahara said. *It's possible that the other leaders agreed with Red's decision to leave Britt. If that's what happened, it's doubtful that any of them would hear our cause. They might agree with Red about the elves.*

We have to try something, Anders said. *If Red doesn't see reason, perhaps the others will. It's our only play that could work. We'll just have to assume that Red is hiding the truth about Britt's leaving with everyone. Maybe if they learn the truth about it some of the ships will sail with us.*

How will we make this information available to the warriors? They're scattered across the islands; it would take days to tell them all, she said.

Red said there was going to be a feast for the blood moon celebration at his lodge tonight. He wants us gone, so we'll act like we're leaving. We can return under cover of darkness and enter the feast. We'll tell everyone all at once. They'll all be there and will hear what we have to say whether they like it or not.

I guess that's as good a plan as any, Zahara agreed.

Anders and Zahara flew over Red's lodge before leaving Argon. They headed out over the ocean and away from the islands. Zahara made sure she was out of sight of the islands before she began circling. Since it was afternoon, this plan meant that they had to fly for hours. Anders and Zahara grew increasingly jaded as they circled the same spot waiting for nightfall. After what seemed a lifetime, the sunset beyond the vast ocean horizon.

The blood moon had yet to rise, so Anders and Zahara were able to fly closer to the islands without being seen. They first came to land on an uninhabited beach of a nearby island within sight of Argon. Anders could see flaming torches lit among the streets of the island city. Hundreds of more longships had arrived since they'd left that afternoon. From a distance, it looked as though the beach was clear of people. He reached out with his mind to make sure there wasn't a crowd on the beach at the edge of the city. Confirming his suspicions, he sensed the majority of the people were in the city, and gathered around Red's large lodge.

It's safe to go over, Anders said.

We'll have to be extra sneaky once we're over there. If the warriors catch us sneaking around before we get a chance to expose Red, they'll likely think we're there to cause harm. I don't want to face an army of Rollo warriors if there's any hope of keeping them as allies.

Okay. We'd better make sure we get this right then, Anders said.

Zahara flew silently over the water. Instead of landing on the beach as they did before, they decided it was best to fly straight to the lodge. The city was dark and quiet as they glided over the thatched roofs of Argon. Anders expected to see a large number of Rolloans gathered outside Red's lodge, but to his surprise, there weren't many at all.

Cupping the air with her large leather-like wings, Zahara slowed herself and landed softly outside the lodge. The few people in the streets didn't think much of their arrival. Half of them didn't even notice they'd landed, their drunken stupor blinding them to the goings on around them.

Anders leapt down from Zahara and walked up to the closed doors of Red's lodge. He could hear the laughs and loud chatter of the warriors within the building. He took several deep breaths to calm his nerves before he grabbed and pulled the brass ring. The large wooden door swung open and Anders stepped boldly inside. The warriors' loud chatter suddenly died as they looked to see the dragonrider enter with his dragon's head following him into the entryway.

Red rose from his seat at the far end of the room, brew horn in hand. "I thought I told you to leave!" he bellowed angrily.

All eyes in the room flashed from Anders to Red and back to Anders.

Anders drew on the magical energy within him and used it to enhance his voice so all could hear him. "I'll go, but before I do, I want everyone to hear why you refuse to come to our aid."

There was a murmur among the warriors, as they looked to one another, clearly confused.

"Like I told you before. We'll not be helping those freaks. Not for you or anyone!" Red shouted. Many cheers arose from the crowd.

Red smiled at the reaction, but Anders spoke over their din, "You may not get along with the elves and that's fine. I'm not asking you to like them. I'm asking for your help in a war that will consume all nations in Kartania. You don't have to do it for your allegiance to Southland or the kinship of the elves, but you should do it for the betterment of the human race.

"Merglan is the most powerful sorcerer this world has ever known. He seeks to rule humankind along with the rest of the world. It may not seem like a threat to you now, but he'll soon be at your doorsteps and no matter how well trained you are, you won't be able to stop him on your own. He'll enslave your children and kill anyone who opposes him. He's taken over Southland now and will be moving to Westland and these islands next. The elves, dwarfs and I are taking this fight to him in Southland. I beg you to listen to reason and help our cause. We'll have a greater chance of defeating him if we can all work together."

Anders' words had some effect on the crowd because some of the people clapped at his call for action.

Red motioned for them to quiet down, "You speak lies!" Red barked. "Our army is strong, far stronger than he will be. Even if the rest of the world falls, he'll never take these islands. We sent him running scared in Eastland and we'll do the same if he tries to come here."

Red earned more cheers and hoots from his warriors.

"I'm not the one who speaks lies. I would tell my people the truth about one of their best captains being forced from their command."

The room fell silent once more. They turned to look at their chief. "What's he talking about?" one of the warriors asked.

Anders knew he was only speculating about what happened to Britt, but he had a strong suspicion he was right.

Red screwed up his face and coughed, clearing his throat. "He's got his facts all wrong."

"You told the members of your navy that one of their best captains, Britt, wanted to leave her post and stay in Westland with her new friends. Did you not?"

Anders looked around the room and saw many of the warriors bobbing their heads in agreement.

"I told them that because that was the truth!" Red shouted. "She told me herself she wanted to stay with them. She'd fallen in love with that dark-haired one, Max."

Many of the people in the room began to talk at this new information.

"I don't believe you," Anders said. "I think you forced her out because she questioned your ability to lead these people," Anders gestured to the crowd.

"I thought I told you to leave. We'll not be helping you

or your cause and I'll not sit here and take this from an inexperienced dandy!" He forced his chair back and he shot to his feet.

Anders stopped him with his mind. He held him still, unable to move or act. The unexpected use of magic drained his energy quickly, but Anders held the spell restricting his movement and his tongue from speaking any further. He spoke to the people in the crowded room, "I came here to ask for help from allies, people who I fought beside in Eastland. I see you as friends and don't want that to change. I'm going to bring the fight to Merglan before he brings it to the rest of the world. I only ask that you make up your minds for yourselves. If you want to stay here with Red, then do that. But if you believe him to be withholding secrets in how he handles things when someone disagrees with him and want to help our cause in Southland, then I ask you to set sail to Southland. We'll be leading the fight at the Drakeshead. If any of you choose to come, you can expect plenty of fighting to be had in the Ramhorn as well. I've said what I have to say."

Anders turned and left the lodge, closing the door behind him. He kept his hold on Red until he and Zahara had lifted high over the city. He wanted to give the people time to think for themselves about what he'd told them. Once he couldn't hold the spell any longer, he released Red.

Do you think that worked? Anders asked Zahara once they'd turned back toward Westland.

I don't know. There were mixed emotions from many in the room. It's hard to say if we convinced any of them to leave. I doubt Red will allow them to leave anyway.

Yeah, you're right. He'll probably banish anyone who leaves, saying that they can no longer be Rollo citizens if they choose to fight with us.

We'll just have to wait and see what happens over the next week, Zahara said.

As they flew through the night, Anders' thoughts wandered to the events of the week ahead. When they returned to the elves and dwarfs, they'd be going to war once again. He worried that he might not live to see Maija again. He wondered how she was faring in Nagano, whether she'd found the dragon and if they'd become friends. He missed her terribly but knew their destinies involved two separate paths now.

TWENTY-TWO

LAZURAN'S POWER

A nders nodded off as he rode, bobbing in and out of sleep as they flew through the night. He and Zahara had gone days with only several hours of rest each night. The chilly air of the night sky was no longer cold enough to keep him alert. When they'd flown from the elven forest, the chill at altitude had held him on guard, but as the days passed in their travels, the chill became numbingly normal. The constant air rushing past his ears turned to white noise and the persistent whooshing of Zahara's wings lulled him to complacency. His connection with Zahara relaxed after they'd taken a brief pit stop along the Bareback Plains earlier that day. After flying over open water through the night and south along Westland's coast most of the morning, they found a small oasis of trees along the coast and took shelter. Using the concealment spell Natalia taught them before leaving the Everlight Kingdom, Anders and Zahara were allowed several worry-free hours to catch up on their sleep before they set out to continue on their route.

Avoiding land during the day, they were somewhere

over the Marauder's Sea later that afternoon when Anders felt Zahara's connection go completely silent. He might not have noticed, but when she unexpectedly steered at a downward angle, Anders almost slid out of the saddle, having not bothered to bind himself to it with magic after their last stop. Catching himself on one of the saddle handles, Anders shouted into her mind waking her from her state.

What was that about? Anders asked as she corrected her trajectory.

Sorry Anders, I nodded off there. I'm so tired. Ever since we left Mount Orena I've not gotten a full night of sleep.

I know, I'm getting complacent and allowing myself to continue blankly as well.

I wish we could stop and sleep for days, Zahara said. Anders felt their connection re-establish itself. He could now sense her longing for a soft patch of grass in the warm sun.

I know, I want the same thing, but we've got to continue at least until we are close enough to make a connection with Ivan. They'll need our help in the coming battle and if something went wrong with their plan, I'd feel responsible.

You're right; we have too much at stake to stop now, but maybe when we're closer we can rest for longer than a few hours at a time?

Yes. Once we're back in the safety of others, we'll be able to catch up on our sleep, but for now, we must continue.

Zahara and Anders pressed on through the night and edged closer to their counterparts sailing south along the coast. Anders found himself worrying more about his cousins, Britt, Max and Bo back in Grandwood. He knew something wasn't right after his conversation with the Rolloan girl. He'd had days to think it over, but couldn't act due to his responsibilities to the elves and trying to stop

Merglan's progress. The more he dwelled on it, the more frustrated he became. He had too much time on his hands during the long flight, enough time to start second-guessing his duties. He knew if he abandoned Ivan, Nadir and Natalia now and found his cousins living comfortably at their farmhouse near Grandwood, Ivan and the elves would never let him live it down if they survived. Anders and Zahara were the last hope at stopping the deadly sorcerer and his dragon from taking over Kartania.

Forcing himself to forget his worries for Thomas, Kirsten and the others, for the time being, Anders found his mind returning to Maija. Her beautiful amber hair and brown eyes. The way she smiled when Anders looked at her. The softness of her lips and the touch of her hand. He longed for her and for their lives to return to the ease of when they first met. Just imagining spending time together lulled Anders into a dreamlike state once more. This time, though, it wasn't Zahara's tilting that woke him. A sudden surge of energy passed through his body sending a tingling sensation from the tips of his fingers up, straight through to his heart. He lost his breath for a moment and thought he might collapse. Zahara seemed to feel it, too, because Anders felt panic flash through her mind, but quickly leave her once she realized she was okay.

Zahara are you okay?

I think so. Are you?

I thought for a moment I was being attacked. Did you feel that, too?

Yes, the tingling that ran from my limbs to my core, I felt it the same as you.

What do you think that was?

I'm not sure. It could have been the edge of an airmine

that we set off. I had a similar sensation when we hit the last one over the Eastland Mountains.

Anders recalled when he'd been thrown from her back. He couldn't remember feeling the tingling sensation, only the emptiness of sky beneath his body and falling endlessly while he watched the air around him rush past, waiting for the ground to catch up with him.

I can't remember feeling that the last time, but I wouldn't be surprised if Merglan anticipated we'd come this way from the Everlight Kingdom and planted several along the coast.

That sounds like something he'd do; that's a cheap trick, Zahara cursed, anger rising within her.

We'd better fly farther off the coast, just in case he's left more as a trap.

Zahara tilted, carrying them away from the coast and out over the open sea. Though they struggled to stay awake, Anders and Zahara flew through the night without a problem. From their height, Anders could see the sliver of light beginning to creep up beyond the horizon. He knew daylight would be coming soon and they were coming closer to areas where orcs might be making their way down to the Goblin's Grove. Just as he began to scan the space below for any sign of enemies, Anders thought he felt a familiar presence. He wasn't sure because it vanished when he recognized it. He was terribly tired but decided to investigate, telling Zahara to double back and pass over the area again. As they did, Anders focused his energy more specifically to pinpoint the sensation he thought he'd felt. Combing the waters below with nothing but rolling waves, he felt it – the hardened and callused mind of his mentor and traveling companion, Ivan. As soon as Ivan noticed another sorcerer's mind discover him, Anders felt his walls shoot up, blocking him from all communication.

Realizing what he'd done, Anders and Zahara quickly sent feelers out to contact Natalia or Nadir. Luckily Nadir's mind didn't react as quickly as the riders' so Anders could send him a message before Nadir shut him out completely. Once Nadir relayed the message to Ivan and Natalia, they opened their minds to communication again.

Anders, Zahara, I'm surprised to see you have returned sooner than expected, Ivan said speaking in both their minds.

We've been flying straight through each night and stopping to rest for only a few hours each day. We're over-worked and desperately need rest. My wings are getting stiff and I can hardly keep my eyes open any longer, Zahara said, her voice weary.

I've been there before. I know exactly what that feels like myself. Unfortunately, it's too risky for you two to stop inland now and I doubt you'd fit on our boats. Now that we've joined forces with the dwarfs, the elven ships are packed to the brim with warriors.

Why can't we stop and rest on shore for a day and catch up with you later? Anders asked. *It wouldn't take us more than half a day make up the difference.*

I've sent a messenger bird ahead to the Lumbapi people informing them of our plan. I received word back. They told us that Merglan has been moving orc forces from the Goblin's Grove over to Southland over the past several days. From there the orcs have been marching toward Kingston. I'm confident Merglan's mind is focused on this task and doesn't know of our planned attack. If we want to keep it that way, we can't risk you two being found out by a group of orcs passing through to Goblin's Grove. We've intentionally made sure our ships are sailing well out of eyesight from the Eastland coast-

line, but we'll soon be close enough to the narrows between Eastland and Southland where we could be spotted. We plan to pass through the narrows at night and dock near the Drakeshead to join the guerilla forces of the Lumbapi people.

Anders felt a wave of paranoia and stress wash over him. Zahara shared these feelings knowing neither of them had much strength left. He spoke only to Zahara saying, *I don't think I'll be able to go much longer without rest and if we encounter foes along the way to the Drakeshead, we'll need to fight. I'm not alert enough to be of any use.*

I will crash into the water if we continue for much longer.

Anders voiced his frustrations with Ivan, *We can't continue that far without rest.*

The silence between them grew as Anders waited for Ivan's reply. It didn't come.

What if we try to draw on some of the energy in Keanu's sword? Anders asked, recalling how Ivan had told him the crystals could be used to store energy.

Anders could feel Ivan's rage beginning to build, *I expressly told you not to experiment with the crystal. We don't understand what it could do to you.*

But you yourself have mentioned several times that we know it can be used to store energy and that energy can be summoned upon when needed. I'm not suggesting we attempt to use the crystal to cast a spell, I'm suggesting Zahara and I withdraw a small amount of its energy to keep us awake until it's safe to land, Anders pleaded.

I don't know. It's not a good idea. What if it alerts Merglan to our presence? Ivan said cautiously.

Zahara just told me she's going to crash into the sea if she has to continue. We could risk resting on shore, but as you said, we will most likely be found out if we do that, Anders said.

Ivan groaned in his thoughts, *I guess you make a valid argument. Okay, you can attempt to draw on a small amount of energy from the crystal, but Anders,* he paused and waited for Anders' reply.

Yes, Anders said after several long breaths of mental silence.

Don't let the power consume you. You must break the connection almost instantly once you draw on the energy. I don't know what will happen if you don't break the link.

Okay, I won't get carried away, Anders said dismissively.

Anders and Zahara could now see the small armada of elven ships slowly gliding across the dark blue sea below. Ivan's connection with them heightened and Anders could sense his frustration. *Zahara, make sure he doesn't take too much, this will affect you both,* he warned.

Okay, Zahara said as they neared the ships.

Good, Ivan said. *It's getting light out now, so come down and fly low alongside our ships. That way we can keep an eye on you if something goes wrong.*

Zahara glided down, closing in on the ships. Leveling out at the same elevation as the masts, she slowed herself to match the pace of the elven ships. Anders could see that each one of them was packed with elven and dwarfish soldiers. Coming alongside the lead ship, they caught sight of Nadir and Ivan for the first time since leaving for the Rollo Islands. Remli, the dwarf king, stood beside Nadir. Anders thought the three leaders to be an odd group. It took something quite important for all three of these incredibly independent leaders to agree on a shared goal and forge an allegiance to accomplish it.

"Hello, dragonrider!" Remli bellowed out to Anders as he and Zahara planed level with the ship's deck. The dwarf waved his stout arm, his long red beard mimicking his arm's motion, swaying back and forth.

Anders waved, too tired to shout a response.

Remli laughed and used the backside of his arm to slap Nadir playfully.

Nadir looked down scornfully at the dwarf king, not smiling. Remli realized his comrade didn't share the same amusement as he, so he awkwardly averted his attention.

Anders thumbed at the sword, not sure when he should attempt to summon the energy they so desperately needed, when Zahara asked Ivan, *What's the strategy from here on out?*

The plan will be to pass through the narrows while it's dark tomorrow night. From there it's only a few more hours of travel until we'll reach our destination. We will need to continue our course, slowing down a bit later in the day so we can time our passing just right. If we stay out away from the coast until then, we have a good chance of passing through unseen. There is a possibility that we could run into a ferry-boat carrying orcs across the narrows between shores. In the letter the Lumbapi sent us they warned of this. The orcs have been crossing during daylight hours, but from what it sounded like, the ferry traffic has slowed. Once we meet up with the Lumbapi, they'll show us where the orc host is gathering. We'll launch our attack and hopefully catch them off guard. If we can attack them while they are disorganized, we'll be able to send them scattering and have an easier time battling them in smaller disorganized groups than as one cohesive unit.

That sounds like a plan if I've ever heard one. What about Zahara and me? What will our role be? Anders asked, moving his hand from the sword's hilt to the saddle handle. Talking was keeping him awake, for now.

You and Zahara will wait until our ground troops have launched an attack, then you'll fly around and take them on in the rear. I'll send you along with some elven special forces to sandwich the orc army between us.

Okay, that all sounds good, but what if Merglan comes out to play?

If he does, we'll need our team of sorcerers to focus all of their attention on him. He's dominant in single combat, but if we can combine our powers, we'll have a better chance at holding him off.

Who's our team of sorcerers?

Well, there's you, me, Natalia, Zahara and Solomon.

Solomon? As in the old wise man we met just outside Brookside? Anders asked surprised.

Yes. He's more powerful than he looks. And he'll be there alongside us in the fighting.

Did you pick him up along the way or something?

No, Solomon journeyed to Southland before Merglan showed his presence. He's been helping the Lumbapi organize their guerilla-style warfare against Merglan. So far, he has managed to keep their camps hidden from Merglan and Killdoor.

That's amazing. I thought it was interesting that you would hold his counsel in such high regard, Anders said.

Zahara hadn't met the old wise man who Anders had been introduced to while passing through Brookside on their way to rescue his cousins, so Anders spent the next several minutes explaining to her how they knew this sorcerer and why it surprised Anders to learn of his abilities.

Anders informed Ivan of their encounter with Red and other Rolloans on the Rollo Islands. He noted how Red reacted to the call to action and told Ivan his suspicions about Red's abandoning Britt and the others. Ivan seemed concerned with the news and hoped some brave warriors would come to their aid. He didn't say it, but Anders could sense his concern for Britt and what Red might have done to her. There wasn't time to deal with the matter now as they were voyaging to war. If they survived, Ivan and Anders would have to talk some sense into Red, but for now, they were forced to let the matter lie.

As they flew, Anders felt more revitalized than he had when he and Zahara were flying alone. At least now when he became too sleepy to keep his head up, he could talk with someone who wasn't as drowsy as he and Zahara were. Anders was beginning to think that he might not need to draw some of the energy stored in the hilt of his sword, that was until he and Zahara fell completely asleep.

Splashing violently into the sea, Anders woke up as he slammed into the water having been thrown off Zahara's back. The bond he held with the saddle broke when he dozed off and was useless when he needed it. He gasped for air as his mouth filled with saltwater. Frantically, he flailed in the water as he scrambled for the surface.

Popping his head into the fresh air, Anders coughed up the water he'd inhaled upon impact. Treading water in the rolling waves, he could see Zahara flapping her enormous wings. As he bobbed in and out of sight of his dragon, he watched helplessly as she attempted to rise out of the water. Anders tried to swim toward the ships, their sails carrying them at a steady rate. It was no use; he wasn't going to catch them. He bobbed in the water until Zahara rose from the sea. Circling back and plucking him out of the water with her large claws, she flew high into the air. With a flick of her talons, she tossed him out away from her body as she dove under him, scooping him onto her back. Anders landed lightly on her back and resumed his position in the saddle.

Okay, that's it, Anders told Zahara. *I don't care about the cost; I'm drawing on some of the crystal's energy. We need it if we're going to make it to Southland.*

Anders, be careful, she warned. *Only take a little. We don't need much to keep us awake.*

Okay, I'll be careful and only take a small amount, he assured her.

He reached his sword hand down across his body and pulled the steel blade from its sheath. The sapphire crystals along its handle sparkled brightly in the afternoon sunlight. The largest of the crystals was molded into the pommel of the sword with a steel circle casting it in place at the top of the hilt. Anders took a deep breath to slow his suddenly rapid heartbeat. He was nervous. The crystals had the potential to be extremely dangerous.

He hesitated, not knowing exactly how to summon energy from the sapphires. Anders recalled his studies. He'd read about how sorcerers could use magic, by spoken word or by emotion. Since he didn't know what word might be best for the occasion, Anders tried with his mind. He sent his mind to the largest crystal, attempting to forge a link between it and his consciousness. To his surprise, the crystal felt alive; it even registered as a living being to him. Anders pulled his mind away, suspicious of a crystal that could be living.

Did you feel that? he asked Zahara.

No. What was it?

It felt, alive.

It's probably just the energy inside that you're sensing. I don't feel any kind of being, she assured him.

Anders shifted in his seat, preparing to form a link with the crystal. He reached out and felt its energy, strong, powerful and bright. Anders probed the crystal in the same way he would probe someone's mind. The crystal opened and received him. Turquoise strands of energy wisped out from the sapphire crystal in his sword's hilt. Anders' eyes bulged as he watched the vine like tendrils slide out and slither up his arm like snakes. The wisps of light slid into his body as if his skin were transparent passing into him with ease.

The energy surged into his body like nothing he'd felt before. The crystal's power passed through his bond and into Zahara as well. The energy was electric, a surge that pulsed into them, vibrating through their very beings. As Anders embraced the crystal's energy, he could feel every inch of his body growing stronger, every strand of muscle increasing in strength. He felt more alive than he ever had in his life. At first, the sensation scared him, but as he let the warmth of its grasp take hold, he wanted more; he needed more.

Anders that's enough, Zahara said sharply.

Zahara's voice seemed far away. He wanted to ignore her, *Just a little bit more*, he responded. As he did, Anders thought he could hear the faint calls of someone or something's voice. For a moment he thought it was Zahara, but the direction in which it was coming from was wrong. It sounded as though it had come from within the crystal. He strained to listen for the cries when a booming voice rang through his head.

ANDERS, ENOUGH!!! Zahara roared in anger. He'd gone too far, and she feared for him; she could feel him slipping away, going deeper into the crystal's consciousness.

Anders pulled his mind away from the sapphire and the tendrils of energy snaking into his skin vanished. He blinked, suddenly aware of his surroundings. He was aware, actually, of everything. Suddenly he felt eyes on him. All the eyes of the elves and dwarf soldiers were on him. He looked down at them. When he did, they returned to what they were doing.

Zahara's roar must have drawn their attention, Anders thought.

Anders, Zahara said, her voice much calmer and quieter than it had been before. *That was too much.*

I know, Anders said ashamed. *I couldn't help myself. I felt like a moth drawn to a lamp, I couldn't control myself. It felt so good. I wanted more.* Anders shuddered at the thought of losing control and becoming entirely enveloped in the crystal's energy.

If we need to use that again, I'll be the one to draw it out, Zahara scolded him.

Alright. You do it next time, Anders agreed.

As NADIR and Ivan led the elven ships closer to the narrows, Anders and Zahara buzzed with their newly harnessed energy. Anders' senses felt finely tuned. He could sense the expanse of water tightening between the two landmasses before them, the eagerness and fear emanating from those on the ships at their side, and the light disappearing on the darkening horizon. He felt the workings of the world itself, an ebbing and flowing of energy.

"We've timed it perfectly," Anders heard Nadir say to Ivan. Even Anders' hearing had sharpened considerably. "With the cover of darkness, we should pass right through the narrows unseen."

"Now we just need to hope there aren't any orcs still crossing," Ivan replied.

"If there are, I'd likely give them a wallop that they'd

knew he was different from Merglan. Now all he could do was prove it, to himself and to the world. He wouldn't let the hatred take him, he couldn't.

THE DRAKESHEAD FORMATION of Southland comprised nearly a full quarter of the island's mass, stretching as far north as the Split Mountain River flowing east to the sea and as far west as the Lumbi Lakes south of Split Mountain. Though the province was vast, it didn't seem that way to Anders and Zahara as they circled above the trees. They could smell the smoldering cook fires of the native Southland people. From the air, Anders and Zahara could hardly make out the distinguishing elements of an army camp. Their soldiers remained in tight camping formations. Before gliding down to land on shore and await the ships, Zahara and Anders flew a few hundred yards down and stopped at a small cove, hidden from the open expanse along the beaches.

Anders climbed down off his dragon's back, his legs shaky from having been in the saddle for so long. He knelt on the rocky coast and dropped his hands down into a small tidal pool left behind by the receding tide. Taking a handful of sand from the base of the pool, he began to scrub the stains off his hands. Three times he grabbed a fresh handful of sand from the bottom of the tidal pool and scrubbed vigorously until the dark stains were gone from his skin. Next, he dipped his head in, washing his hair and face in the same way he did his hands. After several minutes, he rose from the pool and walked back to Zahara.

She entered his mind and said, *It's not all off.*

He examined his hands, rolling them over to examine

each part of his extremities. Then he wiped his hand through his hair again and looked at the residue from his hair, still clean of blood. He looked up at her and shrugged, *I don't see any more on me.*

Your sword, she said shortly.

Anders looked down at Lazuran's handle. The embedded crystals usually shone a faint blue, but with blood covering them, they shone a deathly red. He shuddered again at the thought of what he'd done. He quickly pulled the blade from its sheath and brought it down to the rolling waves continuously slapping the rocky coast. The blade was too long to submerge into the tidal pool he'd used before, so he plunged it into the sea. Not willing to dull his edge, he used the leather cuff wrapped around his wrist to scrape the loosened blood clean from his sword. As he cleaned his weapon, Anders' attention was repeatedly drawn to the crystals in the hilt. The more he looked at them, the more of his attack he could remember. Flying through the air, landing onboard the ship, hacking and slicing the screams away. Anders swatted the air in front of him as if a fly or bug were bothering him. He dropped the sword as he stumbled back over the rocks. Tripping and falling on his backside, Anders sat winded among the slippery rocks. He placed his head into his hands and began to cry again. He cried for many reasons: for the mess he'd made in slaughtering the orcs; for the daunting task that he must complete now that they had reached the island; and for the loved ones he'd lost or had been separated from.

He wept like a child for several minutes before Zahara interrupted him. She knew he needed to face his emotions and what he'd done.

She sat down at his side facing the sea and said, *I know you didn't mean to do what you did. You can't blame yourself for an action that you had no control over. Now that we know what can happen when we use the energy, we can find a way to control it.*

How do you know I can control it? I can't seem to control anything. After all we did to rescue my family, they're still in danger. After all the time I spent with the girl of my dreams, she still left me. And after coming all this way to fight an unbeatable foe, I can't control the power that will give me the best chance at victory. It's hopeless, he said swiping at the tears with his sleeve.

That's not true. Things aren't hopeless, Zahara said soothingly.

It seems like they are to me, Anders said.

That's right. It only seems like they are. Take a look around, see where we are and who we're with. These elves, dwarfs and humans are willing to risk their lives to prove that hope still exists. They're about to walk into the greatest battle this world has ever seen and all to prove that hope and goodness are greater than evil. So, when you feel like all of your problems are weighing you down, just stop and look around. I'm here with you. And as long as I'm here with you there will always be hope in the world. Together we're going to make Kartania a better place. Zahara wrapped Anders up in one of her long wings and held him close.

Anders didn't respond for a moment. Zahara's comforting presence and gentle touch were more than enough to brighten his spirits. After several long breaths, he found his feet. He wiped the debris from his rear and collected his sword, still awash in the rolling waves along the shore.

Sheathing his weapon, he said, *Well, come on then. We'll need to inspire the others if we're going to win this war.*

Zahara smiled and came to his side. She was happy that

her bonded partner had returned to his usual self. She knew he might change, but no matter what happened to them in the future, she knew that he was right by her side with his heart in the right place.

The Lumbapi people were coming out of the trees in large numbers when Anders and Zahara landed alongside the ships. The elven vessels were designed to make landfall with much more grace than standard merchant ships with large bulbous hulls. Ivan, Nadir, Natalia and Remli were already walking toward the group of gathering natives when Anders and Zahara joined them.

Everything alright? Ivan asked as they matched their stride.

We got things sorted out, Zahara reassured him.

Good, Ivan said, eyeing Anders intently.

Anders hadn't felt this awkward around Ivan since he confronted him about the orc ambush. He turned his attention to the approaching people, ignoring Ivan's glare.

"Ivan," a thickly accented woman said. "We are glad to see you in such dire times as these." As the Lumbapi woman spoke, Anders took note of her impressive features. The woman's shoulders were broad, toned and muscular. Her complexion almost matched Maija's tanned hue. This woman's hair was short and straight, unlike Maija's, whose hair was long and wavy. The Lumbapi woman's lean muscles weren't the only attributes about her that were visually impressive. She wore a headdress of flowing colors that would rival any rainbows Anders had ever seen. Her short sleeves exposed a set of tattoos along one arm and her nose was pierced through the septum. Rings and jewelry adorned her fingers and wrists, but not her neck. In the place above the cleft of her breast, she wore a string of bones. Anders looked closely at them before he realized they were claws, no doubt from a predator native to this land. Despite her jewels and trinkets, she wore the very basic browned boiled leather, typical armor for a guerilla-style warrior who needs to use speed to her advantage during battle.

"Princess Inama," Ivan replied. "We're the ones who are glad to see you. The passage south was more treacherous than we'd anticipated."

"Did you encounter any enemies crossing the narrows?" she asked, raising her ornately decorated eyebrows to take a better look at Zahara and Anders stepping into the torchlight.

Before Ivan could answer, the impressive sight that Zahara had come to be startled those surrounding the princess, even she stepped back, startled when Zahara shook the sea spray off her scales before sitting down on the loose gravel beach.

Ignoring the defensive positions the Lumbapi greeters had taken, Ivan spoke as if nothing were amiss, "The dragon and her rider found a vessel carrying orcs across, but our ships sailed around them without their noticing. We haven't encountered any more since then."

Anders knew Ivan wasn't disclosing with them what he'd done to keep up appearances. For all Anders knew, the fact that he'd killed an entire ship alone might frighten the Lumbapi people so much that they'd be unwilling to join the fight. To his relief, the princess and her companions straightened themselves and stepped closer once again, all the while keeping a wary eye on Zahara.

"I'm glad you and your companions were able to make it here in time," Princess Inama said, greeting Ivan formally with a hug and kiss on each side of the cheek, as custom dictated among their people. She did the same to Natalia as

Ivan introduced her. Anders noticed she made her pecks short, making sure not to linger as Ivan had.

"Princess Inama, this is Nadir, recently named King of the Everlight Kingdom," Ivan said introducing him. The princess proceeded to greet him in the same way she had Ivan. "And Remli, Dwarf King in Hardstone."

Remli puffed out his chest trying to make himself look taller. He grinned through his thick red beard and said with a chuckle, "It's a pleasure to meet such a lovely young warrior like yourself. Careful when you kiss these cheeks, my dear, they're shrouded by fire. If you're not careful they might warm you, leaving you with a longing to be near the flames."

Ivan and Nadir shook their heads as they often did when Remli spoke, and Anders chuckled to himself as the princess eyed the dwarf curiously before continuing with her greeting. When she was done kissing him, she acted as if she'd been startled.

"What is it, my dear?" Remli asked more seriously, concern spreading across his reddened face.

"Why I've just kissed fire and my lips are unburnt. I must be the only woman in history to be able to resist your charm," she said mockingly and with a devious smile.

Remli bellowed a hearty laugh and said, "And she's got a good sense of humor! Oh, what a catch this one is."

"You're too kind your majesty," the princess said and turned her attention to Anders. "And I think I can guess who this is."

"You can?" Anders asked, surprised at her confidence in being able to identify him.

"Why of course. You are the dragonrider, Anders. And this is your beloved dragon, Zahara. You don't think the tales of your accomplishments at Black Water Bay went unnoticed, do you?" she asked incredulously.

Anders blushed almost as darkly as Remli had. "I wasn't aware that people knew about us. The elves have known for a while, but other than the Rollo Islanders and dwarfs, we've not had much contact with the rest of Kartania," he replied modestly. As he spoke, he realized he'd been introduced to over half of the nations in Kartania over the last several months.

"Surely you don't think you could take on Merglan's forces and go unnoticed for driving him away. Why our people have heard about it ever since Merglan returned to Southland. It has given us hope that he can be stopped."

"Really?" Anders asked, thinking that he was among the outliers in thinking that Merglan could be defeated.

Princess Inama greeted Anders in the same way as she had the others. He blushed when her lips touched his cheeks and returned the kiss on hers. He quickly felt embarrassed as he glanced to Natalia, wondering what Maija would've thought about the way they greeted each other. The princess smiled, stepping away from him and addressing Zahara with a polite and straightforward bow. Just then Nadir piped in.

"I think that is enough of pleasantries; why don't we discuss strategies."

"As you wish, your majesty," the princess said. She turned sharply and waved for them to follow her.

Nadir and Remli barked a few orders to several elves and dwarfs who'd been awaiting assignments. They were directed to conduct preparations at the ships as the group of leaders began following the princess. Anders wasn't sure if he should follow them or help the dwarfs and elves offload supplies. His expression must have been telling because Ivan motioned for them to follow the princess.

Anders and Zahara trailed the other leaders as they walked uphill into the dense forest near the beach. The forest acted as a great barrier and protective shield from anyone or thing searching from the outside. If it weren't for the flight, Zahara and Anders would never have known anyone was camped there.

Once deep enough into the trees, they began to see tightly formed groups of tents, rows in neatly constructed lines, organized in such a way to be screened from a visual scan of the area by the thick, low-hanging canopy. In addition to the strategic placement, the tents were woven of a fabric designed to blend in with the forest canopy. The closer Anders looked as they walked, the more Lumbapi people he saw. Where once he only recognized a few tents, he now saw hundreds, disguised in the forest undergrowth.

Anders and Zahara walked past sentries standing guard along the outposts of the tent community. Campfires rolling a shallow smolder somehow remained undetected under the forested area. The fires were hot enough to cook on, but not large enough to produce a column of smoke. Many of the Lumbapi soldiers wore no uniforms like the elves and dwarfs. Instead, they wore clothes similar to those Anders saw on people living in Westland, not the typical attire of a highly functioning rebel army. They passed people tending to livestock and other domesticated animals raised for food. Dogs the size of small horses wandered the camp, sniffing at Zahara as she walked by.

Finally, the princess stopped at a larger group of tents that appeared to be army headquarters. When they approached the largest of the tent doors, the fold in the tent wall separated and two small spiked creatures scurried out.

Anders watched a familiar figure emerge from the tent door to call after the creatures, "Rufus, Ulgna! Come back here."

Solomon, the small old wise man Anders had visited back in Brookside, lifted his arms in joy upon seeing the travelers. "Jumping grasshoppers, look who it is!" the old man shouted, scuttling over to them.

Ivan smiled and held out a hand in greeting. Solomon swiped Ivan's extended hand out of the way and wrapped his thickly dressed arms around the sorcerer. At first, Ivan's arms didn't move an inch, but when he realized the old man wasn't letting go of him anytime soon, he returned the gesture, patting him on the back as he quickly hugged him.

"It's good to see you," Solomon said, releasing his grip on the weathered warrior.

"You, too, old friend," Ivan replied.

Solomon peered down his half-moon spectacles at the remaining four of them. His eyes went from one to the other and when they landed on Anders and Zahara, he gasped. "Oh dear." He put his hands over his mouth. He came over to Anders and said, "I recall the last time I saw you, you were starting out on an adventure."

Anders nodded, "Yes, and you gave me some strange advice before I left your house." Anders eyed the old man curiously.

"I did?" Solomon asked.

"Yes. You told me the path ahead was a dangerous one and that I should follow my heart."

Solomon looked to Zahara and back to Anders, "Well, it seems that you took my advice."

Anders nodded, "Yes. I guess I did."

Solomon smiled the quirky smile he always seemed to wear and turned his attention to Remli and Nadir. The way they greeted him made Anders think they'd been old friends, reuniting again after a long time apart.

Once the pleasantries were finished, Anders and Zahara followed the others inside the large tent where a fire roared in an iron fireplace. The smoke funneled up through a chimney and out the top of the tent. The smoke burned clean and hot, so it didn't emit a large plume. Upon entering the tent, Ivan, Natalia, Nadir and Remli began discussing strategies with Solomon and the Lumbapi over a large map laid out on the center table. Rugs lined the floor of the room and Anders chose to sit with Zahara in the back of the tent close to the fire. The talk of war and where Merglan's forces were gathering quickly turned to murmurs in Anders' ears. He and Zahara soon fell fast asleep, nestled together on the tent floor comforted by the fire's warmth.

TWENTY-FOUR

RYEDALE

A nders opened his eyes and looked out at the hazy space inside the sizable Lumbapi tent. He and Zahara were still nestled, laying comfortably on a thick rug that spanned the floor. He sat up slowly, stretching his arms wide and yawning long. The once-crackling fire at their backs had burned out, and he noticed the absence of the furnace-like heat pulsing against his backside. Anders examined the room. Sweeping his sleepy eyes around the darkened innards of the enormous tent, he couldn't see anyone else inside. As his eyes adjusted to the dim glow of light coming in from outside, he became sure that he and Zahara were the only ones left inside.

Anders rose to his feet and walked around to Zahara's head. Shaking her gently, he called to her, "Wake up. Zahara, it's time to wake up." She stirred but didn't open her eyes. Anders placed his mouth near the edge of her cone-shaped ear and said again, "Zahara, wake up."

This time Zahara's head bolted upright, nearly tossing Anders through the air when she came to full attention.

Her head passed quickly back and forth sounding out the room. Her scales clacked against themselves as she did so.

Anders caught himself on a chair that had been pushed away from the long table in the center of the room. *Hey, wow. Nothing to be startled about, it's just me,* he said connecting with her mind and soothing her instantly. He felt her worry subside when she realized where they were. *I was just telling you that we should get up. I think we slept here through the night.*

It looks like it. Where is everyone else? she asked.

I'm not sure. I just woke up myself and haven't had a chance to look around yet. But judging by the light coming in through the cracks, it's morning. We should try to find Ivan and the others and get up-to-date on their plan.

Zahara joined him as they pushed back the fold in the tent and ventured outside. The morning breeze blew gently around the tent. Anders expected to shiver as he'd become used to the morning chill of living at a more northern latitude, but they were in Southland now. Where a late summer breeze in Westland would've chilled him to the bone if he hadn't been wearing a coat, the Southland morning air was pleasantly brisk, but not chilling in the slightest.

When they'd been with the Rollo Islanders' war party, their camps had always been stirring with activity come morning. Warriors sharpened their blades and donned their armor. People warmed themselves by fires lit to cook their first meal of the day. Water gatherers refilled drink containers from nearby streams. But as Anders searched through the hidden Lumbapi camp, he didn't see any such movement. No one was starting a fire, cooking meals or gathering water. In fact, he didn't see a single person moving about the camp.

He looked to the east to make sure that it was, in fact, morning and that they hadn't slept right through the day and into evening again, which wouldn't have been that surprising because they'd been so sleep-deprived that he could easily see how that might happen. His notion of it being early morning, however, was correct; the sun was rising in the east. He thought it strange that nobody was moving about the camp.

Is it strange that we're the only ones up right now? Anders asked Zahara.

Yeah, she replied slowly. *Where is everyone?*

Anders reached out with his mind. He couldn't sense anyone inside the hundreds of tents within this camp. He tried to reach farther past the tents to check the ships, but something was blocking him from sweeping out beyond the camp boundaries.

I almost forgot, Ivan told us Solomon has protected their camp with spells. I can't sense anything beyond the tents, Anders said with frustration.

With a snort, she confirmed that she couldn't reach out that far either.

Come on. We need to get to the ships, something isn't right, Anders said and began to run. Zahara pushed herself up and launched forward, her claws tearing at the soil as she left the ground. She tilted her wing scooping Anders up as she glided past him. He quickly gained his wits and found his seat in their saddle. Zahara maneuvered herself with skill and grace as they flew low under the canopy of the forested camp. Dodging evenly spaced trees, she led them to the edge of the tree line and burst out from the foliage in a dramatic and startling display.

When they shot out of the forest and over the rocky shoreline, they saw the small armada of ships hugging the shoreline and a host of elves and dwarfs assembled among the space between trees and sea. Zahara had to pull up immediately to avoid buzzing their heads. She barely got her body up and over the spear tips of the elves. When she was high enough to clear them, she angled back down and flew in a wide arc, circling back toward shore.

The elves and dwarfs gathered near the ships were so startled by the dragon bursting forth from the woods and nearly crashing into their heads that they scattered in self-defense. The armed soldiers calmed themselves when they realized they knew the dragon and her rider. Anders ogled in surprise at the terror that he and Zahara had caused. He blushed with embarrassment as they landed near the head of the allied forces.

Anders climbed down from Zahara's back as Nadir and Remli approached.

"You gave us quite a scare!" Remli bellowed, brushing the dirt off his pant legs and sleeves resulting from his dive to the ground when Zahara popped out of the trees. "I thought Merglan and Killdoor were here at last. I nearly messed myself at the sudden excitement. I haven't been that startled in all my years." Remli straightened his belt and brushed his beard with his thick stout hands.

"You really shouldn't do that," Nadir scolded them. "We could have attacked you with our archers and we can't risk you getting shot by friendly fire before we even begin our attack." The elf king seemed more in control of his facilities than the dwarf.

"We're sorry," Anders insisted. "We woke up and every-body was gone; the tent was empty. When we ventured outside, we saw that the camp was deserted as well, so we searched with our minds but the protection spells on this place are cast with skill; we couldn't reach out beyond the camp. We panicked and came here straight away." He chuckled slightly at the amusement of it all.

Remli frowned a bit and Anders let out a couple more half-hearted giggles then stopped. The dwarf eyed him with what seemed like intense hatred, then he, too, burst out laughing. Anders and Zahara joined in once more. Even Nadir cracked a smile at the hilarity of the confusion.

"Wait a minute," Nadir said, returning to his scornful expression. "You said you'd fallen asleep in the tent last night? As in when we arrived here?"

Anders quickly stopped laughing and straightened at the question, "Yeah. Right after we landed, I went to the tent with you all. Zahara and I were so tired that we fell asleep on the floor by the fire."

"And you just woke up, saw the sun was rising and assumed you had just slept there for the night?" Nadir asked.

"Um, yes? That's how it happened," Anders replied, slightly confused at why this might seem strange.

Remli continued to chuckle, "Oh, laddie, you have been out far longer than that."

"Really? But we woke up with the rising sun, right?" Anders asked.

"Yes, that's technically correct, but it's not the next morning. You two have been asleep for nearly two whole days," Nadir said with raised eyebrows.

"What!?" Anders shouted in disbelief. "How can that be? Why didn't anyone wake us up?"

"Ivan told everyone not to disturb you two, that you needed to get as much rest as possible before the battle," Nadir informed them.

"What did we miss? Have the orcs advanced farther into Southland?" Anders asked.

"We've been scouting with the Lumbapi the last forty hours, observing the enemy's army and their movements," Remli chimed in.

"My stepmother is heading their army," Nadir said through gritted teeth. "She's been assembling orc forces from the Eastland territories. The traffic slowed and it looks as though they are going to march soon."

"Where're Ivan and Natalia?" Anders asked, relaying the question for Zahara.

"Ivan's with Solomon, watching the enemy's movements. Natalia is with Princess Inama scouting a strategy of where best to attack. While they went on ahead, we came back to assemble our troops. They've planned how to launch our attack. It sounds risky and a bit unconventional, but the Lumbapi have been successful in their strategies against Merglan's forces so far. They know the lay of the land better than we do and they know how best to strike larger forces with fewer people," Nadir said.

Remli nodded in agreement.

"So, when was anyone going to come and get us? Or were you going to win this war without us?" Anders asked, irritated that he'd not been involved in the strategizing.

"Trust me, young rider," Remli said. "We thought it was best for you to be involved in the process, but Ivan insisted that you not be bothered until absolutely necessary."

Anders snorted in frustration. Crossing his arms, he realized there was nothing he could do about it now. He suspected that it might have something to do with the episode he had after drawing on the crystal's power. He thought about the events leading up to this moment. He was still trustworthy; it wasn't fair that Ivan would hide something so important from him at such a crucial time in the war.

It was for the best that we rested, Anders, Zahara's soothing tone came into his head.

Her familiar voice brought a calming presence to his mind and pushed back his frustration with Ivan.

We need all the strength we can get if we are to go into battle, she told him.

He knew what she was telling him was right, *I know. It's just frustrating to be treated like an untrustworthy child. I'm still the same person I was when we left the Everlight Kingdom.*

We know that. It's not about that; it's about us being fully rested for the fight. We'll be relied upon heavily and we must be ready mentally and physically, she said.

"You know it's rude when you do that," Remli said to Anders.

Anders came out of the trance-like state he'd been in while talking to Zahara. "What?" he asked.

"When you two talk to each other telepathically while others are mid-conversation with you," the dwarf king scolded.

"Oh, I'm sorry. I didn't realize we were doing that," Anders said, embarrassed once more.

"I've been around enough riders to know when you're having a conversation, but I guess I didn't view it as rude until our dwarf friend pointed it out," Nadir said.

"I didn't realize that I was being rude. It probably looks strange watching me stare off into space while Zahara and I speak. I'll try to let you know that I'm talking to her before I interrupt our conversations again," Anders said to Remli.

"Yes, you do look strange when you stop talking to us

and start talking with Zahara, but I understand. It would just be a courtesy to let us know when you're about to go all canvas-faced," Remli said.

Anders and Zahara waited patiently for Ivan to return. The morning sun rose higher into the sky while he and Zahara made sure they were battle-ready. Anders still wore the leather armor that the Rollo warriors had given him after the attack at the Glacial Melt Bays. Its thick chest plate and padded arms bore deep scratches and cuts from the fighting it had seen. He wasn't sure who had owned it before him, but the fit was snug, and the light-weight leather allowed him to move faster than the steel-plated alternative. His helmet was hard and light as well and stayed strapped to the front of the saddle. Shin and wrist guards wrapped his extremities. They had proven useful in protecting his arms and legs from sliding blades during sparring practices.

Anders pulled the whetstone from his pouch and ran it along the length of Lazuran, making sure to stroke the edges of his sword with equal counts and pressure. The elven blade was sharp. The steel used to forge the sword was a kind that would not dull easily, but he wanted to make sure every part of his armor and skills were on point for the battle to come. He sheathed the blade opposite the dagger he wore on his belt once he saw the soldiers beginning to form into their ranks.

In a matter of moments, Ivan emerged from the trees. Accompanying him were the Lumbapi princess, her father, Solomon, Natalia and two other Lumbapi soldiers disguised as farmers. Anders followed Nadir and Remli as Ivan waved them over to a cluster of large boulders. Anders joined them in kneeling to create a tight circle within the boulders so they could speak in privacy. Zahara peered down, her massive head looming above.

Once they'd gathered around and Ivan had their attention, he spoke, "The orc forces have just begun to march. They're heading north by northwest up the Kingston Road toward the capital. Lageena is heading their army. They're marching slowly and will continue to march slowly as they have accumulated a large number of orcs. Our scouts saw fairnheir, but no kurr among them. I suspect with the death of Thargon, the kurr have scattered among the Eastland territories and will be disorganized until one of them rises to the challenge and calls them together once again.

"With an army of mostly orcs and some humans, they'll not be able to rely on the kurrs' strength to plow through our lines as they did at the fortress. I've never seen Lageena organize a battle or force as large as this one, but I know she gained a lot of strategic experience as commanding queen and leader of the elves for so many years."

"The ex-queen is not to be underestimated," Nadir said, emphasizing the 'ex.'

"Right, as we've come to find out, she can be much more dangerous than she appears," Ivan continued. "We know that the orcs will be pillaging towns along the way as they march. There's a town, Ryedale, within a day's march of the orcs. Ryedale is long and narrow, because of its unique location. The town was built in a canyon bottom bordering the southern banks of the Split Mountain River. Nine streets form the town, extending east to west along the canyon's bottom for roughly a mile. They've got plenty of buildings, most are one or two stories tall, with three stories being the tallest. These wooden structures will serve as our defenses. The Lumbapi soldiers have already begun making their way to Ryedale. By using the back roads and trail systems, we can make it there before the orcs. The Lumbapi people will disguise themselves as villagers and townsfolk. They'll insert themselves throughout the town before we arrive with our armies. The Lumbapi have been using this tactic to fight back against Merglan's human forces with great success. Usually, they'll wait until the enemy has entered the city before ambushing them with small groups, attacking from all sides before the enemy knows what's hit them. In the past, they have retreated, leaving disoriented and damaged. This strategy has worked for them so far."

"So, where do we come in?" Anders asked.

"Anders and Zahara, you two will be with Nadir and the elves. You'll be part of the team that surrounds Ryedale but remain hidden until the orcs are well within the confines of the town. They'll be pushing people around and trashing businesses, farms and other resources. The Lumbapi and I will attack them from within the town, using the buildings and protective structures to our advantage while the orcs flood the streets. Lageena will be wise to this tactic of fighting and hopefully assume us only to be a small force of Lumbapi. On any other day she would be right, but not today. Today we'll have the whole Lumbapi army within the town and the elves surrounding her to the western half of the town."

"What about the dwarfs?" Remli asked, looking offended that his fighters hadn't yet been assigned a task.

"You and your dwarfs will hit the orcs from the rear. We'll place you near the road and once we've begun the attack, you and your soldiers will close in, leaving them nowhere to run. If all goes to plan, we'll be able to make a huge dent in Merglan's forces," Ivan said with a twisted smile on his face.

Remli bellowed, "We'll give them a good walloping, we will!"

"I like your enthusiasm dwarf, but what if nothing goes to plan?" Nadir asked. "What if Lageena figures out we're trying to trap her in Ryedale and she bypasses the town completely?"

"Ah, that's a great question," Ivan said still holding his sly smirk. "The Lumbapi have picked this town because of its potential for fortifications, but also its geographic location. Ryedale is nestled in the bottom of a steep but shallow canyon. Two smaller rivers converge just above Ryedale, forming the main stem of the Split Mountain River. The water is deep and wide here. It flows east through the canyon and along the northern borders of Ryedale, preventing any easy escape in this direction. The canyon walls also provide a funneling effect, so they can't easily escape once they've committed to journeying up the road."

"So, we'll use the natural landscape to our advantage. The river provides a barrier to the north, deadly to armored orcs attempting an escape. The canyon's slopes provide a blockade and allow us to surround them along the rim to the south and southwest. While we close off the possible escape routes to the south and west, you'll take them by surprise from within. Our forces will take hold of the western and southern flanks while the dwarfs block them in from the rear, effectively pinching off their escape to the east?" Anders summed up concisely.

"That paints the picture," Ivan said.

"It sounds like a sure thing," Nadir said hesitantly. "Like it's going to be too good to be true if you know what I mean."

"The fighting will be tough, and we'll be greatly

outnumbered, but we'll have all the advantages if everything goes to plan," Ivan assured him.

"Okay. What are we waiting for? We'd better get a move on if we're going to be in position before they reach the town," Remli said, scrambling out from the shelter of the boulders.

"The trails are narrow, and the path is grown in so you'll need to follow on our heels so no one gets lost," Ivan called to Remli and Nadir as they gathered their troops to begin the march.

Ivan addressed Anders and Zahara separately, "I'm sorry I didn't keep you two in the loop on this one, but you needed your rest, especially you, Anders. I know how the crystal affected you and we can't risk you going rogue on this one."

Anders opened his mouth to defend himself, but Ivan cut him off, "I don't want to hear it. I know that you'll be on the level now that you've gotten some rest. I'm counting on you two today. You'll need to be there to inspire the troops as we go to battle. Since this is a stealthy operation you can't fly above us, Zahara, and the trees will be too thick along the path to fly in the forest. You'll have to walk with the rest of us; can you do that?"

"We aren't stubborn sky hogs," Anders answered for both of them. "We'll keep up on the ground."

"Good. Well, let's get to it," Ivan said as he led everyone to a path that wound tightly into the forest.

ANDERS AND ZAHARA followed a lightly worn game trail through the thinning tree line. Nadir led the way as they sought out their positions along the shallow canyon's rim.

When they approached the place where they'd be stopping with half the elven army, Anders became keenly aware of the lack of cover. They'd been hiking all morning through a thickly blanketed forest that covered their presence to the naked eye. When they began the ascent up the hills leading toward the canyon, Anders could see farther through the forest than before, but he hadn't thought much about being spotted by the enemy forces marching up the valley along the Kingston Road. Now that they'd come closer to the canyon's edge, the vegetation had become sparse and the possible cover was shorter than it had been in the forest.

Nadir stopped behind one of the last remaining clusters of trees. The brush ahead of them turned to shin-high blades of mustard-colored grass. This grassland stretched across the gap between their army and the canyon rim. Turning to face Anders, Zahara and the single-file line of elves winding back into the depths of the forest, Nadir glanced over Anders' head for a moment to check on their progress before he addressed the young dragon and rider.

"Here's where we must part ways," the elf king said. His expression was less angry than it had been over the past several days. Nadir displayed the calming presence that Anders had grown accustomed to when they'd traveled together earlier through the Everlight Kingdom and Eastland Mountains. "Half our elves will remain with you two while I take the rest up the canyon. Once we're in position along the upper end of the canyon, above the town, you will approach the canyon's rim. With the lack of cover from here on out, we'll need to stay low and assign only a few pairs of eyes to watch for Ivan's signal. In order to give us ample time to set up before you approach the rim, wait fifteen minutes before making your approach."

"And you're sure where we are now is directly above the midsection of the town below?" Anders asked.

"Ivan knows this place better than I and the Lumbapi better than he. They directed us to split up here to lay the most effective trap for Lageena," Nadir bit off the end of her name. Anders could tell he was forcing himself to remain in control of his emotions.

"Okay, I'll wait fifteen minutes before crawling through the grass and watching the town," Anders confirmed.

And the dwarfs are already in position, hiding among the rocks and trees below town, Zahara added, speaking to both Anders and Nadir. Nadir nodded and Anders raised his eyebrows slightly. *I thought that would give you peace of mind knowing they'd made it into their respective stations before advancing up the canyon,* she said.

"Many thanks," Nadir said. He looked beyond Anders and Zahara again and waved the predetermined half of the elven army to follow him through the grass and up the canyon.

He gave them a knowing nod before turning and quickly leading the elves through the grass. They crouched as they jogged out into the uncovered landscape, staying lower than the rim of the canyon and out of view of Ryedale. Even at a crouching jog, the elves' speed was unmatched to that of any throughout humanity. Anders marveled as the stealthy group of soldiers sped out of sight.

After half of the elves had rushed past, Anders turned his attention back to Zahara. *I think it will be too risky for you to come with me when I crawl up to the edge of the canyon,* he said. He could feel that she didn't like this assessment, but knew it was for the best.

She rumbled a halfhearted growl of distaste as she turned her head away from Anders' concerned face.

I know you don't want to rely on others to know what's going on for you, but with nothing but this grass to hide us, you'll stick out like a sore thumb, he said. Anders knew what she was thinking and warned her before she did, *and you'll have to keep your mind out of the way. Lageena's close with Merglan and we don't know how powerful she is. If she has the ability to sense where other sorcerers are, then she'll know we're near if we're canvassing the town. If this plan is going to work, we need her to fall for the bait and lead her orcs into the center of the town.*

With a begrudging sigh and curl of her lip, Zahara consented, *Fine. But you'll connect your mind with me again as soon as she's made it midway through the town. I want to be the first to come over the rim of the canyon and descend on the town.*

Zahara, weren't you listening to Ivan just before he left to join the other Lumbapi soldiers in the town? We're not to risk our lives unless the battle goes for the worse. We're going to need our strength if Merglan comes to join the fighting. We'll also need to be on the lookout to see if he and Killdoor are approaching.

She flicked her forked tongue past her sharp teeth and said, *Ugh. We traveled all this way and have gone through so much training to be of use in this war and, when it finally comes down to it, we're told to remain hidden like a couple of cowards.*

Oh, come on now. It's not like that. We'll have a large enough challenge when it comes time to face Merglan and Killdoor. You don't want me to waste all of my energy battling orcs and the traitor queen only to face Merglan exhausted. I'd be forced to use the energy from the crystal again, and we know how that affects me. I'd be a loose cannon and might cause more harm than good, Anders warned. He didn't exactly know where her ferocity was coming from. Perhaps the anticipation of facing Merglan was getting to her and she desperately wanted to stop the murderous rider from gaining more power.

I know you're right, Anders. It's just that I've been waiting for this moment for months and now that it's finally time, I'm overeager to join the fight.

I knew it was something like that. And look who's got their head on straight now, Anders joked with her.

She chuckled, *Okay, I think it's time to get serious. Who are you going to take with you up to the canyon edge?*

It would be stealthier to go it alone, wouldn't it? Anders asked.

Yes, but Nadir said to take two pairs of eyes. What if you missed Ivan's signal and didn't send the elves in on time? If I can't join you up there, I'd want one of the senior elf leaders to go with you.

That's a good point, I don't want to mess this operation up now. Who do you think I should take? Anders asked while eyeing down the line of elven soldiers. He hadn't gotten to know very many of them other than Nadir and Natalia. During his time in the Everlight Kingdom, he'd not spent any time in the capital proper. He'd been busy training away from the elves at the rider facilities.

Nearly half of the elf army stayed in Cedarbridge and I know little of who Nadir trusts. I noticed Ivan speaking to one of the a-typical ones aboard the ship.

Anders knew what she meant by a-typical, she was referring to several members of the elven army who didn't physically match the highborn elves Anders had spent the most time with.

I believe his name is Brosnan, Anders said, looking at the dark wavy-haired elf. *I think he's a safe bet. If Ivan conversed with him and he rode on their ship, he's likely a trustworthy soldier. I'll go talk to him.*

Anders made his way down the line of crouching soldiers, sneakily tiptoeing toward the tan-skinned elf. Approaching him with care to avoid startling him, Anders allowed his feet to land solidly on the ground as he walked and he let out a, 'psst,' as he drew near. Several elves, including Brosnan, took their eyes off the horizon and turned toward him.

Anders pointed to Brosnan and motioned for the elf to come closer. After looking to either side and back to Anders, the elf crept quietly forward. Brosnan was two hands taller than Anders and appeared to be thicker around the legs, chest and arms, but it was hard for Anders to gauge his actual size with the bulk of his plated armor.

Brosnan's brown eyes met Anders' and he asked in a low powerful voice, "What can I do for you, rider?"

"I need someone to join me while I scout the town and wait for Ivan's signal. Zahara said she had a good feeling about you and thought I should see if you'd help me watch for our signal to attack?" Brosnan's square jaw perked up slightly as Anders spoke. "We'll need to crawl through the grass up to the canyon's rim in order to avoid being seen. Can I count on you to be the elf for the job?" he asked.

Striking a serious expression, the elven soldier said firmly, "You can count on me, sir."

Anders grinned and nodded sharply. "You can call me Anders, and I'll call you?" Anders trailed off giving the elf the chance to introduce himself.

"Brosnan," the bold elf said. "Commander Brosnan Strongsword."

Anders raised his eyebrows, "That's quite the title. Appropriately earned I assume?"

"Yes, sir, er, Anders, I mean. Strongsword was given to me when I joined the Everlight Army and commander just before leaving port for this island."

"I see Zahara's choice in my companionship was well selected," Anders said. He motioned for the elf to follow and said, "Come on, Nadir will be in position by now. We need to be on the lookout over town before Lageena shows up."

Brosnan spit at the mention of the queen traitor's name and quietly trailed Anders as they hustled to the front of the line where he'd left Zahara.

Once there, Anders let Zahara know it was time for them to venture to the edge of the canyon. She forced a wish of luck out and nestled down among the last cluster of trees as Brosnan and Anders crawled on their hands and knees through the grass and out toward the canyon rim.

Anders could see the opposite side of the canyon as they crawled closer to the top. He watched the grass on the horizon slowly reveal more of the canyon's steep slopes as they dropped down toward the valley below. A strong afternoon breeze suddenly began to blow as they crawled. Anders dropped to his stomach thinking it was some sort of magical force. Brosnan did the same, but when they realized it was only the updraft rising from the valley floor, they got back onto their hands and knees and continued crawling through the grass. Several times Anders placed his hand directly on a sharp plant with spikes, wincing each time at the burning sensation caused by the small needle-like spines. As he paused to scratch off the ends that stuck into his palms, Anders found himself glancing down more at the otherwise soft ground as they advanced.

Suddenly he saw chimney stacks and peaked wooden rooftops on the horizon. He dropped to his stomach once again and looked back to his right to see his elf companion doing the same. Anders slowly raised his head to take a first glimpse of the town below them. His eyes ran the length of the narrow town and searched for the Kingston Road below, but all he could see was the opposite side of the canyon's slopes.

That's good, he thought to himself. *If I can't see the road, then nobody on the road can see me.*

Slithering like a snake through the grass, he walked himself forward with his elbows and dragged his lower half by wriggling his legs back and forth. Within ten feet, he was able to see the entirety of the canyon bottom. Stopping, he and Brosnan used their hands to part the grass to gain a clear view down into the valley.

Ivan had described the shallow canyon as having steep, cliff-lined slopes bracketing a valley that had been carved by a wide river, but Anders had not pictured how shallow the valley actually was. The exposed cliffs on either side were not very tall; they rose no more than three times the visual height of the town's tallest three-story buildings. The exposed rock bands were roughly as tall as Anders was and quickly receded back into the hillside. The canyon was narrowest nearer the west end of the town, where Nadir and his half of the elf army had gone to hide. The only thing that seemed to hold true to Ivan's description was the size of the river. Just at Ryedale's western and uppermost location, two large rivers joined to create a vast swelling of water that flowed steeply and quickly down past the town.

Anders' eyes followed the river as it ran along the edge of the long and narrow strip of buildings making up the town where Ivan, Natalia and the Lumbapi soldiers were hidden. He saw the Kingston Road as it exited the town in a wash of dirt and gravel, following the river's edge to the east. Anders' heart skipped a beat when he saw the gray and black bodies of orcs marching into view from around the canyon's far end. He froze, staring at them as they funneled up the canyon toward the town.

Brosnan whispered, "Anders, look. They are coming."

CHAPTER

TWENTY-FIVE

ENEMIES CLASH

L ageena posted atop a black horse clad in polished
armor. The black and crimson colors of the king's
army, Merglan's Army, stood out among the
swath of enemy forces marching up the Kingston Road.
Anders lay on his stomach resisting the urge to move. He
wanted to share what he was witnessing with Zahara
through their bond, but the faint blue glow shining from
Lageena's chest confirmed his suspicions that she had a
crystal similar to the one the horrid kurr, Thargon, had
used during their last battle. Anders knew he couldn't take
the risk.

The host of orcs marching up the road easily spanned
the width of the two-way road built to allow for horse-
drawn carriages to pass by one another. The road must have
been worn wider since its original construction because
Anders could see six horses riding abreast with room to
spare on either side.

Brosnan and Anders watched patiently, not exchanging
a word as the initial small group of dark-headed orcs
continued steadily up the road. Watching Lageena in the

lead, Anders remembered to look for Ivan's signal. No doubt one cue for them to advance would be signs of fighting, but from their vantage point a small skirmish could begin and end before Anders and Brosnan would even see it. If the fighting was among a small enough contingent and remained on the northern side of the buildings, it could take place in a blind spot for them. There were areas within Ryedale where Anders couldn't see anyone in the streets for several blocks. It pained him to think that his companions might be jumping into a fight heavily outnumbered anticipating help that didn't come. Precisely for that reason, Ivan had created a surefire way to signal the elves and dwarfs that it was time to launch the ambush.

The granary and flour mill with its towering windmill in the center of town could be seen from all directions. Ivan, Natalia, Solomon and the Lumbapi soldiers were hiding in buildings throughout the town. Several brave Lumbapi had disguised themselves as the townsfolk. The actual townsfolk had been cleared from Ryedale one day prior. Those soldiers hiding in town had picked strategic locations throughout Ryedale to ensure they were well dispersed. Once Lageena had entered the town and her orcs were well within the confines of the canyon, Ivan and Natalia, using their remaining magical abilities, would force the windmill to spin. When the windmill started turning, all three parties united for this crucial ambush would know from their various vantage points that the fighting could begin. Anders just hoped he wouldn't be too distracted to see the mill when it first started spinning, but that's why he'd invited Brosnan to be his second set of eyes.

Anders was somewhat surprised at the seemingly careless way in which Lageena was leading her forces farther west and deeper into the canyon proper. As he understood it, the Lumbapi had been successfully ambushing Merglan's troops throughout the eastern half of Southland. If Anders were in her position, he would have sent scouts ahead before approaching any town. As he was thinking about what he would do differently, Lageena shouted to her orcs and they halted. The sound of her voice as she barked commands rang up the slopes. Anders could easily hear what she was shouting. If he understood Grug, the Eastland orcs' native language, he would've known what she was saying, but for now, he had to use his eyes to make sense of what was happening below.

The Lumbapi soldiers disguised as townspeople continued working in the fields plotted tightly along the river just east of town. When they heard Lageena's commands, they acted their part and fled toward town in fear.

Shoot, Anders thought. *I wish she would've just kept marching into the heart of the town.* For a moment he wondered if somehow she'd read his mind, but after thinking about it, he quickly dismissed the idea because he'd closed off his mind from all outgoing and incoming thoughts.

"What's she doing?" Anders whispered to Brosnan who remained motionless on the canyon rim next to him.

"It looks like she's going to send a group of orcs out ahead of her to check out the town. That's what I would do if I were her," the elf commander whispered.

That's what I thought, Anders thought to himself. "Hopefully the Lumbapi hold off their attack until Lageena commits to entering the town," he replied quietly.

Anders appreciated the lack of response that meant Brosnan agreed.

All they could do was wait for Ivan's signal whether it

came or not. He briefly wondered what they would do if Lageena backed off and decided to bypass the canyon altogether.

I hope it doesn't come to that, Anders thought.

He observed the thick line of orcs cascading down the length of the road. He'd not seen this many orcs in organized formations before. When they'd fought the orcs beneath the Eastland Mountains, they'd been led by Thargon. It had been dark and for all Anders could tell the orcs had been a disorganized mass. Even in battle, he could only see what was immediately in front of him. It wasn't until Zahara came to his rescue that he was able to see the whole of the army and by then the orcs were fleeing in mass. This host of orcs looked to be well regulated and remained in formation as they marched. They stretched the length of the road and around the corner out of Anders' line of sight.

He took the opportunity to search for other threats among them, such as kurr and fairnheir. Anders couldn't quite tell but he thought he only saw two or three large figures that resembled kurr. From his distance, he realized these could just as easily be large orcs. He could distinctly see a pack of fairnheir, however, snapping and barking like mad dogs. They were recognizable even from a great distance. Once Anders had seen one, he could tell what the figures were from a long way off. He hoped the Lumbapi's war dogs were with them. They'd need their help when they encountered the fairnheir on the battlefield.

It didn't take long before the group of orcs leading Lageena set out toward the outskirts of town. They rushed headlong toward the closest buildings. Anders thought they were being reckless and trying to intimidate any Lumbapi soldiers possibly hidden in Ryedale, but when they halted suddenly, Anders understood their tactics. Lageena must have known that if any archers were hidden within the city, they would have no choice but to fire on a squad of orcs rushing into their midst. Unbeknownst to her, however, there were far more than a few Lumbapi archers waiting for her to enter the town, but they wouldn't make a move until Ivan launched his ambush.

Well within shooting range of the eastern edge of town, the orc squad sent to search the streets drew their weapons and began their slow, careful approach. Anders could see their thick broadswords, cleavers, cutlasses, hammers and several maces in hand as they stepped up to the first row of buildings. The orcs slowly made their way into Ryedale, searching around each building as they advanced. Anders could hear screams and shouts as townspeople, or Lumbapi soldiers dressed as townspeople, fled.

The ruse seemed to be working. The orcs became more emboldened the farther into the heart of town they traveled. By the time they'd reached the opposite side of the thin, mile-long town, the orc squad was simply strolling down the middle of the central street. Satisfied that they had managed to cross the length of Ryedale unchallenged, the squad began their return toward their leader. They stormed storefronts, flipping food stands and tables of trinkets on display and smashing windows as they joyfully ventured back to Lageena.

Anders held his breath, hoping that Ivan would hold off on launching his attack. His eyes darted continuously between the motionless windmill and the orc scouting party. Finally, the orcs left Ryedale's limits and rushed full bore to their leader. Seeing that the windmill remained still, Anders breathed deeply with relief. Now they needed Lageena to trust her foolish orc squad and continue marching west up the road as it ran through the center of Ryedale.

He could see Lageena clutching at the glowing crystal that hung around her neck. She had waited until the orcs returned with their report. Turning back to see the length of her army and no doubt gathering confidence that she had greater numbers than any Lumbapi army, she placed her hands on the long mane of her black horse and spurred him forward. The orc squad stepped aside, clearing her path as she trotted to the head of her horde.

The entire chain of orcs began to move again following Lageena approaching the town. Anders kept his eyes on the windmill, making sure he didn't miss the moment it started moving. Out of the corner of his eye, he could see that the line of orc forces continued around the corner and out of sight. Lageena would enter the city and be through it before the entirety of her army entered the canyon. Ivan must have only seen a fraction of her forces. He didn't know how extensive her army truly was. There was no way their ambush could work in this short of a canyon. Ivan was confident that Lageena's army would march beyond where the dwarfs were hidden and could easily attack the enemy from the rear, trapping them within the canyon. Where the dwarfs were stationed now wouldn't be anywhere near the rear of Lageena's army. Anders felt an ache in the pit of his stomach as he watched the windmill remain motionless while Lageena continued her steady approach.

Lageena halted suddenly, just as the orcs had slowed when they first approached Ryedale. She brought her hand up to her chest and fingered the crystal. Her attention remained on the streets for several long breaths, then she turned her head to the left, her gaze sweeping the shallow canyon slopes beginning their rise only a few hundred feet from the Kingston Road.

Anders remained perfectly still, hoping everyone else within sight of Ryedale did the same. Lageena's sweeping gaze stopped, seeming as though she was staring directly at Anders; he thought for a moment she could see him. Only when her cold stare broke did Anders dare to blink again and she continued searching the rim, westward toward the narrowest point of the canyon. Her gaze lingered there. Anders continued to wait for the windmill's first movements.

Breathing slowly, Anders tried to decrease the rapid pounding of his heart. He struggled to keep his thoughts closed off and to himself as he breathed in and out, watching the suspicious eyes of his foe.

While Lageena sat on her horse before Ryedale's eastern perimeter, her orc army continued to march, filling the canyon's base. Anders could see the common disorganized behavior of the orcs beginning to show. Instead of following the movements of their leader, the army just continued to balloon in around those in the front lines, filling the space between the river to their north and the canyon slopes to the south. Lageena must have heard the gathering sounds of her orcs because she suddenly snapped around in her saddle. Cursing, she shouted in Grug at the orcs collecting along the road behind her. Frustrated, she swatted about attempting to direct her army back into formation. Succumbing to the hindrance, the former elf queen spun forward in her seat, grabbed hold of her horse's black mane and dug her heels into its haunches, moving forward into the town.

Anders sighed with relief. She'd been skeptical of entering Ryedale, but due to the lack of discipline among her troops, she was forced to advance if she wanted them to regain their formation.

The orcs' front lines followed their leader as she rode into the heart of Ryedale and halted under the windmill. Anders saw her point toward the west end of town, after which the orcs continued marching past her. It had worked, even if she hadn't fallen for the bait, their plan to get Lageena into the town's center before attacking had worked. Now all Anders needed to do was wait for Ivan's signal, then he'd be able to open his mind and command his half of the elven army to attack.

With Lageena and the front of her army well inside Ryedale, Anders saw the initial signs of the ambush. The orcs were beginning to spread out among the side streets, four on either side, making more room for the cluster gathering in the canyon behind them. Lumbapi soldiers sprang out from buildings and homes, pulling the passing orcs inside and quickly closing the doors just a fast as they'd opened. Orcs at the head of the army began to fall off one by one as disguised soldiers ran past them through the streets, cutting their throats and lopping off their heads. Before the orcs knew what was happening Anders saw the windmill begin to turn.

This was it, Ivan's signal. The ambush had begun.

Anders opened his mental link to all the elves waiting patiently in the thinly spaced trees behind him. He shouted through their minds, *Attack! Now!*

Before he could shout a second call with this telepathic link, the elves were rushing past him. They poured down over the canyon rim with their blades drawn. At their head, Anders could see Brosnan Strongsword speeding toward Ryedale. Zahara leaped from her hiding place and came alongside Anders as the elves sprinted downslope at the unsuspecting orcs.

What are you doing? We need to remain unseen, Anders said as Zahara came to sit at his side.

She growled and lay down in the grass placing her long head low so her profile wouldn't stand out along the rim's horizon.

Anders shook his head but knew there was no stopping her. This was as hidden as she was going to be for the remainder of the battle.

The sounds of war echoed through the canyon as the Lumbapi soldiers exploded from their hiding places. Nearly every building in the small narrow town opened and Southland natives flooded out. Orcs lay dead in the street before the elves from Anders' position descended on them.

The clash from hundreds of elves colliding with thousands of orcs echoed in the canyon below. Despite the elves' speed on foot, their sword skills were only slightly more advanced than a human's. They outmatched the orcs, but the enemy, though slower, had brute force and numbers on their side. Anders and Zahara watched as the elves began to cut their way deeper into the orcs. Once beyond the initial surprise of their attack, the elves began showing signs of their mortality. First Anders saw a wave of orcs pile into the midst of the attacking elves. The elves held them off for a moment but they were gradually overwhelmed by the sheer numbers of orcs. He witnessed a dozen elves crushed by the collective orcs before the other elves could withdraw from the charge.

Nadir's elves had dropped to the canyon bottom simultaneously with Anders' group. They flooded the road, cutting off any chance for the orc army to advance through the city and up the canyon to the west. While Nadir's contingent had secured the west end of Ryedale, Ivan and the Lumbapi battled the thicket of orcs throughout town.

At first, the orcs were unable to defend themselves from the soldiers attacking from all directions. The Lumbapi quickly killed off many orcs along the side streets. Ivan and Natalia had been inside the mill. They leaped out at Lageena as she pranced around on her horse, trying to regain control of the upset steed. Although Ivan had been close to the traitor queen, she managed to slip away from his grasp. Using the powers of her crystal necklace, she blocked Ivan and Natalia's attacks and held them at a distance while she rode back across the eastern half of town. The impact from the elves dropping into Ryedale from the ridgeline pushed many of the orcs into the town's core. Lageena quickly found a wall of orc bodies to shield her from the attacks of her former subjects.

As she gained situational awareness and control of her surroundings, Lageena began to fight back. She used powers that she shouldn't have had access to, halting elves that were advancing too far into her protective wall of orc bodies. In several instances, Anders saw one of the three-story, wooden buildings fall on both Lumbapi and orcs fighting in close quarters. He could only assume that Lageena was somehow using the properties of the crystal to force the buildings down on her enemies, regardless of whether they crushed her orcs as well.

We should take her now, Zahara said, stirring her wings as she and Anders watched the battle unfold.

It's too risky. If we weren't successful on the first try, she'd attack us and we don't know how much power she has in that crystal. We could probably defend ourselves from it, but it would drain our energy and then if Merglan suddenly showed up, we'd be useless. I want to fly down there and help as much as you do, but if we're going to win this war, it's in everyone's best interest to stay here, Anders said.

But what if we got her on the first try? What if we stopped her now?

They'd be leaderless, but they'd still outnumber us ten to one, Anders warned.

With this field advantage we've taken and the power among us, I think we could snuff them out, Zahara said hopefully.

Anders thought for a moment, *You could be right. And if we took out Lageena now that would surely draw Merglan out, which in the end is what we're trying to accomplish. But I'm not sure if this is the way we want to fight him. If Ivan or Natalia were with us, they could help us battle Merglan.*

That's the spirit. What are we trying to accomplish here? Didn't we come here to end this? I say we go after Lageena now and if Merglan comes, whether we get her or not, then Merglan comes and we'll face him if that happens.

Anders chewed on her idea. He knew elements of her plea were true. What were they doing there if not to fight Merglan?

Alright, I've made up my mind. We'll wait to see if Ivan or Natalia can get Lageena on their own. If she escapes, then we'll go after her. Sound good?

Zahara purred, *Sounds like a plan.*

Anders watched as the fighting continued in the streets. Initially, there had been chaos among the orcs as they scattered throughout the town with Lumbapi attacking them from all angles, but as the fighting continued, the orcs began to take control along the eastern edge of the town where their numbers were greatest. Lageena commanded her forces to fall back to the collective horde that had been piling up in the space outside town. The elves from Anders' half of the army fought fiercely to prevent as many orcs as possible from making it back outside city limits, but they were greatly outnumbered and suffered punishing casualties.

The Lumbapi and Nadir's elves began to collect in the west-end streets while Anders' elves swarmed along the southern slope of Ryedale. Orcs hit by the elf and human armies withdrew, backing themselves up against their own forces as they continued to balloon in the canyon's bottom. Anders began to shift uncomfortably as he watched Lageena gather further protection from her orc army. If he and Zahara had attacked with the elves in the beginning, they would have had a decent chance at taking her out.

They'd been watching from their perch atop the shallow canyon rim for nearly an hour before Anders caught first sight of the dwarfs. They were fighting their way across the steep southern slope of the canyon, using the topography to their advantage as they held off the rear of the orc forces. Anders hadn't seen they'd first attacked, as the line of orcs stretched out down the road past out of sight. The dwarfs must have found the rear of the vast army and struck once the sounds of battle began echoing through the canyon. He wasn't sure how effective they'd been at pinching them into the canyon. The dwarfs were meant to trap the orcs into the canyon, but it seemed like they'd become trapped themselves.

Concern for his dwarf friend, King Remli, came over Anders as he watched several fairnheir rush up the slopes and into the group.

"No," Anders gasped when he witnessed the beasts tearing into the stocky soldiers scattered along the south-facing slope.

To his surprise, however, the fierce dwarfs weren't

much affected by the large houndlike beasts. They'd met them in battle before, undoubtedly. Soon the dwarfs' battle-axes were hewing through the fur-bearing animals.

Although the dwarfs fought fiercely, Anders knew they were even more greatly outnumbered than the elves and Lumbapi. Now that the entirety of the orc army separated them from their allies, the dwarfs were in grave danger.

Seeing the likelihood of success in driving the orcs back gradually lessen as the battle unfolded, Anders decided they had to act if they were going to have any chance at victory. If Merglan was going to show up, Anders figured he would have done so by now. Clearly, Lageena didn't feel the need to alarm him or else Merglan trusted her enough to fend for herself. It was time for Anders and Zahara to join the fighting.

Anders rose to his feet. Zahara pushed herself to her feet as well, ready to make their move.

Remli and the dwarfs are getting pinched off. They'll need to make it back if we're going to hold the town, Anders said to her.

What do you want to do about that? she asked.

I say we attack Lageena. We can catch her by surprise if she doesn't spot us coming. It might cause a big enough distraction that Remli and his dwarfs will be able to reach the elves and Lumbapi soldiers. Anders moved to climb on top of her back and Zahara knelt to make it easier for him. *I'll warn Ivan so he and Nadir will be ready to make a path for Remli to come in.*

Anders opened his connection with the old rider and spoke in an authoritative tone, *Remli's been blocked from getting back and Lageena is protecting herself more strongly as the battle continues. Zahara and I...*

Anders no, Ivan said as he heaved a heavy swing from his sword down on an attacking orc.

We're going to create a distraction, Anders finished and then he blocked Ivan from his communication link. He unsheathed Lazuran and flexed his grip around the hilt of his sword. *Let's go.*

Zahara leapt over the canyon rim, spreading her large wings as they sped down toward the former elf queen mounted on her black horse. Anders locked eyes with her as she became aware of their presence and he began to summon the shared energy between himself and his dragon.

A BLINDING display of white light flecked with blue illuminated the narrow canyon. Anders summoned a pulse of electric magic. Shooting it out in a wave, he directed their combined energy at Lageena. She'd reacted more quickly than Anders anticipated, holding her crystal out in front of her body like a weapon. When their pulse of battle energy closed in on Lageena, it shattered into thousands of reflecting shards as it collided with the barrier she'd summoned through her enchanted crystal.

Zahara rushed headlong toward the bright explosion of light, never wincing or turning from her target. Anders already held the sword in his hand, ready to strike when they came within distance. He intended to kill the queen, or seriously maim her. The pulse of energy directed at her was their first swing in the surprise attack on the traitor queen. He knew it might come down to the sword in the end if they weren't able to make a successful attempt with magic. He also knew that if she had to hurry to defend herself with the crystal, she wouldn't be ready for the attacking swing of Lazuran from the back of a speeding dragon.

The shards of refracted light bounced off Zahara's iridescent scales as she barreled along the path of their ineffective magic attack. Making an impulsive decision, Zahara rolled as she passed just over the heads of the orcs surrounding Lageena. Anders sensed her move and hooked his legs under her wings. While holding onto the saddle handle with one hand, he let Lazuran be thrust above his head, watching the shifting tip point groundward.

For a moment he saw the wide-eyed elf hesitate as she saw the inverted dragon crashing down on her with Anders' elven blade coming swiftly toward her exposed head. While he pulled the sword through the air, bracing for its impact, Lageena suddenly laid back, releasing her feet from the stirrups. She flattened herself on her horse's rear end as Lazuran passed through the air where her head had been a split second before.

Anders cursed as he whiffed forward and nearly launched himself out of the saddle. As he felt his legs lifting out of Zahara's armpits, he secured the magical lashing to the seat of the saddle and gripped the handle tightly as she righted herself.

Once Zahara had rolled around to flying upright again, Anders shouted in frustration, "Ahh!"

You missed? Zahara asked in disbelief.

Anders looked over his shoulder as he adjusted back into a comfortable position in the saddle. *Yes. I had her, but she fell back on her horse. My blade must have missed her by inches,* he said in disgust.

It's not likely that we'll get an opportunity to strike at her like that again, Zahara said in frustration.

I know, I'm sorry. I can't believe I missed, Anders said.

He kept his eye on Lageena's movements as Zahara flew in an arching turn back up above the canyon rim.

To his surprise, the former elf queen had already moved her mount away from Ryedale and closer to the riverbank. Her orc army had swollen to the entire width of the canyon bottom and extended east down the road much farther than he'd imagined. Looking down at the entire battle from this new vantage point, Anders saw how greatly outnumbered their mixed army really was. He glanced to see that the dwarfs were taking advantage of the distraction. Remli was leading them quickly along the top of the rim while the orcs were all looking to the sky, watching the dragon.

Encouraged by their plan's effectiveness to draw attention away from their dwarf allies, Anders turned back on Lageena. *Let's give her another go,* he said to Zahara, her body already turning toward the open space where the traitor queen had fled.

Lageena had rushed her horse out near the banks of the river, away from any visual barriers that might offer Anders and Zahara advantage launching another attack, whether physical using Zahara's power or using their combined manipulation of magic.

Her horse stamped nervously as she shouted commands in Grug to the orcs. It was apparent that she'd ordered everyone to clear a space around her.

Zahara speared back down along the canyon wall, trying to gain speed before Lageena could prepare for their second attack. She sat mounted in a circle of trampled grass, surrounded by a sea of orcs parting ways around her as they continued into town. Lageena held her horse steady, facing Zahara and Anders' approach.

Zahara tucked her wings and Anders focused on Lageena's position. He began to summon more energy as they approached. He knew she would likely be the one to attack this go-round and he wanted to be ready to deflect whatever she attempted to throw at them.

The sound of rushing arrows suddenly arose as Zahara's tucked body came screaming down closer to the ground. Several arrows flew past Anders' exposed upper half, others deflecting off Zahara's scales before he reacted. Speaking the words and quickly summoning a shroud of energy, Anders created a thin shield covering the two of them from the small projectiles. Once he'd done this, the wooden shafts clanked and twanged as they bounced off the energy spacer between his dragon and their deadly paths.

Seeing Anders' momentary focus on the arrows, Lageena seized the opportunity to hurl a ball of the crystal's energy at them. Anders didn't have time to react and would have become consumed by the energy's trajectory, but Zahara moved for him. She quickly dodged the speeding light as it sparked along the outer edge of the shield Anders' had created.

Although they'd managed to dodge the attack, Zahara's track on Lageena had been compromised. She couldn't complete their charge; they'd have to circle back before making another attempt. Anders held onto the energy. Though it strained him physically, the arrows continued to bounce off them until they'd climbed back out of range.

Anders panted, short of breath from holding such a significant barrier for so long. *Well, that didn't work as well the second time around,* he said between breaths.

No, some of those arrows cut my wings before you could begin blocking them, Zahara winced.

We'll need to think of something else if we want to get close enough to attack her without the orcs shooting at us.

I might have an idea, Zahara said and she soared above the canyon walls and westward away from the town.

What are you doing? Lageena's back there, Anders said pointing behind them with his sword.

I know, I have a plan.

Anders trusted her as she flew them out of sight of the battle. Turning around, she dropped back down into the canyon, flying low, just above the ground. She rushed back toward the western edge of Ryedale, banking down into the trough of the riverbank. Anders leaned forward as they flew just inches over the wide river using the riverbanks to conceal their attack. Anders prepared to fire a spell that Ivan had taught them using a large blade of energy extending from his sword, hopefully, he'd be able to sweep it at Lageena when Zahara flew up out of the riverbed.

Once beyond the town's eastern edge, Zahara waited for two short breaths before initiating the assault. Anders heard only the whooshing of her wings catching air as she bolted up from the river. His arm was raised and pointed at where he imagined the former queen would be. As soon as she came into view, Anders shouted, swinging Lazuran down at the elf, not taking great aim before the blue light extended from his sword.

He watched Lageena's horse rear at Zahara's sudden approach behind them. The slash of energy exploded as it struck the ground next to Lageena. The splash of energy knocked her off her horse and she fell to the ground. Zahara quickly turned and buzzed over the orcs lining the road around the elf. She ripped into them with her claws as she flew just over their heads. The sharp eyes of the enemy archers hadn't seen her coming. No arrows were fired until they'd already passed.

Zahara climbed through the air back to the height of the canyon rim. Anders watched the last of the dwarfs rush over the top to town. He let out a sigh of relief. Their plan to create a distraction had worked. The dwarfs would make it back to the right side of the fighting, but for how long Anders didn't know. The orc army greatly outnumbered theirs. Since their plan to pinch them into town had failed, they would soon be forced to retreat to higher ground and hope the orcs didn't pursue.

I think I got her that time, Anders said excited but feeling fatigued from having used more magic.

Your aim was off, but the blast was effective. I saw her fall to the ground, but I'm not sure she'll stay down. We'll need to get another shot at her if we want to make sure, Zahara said turning to fly over town again.

Anders looked toward Lageena's last location. She was already back on her feet, holding the lead rope of her horse, trying to keep him from rearing with fright. While he spotted their target, Anders became aware of a line of elves and humans making a push through the orcs toward the river. Bright flashes and crashing led their charge.

Zahara, I think Ivan and Natalia are making a push to get at Lageena. We can help them.

Zahara saw the bright flashes snapping in quick succession as a pod of elves hacked their way deeper through the eastern reaches of town.

You'll need to distract Lageena while I help them push from the ground, Anders said. He could sense Zahara's confusion, so before she could reply, he explained, *Each time we get close enough to attack, the orc archers force us to veer away because I'm exposed. The shield works, but it drains my energy more and more each time. Their arrows can't penetrate your thick scales. You can continue the assault on her*

461

while I help the others advance toward her. It's our best strategy.

Zahara flew low into the city, tilting her body so Anders could jump off and join the fighting on the ground. As she did, she said, *Don't make me regret this.*

As Anders unleashed himself from the saddle, he replied, *Keep Lageena distracted until we're close, then join us on the ground.* He slid down the length of her wing as she arced around a set of two-story wooden homes. Anders landed feet first on the ground, cushioning himself with a surge of energy as he rushed toward the advancing group of elves.

Zahara straightened herself and climbed, spotting Lageena as she searched frantically to locate the dragon. Clearly, the sneak attack from the riverbed caught her off guard; her jerking movements led Zahara to believe that they had her frightened. She flapped her wings to gain speed, then dove directly at Lageena, hoping she could keep the evil elf woman distracted long enough for Anders to help the others break through to her.

Arrows snapped as they struck her in the breast, several of them cutting into her broad wings. She fought through the pain, focusing on her task. The traitor queen was the first to act, sending a flash of light toward Zahara. With her heightened awareness, Zahara easily swerved around the attempt at her life and barreled directly at the elf. With Anders off of her back, she didn't fear the arrows would hurt him. This meant that she could fly in close. She released a deafening roar and lashed out with her talons as she cupped out of her dive. The traitor queen spurred her horse and the creature carried her out of the way, Zahara finding her claws clutching at nothingness. Zahara kept her eyes on Lageena as she turned, keenly aware of her long tail.

A blue light sparked in Lageena's hand, but before she could release the magic, Zahara flicked her tail. The motion strained her body and she momentarily had to retract her wings to avoid hurting herself with the unnatural pull. Her tail crashed into the elf's horse, sending it toppling to the side as Lageena again fell from her mount.

Zahara spread her wings, catching herself just before touching the ground, orcs climbing over one another to flee the area where it looked as though she might crash. She pushed down with her legs, the force crunching orcs under her weight as she kicked herself back into the air. She shrieked as spears and arrows cut into the folds of her wings. Powering through the pain, Zahara flapped furiously, climbing out of range of the orc archers. She arched her head to locate the traitor queen, a smoldering crater of orc bodies left in the place where she'd sent Lageena tumbling from her horse.

CHAPTER
TWENTY-SIX

MERGLAN

Anders drew on the stores of energy within his body and tried something he'd never done before. As he fell from Zahara's wing, he separated a fragment of the summoned energy and sent the sliver rippling down through his legs. The energy acted as a buffer, and though it may have looked as though he'd crashed onto the ground from a great height, Anders landed softly, the energy slowing his momentum at the last moment before his feet touched the ground. He grinned and sprinted to catch up to the elves slashing their way through the orcs with renewed effort.

Flashes of blue light sparked as Anders' companions fought their way deeper into the cluster of orcs. Anders knew his skills would best be used to aid in leading the charge, but a moving wall of bodies blocked his path. Searching for a break in the thicket of orcs surrounding the group, Anders realized he might have to cut his way through the orcs to reach the front line of his group's charge, a nearly impossible task. As he closed in on the elves, Anders had an idea. Using the same principles as when he landed, Anders sent another burst of energy down one leg, while simultaneously pushing off of that leg with force. To his surprise and relief, he launched into the air and flew. Elves glanced up at him, taken by surprise as he sailed over their heads and came crashing down in a pile of orcs just beyond the main front in the urban battle.

The orcs hadn't seen the sudden attack coming when Anders landed, quickly gaining his footing. Sweeping Lazuran in three long strokes, the sharpened blade cleared an area that would enable him to fight more strategically. Landing in front of the others had not been his goal, but this way he would only have to cut through several lines of orcs before his companions could reach him. Many of the orcs battling along the front line hadn't seen him as he flew over their heads, which gave him the opening to quickly slash his way toward his friends. He moved with purpose, knowing the orcs behind him would soon be nipping at his heels with their thick blades.

While he used Lazuran to clear a path through lines of unsuspecting orcs, a series of blinding lights flashed and Anders instinctively shielded his eyes. The light momentarily stunned the orcs around him, allowing several figures to rush into the space he'd cleared. As Anders lowered his forearm, he found Natalia heaving her blade into two orcs at once, cutting down several more with swift motions as she came to his side. The other figure moved with the grace and skill of a seasoned soldier, but Anders didn't recognize the slender form. As the spear spun, dancing elegantly within its wielder's hands, Anders suddenly knew the figure to be Inama, the Lumbapi princess. She spun and flicked, killing orcs with ease as she advanced past Anders; Ivan, Nadir and Solomon followed. Ivan used his broadsword blocking and attacking with skill alongside Nadir, his elf companion who mirrored his movements. Anders became momentarily stunned when he saw Solomon burst through, wielding only a shield and defending himself from orc blades.

Inspired, Anders spun Lazuran with a quick rotation of his wrist and joined his comrades as they led the charge, cutting through chaos and advancing toward Lageena. Moving as a cohesive unit, those in front broke through the orc ranks. The elves supporting their charge cleaned up any left standing as they passed through. They had no need for communication; each individual seemed to understand how to continue the group's momentum. Even Ivan was silent aloud and telepathically. All were focused intently on their tasks, working toward their shared goal. They had to kill the elf queen-turned-traitor. They had to kill Lageena here and now.

Anders fought with speed and skill, blocking and dodging blows meant to end his life. He didn't think about manipulating Lazuran with his hand, he just felt the blade. The sword seemed to have a power of its own, leading him through the movements instead of him leading the blade. An awareness consumed him, one that brought clarity to his movements. He could see his moves three or four ahead of his actions. Lazuran guided his hand to swiftly kill the orcs in front of him. He quickly passed the others, clearing a path through the orcs, multiple sword lengths wide and gaining distance ahead of his fellow soldiers. Several more flashes of blinding light brought Anders back to reality. He slowed his pace, letting the others catch up. He glanced up and saw Zahara screaming down toward the ground, enemy arrows deflecting off her scales as she dove. Based on her trajectory, they were getting closer, pushing past the eastern edge of Ryedale and out into the broader valley.

Anders glanced over his shoulder to see the shingled rooftops rising from the sea of orcs. Suddenly, he grasped the gravity of his actions. In advancing the group of elves so rapidly, they'd become an island within the vast expanse of enemy fighters. Anders understood. This was how they would have to end the war. They would have to cut off Merglan's influence by eliminating his powerful supporters, such as Lageena. They had to stop her or die trying.

His companions caught up, Inama and Nadir killing with skillful precision. Natalia and Ivan, appearing physically stressed, but continued to use what energy they could summon to attack the orcs while advancing with their blades. Solomon somehow forced his way through a sea of orcs using only a shield and magic to aid him.

How is he doing that? Anders wondered as he raised Lazuran to block an orc sword. The old man moved with the speed and strength of the elves, yet he was ancient. Anders couldn't see or sense a dragon near him and he didn't have a crystal in his possession as Lageena did, as far as Anders could tell.

Zahara released a deafening roar, the sound booming throughout the canyon. Anders' heart nearly stopped as he feared the worst. He fought with renewed vigor when he caught sight of his dragon pulling out of her dive. He let Lazuran take control once more and danced a deadly step as his blade killed more orcs. As the gap between their group and Lageena narrowed, Anders sensed the intensity within their group increase. Though she'd seemed untouchable when they started their push through Ryedale, their chance to take Lageena was rapidly approaching.

Suddenly Zahara tucked her wings and dropped in a sideways jerking motion. Anger welled in Anders at the possibility that Zahara had truly been hurt. He frantically

467

hacked and stabbed out into the thicket of orcs. A bright light flashed among the muddled orc heads before him and for an instant he thought he could hear a voice, calling to him from inside Lazuran's hilt. Before Anders could react, an explosion of light and energy erupted near Zahara's most recent location. The orcs in front of him were lifted off the ground and thrust toward him. They slammed into Anders, driving him through the open space at his back, hitting him hard and leaving him dazed.

Anders groaned under the crushing weight of several orcs, trying hard to breathe. He struggled to move but couldn't force the hefty creatures off. He began to panic, his rapid breaths leaving him light-headed. In an act of desperation, he summoned his magic and sent pulses out of his body in every direction. The bodies of the orcs bounced in response to the energy and rolled to the sides. Before more could slide over on top of him, Anders scrambled to his feet and leapt up, orc bodies rolling back into the space where he'd been knocked down. Landing lightly on top of them, Anders felt lucky that he hadn't lost his grip on Lazuran. He spun, ready to defend himself.

To his surprise, he found he was standing alone near the center of a smoldering crater. All of the orcs around him lay flattened, forming a burning layer uniformly covering the sunken half sphere in the ground. The center of the depression, not far from where he stood, was near where he'd last seen Lageena. Feeling a throbbing ache from the impact, Anders searched the area around him. Ivan and Natalia had been close by when the explosion occurred, but he stood alone among the wreckage.

Starting in the area where he'd last seen them, Anders pulled at the bodies of lifeless orcs. Suddenly he saw movement. An orc rolled onto its side and Ivan emerged.

Rushing to his side, Anders helped Ivan climb out from under the pile of dead bodies.

"What happened?" Anders asked, hoping Ivan would have an explanation.

"Lageena," Ivan said in a dry voice. "Where's Lageena?"

Anders turned, looking toward the area where he'd seen the light originate before the explosion. At the center of the crater lay Lageena's black and crimson plated armor, her body sprawled out and motionless in the smoldering dirt. Anders and Ivan ran over the bodies of the decimated orcs.

Anders, he heard Zahara's voice at last. *You're alive!* she said with relief.

Anders glanced up as Zahara flew over the crater. Lageena's body lay at the center. As they neared her, Ivan slowed his pace, Anders staying in stride with the old rider. *Zahara, how did this happen? Did you do this?*

Zahara dropped, circling in to land near them, *No. I hit her with my tail when I missed grabbing her with my claws. She was summoning something, and it must have gone off when she crashed. When I turned back, I saw this crater of destruction where she'd fallen, and I thought I'd lost you.* She touched down near Anders, slowly approaching the unconscious elf.

The horse Lageena was riding pinned one of her legs, as she lay motionless on the ground.

"Is she dead?" Anders asked Ivan.

Ivan cautiously stepped closer to the queen, his sword pointed down at her body. He glanced to Anders, his eyes flickering beyond him, then returning. Anders turned to see what he'd noticed. The orcs were descending on them, rushing into the crater and trampling over the dead bodies of their kin. Anders bent his knees and Zahara whirled around to see the orcs closing in. They backed up closer to Lageena as they prepared for this last stand.

"No, she's still alive," Ivan said shortly, stepping over Lageena's body. "This ends now!" Pulling his blade back, he aimed the tip to strike Lageena's throat. Plunging it swiftly down toward her, Ivan's sword was met with resistance. Lageena sat up once Ivan's blade was locked in place midway through its strike. She grabbed him by the leg and clutched the crystal around her neck. An orb of light enveloped them, separating Anders, Zahara and Ivan from the rest of the world. The orb retracted and Anders heard a loud snap; they were thrust into darkness.

Anders spun, whirling his head back and forth, trying to make sense of his surroundings. No longer on the field of battle where they'd been half a second before, wherever he was now darkness enveloped them, and the air smelled dank. He found Zahara at his side where she'd been when they were in the crater. Ivan also remained to his left as he'd been moments before. Their positions hadn't changed, just their surroundings.

He heard a shrill laugh as Lageena spun away from them, her armor boots clacking against stone as she created a space between them.

Anders startled, *Hadn't she been trapped under her horse?* As his eyes adjusted to the darkened area, he couldn't see any signs that her horse had been near them.

"What have you done to us?" Ivan demanded, slashing his blade at her.

She chuckled, easily dodging the sweeps, skipping back across the stone floor. Her steps echoed along with Ivan's words in the hollow room.

Anders was hit with a horrible realization. Lageena had

used the same spell that she'd used to escape Cedarbridge, only this time she took them with her.

As her laughter died away, they could hear the footsteps of someone or something marching toward them. Out of the darkness emerged a figure dressed in black. They saw the long silver sword before they could see the man. He stopped alongside Lageena, standing just a few feet in front of them.

Ivan growled through clenched teeth, "Merglan."

NADIR SHOVED at the body of a dead orc. Rolling the charred creature onto its back allowed him to sit up. He took off his helmet and gasped for air. His head throbbed with a terrific pounding and his chest felt crushed though he was still alive. Confused about how he wound up under the orc, Nadir blinked, trying to clear his vision. Though his head ached and his ears rang with a high-pitched whining, he suddenly snapped back to reality.

The battle, he thought searching his surroundings frantically. He sat waist-deep in a crater of smoldering orcs, most lying flat on their faces. He remembered the blinding flash of light as he leapt over a falling orc he'd cut down; then the collision. Orcs launched forward, crashing into him and piling one atop the other as they took the brunt of the exploding force.

Before he could clearly conceive of what had happened, he saw a wave of orcs charge over the fallen corpse at the far side of the crater. They charged toward a dragon and her rider near the center. *Anders and Zahara,* he thought, rising to his feet. *They're in trouble,* Nadir reached for his elven blade, but it wasn't at his side. *The explosion,* he recalled as he scanned the pile of bodies for his weapon. He found his sword protruding hilt deep from the belly of the orc he'd rolled off of himself. Pulling it free and turning to advance toward Anders and Zahara's aid, he hesitated. They were no longer there! He was sure they'd been there a moment ago; both of them, and someone else.

The orcs seemed to turn their attention to him, a lone figure standing among the wreckage. Frantic and aware of how alone he was, Nadir turned left toward the riverbank for salvation. *I could escape in the rapids,* he thought as he ran to the river. He'd rather risk drowning in plated armor than suffer a horrific death at the hands of the orcs. While rushing awkwardly over orc bodies, he heard a muffled shout. Stumbling to a stop, he looked down.

"Hmm, mmh, hu," he heard a soldier attempting to speak from under more orc bodies. Nadir reached down and separated some corpses. A wrinkled hand reached up through the gap and he took hold of it. Pulling hard, the newly named elf king lifted Solomon the wise to the surface.

Coughing, Solomon staggered, trying to find his balance on the uneven surface. "Good grief," the wise man said, brushing the front of his patched leather coat. Seeing the wave of enemy forces charging over the bodies startled him.

"Follow me. To the river!" Nadir exclaimed renewing his run toward the bank.

"Wait!" Solomon shouted, causing the elf to stop short.

Solomon quickly felt at his coat, searching for something in his pockets. With his hand patting three times on his breast pocket, his eyes grew wide. "Ah. Yes, yes," he mumbled to himself as he reached into the pocket and pulled out a spiky creature. A second crawled out, revealing its spiked head to glance at the chaos. He softly muttered something to them, setting the one in his hand down as the other flung itself from his pocket. They scurried with lightning speed toward the oncoming orcs.

Nadir gaped at Solomon with a horrified expression, "Now can we make our escape?" he exclaimed, turning again to the river.

"Not without the others," Solomon said firmly and began searching through the orcs at his feet.

"Solomon, we're going to die if we stay here any longer," Nadir said. As he spoke, however, something extraordinary happened. A wall of flames sprang up between where they were standing and the orcs' frontline. The orcs were nearly halfway through the crater when they were forced to stop by an incredible arc of fire. He watched in awe as it formed a wall of impassible flames as wide as the river that would keep the charging orcs at bay.

"Whu, what? How?" Nadir managed to say.

"Lumbapi razor-backed lizards," Solomon said, standing straight for a moment. "Not quite dragons, but close enough for our purposes. Now come on, help me uncover the others before the lizards' energy drains. They can't keep that wall of fire going indefinitely."

Without hesitation, King Nadir began rummaging frantically through the bodies. Within moments, Nadir and Solomon had managed to uncover Natalia, Princess Inama and an elf soldier from their party. Once above the pile, Natalia was able to use her powers and sense out the remaining elf soldiers. They were far fewer in number than there had been when they started their push toward Lageena.

"How much longer can your lizards hold their flames?" Nadir asked, speaking over the battle cries of the elven and

Lumbapi forces making their stand in the town, the roaring river, and the hiss of flames.

Solomon shook his head, "It's a miracle they've lasted this long."

"Can we push our way back into the town?" Natalia asked, eyeing their group of soldiers.

"It's either that or the river," Nadir said, thumbing over his shoulder to the rushing water along the bank.

"Wait, where are Anders and Ivan?" Natalia said, after taking an inventory of those who'd been recovered.

"I saw Anders and Zahara, at least I thought I did, near the center of the crater. I looked away for a moment and they vanished," Nadir replied, sounding unsure of himself.

Natalia snorted in frustration at his answer. She closed her eyes, searching for Anders, Ivan or Zahara's presence. Opening her eyes again, she said, "I can't feel their presence or Lageena's."

"They probably rode off on that dragon," Solomon said, waving his hand.

"It's possible, but why now and without warning, and what of Lageena?" Natalia asked.

Nadir shrugged, and Solomon said, "We can ask questions later. Right now, we need to act. It's either the river or back through the town."

Natalia suddenly darted toward the wall of flames.

"Natalia where are you going?" Nadir called after her.

Solomon grunted and returned to scrambling over the orc bodies, rolling several over in search of more survivors.

Natalia stopped short of the flame-wall, the center of the crater where Lageena had been before the blast in her line of sight. She examined the ground at a distance, seeing an imprint of unburned soil where the queen and her horse had been. Noticing the width of the flames had decreased just in the short amount of time since she'd been pulled from the wreckage, Natalia knew the lizards couldn't hold the spell for much longer.

Rushing back to Nadir and the others she shook her head, "Lageena's not there. She was, but not anymore."

"Now what?" Nadir asked glancing at the reducing flames.

"Two weak sorcerers, two noble soldiers and two dozen elves against a thousand or more orcs?" Natalia said, shrugging. "Seems like a fair fight to me."

Nadir smiled, "Then we push through."

The two-dozen elves they'd recovered were finishing off orcs who'd survived the explosion when Nadir called them into formation. With Nadir, Natalia, Solomon and Inama at their head, they formed a triangular wedge facing the town. Solomon whistled and the flames subsided. Running with their blades drawn and minds fixed on making their way back through the onslaught of orcs, Nadir charged sword first into the dark mass of bodies barring their way.

Forcing their way into the mass of orcs entering the crater, Nadir fought with all his might. The slow advance up the shallow slope proved difficult. Stepping on dead bodies littering the ground, Nadir operated on blind faith that his footing would hold during this challenging task. The elven blade sank deep into gray flesh as Nadir cut his way out of the crater. Princess Inama sprang over attacking orcs as she used her spear staff to launch herself high into the air. The Lumbapi princess displayed skills Nadir didn't know existed with a spear. It moved in her hands with ease as she twirled, snapped and sliced at her attackers. The spear gave her the advantage of distance from her enemy that a sword did not.

Sweat streamed down the elf king's face as he battered

relentlessly at the orcs. Often, he would sidestep an orc rushing headlong at him, sending the orc back into the soldiers following at his rear. Based on the way they'd begun to creep alongside him, he could tell their formation was beginning to fail. The wedge was excellent for driving through a wide line of enemies, but in this case, the wide line of enemies didn't seem to have an end.

As they neared fringes of town, Natalia used her waning powers to force groups of orcs out of her way, but Nadir could tell her powers were fading. She lagged behind, sluggishly lifting her sword to block the unceasing attacks. In a spinning combination, Nadir glanced behind him, seeing their numbers had decreased severely. Only a handful remained behind him.

"With me!" Nadir shouted as he made a hard push toward the closest building.

Solomon struggled to keep up, blocking rapidly with his shield as he followed the elves. He no longer sparked flashes of blue light as he had on their initial assault, leaving crippled orcs in his wake. His lizards' energy had been exhausted in the crater. With no weapon to defend himself, the old wise man caught up with the handful of soldiers as they huddled into a small pocket of free space on the western side of a brick building near Ryedale's entrance.

Nadir panted as he, Natalia and Inama created a defensible space for their soldiers. Instinctively the elven soldiers formed a wall, as the orcs flooding the streets and marching to the headwall of the fighting became aware of their small group's presence. Cutting and hewing down attacker after attacker, the small collection of resisting elves and humans was pinned and surrounded once again. This time they had no river to retreat to, only a brick wall that would act as an anvil against them. The orc horde would be the hammer and, no matter how many they killed, the hammer would continue to drop, pounding them tighter against the wall.

As they continued to hold their ground, the pile of orc bodies grew higher until the orcs seemed to be towering over them. Nadir looked to his fellow comrades. Natalia was heaving her sword desperately. She and Solomon were trying to combine enough energy to push the pile of bodies back and create more room. Nadir's elven soldiers were dying with orc blades through their chests. Inama slammed her spear into orcs trying to climb their way into the space. This was how he would die, failing at avenging the death of his father, and as a leader, defeated by orcs. Nadir wondered what would become of his people after this battle. Would they fall to Merglan's rule, torn from their homes and forced to live a life of slavery, their wills bent to that of an evil sorcerer? Would he be remembered as a prince or a king? Would he be remembered at all?

As he thrust the tip of his sword through an orc's head, it tumbled down the mountain of bodies and blocked him against the brick wall. Trapped, he saw Natalia take a blow to the side, an orc's warhammer slamming into her ribs. On the opposite side, Inama struggled to pull her spear loose, the back of it butting into the wall as she tried to pry it free. An orc blade cut her flesh as she arched out of the way to escape a piercing to her core. She cried out and Nadir felt years of frustration boil to the surface. Years of hatred against his stepmother, against how highborn elves treated him as insolent, years of never being good enough. At that moment Nadir rallied to fight back for those who fought by his side, to whatever end.

With a surge of adrenaline, the elf king lunged at the orc who'd cut Inama, cleaving the top half of his head clean off with the razor-sharp edge of his sword. Spinning, he heaved down with a backhanded arc of his blade, burying his sword deep into the skull of the orc with the warhammer. Jerking it free, he hewed three more orcs, cutting their heads off as he climbed to the top of the pile. He raised his sword to fell another attacker but stopped before he brought it down.

"Nadir!" Remli bellowed, his dwarf warhammer in hand, crimson with orc blood.

Nadir staggered, lowering his blade in sheer awe. He could hardly believe his eyes, the dwarf king had somehow made his way from the flank of the battle, running across the canyon rim and descending into town. Remli's stout soldiers bored their way through the orcs, much as they had bored through the granite underbellies of the mountains when mining, hammering their way through.

Nadir panted, words falling short to describe his relief. He grabbed the dwarf king, wrapping his long arms around him and locked him in an embrace.

"Get off," the dwarf said, wiggling free of Nadir's grasp. "Are there any others?" he asked quickly.

Nadir nodded and pointed down the backside of the hill of orc bodies. He turned to join him, but Remli climbed too quickly for the tired elf to keep up. The dwarf pulled Inama, Solomon, Natalia and two more injured elves from the pit. On the front side of the mound of bodies, the dwarfs fought fiercely, clearing a path for escape through the town's streets.

"MY DEAR FRIEND," Merglan said with a deceitfully calming voice. "Have all proper forms of nobility been cast from your life? Don't you recall how to properly address royalty?"

Ivan glared at the evil sorcerer as he clutched his sword.

"It's your majesty," Merglan said dismissively, turning his gaze to Anders and Zahara. "I see you brought guests."

Anders summoned a well of energy from within and cast the spell that would direct the energy from the tip of his sword. He swung Lazuran at Merglan with blinding speed. Anders' eyes widened as he watched the energy shoot forth from the tip of his blade and arc down at the unsuspecting foe. The energy shattered, refracting into thousands of pieces as the swath of energy collided with Merglan. The energy meant to deliver a killing blow was somehow reversed at the last moment and sent directly back into the sword. The sudden change of energy bit into Anders' arms as it passed back through. The surge caused him to drop Lazuran and stumble backward.

Zahara expelled a roar from deep within. She lunged at Merglan.

The evil sorcerer didn't flinch as her large jaws closed in on him. Suddenly, a large black tail swung down between them. The scaled muscular tail collided with Zahara's neck, first tossing her to her side and then sending her skidding across the room. She yelped at the unexpected blow as Killdoor landed beside his master, resuming his consumption of Lageena's dead horse.

"Nice try, but did you really think that would work?" Merglan asked flatly.

Ivan shouted and sprang at him, Anders following his teacher as he scooped Lazuran from the ground. Merglan stepped toward them and met Ivan's blade with his own. He blocked the attack, sending Ivan spinning past him. He struck out at Anders. It was all Anders could do to deflect the sharp bite of Merglan's sword as the man attacked. Even when sparring with Ivan and Natalia at the same time, he'd never had so much difficulty keeping up with an attacker's sword. He stepped back, trying to gain some separation when Ivan jumped in again. Distracting Merglan for a moment, Anders was able to regain his composure and the two worked simultaneously to gain an opening on the sorcerer.

Ivan cried out in pain as Merglan's blade slid past his and cut deep into his arm near the elbow, forcing Ivan to drop his blade. In an instant, Merglan reached out to Anders and stopped him mid-swing, holding his body perfectly still with a powerful spell. Merglan held his blade in the other hand up to Ivan's throat, eyeing him sternly. Anders wanted to cry out, but he couldn't. As hard as he tried to push, he couldn't move his body. He dared not open his mental barriers to Zahara for fear of what Merglan would do to them if he broke into their minds. He couldn't see her, but from the sound of it, Zahara and Killdoor had begun fighting as well.

Merglan held his blade to Ivan's throat, also breathing heavily from the physical bout. Pulling his blade back and turning, Merglan walked to Lageena's side. Ivan reached for his sword with his left arm, but Merglan used the same spell with which he was holding Anders immobile, bending Ivan's physical body to his will as well. Sheathing his sword, Merglan addressed Lageena, "Everything went according to plan?"

Lageena ran a finger under her collar and pulled up the necklace with the crystal. Somehow it seemed to glow less brightly than it had before. Taking it off, she handed the necklace to Merglan and said, "More or less. The dragon and her rider came up with some unexpected attacks, but I figured them out."

"Good," Merglan said, looking at Anders and Ivan as they continued to stand motionless. He called to Killdoor with a stern voice, "Keep her alive Killdoor. We need them functional if they're going to be of use to us."

Anders wanted to scream. He could hear Zahara scrapping with Merglan's dragon, their talons scraping against their hard scales as they battled.

Merglan turned his attention back to Lageena. He held up the dull crystal, examining it in the dimly lit room. "This one's done," he said, reaching down into his pocket and pulling a similar sapphire crystal from his cloak. This one shone with a bright radiant light-blue hue. Before handing it to Lageena, Merglan clutched it against his chest and mumbled several words Anders' didn't recognize. For a moment Merglan glowed the same hue as the crystal. At that moment Anders gained control of his body. His sword swung forward and he took several steps before the spell took hold of him again. Merglan seemed to show a hint of exhaustion as the blue hue vanished. He placed the new sapphire necklace over Lageena's head and said, "Return to the battle and finish the job."

Lageena straightened and saluted Merglan. He waved her away and she disappeared in a brilliant flash of light.

TWENTY-SEVEN

THE SAPPHIRE SOUL

Remli led the haggard group of elves and two humans out into Ryedale's streets. The small army of dwarfs followed, their battleaxes and war hammers battering aside the brutish orcs as they retreated. Natalia cringed, forcing herself to move through the pain, her mental strength wavering as she struggled to keep moving. Nadir coaxed the others along. When he saw Natalia, bloodied and broken in the middle, he slung her arm over his shoulder.

Natalia cried out, the sudden movement sending pain streaking through her midsection. "Ah!" she cried, though her scream was cut short by her need to inhale and exhale quickly.

Nadir helped carry her along, keeping pace with the others. He knew Natalia's ribs were battered and broken on the side that took the hammer blow. From the way she was fading, he wondered if her bones were the only things broken by the hammer's strike. Stopping to address her condition wasn't an option; the best he could do was get her to safety.

Battered relentlessly by the onslaught of orcs, the Lumbapi and elven soldiers struggled to hold the front line until their commanders returned from striking out after Lageena. Though their numbers dwindled as they were slowly forced back little by little, the mixed elf and human force still held a quarter of the west end in Ryedale. Descending from the canyon's rim when Lageena's blast occurred, Remli and his dwarfs exposed themselves greatly by choosing to force their way through the midst of Ryedale in an attempt to save the squad who'd been decimated in the blast.

Nadir nearly carried Natalia as Remli led the crew along Ryedale's riverbank, forcing orcs in their path off the edge into the tumultuous waters below. To his surprise, Nadir saw Solomon and Inama force their way to the front of the dwarfs, joining the final push toward their allies. Solomon pushed orcs aside with his shield and Inama, seeming to be unaffected by the large gash on her side, wielded her spear with excellence. After a short while, they appeared to be gaining momentum; even Natalia miraculously seemed to be holding a steady pace, keeping in stride as Nadir supported her.

Suddenly Nadir heard a wicked snapping and popping from behind. He glanced over his shoulder toward one of the nearby buildings. He'd heard that sound before when Lageena began toppling the multiple-story tall buildings at the beginning of the fight. Though he waited for the two buildings on either side of the street to collapse around them, the structures remained standing.

When Nadir returned to his focus on their retreat, he thought the orcs' ranks seemed to have thinned. The dwarfs, now running at a dead sprint, neared the wall of elves and humans. A wave of relief washed over him when he realized that they would soon enjoy the safety in numbers they'd been lacking.

Why have the orcs fled from this one area? he wondered as the elven and Lumbapi ranks opened to receive them. *Is the dwarf force strong enough to scare them into abandoning their hold?* Nadir and Natalia brought up the rear of the group, most dwarfs rushing ahead to join the allied ranks.

Turning to look back one last time, Nadir dropped his hold on Natalia, her momentum sending her stumbling forward as she tried to continue her pace unsupported. Nadir stopped in his tracks. A figure in black plate with crimson trim stood alone in the street, the orcs clearing an opening around her. His feelings of relief were washed away by anger and rage.

Lageena, he clenched his jaw at the thought of her blasphemous name.

A dwarf hurrying to join the safety in numbers, two red braids swaying across his back beneath his helmet, skidded to a stop when he saw the elf king had stopped. "What are you doing? You have to keep moving!" the dwarf shouted, jogging ahead to assist Natalia.

Others from the rear group of dwarfs began to rush back to see what had caused Nadir to stop. Nadir glanced down at the dwarf now helping Natalia along. Nadir called to the dwarf with red braids, "Take her the rest of the way."

He hesitated, seeming unsure if he should follow the command, but did as the elf king ordered, instructing Natalia to rest her weight on his head while several other dwarfs also came to their aid. The dwarfs began hauling Natalia toward the allied soldiers.

Nadir drew his sword from its sheath as he walked purposefully across the open ground toward Lageena. She stood firm, knowing he would come to her. Nadir saw her clutching the crystal that allowed her to wield powers that should've been impossible. Every instinct in his body screamed at him to turn and run behind his friendly lines to be safely protected by his soldiers. For his father's sake, for his own sake, he wouldn't allow himself to miss this opportunity to face her.

Why isn't she destroying me now? he wondered as he tried to gather inner strength. He was so tired. He'd been doomed twice already, staring death in the face, but had somehow escaped each time. *She could wave that glowing sapphire of hers and put an end to me right now. Why isn't she?* he thought as he gripped his sword tighter, waiting for a bolt of lightning to come flying from her necklace. He knew the energy that created the crater was more than anything Anders or Zahara could've generated. That meant it must've come from the crystal. But how was she here? She'd vanished in the explosion. Natalia saw her imprint in the smoldering soil. Anders and Zahara were near where she'd vanished when they, too, disappeared. Now that Lageena had returned, did that mean another rider pair had been destroyed?

Lageena reached up, again clutching the crystal around her neck. Nadir froze, ready to dodge whatever she threw at him. She shot her other hand forward, a ripple of blue light flying from her palm. Nadir leapt to the side, but as the energy shot past him, he saw that he hadn't needed to dodge it. She'd missed. Maybe she didn't know how to use the crystal very well.

He heard the clash of metal as the ripple of energy erupted along a charging front of elven soldiers. He turned to see them flattened backward by the powerful blow. Of course, his soldiers would charge her. These elves were loyal to a fault; they'd follow him anywhere.

Rage rose in Nadir again, the same rage he'd felt the moment he thought he'd die. Nadir shouted as he tapped his elven speed and ran toward his father's murderer. Lageena quickly drew her blade, letting go of the crystal and clashing blows with Nadir. He hit her with such force that the former queen stumbled back exposing an opening as she flailed to keep her balance. Nadir slashed his sword across her black armor, sparks flying as the blade dug a deep scratch across her chest. The hit sent her toppling over, so Nadir's second swing barely clipped the top of her helmet. He stumbled forward, almost losing his balance and falling on top of her.

Lageena rolled to the side as she fell. When she rolled onto her back, she saw Nadir coming down on her with a finishing stab that would pierce her plated armor. Crystal already in hand, she released a small force of energy into Nadir.

Nadir forced his blade downward at Lageena but as he did, she sent a pulse of energy into him, launching him up and away. Now he flailed, falling hard on his back, his bare head colliding with the ground. Colors flashed as he tried to blink away the pain.

Get up, he told himself. Nadir rolled through the pain. Grabbing his blade from the dirt, he wheeled around to face Lageena. She charged at him, sword blazing. Nadir blocked her wild swings, his head swirling in pain as he struggled to keep pace with her speed. Sidestepping a thrust, Nadir pulled Lageena by him, sending her falling face first into the road.

He panted as he backed away from her, tired and breathing heavily. As Lageena quickly rose to her feet and faced him, blade out, Nadir asked, "Why did you do it?"

Lageena smiled through her visored helmet and

attacked. Although Nadir's arms were heavy and sluggish, he was superior with the sword. As she tried to gain an opening, Nadir held his own. With his fatigue yet superior skill, Nadir and Lageena seemed to be evenly matched. He was too weak to advance on her but sharp enough to avoid a killing blow.

He backed away as she lurched forward, breathing heavily through her helmet. "Why did you kill my father?" he shouted in frustration.

"Your father was weak," she spat.

"No!" Nadir shouted. "My father was kind but never weak."

Lageena lunged at him. Nadir blocked her swings at first, but she gained a strike against his side, clanging off his armor and sending him winging to the side. Lageena saw her chance to strike as he regained his footing. She rushed him but Nadir expected her and forced himself toward her with one last huge effort. They collided, blades outstretched about to strike. Nadir tackled Lageena, dropping his sword in the confusion. He rolled on the ground with her, squeezing her tight as he struggled to gain the upper hand.

Grunting, Nadir rolled Lageena under him, planting his knees into the ground and stopping his momentum. She still gripped her sword and tried to swing it at him. He punched at it, swinging his arm in a backhanded fist into hers. She dropped the blade and he forced his other fist down hard into her helmet. Her head bounced off the ground as he smashed her helmet with three swift punches dealt from his gauntleted fists. In his excitement, he didn't realize that she'd been reaching for the crystal. It was too late, Nadir flew into the air, hit by an explosive wave of energy pulsing out from the crystal.

He landed hard on his shoulder and rolled uncontrollably across the open ground. When he tried to get up, Lageena flew to him with a blade in hand. In a force of energy, she drove Nadir down into the ground even harder. The air escaped his lungs from the force. He gasped but she didn't let up. He could see light glinting off the blade of a dagger she held in her hand. Her crushing weight continued to pin him to the ground as he struggled to catch his breath.

Lageena pulled the bent visor off her helmet in a rage as she stared at Nadir with bloodthirsty eyes. She flared her nostrils and exposed her teeth, clearly out of control. She spat, "I killed your father because I wanted to, just as I killed your mother and now you!" Lageena's dagger erupted into flames as she raised it over her head, twirling it point down.

Nadir turned his head, straining for one last breath before she could kill him. The force she was using to press down on him was overpowering and the veins in his neck bulged as he struggled to turn his head. He blinked when he saw a figure in slate gray armor rushing at them. His eyes widened as he watched a stout dwarf with two red braids lower a shoulder and tackle Lageena just as she stabbed at Nadir. In an instant, Nadir could breathe.

Sitting up, he caught a glimpse of the dwarf soldier forcing Lageena's flaming blade into her own chest, the flame extinguishing as it penetrated. Nadir sat up in disbelief. The roar of elf, dwarf and human soldiers rushing past him and colliding into the enraged orc army became white noise in his ears. He sat on the bare ground in his battered and bloodied plate armor transfixed by the dwarf who still held the hilt of the blade pressed deep into Lageena's chest. Lageena twitched several times, but the dwarf held her still, the soldiers steering around her as they collided with the orc horde.

In the moments when Merglan had clutched the crystal, Ivan also had broken free of his spell, grabbing his sword and taking several steps toward the sorcerer before he, too, became paralyzed again.

With Lageena gone, Merglan turned back to Ivan, "Ivan, back to our chat." He strode several steps closer to the old rider and continued maliciously, "What's it been, nearly two decades since we last saw one another? My how the time has flown. That was an interesting day. You came after me with Jazz. Too bad you couldn't save her, I quite liked her. You two would've made an excellent addition to my team. What's that, I can't quite hear you. Your mental barriers are up, not that I couldn't break through them if I wanted to," he said, waving his hand and releasing Ivan from his hold. Anders remained frozen.

Ivan stumbled forward, catching himself before he fell, "You twisted son of a..."

"Tsk, tsk, Ivan. You wouldn't want to curse in front of your youngest, would you?" Merglan smirked smugly.

Ivan thrust his blade at Merglan, but he sidestepped the weak jab while drawing his own blade. "What? Did I push the princeling's buttons?" Merglan said, swiping aside another weakly attempted stab from Ivan.

What's he talking about? Anders thought to himself. *Ivan isn't a prince, is he?*

Ivan wavered, his energy draining from both the physical parrying as well as having to keep Merglan from entering his mind.

"What's the matter, Will? Can't summon the energy like you used to?" Merglan batted aside Ivan's sword as he fumbled to strike at the sorcerer once again.

Dropping his sword, Ivan fell to his knees, clutching at his head and shouting, "No!"

Merglan focused his mental energy on Ivan, trying to break through his mental wall.

Silently observing this exchange, Anders felt the hold on his own body lighten. He moved forward somewhat sluggishly trying to quietly close in on Merglan. He saw Zahara out of the corner of his eye trying to snake her way past Killdoor to help him. Killdoor was much larger than Zahara and faster; he kept her pinned.

Anders dragged himself with all his strength, realizing he wouldn't make it the short distance to Ivan before Merglan broke into his teacher's mind. Anders drew on his remaining energy, weak as it was. He focused, channeling it through his body as he struggled to raise his arm toward Merglan. He somehow managed to send a bolt flying from his palm. Merglan saw the flash but was too consumed with Ivan to deflect it. The bolt hit Merglan's shoulder, knocking him over and sending him skidding across the stone floor.

As Merglan fell, his spell on Anders and Ivan broke, releasing them. Anders dashed to Ivan, helping him to his knees. At the same time, Zahara leapt over Killdoor, spraying flames down on him and sending him shying away briefly. She rushed to their side.

As she landed, Merglan recovered from Anders' attack. Rising to his feet, he began to laugh a deep and horrid sound that grew out of years of hatred and scorn. He flashed his arms out and locked all three of them in place. He seemed to glide through the air as he came toward them. Blood trickled down the side of his face where his head had hit the stone floor.

Coming to a stop, he said, "You think you can defeat me, boy?"

Anders felt a crushing weight bearing down on him as Merglan tried to search his mind. Anders willed him out, but the sorcerer persisted.

"You think you're the chosen one, prophesied to defeat me because you're the son of a prince?" Merglan chuckled as he bore down even harder on Anders' mind.

Anders couldn't move, he could hardly think. While Merglan talked nonsense at him, he focused on keeping him out. If Merglan broke into his mind, he would lose himself to Merglan's will. He couldn't allow it to happen. He wouldn't allow it to happen.

Just as Merglan began to pry open his thoughts, he heard a voice. It was Ivan's. Somehow Ivan had broken through Merglan's mental grip on him enough to speak. "You will not take another from my family," Ivan commanded.

Anders felt the squeeze on his mind lessen as Merglan addressed Ivan, "Who do you think you are, William!?" Merglan shouted. "Or should I call you Ivan since you've convinced everyone into thinking that Kaufen's son is dead and gone?"

"You might take me down in this fight, but I will not allow you to take another from my family," Ivan said through clenched teeth.

Merglan stepped closer, mere inches from Ivan's face, "And you think you can stop me?" Sweat formed on the evil sorcerer's brow. He was breathing heavily from the strain of keeping all three sorcerers paralyzed for so long. Yet he chuckled, "You didn't stop me from killing your father. You couldn't even stop me from taking your beloved wife away in that freak storm. And you couldn't stop me when I killed your dragon right before your eyes."

Ivan spat into Merglan's face, somehow still resisting Merglan's complete control over his body.

Merglan wiped the spittle from his cheek with the corner of his cloak and stared into Ivan's eyes, "You didn't even realize it when I took control of your son."

Anders couldn't believe what Merglan was saying. Ivan was heir to the throne and had been all this time. He was a husband to a wife who Merglan killed in a freak storm, the storm Anders' mother died in. If what Merglan was saying was true, Ivan was Anders' father.

"What are you talking about?" Ivan spat.

"Oh, come on, you can't possibly be so ignorant? The sapphire in his sword," Merglan said, pointing to Anders' hand. "I imbued it with energy from my body when I killed its owner. I knew you and 'the chosen one' would come looking for them. I hatched a plan. I knew you would eventually discover its power. All I had to do was make sure the power had been corrupted, giving the boy the thrill to kill. I felt him use it, Will. I felt when your son channeled my power to slaughter unarmed creatures, and he loved it."

"No," Ivan said.

"Yes. I knew you would come looking for me eventually. When my loyal queen warned me of your departure, I knew you'd be coming into my web. I instilled the hate into your son when he used its power. After that I just needed you to get close to Lageena, then she transported you here, to me."

"How?" Ivan asked in disbelief.

"I learned many things from the Norfolk during my training. I discovered their secrets behind the crystals. They don't all work, but I spent the last two decades of my life harvesting them and restoring their powers. Oh, Will, you wouldn't believe the things these crystals can do," Merglan trembled, his eyes fluttering closed.

"Now!" Ivan shouted and attacked Merglan.

Suddenly Anders felt control return to his body, and he looked to Zahara who turned her head, wide-eyed. Anders took advantage of the situation, leaping onto her saddle as Killdoor attacked. Zahara dodged out of the way, Killdoor's talons scratching across Anders' exposed back as he missed. Anders shouted in pain and Zahara took flight. The darkened room's ceiling rose high into the air above them. Zahara had enough room to turn before Killdoor engaged them again. He scratched at him, biting at his neck as she flapped her wings against him. Anders struck out with Lazuran at the beast, cutting into its scales with the sharp elven blade. Killdoor released his grip and turned in retreat. Anders looked to the ground where Ivan and Merglan screamed, battling each other's minds. He knew Ivan wouldn't be able to hold him for long. He wasn't even sure how he'd been able to break the spell in the first place.

Zahara, what do I do? Anders asked, watching Ivan being crushed by Merglan's will.

We need to escape before he kills us all, she said frantically.

How? Anders asked searching for an exit but not seeing one in the dark room.

Use the crystal in the sword, she said as she prepared for Killdoor's attack. The large black dragon flew at them, releasing a plume of fire as he came at them. Zahara turned, swerving to the side, the flames licking her belly and singing Anders before they escaped the column of fire. *Anders now!* she shouted.

Reluctantly Anders summoned the sapphire's power. Before he could regret the action, he allowed the energy to rise from the pommel of the sword. The tendrils of energy wrapped around his arm and bit into his skin. He drained the energy from the crystal, letting the tempest consume him. The thrill of anger rushed into his veins, pulsing within him. He struggled to control the rage and direct it toward Merglan.

The sorcerer was locked in a mental battle with Ivan when Anders forced his mind to engage. As he locked minds with Merglan, he became aware that his body was now useless in defending himself from Killdoor. He couldn't do anything to stop it. He'd linked minds with the most powerful human in the world, and he hated him for it.

Anders' rage was immeasurable as he wrestled with Merglan's consciousness. The powerful sorcerer gave in at first, unaware that Anders would strike. Recovering from the initial blow, however, Merglan forced Anders back, taking control of his facilities.

Anders, no, Ivan shouted as Merglan struggled to force each one of their minds back. *Get out of here while you can.*

I'm not leaving you here! Anders shouted as he tightened his grip on Merglan. The man's mind was a wealth of strength, unlike anything Anders could have imagined. Part of Merglan's energy was flowing within him now and Anders not only had to force Merglan to his will but control the pure hatred that consumed him.

Merglan suddenly released his grip on Anders and returned to his focus on Ivan. Ivan writhed on the floor as Anders tried to force Merglan to stop. Using the full tempest flowing through his veins, Anders couldn't even divert Merglan's attention.

Zahara dove and swooped around the room, flying expertly as she evaded Killdoor. Each time she locked claws with him, she managed to force the heft of the large dragon away from Anders and escape.

Anders could feel his energy beginning to dwindle. He was running out of time and needed to get them out of there before it was too late. Breaking his grip on Merglan, Anders connected with Zahara again, *I need to grab him when I transport us out of here,* he said.

You're sure you know how to do that? Zahara asked, dodging Killdoor's tail as he swung at them.

No, but I must try. The energy is fading quickly.

I'll get us close, but we'll risk Merglan trapping us again.

Do it. Zahara, he's my father.

Without another word Zahara dove across the room, screaming toward Ivan and Merglan. Anders drew on all the strength they shared and focused their combined energy on transporting them out of there. As Zahara dove, she tucked her wings, slamming into the ground and sliding toward Merglan.

Merglan turned to look at them and raised his hand, but Ivan caught him, blocking his grasp with a last-ditch effort. As Zahara slid along the floor past Ivan, Anders reached out with his hand, grabbed Ivan's leg and released the transport spell. An orb of light consumed Zahara as Anders drained his energy into creating the spell. With a snap, they began to pull away from the room. Anders looked up, his hand still gripping hold of Ivan's leg. Just as the spell began to work and the last stores of energy were pulled from Anders to complete the spell, a hand protruded through the glowing bubble encapsulating them. It grabbed hold of Ivan and pulled him out. Anders and Zahara were drawn away from the room. Transported through space and to a different location.

The dome of light vanished, and Anders slumped in

Zahara's saddle. The spell sucked all energy from his body. The last thing Anders saw before exhaustion claimed him was a red dragon approaching across the sky.

NADIR FELT someone grab him by the armpits and begin to lift him to his feet. Bending his knees, he was able to get his legs under him and rise to his full height. Remli came around to his side and said, "That's the second time today I thought you were a goner."

Nadir sidestepped and picked up his sword from the ground. Wiping the dirt and blood from the blade, Nadir said, "Third actually." He narrowed his eyes, keeping them fixed on the dwarf as he walked over to Lageena's body. Nadir stood alongside the stout soldier. Reaching out to him, Nadir said, "You have my thanks, soldier. Give me your name so I know who I am indebted to."

The dwarf glanced awkwardly to the line of fighting taking place nearby, feeling they should fall back in line and continue their duty, but he couldn't ignore the fact that he'd been addressed by a king.

When the dwarf didn't respond right away, Remli stepped forward, "Your name lad. Give the elf king your name."

Nadir furrowed his brow when the dwarf remained silent, shifting in his armor. Remli groaned and stepped toward the soldier, but Nadir stopped him, grabbing him by the shoulder. He nodded to Remli as if to say it was fine. Nadir held out his hand and the soldier took it. "I don't need your name, because from the moment you drove that burning dagger into her heart, you forever earned a new name in my eyes. I'll call you Burnheart. Now, Burnheart, name a reward. I'm in your debt and I'll do whatever is in my power to see it paid."

At that moment the dwarf named Burnheart reached his arm up and removed his helmet. Nadir raised his eyebrow when he recognized the dwarf. Suddenly he recalled why those red braids had seemed so familiar. Remli gasped, stepping back in surprise. The smooth-faced soldier, queen slayer and Nadir's savior was Remli's own daughter, Maylox.

"No, it can't be," Remli said shaking his head. "You aren't supposed to be here."

Addressing the elf king, Maylox said, "I wish to be a soldier in my father's army."

Nadir turned to the dwarf king, raising an eyebrow.

Remli gawked in disbelief, "But I expressly forbade her from doing this."

Nadir shrugged.

Remli ran his hand through his beard trying to find the right words, "I'm, so, proud." A wide smile crossed his face as he lunged forward to hug his daughter.

Maylox hugged her father, glancing to the line of soldiers fiercely holding back the orcs from pushing through their defense.

Nadir crouched next to Lageena's body, staring into her glossed-over eyes. He stripped the gauntlet off his hand and then held the back of his hand over her mouth and nose to make sure she was no longer breathing. A glint of silver around Lageena's neck caught his eye. A necklace hung, coiling on the ground next to her head. He could see the faint glow from the crystal she'd been using to wield magic. Nadir reached down and picked it up, pulling hard to break the chain from her neck. He held it tight in his hand as he took one last look at his dead stepmother, burn marks on the chestplate where Maylox had driven the dagger into her heart. Lageena's eyes looked wild, crazed and unsettling.

Groaning, Nadir stood. Turning to Remli and his daughter, he said, "Maylox Burnheart. I like the sound of that."

Remli grinned, "Yep. I also like the sound of us living through this, so let's get out of here now."

As the two kings sounded the horns signaling to their soldiers to retreat, they joined the injured who'd already begun sneaking their way out of the canyon. The Lumbapi and dwarfs led the retreat, helping the injured and those slowed by exhaustion to the secret trails that wound through the trees. The elves held the wall, keeping the disorganized orcs at bay while the others climbed to safety in the shadow of darkness. The ravines provided good cover to escape during the night. When Nadir climbed to the top of the narrow canyon and saw the last of his elven forces retreat swiftly up the hill to join them, he gripped the crystal in his hand, wondering what kind of king he would be.

EPILOGUE

"No. No, no, no, no," Thomas whimpered as he tried to shake his sister's limp body awake. "Wake up!" he cried, tears streaming down his cheeks.

Britt watched with a blank stare as Kirsten's flesh turned pale, red streaks extending out from the goblin's bite. Blood seeped out from the deeply cut tissue on Kirsten's left shoulder. Britt had seen hundreds of wounds before. She'd battled humans, orcs, and even kurr, but she'd never seen a wound turn septic so quickly. It was as though the goblin's bite was powered by a rapidly advancing poison.

"The crystal," Britt said pulling herself from her trance. She had dropped the translucent crystal when Kirsten came through the barrier. Dropping the crystal reformed the barrier, severing the goblin attached to Kirsten in two. Britt frantically began searching the forest floor around them. She'd hardly moved from where she was just a moment before when she'd been holding tightly to the crystal.

Max saw her searching and immediately joined in.

"What are we looking for?" he whispered as he raked his hands through the duff-covered ground.

"The crystal," she said. "It can heal her. I know it can." Britt pulled apart clumps of grass at her feet, pushing aside dead leaves and twigs. "It was right here!" she shouted in frustration.

"Got it," Bo said. He'd joined the search shortly after Max.

Britt thrust her palm toward him, "Give it," she said forcefully. Taking the crystal, she quickly pressed it to Kirsten's body, holding it in place on her chest. She held her breath waiting for the magic stone to do something. Nothing happened. Britt frowned and lifted the crystal off Kirsten, looked at it, then shook it and tried again. Again, she held the crystal against Kirsten's limp body, but nothing happened. The red streaking poison in Kirsten's veins continued to spread.

"Maybe we should try it directly on her skin?" Thomas sniffled through his tears, trying to regroup.

Britt tried again, this time holding the light blue stone Governor Rankstine had used to control an entire town against Kirsten's bare skin. Suddenly Kirstin's breathing turned shallow and rapid, as she attempted to breathe through clenched teeth.

"Try on the bite," Max snapped, seeing Kirsten's condition worsen.

Britt moved the crystal directly to the wound, blood coating the crystal. She held the crystal against her friend, closed her eyes and willed the crystal to work.

Kirsten arched her back, seizing out of Thomas' grip. She writhed on the forest floor. Britt opened her eyes, hoping to see the glow emanating from the crystal. To her disappointment, the magical crystal Kirsten had been using earlier in the night failed to work for Britt.

Helplessly, Britt watched as Thomas held Kirsten's head, crying and wishing for her to stop seizing. Suddenly, she did. Kirsten's rapid breathing ceased, and she lay motionless on the ground once more. Britt hung her head, knowing she should've done more to save her friend.

Max placed his hand on Britt's shoulder, lightly nudging. He nodded away from the barrier and mouthed, "We need to go."

She nodded and began to move in toward Thomas. Grabbing Thomas much the same as Max had done to her, Britt wiped the tears from her eyes and said, "We should get out of here. There could still be goblins outside the barrier searching for the one-way passages in."

Thomas held his sister in his arms, crying, not voicing a response.

Britt motioned to Max and Bo, who came alongside Thomas and Britt, bending to help carry Kirsten's body away.

As they got into position to hoist her off the ground, Bo gasped and pointed to her, "Look!"

They followed his gaze to Kirsten's chest. The sapphire necklace Kirsten had found in her mother's dress was glowing. The pink-hued crystal shone dimly at first, but within seconds the light increased, shining brighter with each passing moment. Britt exposed the cleft of Kirsten's chest to show an astonishing feat. The red streaks that had marked the poison traveling through nearly all of Kirsten's veins were receding. The poison from the goblin's bite had made its way to Kirsten's core, but the illuminated sapphire necklace was forcing the poison away from Kirsten's heart. The brighter the necklace became, the more the red streaks dissipated. Kirsten suddenly opened her mouth and inhaled sharply, her breathing returning to normal.

Thomas laughed, a desperate, uncontrollably exhausted laugh. Britt, Bo and Max smiled, knowing that for now at least, their friend was stable. They pulled her limp body up, Bo volunteering to be the first to carry her over his shoulder as they continued their escape.

Max led the group upslope and farther away from Grandwood; Britt followed. Bo carried Kirsten while Thomas walked closely behind, checking to see if Kirsten was still breathing every few minutes. They slogged their way up the steep slopes of the Grandwood Mountains, pausing only to switch off who was carrying Kirsten. Each time they switched, they would have to ensure that the necklace never hung away from her body. Placing the sapphire in a way that it sat between their shoulders and her body was uncomfortable as it dug deep into their muscles, but it was a small price to pay to keep their friend alive.

Sweaty after hiking for hours, and at the same time chilled to the bone from the changing season's evening chill, the group distanced themselves from Grandwood, until they could no longer hear shouts from the trauma-tized city under siege.

Britt rotated to lead and broke trail through the increasingly dense forest. A break in the thick undergrowth appeared. She followed it, welcoming the easier path. Tired and not questioning what caused the break in vegetation, Britt led the group side-slope on the lightly worn path. Still in a haze of exhaustion, Britt thought she could smell camp cooking. Her mouth watered. Distracted, she tripped over a rock in their path, stumbling forward but catching herself from falling face first onto the ground. The jolt spurred her awake and she took a moment to examine their surroundings. They were following a trail. The lightly trampled vegetation had turned into a well-worn path. Without having noticed, Britt had led them out of the thick forest and into an evenly spread stand of old growth pines. Though the crescent moon hung low in the sky, she could see a good distance under the canopy of large trees.

Six horses and a donkey stood sleeping not more than twenty yards to her left. The others behind her had also all been walking under the same complacent spell, not paying attention to their surroundings. Max followed Britt and halted just before walking into her, suddenly realizing what Britt was staring at.

"Who goes there?" a low voice called out from behind the horses.

"What are we going to do?" Max whispered.

Britt looked at Kirsten slung over Thomas' shoulder, the pain in his eyes brought her to a conclusion she wouldn't usually take, but they were desperate. Britt stepped toward the horses, now stirring from the activity around them.

A shadow of a man emerged from the group of animals. "Show yourself," he shouted.

"We're unarmed," Britt called in response. "We need help."

The man jogged over to where they waited just off the trail. He comfortably brandished a broad sword, looking as though he'd used it before. Holding the sword at the ready, he examined the tired young group, Kirsten drooped over Thomas' shoulder. After a moment of looking them over, he waved his sword, "Follow me."

Britt and the others didn't ask any questions; they simply followed the man as he led them past the hobbled horses to, a small camp overlooking the widely spaced trees.

Three large tents arched in a half circle around a smoldering campfire. The man halted them at the fire and said, "Wait here."

They did as he asked and huddled around the embers, soaking up their heat.

The man walked up to the middle tent and pulled open the door flap. Poking his head inside he said, "Rune. Wake up. We have some refugees here who need your help."

CONTINUE READING

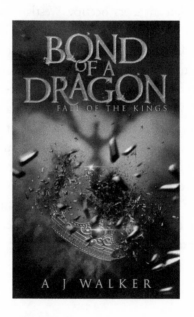

Bond of a Dragon: Fall of the Kings

Anders is lost and without guidance. Merglan's imperial grip tightens on the free nations. A Resistance movement arises to combat venomous magic, but is it too late? In the end, all kings must fall.

When Anders awakens in a foreign land, he finds himself far from the campaign in Southland and anxious to get back. The sapphire's intoxicating grip has given him more than just a craving for power. Its tainted magic pushes him closer to the precipice of becoming more like the evil that he is foretold to destroy. In his attempts to resist the darkness, Anders must work through his pain before he can return to the fight he abandoned so suddenly.

After the allied armies are forced to disband, the five nations begin to feel the effects of the dark sorcerer's imperial rule. Foreign invaders occupy Westland. Southland is flooded with orcs. Humans and dwarfs must band together in resistance. Unlike the elves, who can hide behind their magically protected walls, the other races in Kartania's kingdoms are drastically affected by the absence of an allied dragonrider. With the fate of Kartania hanging in the balance, will these various allegiances unite to combat Merglan's expansion? Can Anders work with his dragon, Zahara, gain back what advantage they once had? Will Kirsten survive long enough to see Westland's revolt? What has become of Ivan and those left behind in Southland?

Get your copy of *Fall of the Kings* to continue your dragonrider experience!

GET YOUR FREE BOOK

Sign up for my newsletter and you'll never miss another A J Walker book launch. You'll receive my prequel novellas, ebook promotions, monthly writing updates and more.

Building a relationship with my readers is the best part about being an independent author. I send out a bi-monthly newsletter with details on new releases, special offers, and other updates concerning my writing progress.

When you sign up for my newsletter, you'll get an exclusive book:

REVIEW

CONSIDER POSTING YOUR REVIEW.

Leaving a book review is a very powerful tool when it comes to getting attention for my books. As an independently published author, I don't have the connections or financial muscle of a New York publisher. Getting my books to the front of the bookstore or in full-page ads in the newspaper is something I'm not able to take advantage of, not yet anyway.

But I do have the advantage of speaking directly to you, the reader. Spreading news about my books by leaving a review not only proves my story's worth to others who might enjoy it, but word-of-mouth and social prof can be more powerful than anything New York publishers can offer.

Honest reviews of my books help attract other readers. If you've enjoyed this book, I would be very grateful if you would spend just five minutes leaving a review — it can be as short as you like.

Thank you so much.
Happy reading,
A J Walker

ALSO BY A J WALKER

In Rulers of Tarmigan Series (an epic fantasy)

Emperor's Fate

Upcoming in Series

Shepherds of Fire

Shattered Dragons

In the Bond of a Dragon Series (a young adult epic fantasy)

Zahara's Gift

Secrets of the Sapphire Soul

Fall of the Kings

Rise of the Dragonriders

Bond of a Dragon Prequel

Dragon Wars: The War of the Magicians

(Available through newsletter sign up.)

Bonnie Glock Mystery Series (an urban fantasy)

Into the Mixed

Finding Justice

Exiled and Forgotten

Dark Fae Rising

Soul Harvest

ABOUT THE AUTHOR

A J Walker grew up in Bozeman, Montana. In his youth, writing fiction and becoming an author was a distant dream, something a young dyslexic didn't think was achievable. A J was diagnosed with dyslexia at a young age. He struggled through most of his education with an elementary school reading comprehension level. When he was sixteen, A J found neurofeedback therapy. With the help of this new technology, he quickly learned how to read and write to the level of his high school peers. Before striving to become an author, A J's love for whitewater kayaking and the outdoors led him to study at the University of Montana. In his university years, A J worked as a wildland firefighter and graduated with a bachelor's degree in the Science of Forestry. Currently, A J lives along the Yellowstone River near Columbus, Montana, with his wife and their dogs.

A J Walker loves hearing from readers, so please feel free to contact him on social media or by sending an email to ajwalker@ajwalkerauthor.com.

Thank you for reading. :-)

CPSIA information can be obtained
at www.ICGtesting.com
Printed in the USA
LVHW072358200623
749997LV00021B/518